**Praise for #1 *New York Times* bestselling author
Linda Lael Miller**

"Linda Lael Miller creates vibrant chara
stories I defy you to forget."
—#1 *New York Times* bestselling au
Debbie Macomber

"Miller is one of the finest American writers in the
genre."
—*RT Book Reviews*

"All three titles should appeal to readers who like
their contemporary romances Western, slightly
dangerous and graced with enlightened (more or
less) bad-boy heroes."
—*Library Journal* on the Montana Creeds series

**Praise for *New York Times* bestselling author
Brenda Jackson**

"Brenda Jackson is the queen of newly discovered
love…. If there's one thing Jackson knows how to
do, it's how to pluck those heartstrings and stir up
some seriously saucy drama."
—*BookPage*

"[Brenda] Jackson is a master at writing."
—*Publishers Weekly*

The daughter of a town marshal, **Linda Lael Miller** is a *New York Times* bestselling author of more than one hundred historical and contemporary novels. Linda's books have hit #1 on the *New York Times* bestseller list seven times. Raised in Northport, Washington, she now lives in Spokane, Washington. Visit her at www.lindalaelmiller.com.

Brenda Jackson is a *New York Times* bestselling author of more than one hundred romance titles. Brenda lives in Jacksonville, Florida, and divides her time between family, writing and traveling. Email Brenda at authorbrendajackson@gmail.com or visit her on her website at brendajackson.net.

#1 *New York Times* Bestselling Author

LINDA LAEL MILLER

JUST KATE

◆ HARLEQUIN® BESTSELLING AUTHOR COLLECTION

ISBN-13: 978-1-335-80429-7

Just Kate

Copyright © 2018 by Harlequin Books S.A.

The publisher acknowledges the copyright holders of the individual works as follows:

Just Kate
Copyright © 1989 by Linda Lael Miller

What a Westmoreland Wants
Copyright © 2010 by Brenda Streater Jackson

Recycling programs for this product may not exist in your area.

Scriptures taken from the Holy Bible, New International Version®, NIV®. Copyright © 1973, 1978, 1984, 2011 by Biblica, Inc.™ Used by permission of Zondervan. All rights reserved worldwide. www.zondervan.com. The "NIV" and "New International Version" are trademarks registered in the United States Patent and Trademark Office by Biblica, Inc.™

This edition published by arrangement with Harlequin Books S.A.

For questions and comments about the quality of this book, please contact us at CustomerService@Harlequin.com.

Printed in U.S.A.

www.Harlequin.com

CONTENTS

Also available from Linda Lael Miller

HQN Books

Visit the Author Profile page
at Harlequin.com for more titles.

JUST KATE

Linda Lael Miller

For Lisa Jackson and Nancy Bush, sisters in crime. Remember the four-to-a-room trip to RWA?

Chapter 1

The exchange was so blatant, so audacious that Kate Blake couldn't believe she'd seen it. It was intermission and the lobby was crowded. People swirled past her, laughing and talking as they waited for the opera to resume. Kate stood frozen in their midst, fingers curved around her glass of orange juice, her indigo eyes wide, afraid even to blink.

She hadn't imagined it. Brad had handed another man a packet of white powder and taken money in return, right there in front of half the population of Seattle.

Perhaps, she thought desperately, it was all a mistake. Perhaps she had only imagined that the packet contained cocaine, and that Brad, the man she'd meant to marry in less than a month, had just accepted money for it.

In the next instant, Brad turned, tucking a folded bill

into the pocket of his coat as he moved. His eyes met Kate's, and it was clear that he knew she'd seen. There was no apology in his gaze, however, only defiance. Then he was looking at his companion again, and Kate might not have existed at all.

She felt dizzy, and then claustrophobic, and she knew she had to get out into the fresh air fast. She set her cup aside and hurried toward the main door.

Outside, Kate gripped the stair railings in both hands and dragged in deep, clean breaths until the choking sensation passed. A glance back over one elegantly bared shoulder told her that Brad hadn't followed. He probably hadn't even noticed she was gone.

She looked up at the dark, star-speckled sky aglow with city lights, and her vision blurred as tears filled her eyes. She was torn. One part of her wanted to go back inside, grip Brad by the lapels and demand to know why he'd thrown everything away; another preferred to pretend that nothing had changed.

Kate inched down the stairs, still grasping the railing with both hands. Brad was the man she'd planned to marry. He was her father's campaign manager. And she'd just seen him break the law in the most brazen of ways.

A thousand thoughts whirled through her head. This wasn't new behavior for Brad; she was certain of that. And yet she hadn't known. She'd been engaged to him and *she hadn't known* what kind of man he was! How could that be?

There were no cabs lined up in front of the theater, since the opera would run another full hour. Kate looked back again, knowing she should go inside, call for a taxi and wait in the lobby until it arrived. But something within her demanded action. She needed to walk, hard and fast, with the cool, clean night wind blowing against her face. She started out in the general direction of her downtown condominium, chin held high, her grandmother's antique brass evening bag swinging at her side.

Hard-eyed street people watched her pass, but there was none of the usual panhandling. Kate supposed that in her present mood she didn't look approachable.

Moments later, as she passed a popular department store, her pace slackened. The breeze had dried her tears. Kate's reflection in the windows regarded her forlornly as she took in her own tall, slender body, the sleek designer gown that had cost the earth, the soft and loose arrangement of her dark hair.

"So who wanted to marry Bradley Wilshire anyway?" she demanded aloud. As she rounded the corner, Kate was careful not to look at her image in the glass, fearing it might answer, *You did.*

Kate pulled her silk shawl around her bare shoulders and shivered. In just a few minutes, she reminded herself, she would be home in her small, elegant condominium overlooking the harbor. She would turn on some classical music, pour herself a glass of low-cal Chablis and spend the rest of the evening soaking in a bubble bath.

Was it possible that Brad was a pusher?

Trying to forget what she'd seen would be useless, she knew, but the ramifications were more than she could deal with, too big to take in all at once.

She was nearly home when she noticed two men standing in front of the cash machine. Kate considered crossing to the other side of the street, but they seemed so engrossed in conversation that they probably wouldn't notice her, anyway.

The man facing Kate was tall and well built, familiar in a disturbing sort of way. In the dim light of the cash machine, she could see he was wearing a tuxedo, and his mouth was curved into an ingenuous smile. She sensed he was aware of her presence, though he gave no sign of it.

"Take it easy now, mate," he said in a thick Australian accent. "If it's money you want, you'll have it, but the machine will only give me so much in a twenty-four-hour period."

An almost dizzying sensation of mingled despair and excitement filled Kate. The voice, the accent—it couldn't be!

It was then that Kate spotted the glint of a switchblade in the second man's hand.

She was filled with instant ire. Thanks to Brad, she'd seen her share of crime for the day, and she was fed up. Without considering possible results, she spun her grandmother's purse on its chain and threw it. When it struck the mugger in the side of the head, he dropped the knife. In the same instant, his knees folded and he sank to the sidewalk in an unlikely position of prayer.

The tall man collected the knife, recessed the blade with an unsettling expertise and tucked it into his pocket. "Nice work, Katie," he said, reclaiming a gold credit card from the slot on the cash machine, "but you shouldn't have taken a chance like that. The bleeder might have turned on you."

Kate sank against the rough concrete wall of the bank, not trusting her knees to support her. "Sean," she whispered.

His white teeth flashed in the night. The mugger started to rise from the sidewalk, but his would-be victim pushed him back down with a light, deft touch of one foot.

Kate thought she was going to be sick and put one hand to her mouth.

"Surprised to see me, are you?" Sean asked.

Kate lowered her hand. Holding her knees rigid and her backbone straight, she started to walk away. "I'll call the police," she said woodenly.

Sean stopped her by taking a light but inescapable hold on her elbow. "No need of that, love," he said in a gravelly tone that made sweet chills ripple over Kate's soul. "They're here already."

Kate glanced toward the street. Sure enough, a patrol car was pulling up to the curb. She considered having herself taken into protective custody until Sean Harris had gone back to Australia, where he undeniably belonged.

"What's going on here?" asked the older of two officers.

Sean explained, and the moaning mugger was hauled unceremoniously to his feet. Kate listened numbly as his rights were read, her teeth sinking into her lower lip. Sean's grasp on her arm never slackened.

"You and the lady will need to come to the station and swear out a complaint," said the younger officer.

"And if we don't?" Sean asked, arching one dark eyebrow.

"They'll have to let him go," Kate answered.

"Can't have that," Sean replied lightly. "My car's just up the street—we'll follow you."

Both policemen touched the brims of their hats in a deferential fashion before hustling the prisoner into the back of the squad car. Sean fairly hurled Kate into the passenger seat of a late-model sports car parked half a block away.

"Well," he said, when they were following the police, "fancy meeting you here, Katie-did."

Kate folded her arms. First Brad's drug deal, then the mugging and now this. Boy, had her horoscope been off target this morning. "My parents would have appreciated a telephone call," she said stiffly, doing her best to ignore her former brother-in-law. "They worry about Gil, you know."

The reference to his young son did not visibly move Sean. At least Kate didn't catch him reacting, though she was watching him out of the corner of her eye.

"They know where we live," he replied, and this time his voice was as cold as a Blue Mountain snowfall.

Kate unfolded her arms and tried to relax. It was almost incomprehensibly bad luck that, of all the muggings she might have stumbled upon, it had to be Sean's. She hadn't seen him since Abby's funeral, and she'd hoped that she would never lay eyes on him again.

She drew in a deep breath and let it out again slowly. "Did you bring Gil with you?" she asked.

"Now why would I drag the poor little nipper from one hemisphere to the other like that?" he countered.

Kate suppressed an urge to wind up her purse again and let Sean have it. "Maybe because his grandparents would like to see him," she said.

"Because they'd like to take him away, you mean," Sean answered, "and turn him into a proper little Yank."

"He's half-American," Kate pointed out, daring at last to turn in the car seat and look directly at Sean. His profile was rugged, like the outback he loved so much. "What's wrong with that?"

They had reached the police station, and Sean was spared having to answer—for the moment.

The next hour was consumed by the dubious process of pressing charges against the mugger. Kate seriously considered turning Brad in for pushing drugs while she was there, but she knew she couldn't do that without consulting her father. An unforeseen scandal might ruin his chances for reelection to the Senate; Kate had to give him time to prepare.

She went to the telephone when she was through issuing her statement and dialed the familiar number.

Her mother answered; it was late enough that the staff was off duty. "Blake residence."

Kate braced herself. "Mother, it's Kate. I'm at the police station and—"

"The police station!" The horror in Irene Blake's voice was unmistakable. "Good heavens, what's happened? She's at the *police station*, dear!"

At this, the senator himself came on the line. Kate winced, just as if she'd been there to see him wrench the receiver out of her mother's hand. "What's this business about the police? So help me, Katherine, if you've been arrested, I'll fire you in an instant."

Kate made an effort to control her temper. "Of course I haven't been arrested, Daddy," she whispered into the phone, embarrassed. "I happened to witness a mugging, that's all."

"Are you all right?" the senator boomed. Now that he knew his career was safe, he could afford to be concerned about his daughter. Kate had never had any illusions about his priorities.

"I'm fine," she answered. "Daddy, the reason I'm calling is that—well—I ran into Sean."

"Sean who?" demanded the senator.

Kate felt a sweet, shivery sensation from head to foot, and looking to one side, she found that the handsome Australian was standing mere inches away. She reminded herself that he'd been Abby's husband, that he was a liar and a womanizer, but the tremulous, taut-bow feeling didn't subside. "Sean Harris," she finally managed to reply, her cheeks burning.

Sean's green eyes danced as he watched her color rise. Apparently he heard her father's question, for he took the receiver from Kate and spoke into it, his tone flippant and cool. "You know, Senator. That no-gooder from down under—the one that married your elder daughter."

Kate squeezed her eyes shut as she heard a burst of profanity explode on her father's end of the line. After a moment's recovery, she jerked the receiver out of Sean's hand and sputtered, "Daddy, remember your heart!"

The senator went right on swearing. He finally hung up with a crash, but not before blurting out a nonsensical sentence that ended in, "...bring that bastard here no matter what you have to do!"

Sean had heard that, too. He rocked back on his heels, his wonderful eyes full of laughter. "There's a welcome for you," he said.

Kate had a headache. She sighed and opened her purse, but there was no sign of the little metal box of aspirin she usually carried. All she found were her keys and a credit card. "He wants to talk to you about Gil," she said wearily. "That's all."

Sean didn't look at all convinced of that, but he offered Kate his arm and inclined his head to one side.

"All right, Katie-did," he said, "I'll face the lion in his den. But I'm only doing it for you."

Kate assessed this man who had caused her family so much heartache and shook her head. He didn't look the least bit remorseful to her.

"Thanks a whole heap," she said.

The lights of Seattle glittered and danced in the rearview mirror of Sean's car as he and Kate drove toward the Blake mansion. Even in the dim glow from the dashboard, she could see he was no longer amused. His jaw was set in a hard, ungiving line.

The confrontation between Sean and the senator would not be a pleasant experience for anyone.

Unexpectedly, Sean reached out and caught hold of Kate's left hand. His thumb pressed against the large diamond in Brad's engagement ring. "Who's the lucky man?" he asked. His tone was gruff, as though he was trying to be congenial and finding it difficult.

Kate's heart ached as she remembered the scene in the lobby at the opera house. She opened the lid of her antique purse, slid the ring off her finger and dropped it inside. "There isn't one," she said sadly.

She felt rather than saw Sean's glance in her direction. "Funny. Abby always said you'd be the one to settle down and have a family."

He couldn't have known what pain that remark would foster—could he? Kate didn't know Sean Harris very well; it had been ten years since he'd married her sister in the garden behind the Blakes' house and five since Abby had driven her sports car off a cliff north of Sydney.

Kate's mother still believed Abby had died deliber-

ately, unable to live with the unhappiness Sean caused
her. Kate didn't know what to think.

She'd visited her sister in Australia several times, the
last being when Gil was born seven years before. Although she'd watched Sean carefully, Kate hadn't seen
any evidence of the emotional cruelty Abby had written
home about. Oh, Sean might have been a little distant
where Abby was concerned, but he'd been crazy about
his infant son. Anyone could have seen that.

"Kate?"

The prompt from Sean brought her back to the present with a start. She pointed one finger. "Turn right on
this next street."

Sean took a new hold on Kate's hand. "I remember,"
he said. "Katie, what happened?"

Kate lowered her eyes. "I thought I was in love," she
confessed. "Tonight I saw Brad do something terrible."

He squeezed her hand. "You're better off out of it if
you have any doubts at all," he said.

Kate had no doubt that was true, but she still wished
she could go back in time and wave a wand and alter
reality. In the new scenario Brad would only be making change for a twenty-dollar bill or giving someone
his business card.

They had reached the foot of the Blakes' long brick-
paved driveway, and the gates opened immediately. Of
course, the senator had been watching for their arrival
from inside the house, the gate controls in his hands.

"I don't know why I'm doing this," Sean muttered.

Kate sighed. "And my horoscope said I'd have a good
day," she said as they passed through the gates.

"You don't believe in that rot, do you?" Sean asked,
and he sounded short-tempered. He couldn't be blamed

for dreading what was ahead, Kate supposed. She wasn't looking forward to it, either.

"Not anymore I don't," she answered.

Senator John Blake was standing on the front porch when they reached the house, his hands shoved into the pockets of his heavy terry cloth bathrobe. Even in slippers and pajamas, Kate marveled to herself, he looked imperious—every inch the powerful politician.

And he was powerful. Careers were made and broken on his say-so.

Sean shut off the headlights and the engine and got out of the car. He walked around to help Kate, but she'd pushed the door open before he reached her.

"Where is the boy?" the senator demanded. No hello. No "What brings you all the way to America?" It was clear enough that Sean wasn't welcome in his own right.

"He's in school in Sydney, where he belongs," Sean answered. He'd never been the slightest bit intimidated by the senator, and Kate suspected that was one of the reasons her father disliked him so intensely.

Senator Blake doubled one hand into a fist and pounded it into his palm. "Blast it all, Harris, that child belongs with his family!"

"I'm his family," Sean said quietly. Kate felt a certain admiration for his composure, even though she wanted her sister's son to visit the United States on a regular basis as much as her parents did.

Kate's mother, Irene, appeared in the massive double doorway behind the senator. "Let's not stand outside, making a public spectacle of ourselves," she scolded. "There may be reporters from those awful tabloids lurking in the shrubbery."

Despite everything, Kate had to smile at that. The

tabloids didn't pick on dull men like her father. They fed on scandal.

Then her smile faded as she stepped into the light and warmth of her parents' house. Once word of Brad's profitable little sideline got out, there would be scandal aplenty.

"What are you doing here?" the senator demanded of Sean the moment they were all inside his study with the doors closed. He sounded for all the world as though he thought Sean should have had his permission before entering the country.

"I've been in Seattle for a week, if it's any of your business," Sean answered evenly. "My company is thinking of placing an order with Simmons Aircraft."

Kate saw the sudden interest in her father's face. Simmons Aircraft was one of the largest employers in the state, and the company was a pet concern of the senator's. "You're still with the airline, then?"

"You could say that," Sean replied. A forest of crystal decanters stood on the bar, and he helped himself to a snifter of brandy, lifting it once to the senator before raising it to his lips. "But you didn't have your daughter drag me up here so we could talk about Austra-Air, did you?"

Kate felt a flash of resentment. Sean made it sound as though her father orchestrated her every move.

"No," Senator Blake responded. "It's about my grandson."

Sean set the snifter aside, then brought a thin leather wallet from the inside pocket of his tuxedo jacket, opening it and extending it to his former father-in-law. Kate caught a glimpse of a handsome blond boy smiling up from a photograph.

It was no secret that Gil resembled his late mother, but surprise moved in the senator's aging face all the same—surprise and pain. "He's a fine-looking lad," the old man said in a strange, small voice. "Does he do well in school?"

"Mostly," Sean answered quietly. "He's got a weak spot when it comes to spelling and the like."

Mrs. Blake hovered close behind the senator's shoulder, peering hungrily at her grandson's picture. "Abby was the same way," she said.

The air in that large, gracious room suddenly seemed to be in short supply. Kate went to the window behind her father's desk and opened one side a little way.

"The boy has a right to know his mother's family," said the senator.

"A few years ago I might have agreed with that," Sean replied, pulling the photograph out from behind the plastic window in his wallet and extending it to Mrs. Blake.

"What changed your mind?" the senator wanted to know. It seemed to Kate that he was having trouble meeting Sean's gaze, but she was wrong, of course. Her father was virtually fearless.

"When a man's son is nearly kidnapped," Sean answered, "it tends to change his mind about a lot of things." He tucked his wallet back into his pocket and glanced at Kate once before telling his late wife's parents, "You're welcome to visit Gil anytime you want to, but I won't send him here. Not until he's old enough to take care of himself."

Kate was staring at Sean, hardly able to believe what she'd heard. Gil had nearly been kidnapped? That in itself was news to her, but it had actually seemed, for a moment there, as though Sean thought the senator might have been behind the attempt.

When Sean walked out of the study, Kate followed, partly because she didn't want to listen to another of her father's tirades and partly because she had to confront Sean. He couldn't go around accusing good people of a crime and then just turn and walk away!

Kate said a hasty goodbye to her mother and father and followed Sean outside.

"I assume you want a ride home," Sean said as he opened the car door on the driver's side. It was the first indication he'd given that he was aware of her presence.

Kate answered by getting into the car. "What the hell do you mean by implying that my father would abduct a child?" she demanded the moment Sean was behind the wheel.

He ground the key into the ignition, and the engine started with an angry roar. "He wouldn't try it personally, of course," he snapped. "He paid someone to steal my son off the playground."

"That's a lie!"

Sean stopped the car without warning and glared at Kate. "Is it?" he rasped. "The man the police picked up admitted everything—he said he was working for a powerful American politician, and I guessed the rest."

Kate felt the color drain from her face. "No," she whispered, stunned. Her father would never do a thing like that. He was honorable and good, the kind of man who belonged in a Norman Rockwell painting. "I don't believe you."

"Believe what you like, love," Sean sighed. "I don't really give a damn."

Kate stiffened in her seat. "If my father was guilty,"

she challenged, "why didn't you take your case to the press? That would have ruined his career."

Sean didn't look at her. He appeared to be concentrating on the road, and his strong hands were tense where they gripped the steering wheel. "I couldn't," he answered in a low voice. "I once loved a daughter of his, you see."

Kate sat back. This had been one hell of a day. "So now you're just going to fly back home and forget that Gil has a family here in the States?"

They had reached the bottom of the driveway. "Yes," he replied. "If you want to see him, you'll have to pay a visit to the land of Oz."

Kate remembered the nickname Australians had given their country from her sister's early emails. The later ones had been filled with anger and fear and a wild, keening kind of despair. "I might just do that," she said. It would be good to get away from what Brad had done, away from her father's campaign.

Sean gave her a quicksilver glance, one she nearly missed. "Really?"

"I'd need to get a visa," Kate told him. "But, with my father's connections, that shouldn't take long."

Kate couldn't tell whether Sean was pleased at the prospect of a visit from his former sister-in-law or not, since the car was too dark and he revealed nothing by his tone or his words. "Where do you live?"

She gave him the address of her building, and he nodded in recognition. It was near his hotel, he said.

"How long are you staying?" she asked as the expensive car slipped through the dark city streets.

He moved his powerful shoulders in a casual shrug.

"Another few days, I suppose. I want to take the plane up at least once more before I make my recommendation."

Kate knew he was testing the airliner his company was considering buying from Simmons Aircraft. "Just how many planes are we talking about here?" she asked.

Sean favored her with a grin that might have been slightly contemptuous. She couldn't quite tell. "You're definitely your father's daughter," he said, and Kate felt as though she'd been roundly insulted. Her cheeks were throbbing with heat when Sean finally answered her question. "Roughly a dozen, give or take a plane. We're phasing out our old fleet."

A dozen airliners. A contract like that would mean prosperity for a good many of her father's constituents.

"What do you do, anyway?" Sean asked.

Again Kate felt vaguely indignant. "I work for the senator."

"I gathered that much," Sean retorted, bringing the car to a sleek stop in front of Kate's building. "Do you actually work, or do you just stand around agreeing with everything the old man says?"

Kate's color rose in anger, and she reached for the door handle, but Sean caught her hand in a swift grasp and held it prisoner. She trembled as he stroked the tender flesh on the inside of her wrist with the pad of his thumb.

"Cold?" he asked, knowing perfectly well she was practically boiling.

She gave a little cry when he tilted his head and melded his mouth to hers, but she made no move to resist him. The old attraction had returned to shame her.

Chapter 2

Kate's telephone was ringing when she let herself into the elegant condominium. She made no effort to lift the receiver, knowing the answering machine would pick up the call.

She listened to her own voice giving a recorded greeting as she carefully folded her silk shawl and set it aside, along with her grandmother's purse. There was a little dent, she noticed with a frown, where the solid brass bag had struck the mugger's head.

Brad's voice filled the room. At least there was one good thing about this whole incident, and that was the fact that Brad's job would be hers now. She was qualified, and she had more seniority than anyone else on the staff. "Kate, I'm at home. Call me immediately!"

"Go to hell," Kate muttered, her arms folded across her chest. Even though the living room was warm, she suddenly felt chilled. She turned down the volume on the machine and, if Brad said anything more, she didn't hear him.

Her mind and senses were full of Sean. Her heart was still beating a little faster than usual, and her nipples felt taut beneath the thin fabric of her evening gown. She kept her arms folded over her breasts in an effort to hide her involuntary response, even though there was no one around to see.

Unlike her parents, Kate didn't keep pictures of Abby out in plain view, but she went to the shelf behind her couch and took down a thin leather-bound album. The names "Abby and Sean" were embossed on the cover in gold lettering, and Kate felt a lump thicken in her throat as she opened it to the first photograph.

It showed Abby sitting at her vanity table in her frilly room, her wedding gown a tumble of satin and lace and pearls. Kate saw herself, ten years younger and wearing a pink bridesmaid's dress. In the photograph she appeared to be pinning Abby's veil carefully into place, though in reality that task had fallen to a hairdresser.

With the tip of an index finger, Kate touched her sister's glowing, flawless face, her golden hair and wide brown eyes. *Abby.* The senator had called her his Christmas-tree angel.

Tears brimmed in Kate's eyes, and she closed the album and put it carefully back among the others. She couldn't think about Abby, not with Sean's kiss still burning on her mouth.

Kate kicked off her shoes and felt her feet sink deep into the plush pearl-gray carpet on the floor. With a sigh, she wandered into her bedroom and slipped out of the dress, her pantyhose and underthings. A long, hot shower soothed her a little, though the pounding massage of the water made her more aware of her body than she wanted to be.

Clad in a striped silk nightshirt, her shoulder-length brown hair blown dry, Kate climbed into the brass bed that had once graced one of her grandmother's guest rooms and pulled the covers up to her chin.

She wouldn't think about Sean. It was that simple. She had a good mind; she could direct it to other matters.

However, it would not be directed. Against Kate's will, she remembered the first time she'd seen Sean Harris.

She'd been nineteen at the time, and he'd come to the house with Abby. Attracted by his good looks, his sense of humor and his lilting accent, Kate had fallen in love. Although he had never said or done anything to encourage her, Sean had always been kind, and Kate had gone on adoring him long after he'd become her brother-in-law.

Then those emails had started arriving from Abby. Sean was a chauvinist, she'd claimed. He hated her, delighted in humiliating her.

"Why didn't you leave him?" Kate asked in the darkness of her room. She squeezed her eyes shut as memories of the funeral invaded her mind, unwanted and painful.

Sean had brought Abby home to be buried in the family plot, though Gil, only two years old then, had remained behind in Australia. Sean's grief had loomed over him, like the dark shadow of something monstrous.

Even then she had loved him, though she wouldn't have admitted that to herself. The guilt, coupled with her bereavement, would have broken her.

For the past five years Kate had concentrated on putting Sean out of her mind. Until tonight she'd thought those treacherous, tearing emotions were behind her forever.

Now she just didn't know.

A furious pounding at the front door awakened Kate with a start. She squinted at the clock on her bedside table and saw that it was two-thirty in the morning.

Full of frightened bafflement, Kate scrambled out of bed and found her robe. Reaching the front door, she peered through the peephole and saw Brad.

"Let me in, damn it," he snapped, somehow knowing she was there.

Kate hesitated, then opened the door. Brad was capable of making a scene, and there was no sense in letting him awaken all the neighbors.

The tall blond man pushed past Kate. He'd exchanged his formal evening clothes for a pair of jeans, a lightweight blue sweater and the formidably expensive leather jacket Kate had given him for Christmas.

"Why the devil did you run off like that?" he rasped, his eyes snapping with barely suppressed fury.

Kate bit her lower lip and brushed her sleep-tangled hair back from her face. He was referring to her hasty exit from the opera, of course. "I saw you take money for cocaine," she said slowly and carefully. Even now she could hardly believe it.

She hoped for a raging denial, but Brad only stared at her in hostile puzzlement. "So?" he asked.

Kate felt fury flow through her like venom. "What do you mean, 'So?'" she cried, struggling to keep her voice down. "We're talking about a crime here—a felony!"

Brad shook his handsome head in apparent amazement. "I don't believe this," he said.

"Neither do I," Kate replied wearily. She found her antique purse, opened it and took out the ring. "Here," she said, extending it to Brad.

His eyes widened in his tanned face. "You're not serious."

"I can't marry you," Kate said. Tears filled her eyes as she mourned all her dreams—the suburban house, the children, the dog in the back of a minivan. All of it was gone. It wasn't fair.

Brad refused to take the ring. "Kate," he said reasonably as though speaking to a cranky child, "*everybody* does cocaine."

Kate shook her head. Her cheeks were wet now, and she dried them hastily on the sleeve of her nightshirt. "No," she argued. "That isn't true and you know it. Brad, you need help. If you'll check into a hospital—"

He held up both hands in a gesture so abrupt that it startled Kate into retreating another step. "Wait a second. A hospital? I haven't got that kind of problem, Kate. And even if I did, I wouldn't just walk away from the senator's campaign."

Kate swallowed. "You'll have to resign as campaign manager, Brad. Right away."

He was staring at her as though she'd just told him she'd had supper with a Martian. "Resign? Are you kidding? This is the most important job of my career and you damn well know it!"

Kate did know that Brad had political ambitions of his own. He had left a prestigious law firm to take the job on her father's staff expressly to make contacts among the powerful. "Brad, if you don't resign, my father will fire you."

Brad paled beneath his tan. "Are you saying that you're going to tell him about tonight?"

"I have to," Kate said with miserable conviction. "It would be irresponsible not to."

Brad stood close, his hands cupping Kate's face. Although his touch was gentle, she sensed a certain restrained violence in him and she was afraid. "No. Listen to me. You can't do this—I've worked too long and too hard..."

Kate twisted out of his grasp and put the couch between them, her hands gripping its back. "Go home," she said quietly. "Think about this. We'll talk again tomorrow."

"We'll talk now!" Brad snapped. "If you tell your father about that cocaine, I'll be ruined!"

"Please leave," Kate said. She felt chilled from head to foot. She had almost married this man!

Brad didn't move at all. He only glared at her and spit out, "You're naive as hell, Kate. This kind of thing goes on every day in every level of government. Why don't you stop being such a goody-goody and grow up?"

Kate could only gaze at him, feeling sick to her stomach. Dear God in heaven, how had he fooled her so completely?

After another long and frightening moment, Brad stormed out the door. Kate rushed to lock and bolt it behind him, leaning against it with her eyes closed while she waited for her heartbeat and her breathing to settle into normal patterns.

She'd been dating Brad Wilshire for a year. There

must have been signs that he used and sold drugs, but she hadn't seen them. That fact in itself was terrifying; Kate wondered if she could trust her own instincts. Was she one of those self-destructive women she'd read about in pop psychology books?

After a few deep breaths and fifteen minutes spent pacing the darkened living room, Kate was tired enough to sleep. She crawled back into bed, closed her eyes and dreamed that she lived in a fine colonial house in the suburbs. Sean was her husband and Gil was her son and there were twelve gleaming airliners parked in the backyard.

The jangle of the telephone awakened Kate before her alarm clock could. She grappled for the receiver and pressed it to her ear, muttering a hoarse, "Hello?"

The senator's voice was like restrained thunder. "Brad has been arrested," he said.

Kate was wide awake. "When?" she asked, sitting up in bed.

"Early this morning. He's denying all the charges, of course."

Kate swallowed hard. "What charges?"

"You ought to know," her father responded coldly. "You're the one who turned him in, aren't you? How could you do this when you knew the effect a scandal would have on me?"

"I didn't turn him in," Kate protested quietly. "I would never have done that without consulting you."

"Be that as it may, the story will be all over the morning papers. We've got to decide whether to stand behind Wilshire or cut him loose."

"That shouldn't be too hard to work out," Kate said,

flinging back the covers. "He's guilty—I saw him make the sale with my own eyes."

"But you didn't blow the whistle on him?"

"No," Kate insisted. "I should have, though."

"I take it the wedding is off?"

Kate shoved a hand through her hair. "I don't know how you can even ask that," she whispered furiously. "Of *course* it's off!"

The senator sighed. Kate knew he'd had dreams of his own where Brad was concerned. He'd meant to groom his prospective son-in-law to take his place one day. And John Blake wasn't a man who gave up easily. "I think I could persuade him to enter a treatment center."

"Give it up, Daddy," Kate sighed. "Brad will ruin you if you keep him on as campaign manager, and we both know it."

Her father reluctantly agreed and ended the conversation. Kate showered, wound her dark hair into a tidy French braid and dressed in a businesslike black suit and tasteful silk blouse. As her father's press secretary, she was ready to meet the newspaper reporters.

It was a good thing, because they were waiting for her the moment she reached the elegant mansion on the hill, clustering around her car, shouting questions and shoving microphones and cameras into her face.

"Is it true you turned your lover in for pushing cocaine?" called one man.

Kate looked at him with distaste and hustled toward the front door. "The senator will have a comment for you later," she called over one shoulder.

Someone grabbed her by the arm, and Kate wrenched free, infuriated by the presumption of such a gesture.

Inside the house she found her father surrounded by aides. There was no sign of her mother. Although Irene was a seasoned campaigner, she tended to get headaches when the water got rough.

"Are you ready to issue a statement?" Kate asked, shouldering her way through to her father's desk.

He looked up as though surprised to see her. "Yes," he said. "Tell those vultures out there that even though we bailed Wilshire out of jail, we're washing our hands of him as of today. He's off my staff."

"When will you name a new campaign manager?" Kate asked. She fully expected her father to give the job to her, since she'd earned it. In fact, in many ways she was more qualified than Brad had been.

"Right now," the senator said decisively. "Tell the press that I've chosen Mike Wilson for the job." He glanced fondly at the young and inexperienced lawyer standing close by.

Kate turned to leave the room without a word.

"Where do you think you're going?" Kate's father called after her, his tone angry and imperious.

Kate froze at the study door, her hand on the brass knob. "I'm about to issue my last official statement as your press secretary," she replied clearly.

The senator's anger was palpable. It reached out and coiled around Kate like an invisible boa constrictor. "Not until you've told me what this is all about, you won't!"

Kate turned and faced him again. "You as much as promised that job to me. How many times have you said, 'If it weren't for Brad, you'd be my campaign manager'?"

"I was only joking, and you damn well know it. It

takes a man to manage a campaign! Furthermore, I don't have time to indulge your temperament, Katherine. If you walk out that door, you can consider yourself fired."

Kate glared at the white-haired man seated behind the desk. His staff surrounded him on three sides, all of them looking at Kate as though she'd just lost her reason.

She offered a silent prayer that she wouldn't cry and raised her chin. "That will save me the trouble of writing a letter of resignation," she said.

The senator swore, and Kate walked out of his study with her shoulders straight and her head high. Her mother was in the hallway, her perfect complexion gray with anxiety, her strawberry blond hair artfully coiffed. She gripped both of Kate's hands in hers, and her ice-blue eyes pleaded for understanding.

"I know your father is in a terrible mood," she said, "but it's sure to pass once the press backs off a little."

Kate could no longer hold back her tears. She shook her head and put one hand over her mouth.

"What's happened?" Irene Blake demanded.

Kate bit into her lower lip, struggling for composure. Her disappointment and sense of betrayal combined to overwhelm her. "He gave Brad's job to Mike Wilson," she finally managed to say.

Irene's gaze revealed honest bafflement. "And?"

Kate's patience was exhausted. "Mother, that job should have gone to me," she whispered angrily.

"But you're—"

"Don't you dare say 'But you're a woman,' Mother. If you do, I'll never forgive you."

Irene sighed. "Why don't you just go away for a few

days, dear. Fly somewhere tropical and lounge in the sun until you feel better."

Kate sniffed and dried her cheeks with a tissue pulled from her purse. She still had to face the press. "That's a good idea, Mother. Tell Daddy I said, *adiós*, bye-bye and *ciao*." With that, she started toward the door.

"Don't be flippant, Katherine," her mother called after her. "It doesn't become you."

Kate rolled her eyes, opened the front door and stepped outside. Sean was just about to enter, and she couldn't have been happier to see him. He was like a barrier between her and the eager reporters. "Thank God you're here," she whispered.

Sean grinned, looking almost intolerably good in his jeans, cotton shirt and leather jacket. "Trust a Yank to do the unexpected," he said in a mischievous whisper that ruffled the loose tendrils of Kate's hair and sent a sweet shiver all through her system. "I was prepared to be thrown out on my ear."

Kate linked her arm with Sean's and smiled up at him. "Pretend we like each other," she said through her teeth.

"Don't we?" Sean countered, feigning an injured look.

Shouting questions about Brad, the covey of reporters closed around them as soon as they stepped off the porch. Kate held on to Sean and looked straight ahead, pretending not to see or hear the men and women vying for her attention. She wasn't her father's press secretary anymore; there was no reason for her to try to appease the media.

"What the hell's going on here?" Sean demanded good-naturedly, once they were safely inside his car and pulling away from the curb.

Kate pressed the tips of her index fingers to the skin

under her eyes in the hope that she could keep herself from crying again. "I've just been fired from my father's staff."

"Given the sack, were you?" Sean didn't look at all sympathetic. "Best thing for you, love," he said cheerfully. "Now maybe you can be somebody besides your father's daughter."

Kate bristled. "What is that supposed to mean?"

"You've given the senator all your time and half your soul, Katie-did. When were you planning to live your life?"

Sean's words cut close to the bone, and Kate hugged herself in an unconscious gesture of self-defense. She wondered how he could have discerned something like that when they'd spent so little time together.

In that moment, Kate felt like a life-size paper doll. She had no real interests, beyond the senator's career, no hobbies and very few friends. She folded her arms, utterly demoralized.

"There now," Sean said soothingly. "It'll all come right in the end."

Kate turned her attention to him. It was better than thinking about herself. "What were you doing at my parents' house?" she asked.

Sean seemed to have a definite destination in mind, and it wasn't Kate's building. "Actually, I was looking for you. Good old Brad's arrest was all over the news this morning, and I thought you might need a sympathetic shoulder. When you didn't answer your telephone, I guessed that you were probably with your dear old dad."

Kate was beginning to rally a little. "Where are we going?" she wanted to know. The car was speeding along the freeway now; they were leaving downtown Seattle far behind.

"Simmons Field," Sean answered. "I told you I wanted to take the plane up again."

"You're not expecting me to go, are you?"

Sean grinned fetchingly. "Sure. We can have lunch at thirty-seven thousand feet—that is, if you don't mind airline food."

"Me? I'll stay on the ground, thank you. I'm no test pilot."

"That's okay, love. We only need one of those, and I'm it."

Kate sighed. "I'm not dressed for this," she said, grasping at straws. She wasn't afraid to fly, but she didn't like the idea of going up in anything that had to be tested.

"It's a passenger jet, Katie-did—not a barnstormer. Come on, live a little."

Kate nodded grudgingly, and Sean's grin widened. He looked pretty pleased with himself.

They arrived at Simmons Field, and Sean parked the sports car in a space marked Reserved. His eyes moved appreciatively over Kate's trim figure when she got out of the vehicle and stood facing him.

"I could wait for you in the hangar," she offered.

Sean shook his head and drew her close. It felt natural and right to walk within the curve of his arm. "Don't be a coward, Katie-did. I'll take care of you."

My secret dream, Kate thought sadly, recalling how she'd thought Brad would take care of her. The truth was, there weren't any princes out here, though some of the frogs could do a pretty good imitation of one. "I can take care of myself," she said firmly.

Sean made no comment on that. Soon they were mounting the portable stairway that would take them into the gleaming jumbo jet he wanted to test. There was a flight attendant on board, along with a copilot and a navigator.

Kate followed the three men into the cockpit, where she buckled herself into a seat near the door. Sean winked at her before sitting down at the controls. She bent far to one side to watch as he put on a set of earphones and then reached up to flip a variety of switches. The craft roared to life, and Kate wondered if there was an ignition key, like in a car.

She gripped the armrests on either side of her as the plane began taxiing down the runway. She could hear Sean talking to the tower in a rhythmic, practiced voice, and she relaxed a little. Even her father would have conceded that Sean was an excellent pilot.

There she went again, measuring her opinions against her father's. She forced herself to relax, realized her eyes were squeezed shut and opened them to see Sean grinning at her around the side of his seat.

Kate made a gesture with the back of her hand, encouraging him to turn his attention back to the friendly skies, and he laughed as he complied.

The navigator smiled at her from his position close by. "Relax," the older man told her. "He probably won't stall it out with you aboard."

"Stall it out?" Kate squeaked. She didn't like the sound of that. "What does that mean?"

"Never mind," said the navigator.

Kate gripped the armrests again.

An hour later, Sean landed the airplane at Simmons Field, and Kate let out her breath.

A group of bald, smiling men wearing off-the-rack suits met them on the tarmac. "Well, Mr. Harris, what do you think of our baby there?" one of them asked, gesturing toward the sleek silver aircraft.

Sean's expression was strictly noncommittal. "The engines grab a little when you stall it out," he remarked.

Kate swallowed. She'd figured out what that phrase meant, and she wondered if she'd had a near-death experience and never even noticed.

One of the officials recognized Kate. "Aren't you Senator Blake's daughter?" he asked.

Kate winced. Maybe Sean was right; maybe she didn't have any other identity besides that one. She nodded, not knowing what else to say.

"I don't mind telling you," the man beamed, looking at Sean again, "that the senator has been a very good friend to Simmons Aircraft."

Sean's expression was bland. "No worries, mate," he said. "We might be able to deal in spite of that."

Kate bit back a grin.

Sean took her hand, said a polite goodbye to the contingent from the sales department and started off toward his car.

"There's a good day's work," he said happily, opening the door for Kate. "Now we can play." He glanced at his watch. "How about some lunch?"

Kate realized with some surprise that she was hungry. Due to the stresses of a political campaign and an engagement, she hadn't had an appetite in months. She nodded.

They went to a nearby steak house, and while Kate gravitated to the salad bar, Sean ordered something from the menu.

When his plate arrived, Kate stared at it in horror. It was a T-bone steak, and it was definitely rare. "Do you know what red meat does to your heart?" she asked.

Sean rolled his eyes. "Don't tell me you've turned into one of those curmudgeons who eats sprouts and drinks blue milk."

Kate speared a cherry tomato and popped it into her mouth. "It doesn't hurt to be health conscious," she said.

Sean cut into his slab of bloody meat, lifted a piece to his mouth and chewed appreciatively. His eyes slipped briefly to Kate's breasts and then rose to her lips, where they lingered for several unsettling moments. "No worries, love," he said. "I promise you, I'm healthy."

Even though Sean had not said anything out of line, Kate felt her cheeks color. Where this man was concerned, she was nineteen again, full of crazy needs and self-doubts. She dropped her gaze to her salad, but Sean's chuckle made her look back up at his face.

"What?" she demanded, nettled.

"I've missed you, Katie-did," he said.

Kate didn't know what that meant and was afraid to ask. She hadn't suspected that Sean ever thought about her, let alone missed her. "I guess you knew I had a major crush on you," she commented.

He reached out, placed an index finger under her chin and lifted it. "I was flattered," he told her.

She felt her cheeks heat up again. "You were my sister's husband," she reminded him, feeling the old guilt rise up within her.

"It's no sin to care about somebody," he reasoned, and for just a moment, shadows flickered in his eyes, sad and dark. Kate knew he was thinking about Abby, and she felt like an intruder.

"Did you love my sister?" she asked.

"Once," Sean answered, and there was no more talk of past loves after that. They finished their meal, and Sean drove Kate back to her building. He was parking the car, while she waited near the elevator, when Brad appeared.

He looked terrible. There were dark smudges under his eyes, his hair was mussed and he needed to shave. "How could you do it?" he rasped. "How could you sell me out like that?"

Kate automatically retreated when he took a step toward her. He lunged in a burst of rage, and Kate screamed when his hands closed painfully over her shoulders.

The next thing she knew, Brad was sailing backward, colliding with one of the concrete pillars that supported the floors above.

Sean had finished parking the car.

Chapter 3

Brad raised himself cautiously from the floor, one hand on his jaw. He was glaring at Sean, but he spoke to Kate. "It didn't take you long to replace me, did it?"

Kate was shaken. A brutal headache was taking shape behind her eyes. Beside her, Sean was silent, though she could feel his fury. "Please," she muttered, avoiding Brad's eyes. "Just go away."

She saw her former fiancé sway slightly on his feet and caught the scent of liquor. It was early afternoon and Brad was drunk.

"Thanks to you," he said, "I might be going away for a long time. Didn't I mean anything at all to you, Kate?"

Unconsciously, she moved a little closer to Sean, but she met Brad's gaze without flinching. "I didn't turn you in, Brad," she said. The elevator arrived then, and she stepped into it.

Sean followed, while Brad stared at her from outside. "I won't forget this, Kate," he vowed.

Kate covered her eyes with one hand and sank against the back wall of the elevator the moment the doors were closed. "Damn," she whispered. Her stomach began to churn as the headache intensified.

Without speaking, Sean put an arm around her. She leaned against him, too shaken to resist.

When they left the elevator at her floor, Sean held out his hand. "Let me have the key," he said softly.

Dazed, Kate found her key ring in the bottom of her purse and handed it to him. "It's the one with the number engraved at the top," she told him.

Sean opened the door, then surprised Kate by lifting her into his arms. "It's time somebody made a bit of a fuss over you, love," he said huskily, carrying her inside.

Kate didn't even think of resisting when he carried her to the bed and laid her carefully down on top of the comforter. He spoke soothingly as he took off her shoes and tossed them aside, then massaged her calves.

She wondered how Abby could ever have described this man as cruel.

He left her, and she heard the door of the medicine cabinet open and close in the bathroom. Soon he was back with a glass of water and a couple of aspirin.

Kate swallowed the pills gratefully and fell back to her pillows with a little moan. She rarely took aspirin because it always knocked her out.

When she awakened, the room was full of shadows, and Sean was stretched out, fully clothed except for his shoes, on the bed beside her. His hands were cupped behind his head, and he appeared to be asleep.

Kate gasped at the rush of sensations that washed

over her, and lay down again. She was afraid to move or speak, in case Sean would awaken and leave her.

After a long time she became aware that he was already awake, despite the fact that his eyes were closed.

"Feeling better, Katie-did?" he asked in a low voice.

Kate licked her lips. She could feel the hard heat of his body to the marrow of her bones, and she was terrified of what she might betray when she spoke. "Much," she managed.

He opened his eyes and turned onto his side. Lightly he brushed her lips with his own, and rested his hand just beneath the fullness of her breast. "Good," he said.

Kate barely held back a whimper as he brushed his thumb over her nipple. "Sean," she whispered, and the word was a plea. She wanted him to touch her, and *not* to touch her.

He kissed her thoroughly, as he had the night before in his car, his lips mastering hers, his tongue foreshadowing an invasion of another kind. Kate eased her arms around his neck and responded with everything that was in her.

She did not want to think of how wrong she'd been before when she'd fallen in love with Brad Wilshire.

Presently Sean pushed aside her jacket and began opening the tiny pearl buttons on her blouse. She tensed, arching her back in a spasmodic surrender, when he pushed up her bra and cupped a naked breast in the warmth of his hand.

"Please," she whispered. *Please stop, please go on, please be the man I believe you to be.*

Sean slid downward and took her nipple into his mouth in a bold suckling kiss. Kate cried out, entangling her fingers in his hair to press him closer.

He reached beneath her skirt, grasping her through the thin material of her pantyhose, forcing her to spread her thighs for him. He spoke quietly as he caressed her and, fevered, she put her hands behind his head and drew him back to her breast.

He chuckled as he nipped at the peak.

Kate, always cool and professional, was out of control. Between the stimulation of her breast and the masterful motions of his hand, she was losing her mind. She thrust her hips upward, and Sean immediately peeled her pantyhose down to the middle of her thighs. She longed to part her legs, but she couldn't, and Sean took immediate advantage of her position.

Then, with the same finger, he invaded her. She sobbed his name and dug her heels into the bed so that she could lift herself to him. All the while suckling and plying her with his thumb, Sean worked her into a frenzy.

"Take me," she pleaded, clutching him. "Oh, Sean, please—please—take me!"

He left her breast to nibble and kiss the length of her neck. "Not this time, Katie-did," he said, just as Kate exploded and became a part of the sunset.

Her body jerked with sweet aftershocks for several moments, then she fell, exhausted, to the comforter. Sean withdrew his finger, caressed the pulsing bit of flesh where a lifetime of pleasure lay waiting to be shared, then raised himself on one elbow to look down at her. After studying her face, as if to memorize it, he kissed her and then sat up.

Sensing that he meant to leave her, Kate scrambled into a sitting position and laid her hands on his shoulders. "Sean, make love to me."

He shook his head once and then drew gently away from Kate to stand with his back to her. "Giving you pleasure is one thing," he said in a hoarse voice. "Taking it is another."

Kate was completely confused. She hadn't had a whole lot of experience with men, but she knew Sean wanted her as much as she wanted him. Her fingers were awkward as she tossed away her pantyhose and tried to button her blouse. "I—I wanted to give myself to you."

At last he turned to face her. "I know you did, sweet," he said, "but you're not ready for that."

Kate gave up on her blouse and went to the closet, keeping her shoulders straight. "I'll be thirty years old in two weeks, Sean," she said, finding her pink terry cloth bathrobe. Turning, she tossed it onto the bed and began undressing. "Just how ready do I have to be?"

Sean looked at her the way a starving man looks at meat as she deliberately stripped away her jacket, her blouse, her tangled bra and skirt. She saw him swallow convulsively when she lowered her half-slip to stand before him naked.

"My God," he whispered. "Put your robe on."

Kate didn't move.

He shoved the splayed fingers of one hand through his hair. "Katie, if you don't do as I say, I'll walk out of here right now."

She reached for her robe and put it on. The motion of her hands was quick and angry.

Sean rose out of his chair. "In two days," he said gently, reasonably, "I'll be going back to Australia. I can't make love to you and then leave you behind."

There was a sob in Kate's voice as she shrugged and asked, "Why not? Don't guys do that every day?"

"Katie, don't," he pleaded hoarsely.

It had been another awful day, and sure as hell, Kate thought, her horoscope probably promised roses and moonbeams. "You don't have to feel guilty," she said as tears slipped down her cheeks. "After all, I came on to you—"

"Stop it!" Sean rasped, rounding the bed and grasping her by the shoulders. She winced, since Brad's hold had bruised her earlier, and saw her own pain reflected in Sean's eyes.

He pulled her close and held her. "Katie," he said, and that one word explained everything and nothing.

A few moments later Sean released her. "I'll go and get us something to eat," he said.

Kate didn't want food, she wanted Sean, but she knew he wouldn't violate his principles by making love to her. He probably still loved Abby very much, and that would make his guilt unbearable.

When she heard the door close, Kate went into the living room, opened the curtains to let in the sparkling night view of the city and put on some soft music. Her body was still reverberating with the savage pleasure Sean had introduced her to such a short time before.

About half an hour had passed when Sean returned with take-out hamburgers, sodas and french fries. By that time, Kate had lit the gas fireplace, brushed her hair and misted herself with her favorite perfume.

Sean looked at her and shook his head. "I was hoping you would have changed into a sweat suit by now," he said.

Kate smiled. "You're lucky I'm not naked," she told him.

He shook his head again. "I don't think lucky is the right word," he observed, and the paper bags rustled as he took out the fragrant food.

"This stuff is terrible for us," Kate said, just before she took a big bite of her hamburger. She was sitting near the hearth, and Sean joined her.

He glanced at the flickering fire, then the spectacle beyond the windows, then the sound system. "Are you trying to seduce me?" he asked forthrightly.

"Yes," Kate answered, chewing.

He laughed and brushed a crumb from her chin. "I ought to turn you over my knee," he said.

"Kinky," Kate replied, wriggling her eyebrows.

Sean reached out suddenly, yanked Kate across his lap, and gave her derriere a sound but painless swat. Laughing, she struggled to sit up, and in the process her robe opened and her breasts were bared. The firelight played over them with shadowy fingers, and Sean choked on a french fry.

Kate didn't move. She couldn't have, even if she'd wanted to. It was as though the whole world, all of time and creation, was holding its breath.

Like a man bewildered, Sean reached out to touch her. She closed her eyes and let her head fall back as his fingers gently shaped her nipple. Within an instant, he drew back, and Kate trembled with humiliation, unable to meet his eyes when she felt him close her robe.

There were tears glistening along her lashes when she forced herself to look at him. "I'm sorry, Sean," she said brokenly.

He laid his hand to her cheek. "Don't be," he told her. Then he got to his feet and went to stand at the window, looking out. It had begun to rain, and the city lights were shifting, shimmering splotches of color against the glass.

Kate sniffled and rose from the floor. Carefully, almost primly, she retied the belt of her robe, as though to prevent what had already happened. She had to say something; she couldn't bear the accusing silence. "I'm really glad you were with me today when we ran into Brad."

Sean didn't look at her. "Does he have a key to this place, Katie-did?" he asked.

Kate supposed she deserved the kind of disrespect that question indicated, but she still had some pride. She lifted her chin. "What if he does?" she countered.

"If he does, I'm staying the night," Sean answered, glaring at her over one shoulder. "He might decide to come back here and avenge his honor or some such rot."

Recalling the way Brad had grabbed her, Kate shuddered. She'd seen a side of the man in the past twenty-four hours that she'd never suspected was there. "He might," she agreed.

Sean was examining the couch. "Does this thing fold out?" he wanted to know.

"Why?" Kate retorted. "Are you tired?"

He pointed a finger at her. "Yes," he answered. "And you stay away from me, sheila."

Kate wanted to scream and throw things. After all, *she* hadn't been the one to start all this.

She stormed across the room, picked up the newspaper that had been delivered earlier and turned to the horoscope page. She could expect everything to go her way that day, according to the prediction.

"Sure!" she yelled, wadding up the paper and flinging it down.

* * *

Sean's mind was not on the business of buying a fleet of airliners. He'd already read all the reports and blueprints and, most important of all, he'd taken the plane up several times. He was relieved when the last meeting with the Simmons Aircraft people ended and he was free to leave.

He was behind the wheel of his rented sports car, loosening his tie with one hand and turning the radio dial with the other, when the news story broke. Senator John Blake had suffered a heart attack en route to Washington. He was in critical condition in a Seattle hospital.

Even in the days when things were still good between him and Abby, Sean and the senator had not been friends. Abby's lies and the kidnapping attempt against Gil had made things infinitely worse. For all of that, Sean was sorry to hear the news.

His first concern was Kate. She was a little fragile these days, given the falling-out with her father and the broken engagement. She was probably pacing in some waiting room, feeling guilty as hell.

He pulled out into traffic and headed in the general direction of the hospital mentioned on the newscast. When he arrived, there were news vans everywhere, along with a small contingent of reporters. He pushed his way through and strode up to the admissions desk.

"I'm Senator Blake's son-in-law," he told the clerk.

The young woman gave him a look of mingled appreciation and skepticism. "I'll just check that out, if you don't mind. Your name, sir?"

"Sean Harris," he answered, watching the woman press a sequence of numbers with a long manicured finger. That told him all he needed to know, but he waited politely while she relayed his name to someone on the other end of the line.

"That was Ms. Blake," the receptionist said. "She says it's all right for you to come up. It's suite 4102. We have to be very careful, you understand…"

Sean nodded impatiently and walked to the elevators.

Kate was waiting for him when he got off. She was dressed in jeans and a yellow cotton shirt, and her dark hair fell free around her shoulders. Her beautiful blue eyes were swollen from crying, and she kept running her palms down the legs of her jeans.

Wordlessly Sean held out his arms, and she flew into them.

"How is he?" Sean asked after a few moments, still holding her tightly.

She looked up at him and sniffled. "The doctors think he'll be okay," she said. "If only I hadn't—"

Sean laid a finger to her lips. "Don't say it, Kate. Don't even think it. The senator's heart attack wasn't your fault."

She drew back from him, but caught his hand in hers. "I wish I could be so sure of that," she said.

Sean wanted to take her home with him, to shelter and spoil her, to make love to her endlessly. She'd done what a long line of models, businesswomen and stewardesses hadn't been able to manage—she'd won his heart. A fraction of a moment before she'd swung her purse at that mugger's head, before Sean had realized who she was, he'd fallen in love.

He took Kate by the arm and ushered her to a plastic sofa, where they both sat down. Mrs. Blake was probably in the room with her husband, and no one else was around except for a couple of members of the senator's staff.

Kate was studying Sean's face. "You have to go back to Australia," she remembered with a note of resignation in her voice.

He nodded. Gil would be expecting him back, and the other members of Austra-Air's board of directors were anxious to hear his report on the new jet. He'd spent two nights on Kate's couch already, and he couldn't protect her forever, even though he wanted that more than anything.

"Did you have the locks changed?" he asked, worried about Brad Wilshire and his temper.

Despite everything, a grin formed on Kate's pale, fine-boned face. "I didn't need to," she confessed in a mischievous whisper. "Brad never had a key. I just wanted you to stay."

The knowledge made Sean happy, though he tried to hide it. It wasn't proper to jump up in the air and shout for joy when somebody was suffering from a heart attack just a few walls away. "Let's have a promise that you'll come and see us," he said softly, curving one finger under her chin.

She ran her tongue over her lips. "That'll depend on how Daddy is," she answered.

"He's made of iron, love," Sean assured her. "He'll be mean as ever in a few days."

Kate lowered her eyes, and Sean hoped devoutly that she wasn't retreating back into that one-dimensional identity she'd cultivated. "Maybe," she said.

Sean kissed her lightly on the forehead, and then they sat in companionable silence, holding hands and waiting.

An hour later a doctor came out and told them the senator was conscious and asking for his daughter. There was every reason to believe he'd recover.

With a small cry of relief, Kate flung her arms around Sean and squeezed. The embrace ended too soon, for she was anxious to see her father.

Sean glanced at his watch. If he hurried, he could still catch his plane. He would have to stop at Kate's to pick up the rest of his things, but that wouldn't take long since he'd never really unpacked.

"Goodbye, love," he said gently, touching her cheek.

"Your things—you'll need a key—" She rushed to find her purse and gave him her spare set.

A feeling of immense loneliness swept over Sean as he walked to the elevators. He made a point of not looking back; he knew she wouldn't be there.

Two weeks after the senator's heart attack, he was at home, preparing to return to Washington, where one of his aides had been voting as his proxy. Although things were better between Kate and her father, she still had no intention of going back to work on his staff. She didn't know exactly what she was going to do with the rest of her life but, for once, she planned to be the one who made the decisions.

Her passport and Australian tourist visa were in the mailbox when she arrived home from visiting her parents one afternoon. She was really going to do it. She was going to pack her bags, buy an airline ticket and fly to Australia to see Gil.

As for what had happened—or *almost* happened—between her and Sean, well, that had been nothing more than a momentary lapse. A reaction to her disappointment over the breaking of her engagement. Whenever she thought about that night, she was grateful that Sean had been too much of a gentleman to take advantage of her pain and confusion.

"Bring the boy back with you," her father instructed her the next morning when she stopped by the house on her way to the airport.

Kate sighed. "I can't just grab him and throw him on an airplane," she pointed out. "I promise to take lots of pictures, though, and if Sean will let me, maybe I can bring Gil here for a visit."

"Just get him here. There's an election coming up in November, and I want to be seen as a family man."

Kate bent to kiss her father's wan forehead. "Don't get your hopes up," she warned. "Sean doesn't trust you, and he's not likely to do you any favors."

"He has a lot of gall, keeping a man from his own grandson. This wouldn't be happening if my Abby were still alive, that's for sure. She wouldn't stand for it."

The senator's words seemed to imply some lack in Kate. "Abby is dead," she reminded him gently.

She saw the old pain move in his keenly intelligent eyes. "Yes. And as far as I'm concerned, we have Sean Harris to blame for it."

Kate knew there would be no point in arguing in Sean's defense. To the senator, it would be like trying to vindicate the devil. "I'll see you when I get back. Don't overdo."

The senator was already reaching for the telephone. Kate gave him a fond half smile and left the room.

Her mother was waiting in the hallway.

"I know I told you you should get away," she began

immediately, "but I really wasn't thinking of any place so far off!"

Kate squeezed her mother's perfectly manicured, lotion-scented hand. "I'll be fine, Mother."

"That's what Abby said," Irene fretted, "and look what happened to her."

Kate sighed. She had known her older sister better than anyone except, perhaps, for Sean. While Abby had certainly looked like an angel, she'd been spoiled and selfish, too, and her temper had been quick. Kate kissed her mother's cheek. "Goodbye, Mother," she said.

Irene caught at her arm when she started toward the door. "When will you be back?"

"I don't know," Kate answered honestly.

Hastily Irene embraced her daughter. She was not an effusive woman, and the gesture was decidedly awkward. "There'll be another man along soon, dear," she promised, completely misreading Kate's emotions as usual. "You mustn't let breaking up with Brad get you down."

Kate let the comment pass. "I'll see you soon, Mother," she said, and then she was outside and the warm June sun was on her face.

It was winter in Australia, but she didn't care. She would be far away from old entanglements there; she would be able to think clearly and decide what to do with the rest of her life.

The night breeze was cool and fragrant as Kate stood on the balcony outside her hotel room, watching the dark ocean reach out to the pale sand and then slowly fall away. She would spend just this one night in Honolulu before traveling on to Fiji, Auckland, New Zealand, and, finally, Sydney.

She thought about Gil. Judging by the picture Sean had given her parents, the boy was a handsome blond with his mother's wide brown eyes. She hoped he was more like Sean than Abby.

Below, the hotel pool sparkled like a huge aquamarine, and island music wafted up from the open doors of the lounge. On impulse, Kate decided to go for a swim. Quickly she changed out of her white cotton nightgown and into her sleek new one-piece swimsuit. Then, wearing a blue eyelet cover-up and carrying a towel, she took an elevator downstairs.

The sound of friendly laughter came from inside the lounge as Kate approached the shimmering pool. She looked up at the tropical moon, and for a single moment, her loneliness almost overwhelmed her. She plunged into the water to escape it, and when she surfaced, she felt more hopeful. After a short swim, she climbed out of the pool, dried off and ordered a mai tai to carry back to her room.

Four tractor salesmen from Iowa were in the elevator with Kate, and they invited her to their party. She declined politely and got off two floors below her own.

When she finally arrived in her room, the message light on her telephone was blinking. For a moment she was afraid. Suppose her father had had another heart attack? Suppose this time he'd died?

Kate forced herself to call the main desk. "This is Kate Blake in room 403," she said evenly. "Do you have a message for me?"

The operator asked her to wait for a moment, and Kate heard paper shuffling.

"Yes, Ms. Blake," came the answer. "You had a call from Mr. Wilshire in room 708. He'd like you to contact him immediately."

Kate felt cold all over, as though she'd just plunged into the pool again. She managed a strangled thank-you and slammed down the receiver.

Brad was here, in this very hotel. Obviously he'd followed her, and he'd jumped bail to do it.

Kate peeled off her suit, showered and put on a sundress and sandals. When she'd combed her hair, she hurled the few things she'd unpacked back into her suitcase, called the desk and asked that her bill be prepared. She would spend the night at the airport.

When Kate opened the door to leave, however, Brad was standing in the hallway, smiling at her. "Maybe we can still have a honeymoon," he said.

Chapter 4

Kate resisted an urge to flee back into her room and slam the door. Brad would be delighted to see that he'd intimidated her. "I thought you weren't supposed to leave the state," she said evenly.

Brad was dressed for the tropics in white pants and a lightweight sport shirt to match. He folded his arms and smiled ingratiatingly. "The charges against me have been dropped because of insufficient evidence. The person who turned me in wasn't—" he paused, searching his mind for the right word "—reliable."

Kate's opinion of the judicial system plummeted. She indicated her suitcase and said, "Well, congratulations to you and apologies to society in general. I was just leaving. Sorry there's no time to talk."

Brad's gaze swept over her. "I'm not going to give you another chance after this, Kate," he warned. "Either you marry me right away, or we're through."

"Don't look now," Kate answered, "but our relationship has been over since the night of the opera. So, if you'll excuse me—"

Brad shook his head, as though amazed that any woman could turn down a prize like him, and turned to walk away. Kate stepped back inside her room and bolted the door.

She slept fitfully that night, half expecting Brad to break into her room. Early in the morning she showered, dressed and set out for the airport. After breakfast in one of the coffee shops there, she boarded Flight 187, bound for Fiji, New Zealand and Australia.

The trip was incredibly long, with layovers at each stop, and Kate lost a full day of her life when they crossed the international dateline. By the time she arrived in Sydney, she was rumpled, cranky and exhausted.

She took a cab to the hotel where her travel agent had made reservations and, after checking in and taking a shower, she collapsed into bed. When she awakened, it was nighttime, and the bridge stretching across Sydney Harbour glowed in the rainy darkness. Seeing the dense traffic still filling the lanes, she guessed it was still evening.

She was wildly hungry. She called room service, then, sitting cross-legged on the bed, she dialed Sean's number.

A housekeeper answered. "Harris residence."

For a fraction of a moment, Kate didn't know what to say. Should she introduce herself as Abby's sister, Gil's aunt or Sean's friend? "This is Kate Blake," she finally said. "Is Mr. Harris there, please?"

"I'm sorry, miss," the housekeeper replied, "but he's out with friends tonight."

Kate felt a pang of jealousy, imagining Sean on a date with some other woman, but she quickly suppressed that unworthy emotion. She wanted to see Gil; his father's social life had nothing to do with anything. "Will you tell him I called, please?" she asked.

The housekeeper promised that she would and rang off.

Kate's dinner arrived, and she sat on the edge of her bed to eat, feeling strange and far from home. She'd forgotten the keen sense of isolation Australia could give a person—especially when that person was traveling alone.

After wheeling the service cart out into the hall, Kate read for a while and then went back to sleep. A knock at her door awakened her early the next morning.

Never at her best at that hour, Kate scrambled awkwardly out of bed, stumbled over to the door and tried to focus one eye on the peephole. She couldn't see anyone, and was just about to turn around and stagger back to bed when another knock sounded and a young voice called, "Auntie Kate? Are you in there?"

Kate's heart hammered against her rib cage. She wrenched the door open and there stood seven-year-old Gil, looking up at her with Abby's eyes. He had his mother's hair, too, and Sean's infectious grin.

Until that moment Kate hadn't realized how badly she wanted to see and hold this child. With a cry of joy, she enfolded the little boy in a hug, which he bore stoically, and then ruffled his golden hair. "Am I ever glad to see you," she said. "Where's your dad?"

Gil pointed one finger toward the elevators. "He's gone to get a newspaper," he said.

Kate appreciated Sean's attempt to give her a few minutes alone with his son. She just wished they'd called first, so she would have had time to dress.

Gil sat on the bed while she dashed into the bathroom to put on jeans and a turquoise pullover shirt. She was barefoot, both hands engaged in working her hair into a French braid, when she came out.

"You don't look anything like the pictures of Mom," Gil observed, watching Kate with quizzical eyes.

Of course, he would have been too little to remember Abby. A momentary sadness overtook Kate. "Your grandfather Blake used to call her his Christmas-tree angel," she said.

"What did he call you?" Gil asked with genuine interest, and Kate realized for the first time that her father had never given her an affectionate nickname. He called her Kate if he was pleased with her and Katherine if he wasn't.

"Just Kate," she said.

"Dad calls you Katie-did," Gil announced. This time Kate noticed that several teeth were missing from the endearing grin.

She searched her mind for something to say to a little boy. "Do you like to play baseball?"

Gil squinted, then shook his head. "Football," he said. "And cricket."

There was a light rap at the door, and Kate went to open it. When she saw Sean standing there, tall and handsome in his jeans, polo shirt and windbreaker, her heart skipped and her breath swelled in her throat.

"Hi," she finally managed to say.

His green eyes danced. "Hello, love," he responded. "May I come in?"

Kate remembered herself and stepped back. "Sure," she said, feeling like an adolescent.

"We woke her up," Gil commented, from his seat on the edge of Kate's crumpled bed.

Sean's gaze was as soft as a caress. "Sorry."

Kate bit her lower lip. "It's all right," she replied lamely.

Sean smiled at her nervousness. "Get your bags packed, Katie-did, and we'll take you out of here. Plenty of room at our place."

Kate hesitated. Seeing Sean again, she knew she hadn't really dealt with her feelings for him at all. It would be so easy to be wanton. "I...I wouldn't want to impose," she said quickly. "I mean, I can just as well stay here."

Gil looked so crestfallen that Kate went to sit beside him on the bed. She draped an arm around his shoulders. "What's this? A sad face when I've just come all the way from America to see you?"

"Let's take your aunt Kate out for some breakfast," Sean suggested quickly. He looked as disappointed as Gil.

Since it was drizzling, Kate took her raincoat. They left the hotel and walked through the clean, modern streets to a small coffee shop that Sean seemed to know.

A hearty breakfast made Kate feel better—and more adventurous. "Maybe I could stay with you for a little while," she said to Gil, "if you're sure I won't be intruding."

Gil's coffee-brown eyes were alight. "I'll show you

my dog, Snidely," he exclaimed, beaming. "He can roll over and play dead."

"I'm very impressed," Kate told him. "What else can he do?"

Gil's expression turned sheepish. "Not much else, besides chew shoes and make messes in the garden."

Kate laughed. "He sounds like a regular dog to me."

"Except for Georgie Renfrew, he's my best mate," Gil said.

Sean winked at Kate from behind the rim of his coffee cup, and she was absurdly pleased, as though he'd made some grand gesture.

They left the coffee shop several minutes later, and Kate held Gil's hand as they walked back to her hotel. There, she packed her things and then checked out. She, Sean and Gil took a cab to Sean's house in an elegant section of Sydney.

It was as wonderful as Kate remembered, with a view of the harbor and the Opera House, and her room was a small suite, with its own bath and a real wood-burning fireplace. The carpets were a pale blue, the bedspread was a complementary floral print, and there was even a small balcony outside.

"It's beautiful," Kate told Sean softly, but she was already regretting her decision to stay in this house. The place had belonged to Abby first, just as the man had, and Kate felt like an intruder.

Sean touched the tip of her nose. "I see ghosts in your eyes. What's the problem, Katie-did?"

Kate bit her lower lip and turned away. In the distance she could hear a dog barking with unbounded glee. Evidently Snidely and Gil had been reunited. "I'm just a little tired, I guess," she lied.

Gently Sean turned her to face him. "And feeling just a little guilty, I think."

Kate nodded, not trusting herself to speak.

Before Sean could say anything more, Gil bounded in with a huge, hairy dog of some indeterminate breed.

"This is Snidely," he said, glowing with pride.

Snidely offered a yelp in greeting and then rolled over on his side to lie completely still. Kate supposed he was playing dead.

"Good dog," she said to please Gil.

"Take him outside before Mrs. Manchester sees him," Sean ordered.

Reluctantly Gil led the animal out of Kate's room.

Sean traced the outline of Kate's cheek with one index finger. "We'll talk later, love, when you're settled in and rested."

Kate nodded.

Sean bent his head and kissed her lightly on the lips, and Kate was almost knocked off her feet by the jolt that passed between them. In that moment she would have given her soul to lie beneath Sean, to share her body with him.

But he left her standing in the middle of that beautifully decorated room, listening to the patter of winter rain against the windows.

Kate was curled up in a chair, reading a paperback she'd brought with her on the plane, when the housekeeper rapped at the half-open door and stepped inside the room. Mrs. Manchester was a heavily built woman with friendly blue eyes and salt-and-pepper hair pulled back into a loose chignon. She smiled at Kate and went to the hearth to build a fire.

"Nothing like a cheery blaze on a wet day," she commented, dusting her hands together and looking back at Kate as the fire crackled to life. "Would you like some tea, miss?"

Kate shook her head. "No, thank you," she said, and an unexpected yawn escaped with the words.

"Seems to me you might want to lie down and take a nap," Mrs. Manchester observed. "Traveling so far takes such a lot out of a person."

The bed did look comfortable, and the dancing flames on the hearth gave Kate a cozy, protected feeling. "I think you're right," she said, and kicking off her shoes, she crossed the room to stretch out on the bed.

Mrs. Manchester kindly covered her with a beautiful knitted afghan and slipped out, closing the door behind her.

Kate drifted off to sleep and dreamed of a campfire under a sky ablaze with silver stars. There, in that imaginary world, Sean lay beside her, his hand on her breast. She whimpered and stretched, wanting more of his touch.

"Kate." His voice penetrated her dream, low and husky.

She stretched again, still asleep, still needing.

She felt his fingers at the buttons of her shirt. Cool air whispered over her skin as he took away her bra. The feel of his mouth on her hardened nipple brought her awake with a start.

Although Sean was in the room, he was standing by the fireplace, and Kate was still fully dressed. Her disappointment was keen.

"That must have been a pretty erotic dream," he said, throwing another log on the fire before approaching the bed.

Kate blushed in the relative darkness of the room, but her words were bold. "It was. You were making love to me beside a campfire."

"Rest assured, Katie-did," he said, bending to kiss her forehead, "I'm not about to make love to you."

Kate glared up at him. "Why not?" she asked, insulted.

"Because the guilt would eat you alive," Sean answered. "For you at least, there would be three of us in the room—you, me and Abby."

Kate closed her eyes. As much as she wanted to cry out that he was wrong, she knew he wasn't. She tossed back the afghan and sat up.

"Mrs. Manchester made tea," Sean said, indicating a wheeled cart sitting beside the fireplace.

Apparently they were going to pretend they hadn't discussed sex. Kate smoothed her hair and disappeared into the bathroom for a few minutes. When she came out, she had recovered her dignity.

She sat down in one of the two wing chairs facing the hearth and poured tea from a small china pot into a matching cup. There were strawberry scones, too, and various cookies she knew Sean would refer to as biscuits. Kate took a raspberry scone, even though she normally didn't eat sugary foods.

Sean was leaning against the fireplace mantle, watching Kate as though she were a complex puzzle. "Why are you here?" he asked.

Kate took a sip of strong tea before answering, "I wanted to see Gil, of course."

"If that were all of it, you'd have been here a long time before now."

Avoiding his gaze, Kate reached for a cookie. The

man made her nervous, and when she was nervous, she ate. She shrugged. "I guess you could say I'm looking for myself," she replied. Her indigo eyes rose of their own accord to his face. "You were the one who said I needed a life of my own."

Sean poured tea into the second cup, added generous doses of sugar and milk and sat down in the chair across from Kate's. "Are you serious about that?"

Kate nodded. "I turned thirty a few days back, Sean, and look at me. I've never been married, never borne a child, never even worked at a real job that I landed on my own."

"And now you're out for an adventure?"

Kate considered for a moment. "Something like that."

Sean set his teacup down in its saucer. Even in the firelight Kate could see the mischief dancing in his eyes. "I think I can provide you with one of those," he said.

Before Kate could think of a response, Gil burst into the room with Snidely loping at his heels. "Mrs. Manchester's gone out to see her sister," he explained, "so I brought Snidely inside straight away." He glanced at the scones and biscuits.

"Have one," Kate said, watching him with delight.

Gil hesitated, looking to his father for permission. Sean must have given it silently, for the boy closed one grubby hand around a scone. After saying thank you and breaking off a small piece for Snidely, he ate hungrily.

"Are you going back to America soon?" the child asked when he'd disposed of the scone.

"I don't think so," Kate said, wondering if Gil was

anxious for her to leave. She was probably disrupting some planned excursion with her unexpected visit.

"I hope you stay a long time," Gil responded. "You're not scared of Snidely and you don't go 'round saying he smells. I like that in a woman."

"It's certainly a trait I always look for," Sean agreed, deadpan.

Kate laughed and rumpled Gil's hair. "Well, I happen to like a discerning gentleman," she said.

"We'll try to dig one up for you," Sean replied.

Snidely was following his own tail in an endless circle. Outside, the winter rain drizzled against the windows, and the fire crackled on the hearth. Kate wanted to stay in that room with Gil and Sean forever.

As it happened, though, Sean rose out of his chair and said, "We'll leave you to yourself for a while. Dinner's in a couple of hours."

Kate wondered if she was supposed to dress up. It didn't seem likely that dinner would be formal when Mrs. Manchester was out of the house.

Feeling rumpled from her nap, she took a long, hot shower. Then, not knowing what was expected of her, she got into a striped dress in shades of pink and a pair of sandals. She wore her dark hair down and applied a small amount of makeup.

Sean's eyes lit up when she walked into the living room. He was wearing black pants and a beautiful cable-knit sweater, and his dark hair caught the light of the fire.

"Now I'm sorry we're having dinner at home," he teased, deliberately intensifying his accent. "I could make all me mates jealous if I showed you off."

Kate laughed, but his words pleased her. It had been a long time since she'd felt so attractive.

Sean offered white wine, and she nodded. When he brought her the glass, she asked, "Where's Gil?"

"He'll be along when he's done dressing. He had a bath—and Snidely got into the tub with him."

Kate laughed again at the picture that came to her mind, and then took a long sip of her wine because she felt so nervous inside. It was as though she'd regressed from thirty years of age to thirteen, and she couldn't for the life of her think of anything intelligent to say. She followed the sip with a gulp.

Sean was just about to say something when Gil bounded into the room, looking scrubbed and handsome in pants and a white shirt. "May I stay home tomorrow and look after Kate?" he asked with a hopeful lilt in his voice.

"Actually, no," Sean responded immediately.

Gil's disappointment was only momentary. After an instant, he was smiling broadly again. "Well," he said, "if you're going to be that way about it—"

"I am," Sean assured him.

Watching her nephew, Kate was thinking how much her parents would enjoy knowing him. She made a mental note to approach Sean, when the right moment arrived, about letting the boy visit.

The three had a simple dinner of meat pies and salad left behind by the very efficient Mrs. Manchester, and then Gil went off to do his homework. The next day was Monday, and school would be back in session.

"I'm sorry I haven't asked you before, Kate—how's your father?" Sean asked as they sat at a small table in a glass alcove, watching the rain fall.

"He's getting better every day," she answered. She studied Sean, wondering if she dared mention the possibility of a visit from Gil in the same sentence with her father. She decided against it. "I called home as soon as I arrived at the hotel, and Mother said he was almost ready to go back to Washington."

Sean turned his wineglass in one hand. "Have you let them know you're here?" he asked.

"I called the hotel and left word at the desk," she answered, yawning. "If any messages come in, they'll call me."

"You're still not over the jet lag," Sean remarked. "You'd better get some sleep."

"Will I see you tomorrow?"

Sean shook his head. "Not until late. I've got business meetings all day."

And Gil would be in school. A feeling of loneliness swept over Kate, and she lowered her eyes.

Unexpectedly Sean put his hand under her chin and raised her face. "Come away with me, Kate," he said hoarsely, getting to his feet and drawing her to him. "I'll show you the adventure of a lifetime."

Despite all her fine resolutions, Kate was powerless in his arms. Something melted deep inside her at the memory of that afternoon's erotic dream. "What kind of adventure?" she asked, her eyes wide as she looked up at him.

"I've got a little plane. I could show you some of the outback."

The idea intrigued Kate more than she would have dared to admit. "What about Gil?" she asked. "Would he go along, too?"

Sean shook his head. "He's got a school trip coming up. We could go then."

"When?" Kate wanted to know. She felt herself melting like a candle as Sean gently caressed her breasts.

"Day after tomorrow," he answered on a long, weary breath.

Kate closed her eyes. She wanted Sean to bare her as he had that other time on her bed at home, but she knew he wouldn't. He was only torturing her, and himself. "Just the two of us," she mused aloud. "Interesting."

Sean bent his head and nibbled the covered peak of one breast. It went taut between his lips. "It'll be very interesting," he promised.

Kate was burning inside. The guilt she'd felt earlier was fading. Sean had a right to happiness, and so did she. No law, moral or civil, said the two of them had to stay apart for fear of defaming Abby's memory. "I think I should go back to my hotel," she said.

Sean lifted his head quickly, his green eyes full of questions. He voiced only one. "Why?"

"Because there I wouldn't feel as though Abby's watching me from beyond the veil," she answered.

"Gil won't understand," Sean reasoned.

Kate didn't want to do anything to hurt her nephew, especially when she was just getting to know him. "You're right," she conceded, deflated.

"There's another place we could go," Sean said thoughtfully. "Wait here."

Kate sat watching the fire and willing her agitated body to calm itself. Presently Sean returned, his hair sparkling with droplets of rainwater, accompanied by a teenage girl.

"This is Angie," he said to Kate. "She lives across

the way, and she's Gil's favorite babysitter. Angie, this is my good friend Kate Blake."

The pretty blonde girl smiled at Kate. "That I am," she said. "Gil's favorite babysitter, I mean. Pleased to meet you, Miss Blake."

Kate nodded to the girl, but she was looking at Sean.

He beckoned to her with one hand, and against her better judgment, she stood and took his hand.

They were inside his car, a British sports model with a convertible top, and speeding down the driveway before Kate could catch her breath. She certainly hoped Sean didn't fly the way he drove.

"Where are we going?" she finally asked when it was clear that no explanation was forthcoming.

"You'll see," Sean answered.

A few minutes later they pulled into the parking garage of a towering building overlooking Sydney Harbour and the Opera House. Kate looked at Sean questioningly as he hauled her out of the car and strode off toward a bank of elevators, still gripping her hand.

"Sean!" she protested.

Inside, he pulled her close and kissed her so thoroughly that when he drew back, she was momentarily disoriented. He chuckled and kissed her again.

"Where are you taking me?" she demanded when she could gather the breath to speak.

The elevators whisked open on a small, beautifully decorated lobby. "This is the penthouse," Sean explained at last. "My company keeps it for visiting dignitaries."

Kate lifted an eyebrow as he unlocked the door. "Is that what I am?" she teased.

Sean winked. "Austra-Air wants to make sure your

stay in Oz is memorable," he assured her. Then he opened the door, and Kate stepped into the penthouse, instantly bedazzled.

The outside walls were all glass, and Kate could see, through the rain, the lights of the bridge and the Opera House and the ferry boats crossing the water. All around them, in fact, lay the city like a kingdom made of colorful jewels.

"Oh, Sean, it's magnificent," Kate whispered.

He closed and locked the door. "So are you," he whispered, drawing her close again.

She reveled in the muscular hardness of his body as he bent and nibbled softly at her neck. When she was nearly too weak to stand, he led her into the darkened living room, where huge couches and chaise longues sat in the shadows. He removed her dress with a minimum of trouble, pleased to find she was wearing only panties beneath it.

Kate groaned as he laid her out on one of the large chaises, the city spread before her like a gift, and eased her panties down over her hips. Something nagged at her—the realization that she'd been so wrong about another man in what seemed to be another lifetime—but she couldn't break free of Sean's spell. It was entirely too powerful.

"Do you want me to love you, Kate?" he asked.

"Yes," Kate managed to whisper. "Oh, yes."

Gently he lifted her legs so that they rested over his shoulders. His hands caressed her inner thighs. "Prepare for some slight turbulence," he teased.

Chapter 5

After a few minutes of Sean's loving, Kate was frantic for fulfillment. A delirium of pleasure caused her to writhe and toss her head from side to side even as she pleaded, "Sean—I don't want to—not without you…"

Breathing very hard, he stripped off his sweater and tossed it away, then got to his feet. He lifted Kate into his arms and carried her into a nearby bedroom.

Her skin, covered with a fine film of perspiration from her exertions, felt deliciously cool. She watched her man as he removed the rest of his clothes and then came to her.

"Kate," he whispered hoarsely, just before his lips covered hers in a masterful kiss.

She responded with her whole being, her doubts falling away behind her like the tail of a comet. The throbbing heat in her body was building toward a crescendo again, and she began to twist and thrash beneath Sean. She was wildly impatient.

He buried his face in her neck, chuckling. "So it's like that, is it?" he teased in a husky rasp.

Kate arched her back, and in that moment, Sean's control snapped. He found and entered her in one fiery stroke.

For Kate, for that instant, all of creation froze like the slides in a broken kaleidoscope. In the next, the universe splintered into colorful pieces, for she had been too greatly aroused and too long denied. Her body bonded itself to Sean's, and with a primitive cry, she gave of herself, body and soul.

Her triumph excited Sean, and with a groan, he began increasing his pace. Kate urged him on with soft, breathless words and the motions of her hands. She met each thrust with a swift rise of her hips, taking him far inside her.

He muttered something that might have been either a prayer or a curse when the quest became urgent, and then, with a hoarse shout, he stiffened, gasping her name.

Her hands soothed the moist, muscle-corded expanse of his back. "I'm here," she whispered.

Sean trembled violently as he surrendered, then sank down beside Kate on the bed of shadows. "God," he muttered. "My God."

They lay still and silent for a long time, and then Kate started to rise from the bed. Sean immediately pressed her back down.

"I'm not through with you yet, love," he told her. "Not nearly."

Kate gave an involuntary groan as he found her breast in the darkness and weighed it in the palm of his hand. His thumb moved over the responsive nipple, shaping it. Preparing it.

She twisted onto her stomach, gasping, knowing she needed a few minutes to rest. But Sean was granting no quarter; he reached beneath her, and she flung back her head like a wild mare when he found what he sought.

"Stop," Kate murmured, even as she ground her hips in an involuntary response.

"Not until you're satisfied," Sean replied.

Kate could not turn onto her back again, for she was trapped by her own needs. "Oh, Sean—Sean—"

"Almost there," he told her, intensifying his efforts to drive her mad. "Almost there..."

Kate was damp with perspiration from her head to her feet. Her legs were stiff and wide apart, and her toes curled into the bedspread, seeking purchase. Her hands were pressed against the mattress, raising her upper body from the bed. "Oh," she cried, lifting her eyes to a ceiling she couldn't see. "Oh—*oh*..."

"It's going to be a long night, love," she heard Sean say gently from somewhere beyond the exploding lights and shooting flares of her climax. "A long, sweet night."

Kate awakened feeling as though she were lying in the light of a gentle sun, her sated body wrapped in the softest silk. Expertly Sean had put her through her paces, draining away all her tensions.

He bent and kissed her. "We'd better go, love. Mrs. Manchester will get the idea we're up to something."

Kate laughed and then stretched. "I don't think I can move from this bed," she said.

"That's fine, too," Sean answered. He was fully

dressed again, but he pretended he was about to take off his sweater.

Kate bounded out of bed and hurried into the bathroom. One more session of Sean's singular brand of loving would turn her into a madwoman for sure.

She took a hasty shower and got back into her panties and dress, which Sean had thoughtfully brought from the living room. He was there when she came to him, looking out at the city lights and sipping from a crystal glass.

"What's that?" Kate asked.

"Vodka," he answered.

Kate wrinkled her nose. "Bad for you," she said.

"We're fresh out of carrot juice," Sean explained. "Let's go, love."

They took the elevator down to the parking garage and walked to Sean's car. When Kate was seated in the passenger seat, Sean walked around to the driver's side and got in. The engine roared to life and Kate felt sad to be leaving a place that had been hers and Sean's for a house that had been Abby's.

"I'll sell the house," Sean said, and Kate was convinced he'd been reading her mind. "It's that simple."

"It isn't, and you know it," Kate argued. "You have a child—my sister's child. I live in one hemisphere, and you live in another. There are just too many differences."

"What about tonight?" Sean argued. "Was that a difference?"

Kate swallowed. "A few more nights like tonight and I'll be a candidate for a nursing home. I must have had six..." Her cheeks went hot as she fell silent.

"Seven," Sean replied, "but who's counting?"

"That was only physical," she said. "You can't build a relationship on that." She prayed Sean would say he loved her, so she could tell him her real feelings for him.

"Come on, Kate. Men and women have been building 'relationships'—I hate that word—on *that* for a few million years." He shifted gears as they began moving uphill. "Beware of me, Katie-did—now I know how to bring you right into line."

Kate's face throbbed with renewed heat, and she was grateful for the darkness. "That was a chauvinistic thing to say!"

"Nevertheless," Sean replied with a shrug, "it's true."

And it was, although Kate would have died before admitting it. All Sean had to do was maneuver her into certain positions, touch her in certain ways, and she was lost.

"The way it is with us," he began after a long silence. "Was it like that with Brad?"

Kate knew he was really asking if what they had was new to her, so she didn't resent the question. "Brad and I never made love," she admitted, "so I wouldn't know."

Sean pulled the car over to the side of the street and stopped so suddenly that Kate was stunned. "What?" he demanded.

"I said, Brad and I never made love—"

"How the hell did you manage that? You were engaged to the man!"

Kate's eyes were very wide. "You sound angry."

A closer look proved that he was more indignant than angry. "I feel so cheap," he said.

Kate couldn't help laughing. "I think that's supposed to be my line," she told him.

"You were saving yourself for marriage with him," Sean pointed out. "With me, it's a fast roll in the straw and 'thank you very much I've got a plane to catch'!"

Kate only shook her head, baffled.

Sean wrenched the car back into gear and pulled onto the road again, muttering a swear word.

Kate squinted at him in the darkness. "Did I miss something here? I haven't been to bed with anyone since college, and you're upset because you're the first?"

"Who was he?" Sean barked.

"Who?" Kate countered, getting angry herself now.

"The guy in college!"

Kate laughed again. "My God, I don't believe this!"

Sean's hands tightened on the steering wheel, then relaxed again. "Were you in love with him?"

Kate sighed, turning her eyes to the rain-misted view. Even in that weather, at that hour of the night, it was magnificent. "I thought so. His name was Ryan Fletcher, and we were going to be married."

"What stopped you?"

"Abby brought you home, and I realized what love really was."

Sean was quiet for a moment, then he said something that surprised Kate to the core of her being. "I married the wrong sister, I think."

Kate reached out and laid a hand on his thigh. She felt the muscles tighten to a granite hardness beneath her palm. "What went wrong between you and Abby?" she asked. "You were so happy once."

"Maybe I was. Abby changed her mind about life with me about five minutes after our plane took off from Seattle. She didn't like being married to a pilot, she didn't like sex, she didn't like Australia."

"Why didn't she leave you, then, and come home?"

Sean gave Kate a sidelong look. "This was home," he said flatly.

"Not to Abby," Kate pointed out.

"And not to you," Sean replied.

"We're not talking about me," Kate countered.

"I think we are," Sean argued. "You couldn't stay here with me and be happy any more than Abby could. You're a Yank, and you belong in the States."

Kate sighed. "I'll decide where I belong, thank you very much."

"You belong in my bed," Sean answered, "and if you think you can deny me, I'll have to prove my point."

Kate knew better. Sean could take her anytime, anyplace he wanted; her responses were evidence of that. All the same, her pride made her keep a defiant silence.

They had reached Sean's house, and the garage door opened at a command from a button on the dashboard. The inside was only dimly lit.

Kate started to get out of the car, but Sean stopped her by gripping her wrist in his hand. He gave her a soft, savage kiss. When it was over, her knees were so weak that she could hardly walk inside the house on her own, but she wouldn't let Sean support her. He'd done quite enough.

In her room, Kate quickly undressed and put on a flannel nightshirt. She brushed her teeth and climbed into bed, determined to sleep.

She couldn't. For much of the night she relived the things she and Sean had done together, and by morning she needed him again.

* * *

With Sean in meetings and Gil in school, Kate had a day strictly to herself. The first thing she did was place a call to the United States, using her credit card.

Her mother answered on the second ring. "Hello?"

"Hi, Mother," Kate said, feeling shy with this woman, as though they were strangers with little common ground. In many ways, of course, they were exactly that.

"Kate," Irene confirmed, sounding a little annoyed. "Well, how is our world traveler?"

Kate suppressed a sigh. "I'm fine," she replied. "How are you and Daddy?"

"I'm very well, thank you, and your father is almost his old self again. We're off to the house in Washington tomorrow, as a matter of fact. Have you seen Gil?"

"I'm staying in the same house with him. He's a wonderful boy, Mother."

"Of course he is," Irene answered, sounding impatient. "He's Abby's child, isn't he?"

Kate could not have explained the emotions her mother's words aroused in her, and she was glad she didn't have to. She was also glad to be more than ten thousand miles away. "I think Sean had something to do with the project," she pointed out.

Irene sighed. "Which brings me to the most obvious question of all. What are you doing staying under that man's roof?" She made it sound as though Kate had taken a room in hell in order to have regular chess matches with the devil.

Kate thought of the sweet torments Sean had subjected her to the night before and wanted him more than ever. It was all she could do not to answer, *I'm here because I'm addicted to his lovemaking.* "It's a big house, Mother," she said instead. "They've got lots of room. Besides, this way I can be close to Gil."

"I'm not at all sure your father will approve. You haven't taken up with that man, have you?"

"*That man* has a name. It's Sean."

"Very well then, Katherine—are you involved with *Sean*?"

Kate wanted very much to answer yes, but she didn't quite dare to do it. "I'm his friend," she said, and her lips curved into a wry smile as she thought what an understatement that was.

"He's a monster—directly responsible for your sister's death."

Kate closed her eyes. "You know that isn't true, Mother. You remember what the coroner said. She'd been drinking and taking pills."

"Only because Sean Harris drove her to it. Australian men are chauvinists, Katherine. They use you up and throw you away when they're finished."

"I didn't call to argue about Australian men," Kate said firmly.

"Don't hang up!" Irene said quickly.

"We may not be the best of friends, Mother," Kate answered, "but we haven't reached that point."

"Your father will want to know whether or not you'll be bringing Gil back to the States and when."

Kate was developing a headache. "I haven't spoken to Sean about that yet. I need time."

"Just remember that your father isn't getting any younger, and he has a weak heart. It would mean the world to him to see his grandson."

Guilt swept over Kate like an ocean wave, but she stood strong against it. It wasn't her mission in life to effect a reunion between her parents and Gil. "I'll do my best," she said. "Goodbye, Mother."

"Goodbye, Katherine," her mother responded.

It would have been easy for Kate to lapse into a low-grade depression at that point, but she was determined not to let Irene get her down. She hung up and went to find Mrs. Manchester.

After conferring with the housekeeper about the best places to shop, Kate called a cab and ventured into downtown Sydney. Soon she was happily embroiled in purchasing the things she would need for her mysterious adventure with Sean. She bought several pairs of jeans, heavy flannel shirts, special underwear, socks and hiking boots. Then, lugging her bags, she found a model airplane for Gil, a fancy collar for Snidely, a book for Sean and a small box of imported chocolates for Mrs. Manchester.

It was midafternoon when she arrived back at Sean's house, where Gil and Snidely met her at the gate.

"I was afraid you'd gone back to America without saying goodbye," Gil told her.

Kate shifted all her packages so that she could ruffle his hair. "I'd never do that," she said gently. "Didn't Mrs. Manchester tell you I was out shopping?"

Gil shook his head. "All she said was to keep Snidely out of her clean house," he said. His brown eyes took in the bags she carried, one of which was clearly marked with the name of a local toy store. "What have you got there?"

"Help me get them inside and I'll show you," Kate answered, handing over half her burden to her nephew.

He accepted graciously, and the two of them went as far as the screened porch, Snidely at their heels. They dropped the bags and boxes on a wicker sofa, and Kate handed the model airplane to Gil.

His brown eyes widened. "Thank you, Aunt Kate," he said, accepting the gift.

"I believe the American word is 'wow,'" commented a quiet masculine voice from the inner doorway.

Kate looked up and saw Sean, and she went warm all over.

"Wow!" crowed Gil.

Kate felt almost shy, despite the fact that she'd thrashed beneath this man's hands and lips and body the night before. "I bought something for you, too," she said, handing him the book. It was an illustrated history of aviation.

"Thanks, Kate," he said. He accepted the book.

"And I didn't forget Snidely or Mrs. Manchester, either," Kate announced, perhaps too brightly. She felt awkward and inept all of a sudden.

Sean set aside the book to help a delighted Gil put the new collar on the dog. Moments later the boy rushed off to the kitchen to present Mrs. Manchester with her chocolates.

"What else did you buy?" Sean asked. The way his green eyes touched Kate made her feel a special intimacy with him, a deep need for more of what they had shared in the night.

Kate shrugged. "Jeans and shirts to wear when we go away," she said.

Sean was very close now. "Smart girl," he said. His hands rested on the sides of Kate's waist; his lips were a fraction of an inch from hers. "Did you buy a sexy nightgown?"

Kate eyes widened. "No," she admitted.

He gave her a light, nibbling kiss that set her senses afire. "Good, little sheila, because you aren't going to need one."

Kate trembled at the portent of his words. She was afraid and excited, wanting to run away and to stay, both at the same time. "Are you making an indecent proposal?"

Sean kissed her again, more thoroughly this time. "Absolutely," he answered, supporting Kate when her knees went limp beneath her.

She looked up at him, dazed. If he'd led her off to bed at that moment, she would have gone willingly, even eagerly, but he didn't. He gave her a swat on the bottom and nodded toward the bag of clothes she'd bought for their trip. "You'd better wash those before you wear them," he said.

Kate batted her eyelashes at him. "Thanks. I never would have thought of that on my own."

He gave her another swat and helped her gather up the bags. They were in the laundry room, cutting off tags and poking things into the washer, when Mrs. Manchester arrived, shooed them off and took over the project herself.

Sean took Kate's hand and led her into the living room. Since it was a bright, sunny day outside, there was no fire burning on the hearth, but Kate knew there would be later. Winter nights in New South Wales were cold.

"Where are we going on this adventure of ours?" Kate asked, perching on the arm of a comfortable sofa upholstered in practical navy blue fabric while Sean poured himself a drink.

"Queensland," he answered. "To a place out beyond Lightning Ridge."

"But it's winter," Kate reasoned.

Sean winked at her. "No worries, love. I'll keep you plenty warm of a night, and sometimes in the daytime, too."

Kate blushed and lowered her eyes. She could hardly wait to leave. "We'll go tomorrow?"

Sean nodded. "Can you wait that long, little sheila?"

Kate glared at him. Sometimes he carried his caveman routine just a little too far. "I can wait forever."

"Don't make me prove you a liar," Sean said, grinning. Then he set aside his drink and approached her.

Kate's breath caught in her throat when he placed gentle hands on both sides of her face and kissed her, his tongue claiming her almost as masterfully as his manhood had the night before.

"Maybe I'd better take you to bed," he said softly when the kiss was over and Kate was still trying to regain her balance.

Kate trembled. His delicious threat was empty, since Gil and Mrs. Manchester were home. Wasn't it?

Sean chuckled at her bemusement and gave her another soul-rendering kiss. When it was over, Kate had to sink down onto the couch, since she couldn't stand on her own any longer.

Gil came bounding in at that moment like a fresh breeze, carrying the box that contained his new model airplane beneath one arm. "Can we put this together tonight, Dad?" he asked eagerly, his brown eyes shining as he looked up at his father.

Kate felt such love for both Sean and Gil in that moment that she couldn't have spoken past the lump in
her throat. Tears of emotion glistened in her eyes, but
if Sean noticed, he pretended otherwise.

"We could get a start on it, I suppose," Sean agreed.
"Have you got all your things packed for the trip to
Canberra?"

Gil nodded. "Mrs. Manchester took care of that,"
he said.

With a wink at Kate, Sean took the colorful box his
son was holding out to him. "This looks like a three-
man job to me," He said. "Want to help?"

Kate wanted to be near both of them. "Sure," she
said with a sniffle.

Gil squinted at her. "Are you crying, Aunt Kate?" he
asked.

Kate shook her head. "Yes," she said, contradicting
her own gesture.

"Women," commented Gil.

Sean laughed, and even though he didn't touch Kate
in any way, she felt as though she'd been held and com-
forted.

The three spent a happy evening putting the model
airplane together, although Sean complained that it was
a job Wilbur and Orville Wright wouldn't have wanted
to tackle. By the time dinner was served, the plane was
only half-finished.

"Looks like the rest of this will have to wait until
you get back from your trip, mate," Sean told his son.
"You've got lessons to do, haven't you?"

Gil nodded and went off to wash his hands before
supper. When he joined Sean and Kate at the table, he
was already yawning. "I'll bring you back a present

from Canberra," he promised Kate. His eyes flickered to his father. "And you, too, Dad," he added.

"Thanks for remembering," Sean said with a grin.

Gil sighed contentedly. "This has been the best night since my birthday," he said.

Again Kate felt silly, sentimental tears stinging her eyes. She quickly lowered her gaze to the delectable seafood salad on her plate. In that moment she mourned all the birthdays and Christmases she'd missed with Gil, just as though he were her own son.

Sean's hand closed over hers, though only momentarily. "You're tired," he said.

Kate nodded. That was true enough. She'd never really recovered from jet lag, and then she'd spent most of the previous night in Sean's arms.

Sean's voice was almost unbearably gentle. "Maybe you'd like Mrs. Manchester to bring your dinner to your room? After all, it'll be an early morning tomorrow."

Kate wouldn't be pampered. She ate what she could of her dinner before excusing herself to hurry off to her room. After a brief shower, she collapsed into bed without even putting on a nightgown.

Chapter 6

That night was cold, but the next day dawned bright and warm. As Kate sipped the bracing tea Mrs. Manchester had brought to her, she looked ahead to the trip she and Sean planned to share and wondered what had possessed her to agree to it. She was not the daring type, as a general rule.

Abby had been the bold one. She'd been the one to skydive, get a pilot's license and go off to Australia to live with a new husband. Kate wondered what had changed her sister from a fearless woman to a little girl writing petulant emails home but refusing to do anything about her situation.

A knock on her bedroom door interrupted Kate's musings, and she uttered a distracted, "Come in."

It was Mrs. Manchester, back for the tea service. She smiled at Kate and waited politely for an indication that she was through.

"You didn't work here when my sister was alive, did you?" Kate asked the older woman, frowning. "I'm sure I'd remember you."

Mrs. Manchester hesitated. Her warm eyes skirted Kate's. "I was here when she died, miss," she finally answered. "I'd just taken over from Mrs. Pennwyler."

"Is she still around anywhere, this Mrs. Pennwyler?" Kate asked. "I'd like to talk with her about Abby."

Mrs. Manchester shook her head. "Sorry, love. The old girl, bless her soul, has gone to live with her eldest son up in Darwin."

"What do you remember about Abby?"

"Mrs. Harris was very unhappy, miss."

Kate nodded. "I know. She emailed often. But I've never understood why she didn't divorce Sean—Mr. Harris—and catch a plane home."

"She had problems," the housekeeper said sadly.

Kate nodded, thinking of the coroner's report. A chill swept over her as she imagined what it must have been like for Abby hurtling off a high cliff that way, knowing she was going to die within seconds.

Mrs. Manchester was putting Kate's cup and saucer and the plate that had held a flaky croissant onto a tray. "Mustn't let the dead get in the way of the living," she said wisely. "Our time is limited enough as it is."

For the first time since she'd started thinking about Abby, Kate smiled. "You're right," she agreed. "Is Mr. Harris up yet?"

Mrs. Manchester laughed. "Up? He's been out and about for hours, miss—just got back a few minutes ago."

Kate looked down at her jeans, flannel shirt and hiking boots as Mrs. Manchester left the room. She hoped she was dressed for whatever Sean had planned.

As if summoned by the mere thought of his name, he appeared, looking around the door at Kate. There was an appreciative glint in his green eyes. "Everything's ready, love," he said.

A tremor of mingled delight and fear went through Kate as the man she loved stepped into the room. Like her, he was wearing jeans and a casual shirt. He carried a slouchy leather hat in one hand. "How do I look?" she asked.

"Good enough to eat," Sean responded hoarsely, and another shiver went through Kate even as her skin flushed hot.

She cleared her throat and averted her eyes for a moment, feeling shy again. "What about Gil? Did he leave on his field trip?"

"While you were still sleeping," Sean said. One moment he was in the doorway, the next he was standing so close to Kate that she could feel the heat of his body. He traced the outline of her mouth with a light touch of his index finger.

Kate trembled visibly, and her response embarrassed and angered her. "I could still back out, you know," she pointed out.

Boldly Sean cupped his hand over one of her breasts. The nipple hardened beneath the stroking of his thumb. "Could you?" he countered.

Kate groaned. "That isn't fair," she managed to say.

Sean was unbuttoning her shirt. Beneath it she wore a stretchy undershirt, rather than a bra, and her breasts and nipples were clearly visible through the thin fabric. Sean admired them for a long moment while Kate's cheeks flared pink. Although she was outraged, she was unable to stop him.

With one finger, he drew the neckline of the undershirt down until one breast was exposed, plump and vulnerable. "Just a little taste of what's going to happen when I get you alone," Sean said, and when he bent and touched Kate's nipple with the tip of his tongue, she tensed with sudden, violent pleasure. All thought of rebellion gone, she cupped her hands behind his head and pressed him to her.

But he was only playing. He abandoned the bare breast and turned to the one covered by the undershirt. Through the fabric, he nipped at it, grazing it lightly with his teeth, and Kate cried out softly, her head falling back.

Again she was disappointed. Sean caressed her naked breast once before covering it again, then he rebuttoned her shirt. She had never been more frustrated in her life.

"Sean, I need you," she managed to say.

He gave her a kiss as exciting as his dalliance with her breasts had been. "Later, little sheila."

Kate ached. "Now," she said.

Sean chuckled and gave her trim backside a swat. "Later," he repeated.

Kate was furious. Sean had aroused her on purpose and now he was just going to leave her to suffer. "I want you now," she insisted.

"Tough," Sean replied. He grasped Kate by the hand, taking up her suitcase with the other. She allowed him to lead her through the house and out into the driveway where an open Jeep was parked.

"Damn you," she whispered angrily. "I want you to drop this Tarzan routine right now!"

Sean tossed her expensive suitcase into the back of

the Jeep as though it were bargain-brand stuff. Then, grinning down at Kate, he lifted her by the waist and set her down inside the vehicle.

Although her pride dictated that she get out of the Jeep, storm into the house and call a taxi to take her back to the hotel, she buckled the seat belt instead.

Sean put the hat on and got behind the wheel. Looking over one shoulder, Kate noticed he'd brought a lot of other things besides her suitcase. She saw a tent, a single sleeping bag, fishing poles and a lot of packaged food, among other things.

"How come there's only one sleeping bag?" she demanded.

Sean grinned at her as he shifted into reverse. He was looking back at the road when he answered, "Spoiling for a fight, aren't you, sheila? Well, watch out, because you're about to get one."

Kate glowered at him and folded her arms across her chest. Her breasts still tingled from Sean's earlier attentions. He was a skunk, she decided, to get her excited and then leave her high and dry. "I wouldn't lower myself," she said.

"We'll see about that," Sean quipped, and then they were moving rapidly down the left hand side of the road.

Kate gasped, forgetting for a moment that all Australians drove that way. Sean put a hand on her thigh. Although Kate knew the gesture was meant to relax her, it only heightened her tensions.

"It'll be all right, Katie-did," he shouted over the noise of the wind.

Kate pushed his hand away and folded her arms again. That made Sean laugh.

They didn't attempt to speak after that. Instead, they

raced through traffic rapidly, leaving the sprawling city behind. After an hour they reached a small airport.

Kate felt as though the breath had been buffeted from her. Her hair, so carefully plaited into a tidy French braid, was flying wildly about her face. Before looking at Sean, she grimaced into the side mirror to make sure there were no bugs in her teeth.

Sean caught her by surprise when he lifted her from the Jeep. Her body brushed the length of his as he lowered her to her feet, and the ache within her intensified until it was nearly unbearable.

"I ought to slap you," she said.

He kissed her until her knees were weak. "Patience, little one," he told her gruffly. "We're spending tonight on a friend of mine's station. You can do all your lovely little tricks for me when we're alone."

Kate decided then that she definitely *would* slap him. She raised her hand to do so, but Sean caught her by the wrist and pulled her close. She was breathless.

Sean kissed her forehead lightly. "Behave yourself," he ordered. Then he left Kate and started unloading the things in the back of the Jeep.

For lack of a better idea, Kate helped. He stowed the tent inside a small twin-engine airplane and went back for more baggage. Once they'd loaded the plane, he got inside and started the engines, then walked around the small craft, making a mysterious examination of everything.

Thinking she might lose her courage if she didn't take definite action, Kate climbed onto the wing, the way she'd seen Sean do, opened the passenger door and got into the seat.

Sean was wearing earphones now, and tuning in the radio. "Buckle up, love," he said to Kate.

She fastened her seat belt, trying not to think about how small and fragile that airplane seemed. As far as Kate was concerned, it was almost as flimsy as Gil's model. She bit down hard on her lower lip and clasped the edges of the seat in both hands.

Sean was talking with the control tower, but Kate didn't listen to his words. Her whole life was passing before her eyes.

Soon the plane was lumbering and jolting along the rough pavement toward the single runway. Kate closed her eyes tight and prayed silently for some last-minute reprieve, like a flat tire or an empty gas tank.

God was not listening to Kate's prayer. The airplane gained the runway and began taxiing along it at an ever-increasing speed.

"Open your eyes, Kate," Sean said reasonably, although he had to speak in a loud voice to be heard over the roar of the engines.

Kate obeyed him, not because of any desire to see, but because her first impulse was always to do just as Sean said. She was going to have to work on that, or she'd end up fetching his slippers and lighting his pipe. "Oh, God," she cried.

Sean laughed as the little craft hurtled into the sky. The ground fell away beneath them while they climbed toward the clouds.

Kate's knuckles were beginning to ache. She released her grasp on the seat and let out her breath. An exhilarating sensation of freedom and excitement had overtaken her horror, and her eyes went wide as she looked down upon farmhouses and fields.

"It's beautiful!"

"I know," Sean answered. They had gained enough altitude, it seemed, for he was leveling the plane off now. He muttered something into the speaker on his earphone and then grinned at Kate. "Control says they're glad you like it," he told her.

Kate made a mental note to watch what she said from then on. There were things she wanted to say to Sean that were none of Control's business. She rolled her eyes at him and gave him a shaky smile.

They'd been flying for over an hour when Sean switched the radio off and removed the earphones.

Kate was alarmed. "Don't you need to stay in contact with the tower?" she asked.

Sean smiled indulgently. "We're too far out for that, love," he said.

"Oh," Kate replied, and she was smiling, too. There were thoughts of revenge in her mind. "I suppose there's no reason I can't repay you for all the frustration you've caused me, then, is there?"

Sean looked a little worried. "I don't know what you're talking about," he said.

Kate unfastened her seat belt and turned sideways. "You will," she promised.

Sean stiffened and gave an involuntary groan as she ran her hand lightly up his thigh.

And that was only the beginning.

By the time the trees and craggy cliffs beneath them had given way to open grassland, Sean was as disconcerted and unsatisfied as Kate. He gave her a hard look as she settled back and refastened her seat belt.

She smiled at him. "How do you like the taste of your own medicine, Mr. Harris?" she asked.

"I'd step lightly if I were you, sheila," he told her. His jaw was clamped down tight, and he shifted uncomfortably in his seat. "As you Yanks like to say, you're on thin ice."

Kate tilted her head to one side. "Just what is it you're threatening to do to me?" she asked sweetly, batting her eyelashes and clasping her hands together beneath her chin. "Beat me? Strip me naked and leave me for the dingoes?"

Sean gave her a wry look. "Wrong. Except, of course, the part where I strip you naked. I like that one."

Kate laughed. "I think we're even," she said.

"Do you? Well, two can play at your game." With that, he reached out and laid his hand on her upper thigh. She tensed as his fingers brushed her most sensitive and private place. Even knowing that he had no intention of satisfying her, any more than she'd satisfied him, she couldn't bring herself to push him away.

She felt a thin layer of perspiration cooling her heated skin. "Sean," she whispered as he tormented her with touches as light as the passing of a butterfly.

He chuckled. "The poet was right. Vengeance is sweet."

"I hate you," Kate gasped, even as her body jerked slightly in response to the whisper-light forays of his fingers.

"Absolutely," he replied.

"Oh," Kate moaned.

"Open your shirt, Kate," Sean said quietly. His tone was warm and inviting and terribly seductive. "I want to look at you."

"No," she murmured breathlessly, even as her fingers rose awkwardly to the buttons of her shirt and began working them.

When her shirt was open, Sean's fingers moved to her breasts. Their peaks strained against the fabric of her undershirt, longing to be free.

"You know what I want now, Kate," Sean said with a gentle kind of sternness that heated Kate's blood to a passionate simmer.

She did know, and it wasn't in her to refuse, even though she knew Sean was only dallying with her. He would leave her unsated until they were in bed that night, and that was hours away. With both hands, she raised the undershirt so that her breasts were bared for Sean's gratification.

He made an appreciative sound low in his throat and began to caress and shape her. With a groan, Kate sunk her teeth into her lower lip and turned her head, looking down at the distant ground, searching for anything that would distract her from Sean's delicious torment.

Half a dozen kangaroos hopped along the grassy ground, moving more rapidly than Kate had ever dreamed they could. She moaned as Sean continued to fondle her, arching her back even as she searched her mind for a way to rebel.

The plane began a gradual descent, and Kate scanned the horizon. There was no sign of a station anywhere in sight. She couldn't even see a single sheep.

"What are you doing?" she asked.

Sean withdrew his hand in order to concentrate fully on the controls. "You win, sheila," he answered cryptically. "I can't wait any longer."

"But this is the middle of nowhere!" Kate cried, coming swiftly to her senses. She pulled down her undershirt and then fastened her buttons.

"The perfect place," Sean answered.

Moments later the plane was bumping crazily along the ground. "What if we can't take off again?" she asked, wide-eyed.

"In a few minutes, love," he answered, "you're not going to need a plane to fly."

Kate's muscles went limp, then tensed again, going taut as piano wire. The plane came to a stop, and she closed her eyes in relief. Her heart was hammering, and she wasn't sure whether it was the unscheduled landing that had caused it, or the prospect of Sean's lovemaking.

He opened his door and climbed out onto the wing, then jumped nimbly to the ground. Kate was still trembling in her seat when he came around, got up onto the wing on her side and opened the door.

His eyes full of mischief and promise, he kept his gaze fixed to Kate's all the while he was unfastening her seat belt and turning her to face him. Her legs dangled outside the plane, on either side of his hips.

"Oh," Kate whimpered as he began unbuttoning her shirt.

He soon had that laid aside and her undershirt up beneath her armpits. Her breasts were warm and swollen under his gaze, their peaks pouting for his attention.

She cried out in mingled relief and despair when his mouth closed over one of her nipples. "A-aren't you even going to kiss me?" she asked.

He drew back long enough to answer, "I'm past that, thanks to your teasing. Now you'll have to pay the piper."

Sean took a long time at Kate's breasts, enjoying

first one and then the other. When he finally pressed her back across her own seat and his, she was almost out of her mind with need. She felt the snap open on her jeans, trembled as they slid, her panties with them, down over her hips.

Ever so lightly, Sean kissed the tangled silk that sheltered Kate's femininity from all but him. She moaned and lifted her hips as an offering, but he only teased her with more kisses. At the same time, his hands were busy removing her boots, pulling her jeans and panties down and off.

When Kate was thrashing from side to side, frantic with need, he raised up. She felt all the familiar doubts and fears, all the old insecurities, but they weren't enough to stop her. She held her breath as he opened his zipper and freed himself. When he entered her, she became a wild thing, clutching at him with her hands and wrapping her legs around his hips.

Although she urged him to hurry, Sean's pace was slow and rhythmic. He meant to extract the last ounce of response from Kate before satisfying himself, and that knowledge only increased her frenzy.

When she was on the edge, he stopped to enjoy her breasts again at his leisure. Kate was woman at her most primitive; she pleaded, she threatened, she wheedled and bargained.

At last, with a low moan of his own, Sean gave in. He began to move more rapidly, and the friction made Kate cry out and stiffen as satisfaction overtook her. She was torn apart in those moments, and reassembled into a new, softer and gentler woman. She had been mastered, like a wild mare broken to ride, and the feeling was glorious.

Sean's release was a violent one. He lunged deep inside Kate and hurled his head back, his teeth bared over a string of savage endearments.

Kate cupped his taut buttocks in her hands as his powerful body bucked several more times, and then he fell to her breasts, gasping for air. Within moments, he was rolling a taut nipple between his lips and then suckling hungrily even as his torso heaved with the effort to breathe.

Kate plunged her fingers into his hair. She would have been content to hold him like that all day but, when he'd had a long turn at both her breasts, he raised his head and pulled her undershirt down. While he fetched Kate's panties and jeans from the wing, she hastily buttoned her shirt.

He bent and kissed both her knees before handing her the rest of her clothes. "You're a bad girl, sheila," he scolded. "Maybe that's why I like you so much."

Kate wished he would have said he loved her, but she'd long since learned that wishes were one thing and reality was very often another. "You're a scoundrel," she said, wrenching on her panties and jeans. "Where are my boots?"

Sean recovered them from the ground and handed them to her, rounding the plane as Kate shoved her feet into them.

He boarded the plane and reached across Kate to close her door, the back of his arm brushing her full breasts. "That'll keep you satisfied until tonight, I hope," he said.

"Your arrogance is not to be believed!" Kate fussed.

Sean grinned broadly and quoted back some of the

outrageous things she'd said to him during her climb to the heights.

"Bastard," Kate said.

The plane engines whirred and the propellers began to spin.

"Have you ever taken off from a place with no runway before?" she asked worriedly, now having something else to think about besides the obnoxious man beside her.

"Only about fifty thousand times," Sean answered, reaching for a pair of mirrored sunglasses on the instrument panel and putting them on with a flourish.

Kate was back to gripping the edges of the seat, although she was so relaxed that it was hard to hold on. She wanted nothing so much as to crawl into some warm, safe bed right there on the ground and sleep for twenty-four hours.

The plane jolted terribly as Sean increased its speed. Finally, with a rattling mechanical grunt, it flung itself into the air. Kate let go of her seat.

"I'm getting hungry," she said.

"I don't wonder," Sean answered, "considering the energy you've burned up in the past few minutes."

Kate hit him in the shoulder, but she was grinning. She felt too damn good to be angry.

After another hour in the air, an enormous flock of sheep came into view, shepherded by a man and three dogs. In the distance, Kate could make out a sizable house and a number of rustic outbuildings.

"Is that your friend?"

Sean rocked the plane from side to side, and the man below waved a hand. "Yes," he answered. "That's Blue. He's the best mate I ever had."

Kate continued to stare at the ground as Sean banked the plane into a wide sweep around the house and buildings and began a descent toward a dirt landing strip below. She could see another plane on the ground, as well as gasoline pumps and a pickup truck with rusty fenders.

"Does he live here all by himself?" Kate asked, thinking how lonely that would be. This part of Australia was so vast and empty, except for the occasional gum tree and the ever-present brown grass.

Sean shook his head as the plane nosed downward. "He's got a wife and kids."

"Kids?" Kate echoed. "Out here? Where do they go to school?"

Sean was busy landing the airplane, so he didn't look at Kate as they landed. "They don't. Ellen teaches them herself."

Any answer Kate might have made was prevented by the jostling impact of touching down. She breathed a silent prayer of gratitude for a safe landing and unfastened her seat belt.

Sean stopped Kate before she could open the door and jump out of the plane. "Don't be trying to put any fancy ideas in Ellen's head," he warned. "She likes her life the way it is."

While Kate was still thinking what an odd remark that was, Sean shut off the engines and got out himself. He came around to lift Kate to the ground as a slender blonde woman came running from the direction of the house, her face alight.

"Sean!" she cried as she reached him and flung herself into his arms.

He gave her a hug and a sound kiss on the forehead and set her down. "Ellen," he said, "meet Kate."

Kate greeted the woman with a smile and an out-stretched hand, even though she was wondering why Sean hadn't mentioned that she was Abby's sister. "Hi," she said.

Turquoise eyes sparkled in a suntanned complexion. "Hello, Kate," Ellen said, accepting Kate's hand with a strong grip. Momentarily she turned back to Sean. "Did you bring me books and chocolate bars?" she demanded.

Sean laughed and gestured toward the plane where the gear was stowed. "Enough to last you six months," he answered.

Kate heard dogs barking in the distance and the bleating of sheep. Soon, Sean's friend Blue would reach them.

She looked nervously at Sean. She wondered if Blue and Ellen had been Abby's friends, too.

Sean glanced at her, and once again she had the strange sensation that he could read her thoughts. He put one arm around her waist and pulled her close, his lips moving softly against her temple.

"Tonight," he whispered.

Chapter 7

When Sean had taken a large grocery box from the back of the airplane, he and Kate and Ellen started off toward the house.

It was a sturdy, practical-looking place, built mostly of natural stone. Smoke curled from two different chimneys, reminding Kate that the day was cool. She'd forgotten in the heat of Sean's lovemaking and its glowing aftermath that it was winter in Australia.

As they neared the house, three children, two girls and a boy, appeared at one end of a long, verandalike porch. "It *is* you!" one of the little girls cried, bounding down the steps to attach herself to Sean's right leg.

Sean laughed and shifted the box in his arms so that he could ruffle the child's flaxen hair. "Hello, Sarah," he said.

Now that Sarah had broken the ice, the other two

children came running, too. They were introduced to Kate as John and Margaret.

"We were doing lessons," John confided. "I'm glad you're here, Uncle Sean, because it was a dead bore."

"John!" Ellen scolded, but there was a smile in her beautiful blue-green eyes.

The bleating of the sheep and barking of the dogs had grown much louder. Sean set the box down on the step and turned toward the mingled sounds, a broad grin stretching across his face. After a moment's pause, he strode off to meet his friend.

Kate started to follow and then stopped herself. Ellen was shooing the children back to their lessons.

"Come in," she said to Kate with a sunny smile. "Blue and Sean will be a while."

Kate returned the smile and went inside with Ellen, finding herself in a kitchen that ran the length of the house. Burnished copper pans and kettles hung on the walls on either side of an enormous brick fireplace. School books, pencils and papers were strewn over a long trestle table, and a rocking chair sat in a sunny alcove.

"Tea?" Ellen asked, going over to an old-fashioned electric stove and lifting a steaming kettle.

Kate was developing a taste for tea. "Yes, please," she said.

"You can sit here with us, Miss," little Sarah put in. She looked to be about ten years old.

Kate sat down at the end of one of the benches aligned with the trestle table. "Thank you," she said. She tried to look at the work the children were doing without being too obvious.

Ellen had gone back outside to fetch the box Sean

had brought while the tea brewed in a blue delft pot. When she returned, she set the box on the end of the table, opposite Kate, and pulled back the flaps.

Kate watched as she lifted out boxes of chocolate bars and stacks of books. "Bless that man," she said as John, Sarah and Margaret looked at the candy with round eyes.

"Just one between you," Ellen told the children, smiling as she handed them a chocolate bar. "Mind that you break it up evenly now."

While the kids were dividing the candy, Ellen turned her attention back to Kate. "Would you like one?" she asked.

Kate shook her head. "No, thank you," she answered. She was more interested in the books.

Ellen laughed as she handed one to Kate. It was a romance novel showing a sweet young thing being swept up into the arms of a dashing buccaneer. "They're better than candy," she said. "I can't get enough of one or the other."

Kate smiled as she looked through the other books. The covers were all quite similar, depicting almost every period in history as well as the present day. At the thought of Sean shopping for these books, her smile widened.

Ellen brought the teapot to the table, along with lovely china cups, too fragile for a station in the outback. "Do you think they're silly, those books?" she asked in a lilting voice, her expression worried.

"No," Kate said quickly. "As a matter of fact, this one with the sheikh on the cover looks pretty interesting to me."

Ellen's eyes sparkled. "Doesn't it, though?" she agreed, pouring the tea.

Before Kate could make further comment, a tall man with auburn hair and brown eyes entered the kitchen, followed closely by Sean.

"And who's this?" Blue demanded good-naturedly.

When Sean answered, there was a note in his voice that Kate had never heard before. "Katie-did, meet my best mate—Blue McAllister."

Kate nodded, feeling oddly moved. "Hello."

Blue hung up his hat and lightweight leather coat before progressing to the table. "Hello," he said, helping himself to one of Ellen's cherished chocolate bars. "I suppose you have a last name, as well?" he asked. "Or is it a well-guarded secret?"

"Blake," Sean said before Kate could answer, and this time he sounded angry.

Kate wondered why.

A look passed between Sean and Blue that wasn't entirely friendly. "You were related to Abby?" Blue asked in gentle tones.

Kate nodded. "She was my sister."

An uncomfortable silence descended, and Kate found herself wondering again why she'd given in to her passions when it was so clear that she and Sean could never have any kind of lasting relationship.

It was Ellen who smoothed things over. She laid a hand on Kate's shoulder and said, "Welcome. It isn't often I get a chance to talk with another woman. I'm glad you're here."

"Thank you," Kate answered, but her eyes had strayed to Sean's face, and she knew they mirrored all the questions she wanted to ask.

He turned away, ostensibly to gaze out the window. Blue suggested having a look at the starboard engine of his airplane, since it had been sputtering, and the two men left the house without a backward glance, John tagging after them when his mother nodded her permission to leave his schoolwork.

"Don't mind the men," Ellen said in her delightful accent after sending Margaret and Sarah off to play with their dolls. "I never met one yet that had half the tact he needed."

Kate wanted to cry, but she didn't. She couldn't quite manage a smile, however. "Were you and Abby friends?"

Ellen hesitated for a long moment. "Not really," she answered reluctantly. "The only time she ever came out here with Sean, she spent the whole of the weekend trying to convince me to leave Blue. Imagine it—me without Blue."

There *had* been a special spark between the McAllisters when Blue came into the kitchen, now that Kate thought of it. "Why on earth did Abby want you to leave your husband?"

Ellen sighed. "She said I was downtrodden, and that I was going to seed out here with nobody to talk to but Blue and the kids."

The remark Sean had made when they landed came back to Kate in that moment. *Don't be trying to put any fancy ideas in Ellen's head. She likes her life the way it is.* "Abby could be pretty thoughtless sometimes," she said, taking a sip of her rapidly cooling tea.

Ellen smiled and shrugged. "She didn't know how it is with Blue and me," she said, and there was something in her tone and her manner that made Kate flash back to the explosive passion she'd felt in Sean's arms a short time before.

She nodded, a little shaken by the experience.

Ellen seemed to sense Kate's thoughts. She hid another smile behind the rim of her teacup. "You're in love with Sean?" she asked a moment later, keeping her face expressionless.

Kate swallowed. "I'm afraid so," she admitted miserably.

Ellen reached out for the pretty teapot and refilled Kate's cup and her own. "Troubles?"

Kate lowered her head for a moment. "You saw how he reacted when I told Blue Abby was my sister," she said.

Ellen looked genuinely puzzled. "Yes?"

"I'm a reminder of a very unhappy time in Sean's life," Kate told her new friend sadly.

Ellen's face brightened. "I think perhaps you're another kind of reminder altogether," she reasoned. "I can't remember when I've seen Sean look so relaxed."

Kate blushed. If Sean looked relaxed, it was no mystery to her.

Ellen chuckled. "I see I've blundered in where I don't belong," she said. Then she graciously changed the subject. "Earlier you said you'd planned to teach once. What did you take up instead?"

Kate gave Ellen McAllister a grateful look. "Political science," she said. "Daddy—my father thought it would be a better use of my time and his money. He wanted me to work on his staff."

Ellen broke off a square of chocolate from the bar she'd opened earlier and laid the morsel on her tongue.

A look of ecstasy flickered briefly in her eyes, then she commented, "Do you like it—working for your father?"

Kate searched her heart. "Not really," she confessed.

"If you could do anything in the world," Ellen began, narrowing her eyes in speculation at all the possibilities, "what career would you choose?"

Kate didn't have to think. "I'd be like you, Ellen—making a home for the man I love. Raising his children."

Ellen put one hand to her mouth in feigned shock. "You mean, you'd actually like to be a—" she lowered her voice to a scandalized whisper "*housewife*?"

Kate laughed. "Yes," she answered.

Ellen squinted at her and took another square of chocolate. "I can't figure you as Abby's sister," she said.

Kate knew the remark was meant as a compliment, but she felt sorry that Abby had missed having Ellen for a friend. "According to Sean, she didn't like being a wife much."

Ellen glanced nervously toward the door, looking for the men, then lowered her voice to a confidential tone. "She took a lover the first year they were married," she said.

Kate was stunned. She'd known that Abby had been unhappy from the first, but she'd never suspected such a thing. "Did Sean know?" she asked.

"Yes," interrupted a taut masculine voice from the doorway. "Sean knew."

Kate raised her eyes to his face. He looked grim and angry.

"I'm sorry," Ellen said quickly. She got up from the table and fled the kitchen in embarrassment.

"If you want to know anything about Abby and me," Sean said coldly, "ask me and not my friends."

Kate was quietly furious. "Now just a minute, Sean Harris. Don't you think you're being a little unreasonable here?"

He shoved a hand through his dark hair, and his broad shoulders slumped slightly. "Until about five seconds ago," he said hoarsely, "I thought Abby's affair was a secret."

Kate went to Sean and put her arms around him, her chin tilted back so she could look up into his face. "She was a fool," she said softly.

He kissed her forehead. "You're prejudiced, but thanks, anyway," he said.

Kate laid both hands on his chest, their torsos fitting together comfortably. "Go and talk to Ellen," she suggested. "She thinks you're mad at her."

Sean held her a little closer. "Couldn't that wait a little while? I'd like to show you where we'll be sleeping tonight."

Kate thought of Sarah and John and Margaret. "We're not going to share a bed under this roof," she said firmly. "There are children here."

Sean moved her to arm's length, his hands gripping her shoulders. "What?"

"It wouldn't be right, Sean," Kate whispered. "We're not married."

"Then we'll get married."

"You're crazy. Where would we get a license? And a preacher?"

Sean sighed. Obviously those things would be impossible to find in the middle of nowhere. "Wouldn't being engaged make it right?" he asked.

"No," Kate said stubbornly.

Sean swore. "Then I'll just have to convince Blue that we should sleep in the barn," he replied.

Kate set the last bacon, tomato and lettuce sandwich on the platter with a flourish. Lunch was ready.

She started when she heard a sizzle behind her and turned to see Ellen cracking eggs into a frying pan. Kate could barely believe her eyes. "Eggs?" she asked.

Ellen smiled at her. "Blue and the kids really like them," she answered.

Kate cast a bewildered glance toward the pyramid of sandwiches she'd prepared, then looked at Ellen again.

"They'll just add them in," Ellen said.

"Oh," she finally answered, sounding a bit lame.

When they all sat down at the long trestle table a few minutes later, it made for a merry group. The children were all talking at once, while Blue and Sean carried on a separate conversation.

She watched the men lift the tops off their sandwiches and add a fried egg, but she let the platter pass her by without taking one. She didn't usually eat this much for lunch but, keeping her eyes on her own plate, she ate what she could.

When the meal was over, Kate helped Ellen with the dishes. Blue and Sean and all the children had gone outside again.

"Are you feeling all right?" Ellen asked, looking genuinely concerned. "You didn't eat much."

Kate sighed. "I'm a little tired," she confessed. "I've never really gotten over my jet lag."

Ellen's lovely eyes were full of concern. "I'll show you where your room is, and you can lie down."

Kate shook her head. She didn't want to waste a

minute of this experience on anything so ordinary as a nap. After all, she might never find herself on an Australian sheep station again. "I'd like to see more of the place," she said.

Ellen was obviously pleased. "Then you shall," she promised with a bright smile. They finished the dishes and walked outside.

"That's the shearing shed over there," Ellen said, pointing out a large building. "We have about two dozen lads come to help us when it's time to crop the sheep."

The bleating of the animals filled the air, and Kate could see them spread out all around the outbuildings like a sea of dusty clouds. "Do they make that sound all the time?" she asked.

Ellen smiled. "Mostly, yes. Of course, they're generally not this close to the house."

"Doesn't Blue have anyone to help him?" Kate asked, imagining what a task it must be to drive so many sheep from one pasture to another.

Ellen squared her slender shoulders and looked just a mite offended. "He has me," she answered.

"But you've got the children to take care of, and the house," Kate pointed out.

"I still have time to lend Blue a hand when he needs me." Ellen sounded proud and a little defensive.

Kate allowed herself to imagine living in such a place with Sean and she understood. When Ellen McAllister lay down beside her husband at night, she was probably bone weary, but she had the satisfaction of knowing that the work of her hands and heart and mind made a real difference.

Kate couldn't remember when writing speeches and

booking hotel reservations for her father had ever given her such a feeling. "You're lucky," she said.

Ellen relaxed. "I know," she answered.

The two women walked for some time, while Ellen showed Kate the large patch of ground where she raised vegetables, the coops with the squawking hens that produced the McAllisters' eggs and provided the occasional chicken dinner, the building where the hired hands would stay when it came time to shear the sheep.

"Don't you ever get lonely, living way out here?" Kate ventured to ask as they entered the cool, spacious living room with sturdy, serviceable furniture and a fireplace that adjoined the one in the kitchen.

A large quilting frame was set up in the middle of the room, and a beautiful multicolored quilt was in progress. Ellen touched it with a fond hand as they passed. "I've got Blue and the kids and the people in those books Sean brings," she replied, starting up a set of wooden stairs. The banister was made of rough wood with bits of bark clinging to it in places. "Most of the time they're enough."

Kate sighed. "I guess nobody likes their life all the time," she said.

Ellen nodded as she looked back. They were on the upper floor when she asked, "What do you like best about your life, Kate?"

The question took Kate by surprise, and so did the realization that she hadn't really *had* much of a life before she came to Australia. "Sean," she answered, her eyes lowered, her cheeks warm.

"It's nothing to be ashamed of, loving a man," Ellen insisted. They had reached a doorway, and she led the way inside. "This is our room, Blue's and mine."

Kate saw a lovely hardwood bed covered with one of Ellen's colorful handmade quilts. There were several comfortable chairs, and two hooked rugs brightened the wooden floor. An old-fashioned folding screen stood in one corner of the room, and a wisp of a nightgown was draped over its top.

With a soft smile, Ellen pulled down the nightgown, folded it and tucked it into a drawer.

As much as Kate liked this woman, she was filled with envy. It wasn't hard to imagine the happiness Blue and Ellen shared within the intimacy of these four walls; it was a charge in the air, like lightning diffused in all directions.

They went through each of the children's rooms, then Ellen opened a door at the end of the hall. It was a small room with a slanting roof, and contained an iron bedstead that was painted white. The spread was another of Ellen's elaborate quilts, this one in a floral design, and the curtains matched. A ceramic pitcher and bowl set was on top of an old wooden nightstand.

Kate drew in her breath. "It's charming," she said a moment later.

Ellen smiled. "I'm glad you think so, because you'll be sleeping here."

Kate was embarrassed again. "Sean...?"

Ellen's eyes sparkled with amusement and affection. "He can sleep downstairs in Blue's study. There's a chesterfield there that folds out into a bed."

Kate bit her lower lip and nodded.

Ellen laughed. "I dare say he'll have his due once you're away from here, though."

Kate had absolutely no doubt of that. She wouldn't be able to resist Sean when he set his mind on seducing her, so she didn't plan to waste her time trying. She looked toward the open window, where lace curtains danced on a rising wind.

"The sky looks angry," Ellen fretted, crossing the room to lower the window sash. "A storm's brewing, I think."

Kate felt an elemental yearning to be alone in this room with Sean, to lie with him beneath the beautiful quilt and feel his arms tight and strong around her. "There must be things you need to do," she said to distract herself. "How can I help?"

Ellen remembered with a start that her wash was hanging outside on the line, and the two women ran to reach it before the rain did.

"What about the sheep?" Kate shouted over the increasing howl of the wind as she and Ellen swiftly wrenched sheets and shirts and dish towels from the clothesline.

"They don't mind a little rain," Ellen called back.

Enormous drops began pummeling the ground, the roof and the windows only moments after Kate and Ellen were inside. They stood near the sputtering fire to fold the fresh-smelling laundry. The kids were back at the trestle table, working at their lessons.

About half an hour had gone by when Blue and Sean came in from looking after the sheep. They were both soaking wet, and Ellen rushed to peel away Blue's jacket and hat. As she was leading him toward the fire, Kate's eyes met Sean's.

She longed to fuss over him in the same way, but she wasn't certain she had the right. After all, this wasn't her house and Sean wasn't her husband.

Both mischief and appeal flickered in his eyes as

he gazed back at Kate. Then, rather dramatically, he sneezed.

Kate went to him. "You're wet," she said helplessly.

"And cold," he answered.

Kate shivered, although she was dry and warm. After a moment's hesitation she took his hand and led him toward the hearth. There was something sweetly primitive in making a fuss over Sean while a storm raged at the windows, and she wished they were alone.

Sean smiled and kissed her forehead, then began stripping off his shirt. Drops of water shimmered in his hair, catching the firelight like diamonds. His chest glistened with moisture.

Using all the determination she possessed, Kate turned away. "I'll get you some tea—"

"They'll be needing more than tea," Ellen said wisely. She took a bottle of brandy down from a cupboard, along with a jar of instant coffee.

Kate stood by and watched, since there was nothing else to do, while Ellen brewed two mugs of coffee and added healthy doses of sugar, milk and brandy. Kate's hands trembled a little as she carried the nutritional disaster to Sean and held it out.

He accepted the offering with a little ceremony. His eyes, linked with Kate's, seemed to strip away her dry clothes, until she felt naked in front of him. She'd lost all awareness of the others.

Sean lifted the brew to his lips and drank, and when he swallowed, Kate felt the brandy coursing through her own system, warming her, melting her muscles and bones.

"You need to lie down," she heard Sean say. The words didn't seem to go with the movements of his lips.

A moment later he set the mug aside and lifted Kate into his arms. She could feel the wetness of his skin seep through her lightweight flannel shirt.

He carried her to the room Ellen had showed her earlier and laid her gently on the bed.

"The children," she whispered in sleepy despair.

Sean grinned as he unlaced her hiking boots and pulled them off. "It's all right, Katie-did. I'm only putting you to bed."

"I wish we could—make love," Kate said with a long yawn.

Sean chuckled. "Believe me, sheila, so do I. But you're right—we can't with the nippers about."

It felt so good to have her shoes off that Kate stretched and gave a little groan, curling her toes as she did so. Sean unsnapped her jeans and slid them down over her hips, thighs and legs. It was so different from the last time he'd removed them.

He stripped her to her undershirt and panties, then tucked her underneath the quilt and bent to kiss her forehead. "Sleep, love," he said softly.

Kate snuggled down between the crisp, chilly covers, giving a little sigh. "It's so—nice here..."

Sean kissed her again, this time on the lips. "All the comforts of home," he agreed. "Except for one, of course."

Kate opened her eyes, but they fell closed again. She hadn't realized she was so tired. "I'm afraid of thunder," she confessed after the sky was rent by a deafening roar.

Sean drew up a chair and sat down beside the bed, holding her hand in his. "I'll never let anything hurt you," he promised.

Kate couldn't remember a time when she'd felt so safe and wanted. Her mouth seemed to be moving without permission from her brain. "I wish we lived in a place like this," she said, punctuating her words with a yawn. "Just you and me and Gil and our babies…"

Sean's chuckle was a rich, sweet sound. "Oh, love, you are making it hard for me to keep my hands to myself. Go to sleep, before I disgrace us both."

Kate stretched and burrowed deeper into her pillow. Soon the rain and the wind and even Sean receded into nothingness, and she was dreaming dreams.

When she awakened hours later, the room was dark and cold and she was alone. For a reason she could never have explained, she turned onto her stomach, buried her head in her arms and wept with grief.

Chapter 8

At dinner Kate was puffy-eyed and quiet, wishing she'd never come to Australia. Maybe she wouldn't be so deeply, hopelessly in love with Sean Harris if she'd stayed where she belonged.

Later, when the dishes were washed and dried and put away, Ellen sat down at her quilting frame and showed Kate how to work a simple stitch. While they sewed, Sean and Blue played a cutthroat game of chess. The children were sitting in front of a television set, watching a picture that intermittently faded and jiggled on the screen.

"Is that good for their eyes?" Kate asked, worried.

"They'll soon tire of it," Ellen answered with a contented sigh, and she was right. Minutes later, the TV was silent and the kids were getting out various books and toys.

Because they got up early and worked hard, the

McAllisters liked to be in bed by eight. Kate, having had a long nap, was wide awake, but she didn't want to disrupt the household, so she helped herself to one of Ellen's romance novels, gave Sean an innocuous goodnight kiss and went off to her room.

About a hundred pages into the book Kate realized she'd selected the wrong reading material for keeping her mind off Sean and all the sweet delights she'd known in his arms. She closed the paperback and turned out the light to stare up at the ceiling with unblinking eyes.

She tried counting sheep next, and was certain she got through the McAllisters' entire flock without missing so much as a lamb. She was still sleepless, and her body was still wanting Sean.

She turned the light back on and started to read again. This time she didn't stop until the happily-ever-after ending, and a glance at her watch told her that it was nearly dawn. Kate got out of bed and quietly got dressed.

Sean was in the kitchen, drinking instant coffee by the hearth, when she arrived there. He'd already built the fire to a crackling blaze.

"Where do they get wood?" Kate asked. She hadn't stopped to wonder before, but the land was barren for miles around.

Sean set aside his coffee and drew her into the circle of his arms as though she'd asked some romantic question. "There's an occasional stand of gum trees about," he answered, his lips a fraction of an inch from Kate's. "And they have some of it shipped in by rail, from a town about ninety-five kilometers south of here."

Kate's breasts were pressed into the hard wall of Sean's chest. "Oh," she said weakly. She was still holding the romance novel she'd read during the night in one hand, and it dropped to the floor.

Sean released her to retrieve it, and his eyes danced in the dim light of the fire as he looked at the cover and then at Kate. "Katie-did," he teased, "I'm surprised at you."

Kate was quietly defiant. "I liked it," she said, sticking out her chin. "In fact, I can't wait to buy a supply for myself."

Sean tossed the book onto the table with a chuckle and then pulled her close again, his hand grasping the waistband of her jeans. His fingers were warm against the bare skin of her abdomen, and he seemed in no hurry to withdraw.

Kate gave a trembling sigh. She was helpless where this man was concerned. "A-are we leaving today?"

Sean nodded, bending his head to nibble at her lips. "Yes, sheila. Provided the runway isn't knee-deep in mud, we're taking off after breakfast." He turned his hand to caress the nest of silk at the junction of Kate's thighs. "If we stay," he continued, answering the question Kate hadn't the breath to voice, "I'll have to take you somewhere private and have my way with you."

At the sound of footsteps on the stairs, Sean stepped back, ending the intimate embrace. Kate swayed on her feet, and he gripped her shoulders, pressing her onto one of the benches beside the table. She was trying to catch her breath when Blue came into the kitchen, whistling softly.

"Good morning," he said, his grin taking in both his guests in a single sweep. "Off to the blue sky, are you?"

"If the runway's clear," Sean answered, and he sounded as distracted as Kate felt.

Blue took the kettle from the stove and poured steaming water into a mug, adding instant coffee and sugar to that. He stooped slightly to look out the window and assess the sky. "Should be all right," he said. "Then again, you could be here for weeks."

"Now there was a conclusive statement," Sean remarked.

Blue's eyes were twinkling in the dim, cozy light of the warm kitchen. "Anxious to see the last of us, are you?" he teased. "I don't mind telling you, I'm insulted."

Sean laughed. "Who's insulted?" he returned. "You and Ellen haven't been to Sydney in six years."

While the men went on arguing good-naturedly, Kate went to the cupboard for a cup, then to the stove for hot water and coffee crystals. She stood at a far window, looking out at the sky. As she watched, streaks of gray shot through the black velvet expanse, following by tinges of crimson and apricot. The spectacle was stunning.

Sean appeared beside her. "What do you see out there, sheila?" he asked softly.

"Magic," Kate replied, glad to be next to him.

Soon the sky had performed all its tricks and the kitchen was full of noise and laughter. Kate set the table for breakfast, while Ellen prepared oatmeal, toasted bread, sausage and eggs.

When the meal was over, Blue put on his coat and hat. Ellen and the children gathered around him in a happy ritual of hugging and kissing. Kate's throat felt thick as she watched.

After Blue had said a morning farewell to his wife and children, he shifted his eyes to Kate. "It was good to meet you, Kate Blake. Come back and see us again soon."

Kate nodded and muttered her thanks as Sean put on his own hat and coat to follow his friend outside.

Ellen was busy clearing the table, her motions too swift and intense for the simple job. It was plain to see that she already missed her husband, even though he would be back in time for supper.

"Daddy forgot his tucker!" Sarah cried suddenly, running to fetch the canvas bag that contained a hearty homemade lunch and dashing for the door.

John and Margaret ran out behind her.

Kate felt a pang at the prospect of leaving this family. She'd never seen one quite like it before, and she hadn't dreamed such simple, unadorned happiness really existed.

When Sean came back inside minutes later, he announced that the runway was dry enough for a take-off. Kate went to gather her things, bringing her small leather suitcase downstairs with her.

The time with Ellen and Blue and their children had been precious to Kate. She hugged her new friend and said a soft goodbye.

There were bright tears in Ellen's eyes. "Don't be a stranger," she said, before turning to embrace Sean.

Kate didn't let her tears fall until she and Sean were inside the airplane and racing along the runway to meet the blue sky.

"What's wrong?" Sean asked with genuine concern in his voice as the small craft shot into the air. The landing gear made a *ker-thump* sound as it moved back into the belly of the plane.

Kate sniffled and dried her cheeks with the back of one hand. "They're so happy," she said.

"And that's something to cry about?" Sean persisted, frowning in puzzlement.

"It is if you realize you've never even *seen* that kind of happiness before, let alone had it for yourself."

Sean was quiet for a long time. When he finally spoke, they were flying at a level altitude. Far below, a small stream looked like a long mud puddle in the brown grass, and kangaroos paused to drink. "Abby thought Ellen ought to leave Blue and get herself a career in the city," he said, and his voice was flat, emotionless.

Kate supposed it was hard for him, even now, to speak of Abby. "Ellen told me," she answered. "Did Abby want a career?"

Sean made a raw sound in his throat that was probably meant to pass as a chuckle. "Definitely not. She made a life's work out of telling other people what to do."

Kate regretted bringing Abby's name up in conversation, but she knew that she and Sean had to talk about her sister. If they didn't, she would always hover over them like a ghost. "You sound as though you hated her," she said.

"Toward the end," Sean answered, "I did."

The subject was too painful; Kate had to back away. "Where did you meet Blue McAllister?"

There was relief in Sean's voice when he answered, "Flight school. He and I went to work for Austra-Air at the same time."

"And Ellen?"

"She was a buyer for a chain of department stores. They met on one of Blue's flights."

Kate was surprised. She'd pictured Blue and Ellen

growing up close to the land. "How on earth did they end up way out here on a sheep station?"

"The station was Blue's dream. Ellen loved him enough to share it."

Kate was quiet for a long time. She looked out at the raw panorama spread out below, trying to remember how it had felt to live and work in Seattle, to be mainly concerned with the course of her father's career. The whole scenario had about as much reality for her as a rerun of a TV movie.

"What's your dream, Sean?" she finally dared to ask.

Sean had one hand on his knee, the other on the control lever. "I want to keep on flying," he answered in a noncommittal tone without looking at Kate.

"There has to be more than that," Kate ventured.

Sean sighed, and she knew by the angle of his head that his eyes, hidden behind a pair of mirrored sunglasses, were fixed on the horizon. "All right," he said, "I'll tell you. I'd like to have a wife who looked at me the way Ellen looks at Blue."

Kate smiled. "That shouldn't be hard to manage. I would imagine you have women falling at your feet, Captain Harris."

At last Sean spared her a glance. "Most of them are only looking for a good time," he said. "I want a woman who can say her wedding vows and mean them."

Back to Abby again. Kate let out her breath. "How about you? Did you keep your vows, Sean?"

His jawline hardened visibly. "I've never gone back on my word in my life," he replied, and Kate knew he was telling the truth. He had been faithful to Abby, even when he was desperately unhappy.

Kate reached out and rested a gentle hand on Sean's leg. "We need to talk about my sister," she said.

"Personally," Sean responded, "I'd like to forget she ever existed."

Kate was annoyed, sensing the depths of Sean's stubbornness. "What about Gil? He's a part of Abby. Do you want to forget about him, too?"

"Of course not," Sean snapped. "If it hadn't been for him, that part of my life would have been a total waste."

Kate drew a deep breath and let it out slowly. "Was it really that bad?"

He turned his head in Kate's direction, but she couldn't see his eyes because of the sunglasses he wore. "It was that bad," he answered.

"Then why didn't you divorce her?" Kate asked, exasperated.

Sean's answer stunned her. "I did," he said. "Two days after I moved out of the house, she drove her car off a cliff."

Several long moments passed before Kate could speak. Even now she was afraid to ask the question that had plagued her ever since Abby's death, but she made herself do it. "Did you take Gil away from her? Is that why she did it?"

Sean shoved splayed fingers through his dark hair. "She didn't want him," he said in a voice so low that Kate could barely hear it. "She brought him to my office that afternoon and left him with my assistant—along with a note saying she was going to meet her lover in Brisbane. They were planning to be married once the divorce went through, according to her."

Kate closed her eyes. As painful as any reminder of Abby was to her, it was a tremendous relief to know that her sister hadn't died on purpose. "Why didn't you tell us that before? My parents and I have always thought she killed herself."

"No one seemed very interested in anything I had to say at the time," Sean answered.

It was true. Everyone had been so caught up in their own feelings and conclusions about Abby's death that very few questions were asked. "I'm sorry, Sean," Kate said softly.

Sean had evidently spotted their destination. He began guiding the small plane downward, and the conversation was clearly over.

The campsite was in the shelter of a grassy canyon, where a small, spring-fed lake was hidden away. Since they had landed a mile off, by Kate's calculations, she and Sean had to carry their supplies a considerable distance.

When several trips had been made, and Sean was satisfied that they had everything they needed, he set about putting up the tent. Kate, exhausted by the treks back and forth between the plane and camp, collapsed onto the ground.

"I wouldn't do that again if I were you," Sean commented without looking up from his task. "We get the occasional milk snake 'round here."

Kate shot back to her feet and looked frantically around. When there was no sign of a snake, she sat down again. "Next you're going to tell me there are crocodiles in the water," she said, gesturing toward the lake.

Sean's white teeth showed in a grin. "Just don't expect me to wrestle one for you, love."

Kate sniffed. "You mean, you wouldn't even try to save me?" she asked, insulted.

"I'd say it would be the croc who needed saving," he replied, going on with his work. He tossed his head, as if to shake away some dreadful image. "Poor devil," he added.

"What kind of Australian are you?" Kate grinned, folding her arms across her chest.

"The kind who can manage the likes of you," Sean responded, finishing with the tent and dusting his hands together at a job well done. "Come on," he said, taking up a tackle box and two fishing poles. "Let's go catch our supper."

"Supper?" Kate echoed. "We haven't even had lunch."

Sean dropped the fishing poles and the tackle box and came toward her, grinning. "Lunch, is it?" he teased. "Now there's an idea I can warm up to. Come here, Katie-did, and give me lunch."

Kate's cheeks were hot, and she retreated a step, unconsciously holding the buttoned front of her shirt together with one hand. She wanted Sean as much as he wanted her—but she wanted him *later*, in the privacy of the tent. "I think we should go fishing after all," she said formally.

Sean was still advancing. Then, suddenly, he stopped in his tracks. A look of absolute horror contorted his features, and he yelled, "Look out!"

Kate sprang into his arms, her heart hammering against her breastbone, only to find that he was laughing. A wild turn of her head showed her that there was nothing behind her. "Bastard," she said, doubling up her fists and slamming them against Sean's chest.

He caught her by the waistband of her jeans, opening

the snap with a motion of his thumb. A slight pull made the zipper come undone. "You were awake all night, wanting me," he said in a low, hoarse voice.

It was true, and Kate couldn't deny it, much as she wanted to. "How do you know?" she threw out lamely.

Sean's hand slid up under her shirt, over her rib cage to the rounded underside of her breast. "It was a wild guess," he replied, and a grin spread across his tanned face as Kate flinched at the passing of a fingertip over her nipple.

"S-someone might see us," Kate managed. As much as she longed for and needed this man, something deep inside her always wanted to erect a barrier. She needed a place to hide.

"Only the 'roos and the snakes," Sean answered with an easy shrug. He was unbuttoning Kate's shirt now, and there was nothing she could do to stop him. Her hands hung uselessly at her sides.

"We c-could go inside the tent," she suggested.

Sean shook his head. "I want to have you in the bright light of day, Katie-did," he answered.

A tremor went through Kate as he slid her flannel shirt off over her shoulders and arms and tossed it onto the grass. Her full breasts swelled against the scanty cloth of her undershirt, straining to be free.

He squatted to untie and remove her boots, then peeled away her stockings. The feel of his hands on her bare feet was so unexpectedly erotic that she shivered. He claimed her jeans and panties next, leaving the undershirt for last. After he'd pulled it ever so slowly over her head, Kate stood naked before him.

She felt no more shame than Eve had before the fall from grace.

"My God, you're beautiful," Sean whispered, his hands resting lightly, almost reverently, on the curves of Kate's hips.

Kate reached back to undo her French braid, delighted by the catch in Sean's breathing as her bare breasts rose. Then she shook her head until her hair lay about her shoulders. In those moments it was easy to believe that she was the only woman on earth, and Sean the only man.

He took off his hat first, tossing it into the grass. Then he removed his shirt. Goose bumps appeared on his skin as the cool breeze touched him, but Kate doubted that he felt the cold any more than she did.

She stepped forward to unfasten his belt and open his jeans. Sean groaned and let his head fall back when she clasped him boldly in one hand, taking his measure with long, gliding strokes of her palm.

He dug his fingers into her bare shoulders as he dragged her close and propelled her into a hard, elemental kiss. When it was over, Kate ached to possess and be possessed. Her body had long since made itself ready for Sean.

"I need you so much," she whispered. "Please don't make me wait this time."

Sean uttered a hoarse chuckle. "I don't think I could manage that," he admitted. Then, in a motion that dated back to Adam, he clasped Kate by the waist and lifted her to the top of his shaft.

She drew in her breath as she felt him nudging the portal of her womanhood, and it came out as a ragged rendering of his name.

He lowered her slowly, begrudging every fraction of an inch she gained, making her pay for it with pleas and promises. By the time she'd taken all of him, she was delirious with need.

Kate shivered as he unsheathed himself rapidly, then began the sweet process of entering her again. "Oh, Sean," she whispered, "please."

But he stopped and tilted her back, only partly joined with him, so that he could take one of her nipples into his mouth. A jolt of pleasure went through Kate at this new contact, and she thrust herself down upon him in response, taking matters into her own hands.

Sean groaned and lifted her again, slowly, slowly, all the while feeding greedily at her breast.

She wrapped one arm around his neck and entangled her free hand in his hair, whispering his name over and over again as a litany and a plea.

Finally Sean reached the limits of his control. He dropped to his knees in the grass without ever breaking contact with Kate, and allowed her her freedom. She began to rise and fall and writhe upon him, her body taking over her entire being while her mind spun in another universe.

When Kate cried out in unbearable pleasure, Sean thrust her bountiful breasts together with his hands and ran his tongue back and forth across the nipples. Kate gave cry after primitive cry while her body bucked spasmodically in release.

She was still in a daze when Sean's moment came. He stiffened violently beneath her and then thrust his hips upward, spilling himself into her.

She prayed silently that he had given her a child, so that she would have something left of him when the inevitable happened and they parted. All her dreams and fears entangled with one another and Kate dropped her head to Sean's bare shoulder and sobbed.

He was still breathing too hard to speak, but his hands roved soothingly over the naked skin of her back and buttocks, and his lips moved against her temple. "What is it, sheila?" he asked softly when he could speak. His hand was under Kate's chin then, and he was looking deep into her eyes.

Kate couldn't speak of parting, not when she and Sean were still joined together. She simply couldn't. She shook her head wildly and pressed her wet cheek against his shoulder. The ghosts of people she'd trusted—Abby, Brad, her father—were all around, taunting her. "Hold me," she said.

He reached out and found his shirt, which he draped gently over Kate's trembling shoulders, and then he put his arms around her. "I love you," he told her.

For a moment Kate couldn't believe she'd heard the words. "What?" she sniffed.

He chuckled, holding her even more tightly. "I said I love you," he answered.

Kate drew back far enough to search his face and the depths of his green, green eyes. "You do?" she marveled.

Sean sighed in a put-upon way. "That isn't the customary response to such a declaration, Katie-did," he pointed out. "Do you love me or not?"

Kate pretended to consider the question. "I love you," she professed in the tone of one making a sudden decision. Then she couldn't tease any longer. "I always have," she added softly.

He kissed her, deeply and thoroughly, and she could feel him stirring inside her. He slipped his hands beneath the shirt and around her rib cage, rising unerringly to her breasts. "Marry me," he said when the kiss ended.

Kate was dizzy, and she could barely see for the stars in her eyes. "Anytime," she answered.

Sean opened the shirt and lifted her breasts in both his hands. "I'll be a demanding husband," he warned, chafing sensitive nipples with the pads of his thumbs. He was getting harder inside her.

"I'll be a demanding wife," Kate answered, giving a small sigh as she began to move upon Sean.

He stopped her movements to prolong the delicious friction. Nibbling at her ear, he said, "I'll want you often."

"Good," Kate breathed, writhing slightly.

Sean groaned at the sensation this produced, then pressed Kate backward into the grass. The fabric of his shirt protected her from the chill of the ground as he withdrew and then drove into her, and she bent her knees in order to receive him.

Satisfaction came to Kate first, so she had the special pleasure of guiding Sean through his. She ran her hands up and down the smooth flesh of his back and whispered soft, soothing words as he fought against the inevitable and then succumbed.

He fell to Kate when it was over, gasping and exhausted, and still she held him. Presently he rolled onto his side, drawing Kate close as he moved. He kissed the top of her head and squeezed her tightly.

"I hope I'm pregnant," she said dreamily.

Sean sat bolt upright and stared down at her. "What?" he rasped.

"I said—"

"I know what you said, damn it!" Sean growled. Then he swore roundly, got to his feet and fastened his jeans.

Kate stared up at him, startled and scared. "Sean—"

"I thought you were protected," he said.

It was like being slapped. "You thought…" She snatched up her clothes and began scrambling back into them. "Damn you, Sean Harris!" she screamed.

He turned away, shoving one hand through his hair. "I won't be able to bear it if you leave carrying a child," he said in a voice so low that Kate barely heard him.

Her eyes were hot with tears—tears of relief and confusion and love. She went around to face him, snapping her jeans as she moved, then pulling her undershirt into place. "Sean, I don't have any plans to leave."

He looked at her with mingled hope and contempt. "You will, love," he said. "As soon as your beloved daddy crooks his finger, you'll be on a plane home."

Kate had to vent her frustration somehow, so she stomped one foot. "I'll give you a *finger*, you officious creep!" she yelled, holding up the pertinent digit.

Sean laughed in spite of himself. "God, but you do need taming, sheila," he said.

Kate kicked dirt at him with her bare foot. "You go to hell!" she shouted, still furious over his remark about her allegiance to her father. Deep down inside, she was terribly afraid he might be right.

"Come here," Sean ordered quietly.

"Drop dead," Kate answered, storming off in the direction of the plane. In that moment she would have given her soul for a pilot's license.

Not to mention her boots.

Chapter 9

Midway between the campsite and Sean's plane, Kate stepped on a thistle and began hopping about awkwardly on one foot in a ceremony of pain.

Sean made an affectionately contemptuous sound as he lifted her into his arms to carry her back to the camp. "You're lucky I don't believe in spanking," he said with a philosophical air about him. "If I did, I'd turn you over my knee right now and blister your delectable little rear end."

Kate glared at him. "Put me down," she said.

"It'll hurt if I do," Sean warned.

The thistle in Kate's foot was already stinging. "Then don't," she conceded grudgingly.

Sean chuckled and set her carefully on a large stone near the tent. Then, squatting down in front of her, he lifted her wounded foot and examined it with a frown.

"Nasty bit of business, that," he commented. "Next time you stomp off in a rage, sheila, wear your boots."

"Don't patronize me," Kate hissed, squeezing her eyes shut when she saw that Sean was about to remove the thistle. There was a biting sting and then relief.

Sean set her wounded foot on her knee. "There's still the iodine," he said, rummaging around in one of the packs they'd brought.

Kate figured the medicine would hurt worse than the injury, and she was right. Tears burned in her eyes when Sean applied the iodine, and her teeth sank into her lower lip.

Gripping her foot in a gentle grasp, Sean put a Band-Aid over the wound and followed that with a light kiss.

Kate braced herself. "Would it really be so terrible if I had your baby?" she asked.

Sean handed Kate her stockings, then her hiking boots. "It would if you got on a plane and went back to the States," he answered, looking not at her but at the sparkling waters of the hidden lake. "I won't have my children living on different continents."

"You asked me to marry you a little while ago," Kate reminded him. "Did you mean it?"

Sean got to his feet. The winter sun was at his back, casting a golden aura all around him. "I meant it," he said. "But there won't be any babies until we're sure it's going to work out."

"That's the stupidest thing I've ever heard," Kate argued, lacing up one of her boots. "If you don't think we can make it, why the hell did you bother to propose?"

Sean cupped his hand under her chin and made her look up at his face. "Because I love you, and I need you," he said forthrightly.

"Well, then," Kate pressed, standing.

"I felt the same way about Abby," he answered tightly. Then he took up the fishing poles and the tackle box again, and he walked away.

Kate still didn't know whether he'd really meant his marriage proposal. It had seemed so, but then he'd made that ominous remark about Abby. She followed him down to the rocky bank of the lake and took one of the fishing poles when he set them down. "I guess you don't trust me much," she observed.

Sean took a jar of fish eggs from the tackle box, opened it and baited his hook. "I think we should live together for a while," he announced.

"No way," said Kate, thinking of Gil as well as herself and Sean. "If you don't have enough confidence in what we have together to marry me, then we're better off to stay on separate continents."

Sean handed Kate the pole with the baited hook. "What do we have, Katie-did? Besides the sexual thing, I mean?"

Kate cast her hook into the water and reeled in the slack in her line. "I don't know. But if it's what I saw back there at the McAllisters', I want a shot at it."

Sean looked at her and grinned. "Me, too," he answered.

They fished in silence for a while, neither getting so much as a bite, and then Sean said, "I've got a flight to Hong Kong day after tomorrow. Come with me."

Kate hesitated. "I don't think so."

"Why not?"

"Because I want to spend some time with Gil, for one thing. And I need to think about what's happening between you and me. In case you haven't noticed, Sean

Harris, it's hard for me to put one sensible thought in front of another when you're around."

He grinned. "I have the same problem."

Kate drew a deep breath. Since they were talking calmly, now seemed as good a time as any to broach the subject of taking Gil back to America for a visit with his maternal grandparents. "Mother and Daddy would love to see Gil," she ventured.

Sean stiffened slightly. "Fine. Let them fly down here."

Kate sighed. "Sean, my father is getting older, and he's not in the best of health. I think the trip might be too much for him."

Sean was quiet for a long time. Out of the corner of her eye, Kate could see that his jawline was as hard as the volcanic rock embedded in the walls of the canyon rising around the lake. "I don't trust him," he said finally.

Kate gave her line a few tugs, hoping to interest a fish. "Okay," she answered, "but it's only fair to tell you that if we get married, I plan to make regular trips back to the States. And if we have a child, I'm taking him or her with me."

Sean's resentment was almost tangible. "Fine," he said. "Let's just forget about having babies and getting married. That will make everything simple."

"Damn," Kate muttered through her teeth. "What did my father do to make you hate him so much?"

"He tried to steal my son."

Kate's pole trembled in her hands. "I know you think Daddy was behind that, Sean, but you're wrong. He would never do a thing like that."

"A month ago you would have told me that what's-his-name wouldn't sell cocaine," Sean pointed out, reeling in his line with a furious motion of his hand and then casting it again.

The reminder of Brad shook Kate's confidence in her own instincts. She *had* trusted her fiancé with her whole heart, and she'd been so terribly wrong. She bit into her lower lip and said nothing, and her pole and the lake blurred into each other.

Sean finally put his hand on hers. "Kate, I'm sorry," he said. "I shouldn't have thrown that in your face."

Kate couldn't look at him. "No. You were right—I trusted Brad. I would have married him."

"Kate."

"What's your secret, Sean?" she asked miserably, still avoiding his eyes. "What terrible thing am I going to find out about you now that I'm so much in love with you that there's no going back?"

He took her pole and set it aside with his own. "I've never lied to you about anything, Kate, and I don't plan to start." He spread his hands. "I'm just what I represent myself to be—a man who loves you."

Kate went into his arms and held on tight to his waist. "If this falls through," she whispered, "I won't be able to stand it."

Sean entangled his fingers gently in her hair and drew her head back to make her look at him. "I'm not going to betray you, Kate," he promised hoarsely.

She gazed into his eyes, letting all her fears and insecurities show. There was no hiding from this man who could turn her mind and body inside out at will. "I'll marry you, if you still want me," she said softly. "As soon as you get back from Hong Kong, we'll arrange for the license."

Sean nodded. "It's a deal, Yank," he said with a grin.

Kate put her arms around his neck and kissed him. "There's one other thing, Sean," she said after a long time. "I can't live in Abby's house."

"Fair enough," he answered. "We'll shop for one of our own after the honeymoon."

Kate was silent a moment, gathering courage for what she wanted to suggest. "We could take Gil with us," she said cautiously.

"On our honeymoon? Not likely, sheila."

Kate forged bravely ahead as though he hadn't spoken. "It's summer in the States," she said. "Gil would love Seattle, and on our way home, we could take him to Disneyland."

Sean's face hardened. "Is that what this is all about? You want to get married so your parents can get a look at Gil?"

"Of course not!" Kate protested, insulted.

He smiled, but the expression wasn't pleasant. "Maybe they'd like to come down for the wedding," he suggested. "I'm sure they'll be pleased to learn that The Fiend has started in on their second daughter after using up their first."

"That's a terrible thing to say!" Kate cried.

"The truth is the truth, Kate," Sean said stubbornly. "When your parents find out I'm back in the family, all hell's going to break loose. You might just have to choose between them and me."

The thought was appalling—and all too possible. "Is that what you wanted Abby to do? Choose between you and them?"

Sean threw down his fishing pole without even bothering to reel in the line. "No!" he shouted. "Damn it all to hell, no!"

Kate put her pole down carefully, just to show him that some people in this world were civilized and could control their temper. With her chin high and her shoulders back, she turned and walked toward the camp.

Sean strode after her, grabbing her by the shoulders and wrenching her around. "I never asked anything of Abby but love and loyalty," he rasped. "She repaid me by getting rid of our baby and taking a lover. *Don't you ever* accuse me of trying to hurt her in any way, because I gave her everything I had!"

With that, Sean abruptly released Kate and walked away, leaving her to stand alone by the lake, staring after him. He disappeared around the canyon wall without once looking back.

Kate's emotions were in such a dither that she couldn't stand still. Her mind rang with words she wanted to forget—*She repaid me by getting rid of our baby and taking a lover.*

The solution, she knew, was to get so caught up in some task that she didn't have time to think. She busied herself gathering rocks to make a circle around the place where the bonfire would be, as she'd seen people do in the movies. After that, she gathered what stray pieces of brush she could find and piled them inside the ring of stone.

An hour passed and there was still no sign of Sean.

Kate dragged a box of canned goods over near the nonexistent fire and sat down to wait, her chin in one hand. Sean would be back, she told herself. He couldn't stay away forever.

She began to tap one foot against the ground. One

thing was clear—marrying Sean Harris in the near future was out of the question. He wasn't emotionally ready for such a commitment, and neither was she.

An overwhelming sadness overtook Kate, and she sighed beneath the weight of it. When they got back to Sydney, she would pack her things and return to the hotel. Once she'd had a few days to get to know Gil, she would get on a plane, go home and try to pick up the scattered pieces of her life.

The trouble was, none of them fit anymore. She was no longer Brad's fiancé or her father's press secretary, and that left her with nothing to be. She was shamed anew by the realization that, for all her efforts, she'd never built a life for herself.

Kate was chewing listlessly on a cold piece of Mrs. Manchester's meat pie when Sean finally returned to camp. He looked at Kate's attempt at a fire and grinned.

"What's so funny?" Kate demanded. She was through putting up with his patronizing manner.

Sean dumped an armload of dry, broken branches beside the carefully arranged rocks. He ignored Kate's question and squatted down to go through the supplies for a meat pie of his own.

"Don't you have anything to say?" she asked when the silence stretched to interminable lengths.

Sean looked up at her, chewing. "Yes," he answered. "Can you cook?"

Kate gave a strangled cry of fury and kicked dirt at him. "No, and I don't intend to learn," she said, "so you can just forget any ideas you might have of getting me to fetch and carry for you!"

"Fine," Sean told her calmly.

"Furthermore, I have no intention of marrying any-body with a temper like yours."

"Good," Sean replied, serenely consuming the rest of his meat pie.

Kate sank to her knees beside him and shoved one hand through her hair. "Aren't you going to ask me to forgive you for deserting me like that?" she asked.

"No," Sean answered. "I'm not."

"You're not sorry?"

Sean shook his head. "It was leave or wring your neck, sheila. I'm still not sure I made the right choice."

Regally Kate got to her feet, marched over to the tent and crawled inside. Then she summarily zipped the zipper.

A marriage to Sean would never work out anyway, she assured herself. And then she lay down on the sleep-ing bag she was going to have to share with him that night and cried until her nose was red.

Some time later the zipper on the tent made a rasp-ing sound as Sean opened it. He crawled in to lie beside Kate, gathering her into his arms. "Don't cry, sheila," he whispered, holding her close.

Kate slipped her arms around his neck; she couldn't help it. "We're hopeless," she said.

He chuckled. "No. Where there's this much love, there's always hope. But you were right before." He paused and sighed. "We need time to think this through, both of us."

For all the reassurance in his words, there was a note of resignation, too, and Kate was anything but com-forted. She couldn't pretend that nothing was wrong, either, because something was. "What did you mean when you said Abby got rid of your baby?" she asked, her voice barely more than a whisper.

Sean didn't put her away from him, but his arms didn't hold her quite so tightly. "Exactly what you think I meant," he answered after a long time.

Kate closed her eyes. "I'm sorry, Sean."

"So am I, but it's over and done. It's a mistake for us to talk about Abby. We're both scared, and we keep dragging her memory out and throwing it between us."

Kate knew he was right, but she wasn't sure they'd ever be able to make a relationship work. Sure, they had passion, but Sean and Abby had probably had that in the beginning, too. Would their lovers' quarrels become vicious battles at some point in the future?

Kate couldn't bear the thought. "Make love to me, Sean," she whispered, desperate for some distraction from her confusion.

He laughed, but the sound had elements of a hoarse sob. "There's a request I'll never refuse, Katie-did," he said. But instead of kissing her, or opening her shirt or jeans, he caught her by one hand and hauled her out of the tent.

"I think you may be an exhibitionist at heart," she commented, disgruntled, and Sean laughed again.

He kept right on walking toward the lake, though, pulling Kate after him.

When he finally let go of her hand, he immediately tossed aside his hat, then kicked off his boots. His socks, jeans and shirt soon followed.

Kate looked at the water with concern. "Are there snakes or crocodiles in there?" she asked.

"Probably not," Sean answered, wading into the water.

He was as magnificent naked as he was dressed, and

Kate couldn't help staring at him. "Come back here," she said lamely.

Sean grinned. "Come and get me," he challenged.

"Damn it, it's winter," Kate pointed out, hugging herself.

"Chicken," he replied.

His insolence made Kate get out of her boots and her clothes and stomp furiously into the water that could be infested with creatures she wouldn't even recognize. When she stood face-to-face with Sean, he chuckled at her angry expression and began to bathe her.

The water was cold, but Kate was transfixed by the gentle splashing motions of Sean's hands. He washed her face, her shoulders, her back and breasts and beneath her arms, and it was a strangely sensual experience.

When he proceeded to the lower part of her body, her breath caught in her lungs and the already taut tips of her breasts grew tighter still. She ran her tongue over her lips as he parted her, cried out when he claimed her with a sudden thrust of his fingers.

"Easy," he said, as the water began to churn around them from the frantic motions of Kate's hips. "Take it slow and easy, sheila."

"I—oh, God—I can't!" Kate cried. His thumb was moving around and around on her, making her slippery even though she was waist-deep in water. "Oh, Sean…"

He bent to take one of her nipples into his mouth, and Kate clutched at him, driven by a need she hadn't been prepared for. Her nails left pink curves in the flesh of his shoulders, but she didn't care. She moved wildly in the water, seeking him.

"Take me," she pleaded.

"Later," he replied. "Right now I want to see your pleasure, Kate. I want to watch you respond to me."

"Oh," she whispered, *"oh..."*

Sean intensified his efforts, greedy at her breasts, a merciless conqueror. When she stiffened violently and cried out in relief, she knew he was watching her every reaction, and that made her gratification even keener.

When the water was still at last, he kissed her and maneuvered her gently onto his shaft. Soon the lake was wild again, and the cries that filled the air were Sean's.

They didn't dress immediately, but dried each other and crept into the tent to lie entwined in sweet silence and sleep. When Kate awakened, Sean was outside, whistling, and she could hear the cheery crackle of a campfire.

Hastily Kate found the clothes Sean had left for her and put them on. When she crawled out of the tent, he was squatting beside the fire, stirring something in a frying pan, and dusk was deepening the shadows that sprawled across the lake.

"What's that?" Kate asked, sniffing.

Sean grinned at her. "No worries, love. It's nothing on the endangered species list."

"Don't tease me," Kate fussed, going to sit near him on the ground. "I just woke up."

He treated her to a brief, smacking kiss but said nothing.

Looking at him, she wondered how she was going to live without him—for a few days or for a lifetime. "Do you absolutely have to go to Hong Kong?" she asked.

"Yes," he answered. "You can still come with me, you know."

She shook her head. "There will be other trips," she

said, hoping against hope that what she was saying was true. "Right now I need some time and space, and so do you."

Sean only shrugged and went back to his cooking. It looked to Kate like some kind of chops, and it smelled wonderful. Her stomach grumbled.

Sean chuckled. "Hungry, sheila?"

Kate nodded, licking her lips.

"Strange thing about love," Sean philosophized. "It either takes your appetite away completely or makes you eat like a crazed shark." He reached out to give the contents of another kettle a knowledgeable shake. "I probably shouldn't give you any dinner, since you refuse to do your share of the cooking."

Kate found metal plates and utensils for them both. "Does setting the table count?" she asked.

"That depends," Sean said, pausing to look at Kate's chest. Her buttons were open, and she was straining against the undershirt.

"On what?" she breathed.

Sean reached over and lowered the undershirt, revealing both her breasts. He bent and kissed each nipple lightly. "On whether or not you're willing to provide dessert," he replied.

Kate held a breast for him with one hand and entangled the other in his hair. "Does this answer your question?" she asked, her voice husky with pleasure.

He suckled for a few moments, then withdrew and righted her undershirt. "Absolutely," he answered belatedly.

The mosquitoes were thick that night, so they retired to the tent after their meal. Kate couldn't see a thing in the darkness, but she could hear Sean undressing as she took off her outer clothes. She was kneeling, clad only in her panties and undershirt, when he reached out for her.

"What do you want, Kate?" she heard him ask in a low, raspy voice. He was close; his hands were resting on her bare thighs and she could catch the clean scent of him.

Kate drew her undershirt off over her head and then took his hands in hers. For an answer, she laid his palms against her swollen breasts. Her nipples hardened.

Sean caressed her for a while, then gently turned her so that her back was to him. He moved one of his hands between one breast and then the other, fondling them in turn, while he moved his other lightly over her belly.

Kate's breathing was quick and shallow, and despite the chill of the night, she was so warm that she was perspiring lightly. She squirmed backward until she found what she wanted and needed, and she took it.

Sean had not expected to be taken prisoner, and he gave a sharp gasp of pleasure.

Bracing herself against the tent floor with her hands, Kate allowed her instincts free rein and became the conqueror. Sean groaned helplessly as she had her relentless way with him, now teasing, now tempting, now taking him in earnest.

He gave up what Kate took from him with a defiant, adoring shout, then turned her and pressed her to the sleeping bag. She still could not see him, but she could feel the caresses of his hands and the touch of his lips, and that was enough.

"You'll have to give an accounting for that, sheila," he promised between deep, ragged breaths. He found her with his strong fingers and began a rhythmic, circular massage that soon had Kate writhing, her hands stretched above her head.

Sean found them and imprisoned them in his fist, holding them where they were. Kate's back arched, and a whimper escaped her as he continued to soothe and torment her at once.

"I love you," she managed as he worked her skillfully toward frenzy. "Oh, God, I love you so much."

"Then stay with me," he answered, showing her no more mercy than she had shown him. "You belong with me, Kate—in my house and my bed."

She moaned.

He took her to the east and west and north and south of heaven itself before allowing her a slow descent to earth.

In the morning they rose early to fish. It was their last day alone together, and that gave everything they did a note of sad festivity.

After lunching on their catch, they took down the tent, packed up their gear and hauled the lot of it to the airplane, where Sean stowed it neatly away. Looking back, Kate could see only a ring of stones surrounding a dead fire to mark their passing. Except for that, the ancient land was undisturbed; they might never have been there, loving and living, laughing and crying, shouting and whispering.

"We'll be back someday," Sean assured her, lifting her chin and planting a soft kiss on her mouth.

Kate nodded and turned her face toward the future, half excited and half afraid.

The small plane left the land with a roar that scattered birds and sent kangaroos hopping wildly toward the horizon. A magical time in Kate's life was ending, and she knew it, and she wanted to cling to it with both hands.

Of course, there was no way to do that.

They landed once, around noon, at an isolated place that sold hamburgers and gasoline to truckers and pilots, and took off again immediately.

"I didn't bring you out here to make you sad, Kate," Sean remarked, having caught the forlorn expression on her face.

She nodded, her hands clenched together in her lap. "I know," she said. How could she explain the feeling of loss she had, and the sense that it would be permanent?

They landed at the small airport outside of Sydney a few hours later, and neither of them spoke as they carried their gear from the plane to the waiting Jeep. Sean had a word with a mechanic, and then they were off.

"I'm moving back to the hotel," Kate said, uttering her first sentence in over an hour.

"Tonight?" Sean asked. There was no challenge or recrimination in his voice.

"Yes."

"Why?"

"Because of Gil. Because of Abby," Kate whispered. "Because we can't be in the same house together without ending up in each other's arms."

Sean shrugged and took Kate to the hotel where she'd stayed her first night in Sydney. He waited until she'd booked a room, then kissed her lightly on the cheek and left.

An hour later her suitcases arrived by cab. She was on the telephone when the bellhop brought them up, but she managed to tip him and wave her thanks without interrupting the call.

"So," she said when the door had closed behind the young man. "What would you and Daddy think if I married Sean Harris?"

Her mother's stunned silence was answer enough.

Chapter 10

"How long will you be in Hong Kong?" Kate asked, holding the telephone receiver to her ear with one hand and towel-drying her freshly shampooed hair with the other.

"Three or four days," Sean answered. He sounded as glum as Kate felt. "You might as well come here and stay, since I'll be gone."

She smiled. "That was a very transparent attempt to get me to feel sorry for you," she said.

He chuckled ruefully. "Did it work?"

"Yes," Kate answered, "but I'm still staying here."

"Have it your way, sheila."

Kate drew a deep, weary breath. "I would like to spend some time with Gil, if that's all right with you."

"It's fine. Listen, love, I'm not very good at small talk. Will you have dinner with me tonight?"

"No," Kate answered, remembering the chops he'd cooked by the campfire. "I had dinner with you last night. I'll see you when you get back from Hong Kong."

Sean sighed. "Good night, Kate."

"Good night," she responded gently before hanging up.

The evening news was flickering on the television screen, so Kate went over and turned up the sound. As events happening overseas were recapped by a brisk Australian voice, a picture of her father's face filled the screen. He was standing behind the president's desk, witnessing the signing of an important bill he'd been trying to push through the Senate for months, and he looked justifiably proud of his accomplishment.

Kate felt a certain homesickness, then cinched the belt of her heavy terry cloth robe a little tighter and sat down on the edge of her bed to eat a supper brought to her by room service. As much as she loved Sean and Gil, it was going to be difficult to live so far from friends and family.

When a silly game show came on, she got up to turn off the TV. She thought of Abby, and wondered how many of her sister's problems could have been solved by an extended visit home.

In a moment, Kate's sister and mother were both inside her head, yammering that it would be a mistake to marry Sean. She shut them up by turning the game show back on.

Kate slept in the next morning, then spent a few leisurely hours shopping. She and Sean weren't planning a formal wedding, but she wanted a special dress just the same.

It was midafternoon when she arrived at Sean's

house to see Gil. He and his dog, Snidely, were play-ing with a Frisbee on the front walk, and his eyes lit up when he saw Kate.

"Is it true?" he demanded, racing toward her but stopping just short of a hug.

"Is what true?" Kate laughed, resisting an urge to ruffle his hair. She knew that some children resented gestures like that, and she wanted very much for Gil to like her.

"Dad said you and he have been talking about getting married," Gil told her, and he looked genuinely pleased by the prospect. "Are you going to be my mom?"

So Sean had said they'd *talked* about getting married, not that they definitely would. Kate put an arm around Gil's shoulders, and they proceeded up the walk. The driver of the taxi she had arrived in honked his horn as he drove away, but she barely heard the sound. She was too busy searching her mind for the proper answer to Gil's question. "I'd be your stepmother," she said at last. "And your aunt. But my sister was your mom, and nothing is ever going to change that."

Worried brown eyes scanned her face. "You wouldn't make me give Snidely away, would you?"

"Of course not," Kate answered quickly. They had reached the steps of the porch, and they sat down side by side at the top. "I think Snidely is a nice dog."

Gil was happy again. "Thanks," he said.

Kate wanted to kiss his forehead or his cheek, but checked herself. He'd probably hate that, think it was corny. "Say, handsome," she said as though struck by sudden inspiration, "how about having dinner with me tonight, since your dad's away? We'll go wherever you like."

The child nodded eagerly. "McDonald's!"

Kate laughed and slapped her hands against her blue-jeaned thighs. "McDonald's it is, then, but we'd better tell Mrs. Manchester before she goes to any trouble making you dinner."

The two went inside and found the older woman in the kitchen, rolling out dough.

"Aunt Kate's taking me to McDonald's," Gil announced importantly, "so you don't have to cook."

Mrs. Manchester smiled. "Well, that's good news," she said with enthusiasm to match Gil's. "I'll just watch the telly, then, and have something simple for supper."

"We could bring you a hamburger," Gil volunteered.

Mrs. Manchester glanced at Kate, her eyes twinkling. "I don't think that will be necessary," she said. "You just go and have a good time, young man, and don't worry about me."

Kate told the housekeeper when she would bring the boy back and called another taxi while Gil dashed upstairs to change his clothes.

"I wish you'd come back and live at our house," Gil told her when they were riding toward the nearest Mc-Donald's in the backseat of a cab.

Kate thought of the plans she and Sean had made to buy another house, one where Abby's memory wouldn't haunt them at every turn. "I think we might end up living together at some point," she said cautiously. "Maybe you wouldn't like it, having another person around when you're used to just your dad and Mrs. Manchester."

Shyly Gil moved a little closer to Kate on the seat. "I'd like it," he assured her in a quiet voice.

Kate was so moved that her throat thickened and, for a minute, she didn't dare look at her nephew for fear of bursting into sentimental tears. "Have you ever thought about visiting America?" she asked when she'd recovered herself.

Gil considered for a long time. "Dad says the place is overrated," he told her finally. "But I'd like to see it for myself—especially Disneyland."

Kate smiled at that. "Disneyland is one place that's everything it's cracked up to be," she told Gil.

He looked concerned. "Disneyland is cracked up? What happened to it?"

Kate laughed. "We seem to have a language barrier here. When an American says something is everything it's cracked up to be, that means it's all that you'd expect of it and more. Disneyland is wonderful."

"Oh," Gil replied, and his expression betrayed both puzzlement and relief. "That's good."

Once they'd reached McDonald's and were happily consuming their hamburgers, french fries and milk shakes, they exchanged idioms and tried to guess at their meanings. This made them both laugh so hard that people turned to look at them.

Kate would have liked to spend more time with Gil, but it was getting late and he had school in the morning. The day after that, however, would be Saturday, and Sean wasn't returning until Sunday.

"Do you have plans for this weekend?" she asked.

Gil's eyes were bright with anticipation as he shook his head.

"Then how about going to the Taronga Zoo with me? It's been a while since I've seen a platypus or a wombat or even a koala."

Gil liked the idea immediately, and he recounted the school field trip he'd just been on all the way home in the cab. Kate had the driver wait while she saw her nephew safely inside the house and said good-night.

When she got back to her hotel room, a bouquet of twelve yellow roses was waiting on her nightstand. The card read simply, "Now and always. Love Sean."

Kate bent to sniff the luscious scent of the flowers, feeling optimistic about all the problems and differences she and Sean would have to work out in order to make a life together. Didn't all couples have to do that?

She took a long, hot bath, read a third of the thick romance novel she'd bought that afternoon while shopping for her dress and fell into a sound sleep.

Since she hadn't found a dress she liked the day before, she went out shopping again after breakfast. At a pricey little boutique tucked away between a pawnshop and a bookstore, she found a lovely ivory silk gown with a trimming of narrow lace around the hemline and along the V-shaped bodice. It was perfect.

After paying for the dress, Kate took it back to her hotel room and hung it carefully in the closet. She was just turning away from doing that when the telephone rang.

She answered with a questioning, "Hello?"

Sean's voice came over the wire as clear as if he were in the next room instead of on another continent. "Hello, sheila," he said. "Did you get the flowers?"

"Yes," she answered, smiling. "They're beautiful— thank you."

"I'll have to exact a certain price for them, of course," Sean teased.

Kate felt warm all over, and she wished he could be right there in that room with her. "Of course," she retorted in a low, sultry voice.

"How's Gil?" was his next question.

"He's just fine. We went to McDonald's for supper last night, and we're off to the zoo tomorrow."

"Sounds like he's pretty comfortable with you."

Kate smiled. "He asked me if I was going to be his mom."

The warmth seemed to fade from Sean's voice, at least for the moment. "What did you tell him?"

Kate sat down, feeling deflated. "I said I'd be his stepmother, *if* you and I were to get married."

"I see." Sean still sounded uncomfortable, but that awful chill was gone from his voice.

Kate was never sure where her next question came from, because she hadn't given it a moment's thought beforehand. "I don't suppose you'd let me adopt him?"

There was a long silence.

"Sean?"

"That would give you the same legal rights that Abby had," Sean reflected.

"I know," Kate answered. She knew she was walking on thin ice emotionally, and she was practically holding her breath.

"We'll talk about it when I get back," Sean said abruptly. Kate wished she could look into his eyes, for then she'd be able to read his thoughts.

"Which will be Sunday?" Kate asked brightly, anxious to soothe him.

"Probably," Sean replied. "I love you, Kate."

"And I love you."

A few moments later they hung up.

The telephone immediately jangled again, and when Kate answered, she was surprised and a little alarmed to hear the operator say, "You have another overseas call, Ms. Blake. This one is from the States."

"Thank you," Kate said, and bit down on her lip as she waited. She felt inexplicably nervous.

"Your mother tells me you're thinking of marrying that Australian," Senator Blake boomed, without so much as saying hello to his daughter first. "Don't you think that's a little idiotic, given what he did to your sister?"

Kate braced herself. "He didn't do anything to Abby. She manufactured her own set of problems, just like the rest of us."

"He'd like to have you believe that. Katherine, I want you to get on the next plane and come home. I need you here in Washington, anyway."

"I'm not going anywhere," Kate answered flatly.

She could feel the storm brewing in and around her father. "Katherine," he said in an ominously quiet voice, "I expect to see you in this office within seventy-two hours. Is that clear?"

She sighed. "I'm sorry, Daddy. I'm staying here, and I'm marrying Sean."

"If you do, by God, I'll disinherit you. You'll be left with nothing but your grandmother's trust fund!"

Kate didn't care about the money she wouldn't inherit, and her trust fund was quite adequate for her needs. But she did care about losing the senator's love and approval. "Do whatever you have to do. I've made my decision, Daddy."

At that, the senator hung up on his daughter with a resounding crash.

Kate was still upset the next morning when she set out to pick up Gil at Sean's house. Her father had no right to behave like such a tyrant, and she was going to tell him so the next time she saw him.

Gil greeted her at the front door, dressed for a day at the zoo. His smile seemed as wide as the distance between Kate and the senator. Once she was inside, the little boy gave her a shy hug. "I've been thinking about going to the States," he told her. "I think I should, since I'm half-Yankee."

Kate grinned. "I think you should, too, but your dad might have a different opinion."

"I could go if he changed his mind, though," Gil told her enthusiastically. He brought a passport from the pocket of his jacket. "See?"

Kate nodded. "You'd better put that away before you lose it or something," she said.

She was distracted from Gil by Snidely's unmistakable bark. "You get out of my kitchen, you great hulking beast!" Mrs. Manchester cried, affronted.

"I think maybe you should go and tie up your dog," Kate told her nephew.

He nodded his agreement and disappeared.

When the boy returned, he and Kate went outside and got into another taxi. They rode to Circular Quay, which was down near the Sydney Opera House, and boarded a ferry that took them across the harbor to the world-famous zoo.

They spent a happy morning examining one creature after another. Some were indigenous to Australia, while others might have been seen in any zoo.

Kate took a picture of Gil holding a baby koala. The little animal crunched nonchalantly on eucalyptus leaves all the while, willing to tolerate the idiosyncrasies of human beings.

When midday came, Kate and Gil had hot dogs and sodas for lunch. Kate reflected that her diet was going to hell on greased tracks; she'd have to get herself back on healthy food soon.

By early afternoon Gil was getting tired, so they took the ferry back to Sydney proper, found a movie house and bought tickets. Kate was glad to sit down, and she didn't really care what the show might be.

It was an action-adventure story, as it turned out, and both Gil and Kate were soon drawn into the plot, as much a part of things as the main character. When they came out two hours later, they were blinking in an effort to focus their eyes.

A quick check of her pocketbook showed that Kate was nearly out of money. "Let's go back to the hotel for a few minutes," she said to her nephew. "Then we'll have supper somewhere."

"Great," Gil agreed. It was an expression he'd heard in the movie, and he seemed pleased with himself for picking it up.

The hotel was several blocks away, but it felt good to walk after sitting for a couple of hours, and Kate and Gil played their game of exchanging idioms again as they went.

When they reached Kate's room, she opened one suitcase, and then another, and then another, searching for her Australian money. She finally found some in her overnight case, which was sitting in the bathroom on the counter.

A knock at the door brought her out, smiling and curious, her wallet in one hand. The room looked as though it had been ransacked, she thought, as she passed by the trail of open suitcases she'd left behind her.

Sean was standing in the hallway when she opened the door, and she was so surprised that she just stood there for a moment, staring at him.

"When I go to America," Gil was saying cheerfully in the background, "I'm going to spend a whole month at Disneyland."

There was a slight change in Sean's expression, but his words sounded normal enough. "Aren't you going to kiss me, sheila?"

Kate realized that he was really there, and not a product of her overworked imagination, and she hurled her arms around his neck. "You're back early."

He removed her arms gently. "Surprised?" he asked, backing her into the room.

"Dad!" Gil shouted, hurling himself at his father. "We went to the zoo and saw a movie and once we had supper at McDonald's!"

"Good," Sean said quietly, ruffling Gil's hair with one hand. He was smiling, but there was something odd in his face as he looked around the room at Kate's suitcases.

Kate felt uneasy without knowing why. "Lucky we came back to get some money," she said to Sean. "If we hadn't, we would have missed you."

Sean was still looking at the suitcases, and it seemed to Kate that he was a little pale beneath his suntan. "Is that so?" he asked.

Kate wanted to shake him. "What's wrong?" she asked, keeping her voice as even as she could.

Sean wouldn't look at her. Instead, he turned his gaze toward Gil, who still stood at his side, looking up. "So, you're planning a trip to America, are you?" he asked.

Dread went through Kate like a cold wind when she

realized the conclusion Sean was drawing from the rifled suitcases and his son's comment about Disneyland. "You don't understand," she said lamely.

"I think I do," Sean said, and his voice was like dry ice.

Gil chose that moment to whip his passport out of his jacket pocket and present it. "I could go anytime I wanted," he said proudly.

"I want you to wait for me by the elevators," Sean told his son, speaking in a voice that was all the more ominous for its quiet, measured tones.

Disappointment flashed in Gil's upturned face. "But we were going to have supper—"

"Go," Sean said flatly.

After casting one baffled, injured look in Kate's direction, Gil obediently walked out of the room and down the hallway. Kate would have gone after him, but Sean closed the door and barred her way.

"Pretty damned clever," he said.

Kate let out a furious sigh. "I wasn't planning to take your son away," she told him, shoving one hand through her hair.

Sean looked at her with contempt, but behind that she saw the pain of betrayal. "I was a fool to trust you. All of it—the talk, the lovemaking—you did it all to get into my good graces, so I'd leave you alone with Gil!"

"That's not true!" Kate cried. "You're deliberately misunderstanding the situation. Gil and I went to the zoo and then to the movies, and I was out of money, so I came back here to get some—that's why the suitcases look the way they do."

Sean didn't seem to hear her. He was like a geyser about to spew dangerous steam, and Kate had a terrible feeling that nothing she could say or do would move him. "Why did he have his passport, then?" he hissed, moving to grab Kate and then stopping himself at the last second. "Why was he talking about going to Disneyland?"

"I don't know why he brought his passport," Kate answered. "He got it out earlier to show it to me, and he probably just stuck it in his pocket."

"Why were you interested?" Sean demanded.

It was no use, and Kate knew it. "We did talk about going to America," she confessed. "But it was a some-day kind of thing—not something immediate."

"You're just like your father," Sean accused. "You'll do anything, step on anybody, to get what you want!"

"No," Kate argued, her eyes filling with tears as she shook her head.

She might not have spoken at all for all Sean seemed to care. "You're like her, too—why didn't I see that you're no better than she was?"

Kate couldn't bear any more. She grabbed Sean by the lapels of his windbreaker and shouted, "Listen to me, damn you. I'm not my father, and I'm not Abby— I'm just Kate! And I'd die before I'd betray you, Sean Harris, because I love you more than I've ever loved anything or anybody!"

With a gentle kind of cruelty, Sean brushed Kate's hands away, turned on his heel and walked out, leaving the door open behind him.

Kate stepped into the hallway, her face wet with tears. "Sean, please…" she called after him, desperate.

"Goodbye," he said coldly without even turning around to look at her.

Kate sagged against the doorframe, closing her eyes

as she heard the sound of an elevator bell. When it chimed again moments later, she knew Sean and Gil were gone.

She went back into her room, like something wounded, and, after closing and locking the door, she sprawled across the bed, too sickened to think or move. It was a long time before she gathered the strength to call the airport.

There was a flight leaving for Los Angeles in two hours. Numb from the core of her soul out, Kate booked a reservation on that flight, refolded everything in her suitcases and called the desk for a bellhop. While she was waiting, she dialed Sean's number.

Fortunately Mrs. Manchester was the one to answer.

"This is Kate," the caller said brokenly. "May I please speak to Gil?"

The housekeeper sounded bewildered and kindly. "He's right here, Miss Blake," she said.

Gil came on the line a moment later. "Are you going, Aunt Kate?" he asked.

New tears welled in Kate's eyes. "I have to, sweetheart," she said. "You understand, don't you?"

Gil was silent for a long time, then he answered, "I guess I won't get to see Disneyland."

Kate dried her cheeks with the back of one hand. "Maybe another time," she said with forced cheerfulness. "I want you to promise to email me, Gil, and tell me all about school and sports and Snidely. Okay?"

"Okay," he replied.

"I love you, darling."

"And I love you, Aunt Kate," the little boy responded bravely.

Kate swallowed. "G-goodbye, Gil."

"Goodbye," came the forlorn reply.

Just as Kate was hanging up the telephone, a knock sounded at the door. The bellhop entered at her hoarse call of, "Come in!"

The young man loaded Kate's bags onto a luggage cart and started off toward the elevator. After a few moments spent struggling for composure, she followed.

All the way down to the desk and all the way to the airport, Kate kept hoping that Sean would show up. She had the scenario all worked out in her mind. He would say he was sorry, that he knew she would never do anything to hurt or betray him, and then they'd kiss and everything would be all right again.

Only it didn't happen that way.

There was no sign of Sean at the airport.

Kate had her passport checked and boarded the plane. Her last fantasy died when the doors of the craft were slammed shut. Sean wasn't going to come down the aisle and collect her and take her home.

She didn't have a home anymore.

Kate curled up in her seat, a bundle of despair and confusion, and stared out the window, watching the city of Sydney recede. She was really leaving—the dream was over.

After a while Kate slept. It was a fitful rest, and she awakened with a violent start when she felt someone's hand on her shoulder. Sean. Somehow, someway, he'd come for her. Maybe he'd been in the cockpit of the airplane all the time....

But it was only a blond flight attendant, smiling apologetically down at Kate. "I'm sorry, miss," she said, "but we're about to land in Auckland. You'll have to fasten your seat belt."

Kate sat up grumpily and fixed the belt. Maybe she'd get off in New Zealand, take a couple of days to compose herself and then go back and talk to Sean again. By now he had to be sorry for what he'd thrown away so thoughtlessly.

But even before the plane touched down, Kate had decided to go on to the States.

She'd done enough compromising. If Sean Harris wanted to talk to her, he was going to have to make the next move.

Chapter 11

The child flung himself at Sean in a rage of pain and disbelief. "I hate you, I hate you!" he screamed, hammering at his father's chest with knotted fists. "You made her go away!"

Mrs. Manchester, who had inadvertently witnessed the scene, hurried off to another part of the house—but not before giving Sean a look that said her thoughts on the matter were similar to Gil's.

Feeling as though he were being torn in two, Sean grasped his son by the wrists to stop the attack. Then he knelt down on the floor of the entryway to look into his son's eyes. "Listen to me," he said hoarsely. "Please."

Gil still looked miserable, but he gave up the struggle. "Kate wasn't going to take me away," he insisted. "We were just going to have supper at a restaurant."

Sean gave a heavy sigh. "I know that now," he confessed. "And I'm sorry."

Gil's lower lip trembled and tears glistened in his eyes. "What good does being sorry do?" he challenged. "Aunt Kate's gone, and she'll probably never come back."

Kate was gone all right. While Sean had been agonizing over the fact that he'd been a fool not to trust her after all she'd been to him, she'd checked out of her hotel room, taken a cab to the airport and gotten on board a plane. By now she was probably halfway to New Zealand.

Sean rose to his feet. He was hurt and he was remorseful, but he wasn't really surprised. Kate had only done what he'd expected her to do all along—she had run back to Daddy when the first misunderstanding arose. Sean sighed, ruffled his son's hair and walked away.

"You could go and get her," Gil called after him in hopeful despair. "You could tell her you're sorry and bring her back."

Sean closed his eyes against his son's pain and his own. In time the hollows and canyons Kate's passing had left in their lives would fill in. All they needed was time.

"It's better this way," he answered, and kept walking.

The first thing Kate did when she reached home was take a long, hot shower. When that was done, she slept for thirty-six hours.

She opened her eyes to a world without Sean and Gil, and cried all the while she bathed and dressed and set out for the supermarket to buy food. She had no appetite at all, but her refrigerator was empty, and she knew she would eventually have to eat.

She encountered Brad in the yuppie section, where the miniature corn cobs and pickled crab apples were sold. He smiled and introduced the woman beside him.

"Allison, meet Kate Blake. Kate, my wife, Allison." He said "my wife" with a spiteful little twist, as though he expected Kate to fling herself down at his feet in despair.

"Allison," Kate acknowledged, properly shaking the hand of Brad's new bride. She was obviously a career woman—she wore a classic suit and there was a briefcase in the shopping cart, with the initials ABW engraved on the brass trim.

The brown-eyed, attractive blonde nodded, reserve evident in every supple line of her body. "Kate," she confirmed.

Kate excused herself and went wheeling off toward the produce section, hoping Brad had given up the life of crime once and for all, for his own sake as well as Allison's.

When Kate arrived home, loaded down with shopping bags, the doorman helped her carry them into her apartment. She was just handing him a tip when the telephone rang.

Until that morning Kate had kept it unplugged, and she wished now that she'd left it that way. She wasn't ready for a round with the senator or her mother.

The caller was Irene Blake. "Welcome back, darling."

Kate sighed. "Hello, Mother."

The doorman waved and slipped out, closing the door behind him.

"I can't tell you how glad your father and I are that you've finally come to your senses. I'm certainly disappointed, though, that you didn't bring Gil back with you."

"Hold on a moment, please," Kate said politely. Then she laid down the receiver, walked into the kitchen and took two aspirin from the bottle she kept in the cabinet by the stove. After washing them down with water, she went back to the telephone.

"I guess I'm not surprised that Sean wouldn't give an inch where the boy is concerned," Irene went on, and Kate wondered if her mother had been talking the whole time she was in the kitchen. "Australian men are notoriously stubborn, you know."

"And American men aren't?" Kate retorted, singularly annoyed.

"Your father is going to be stunned when he learns you didn't bring Gil home with you," Irene continued. "It's little enough to ask, I should think—"

"Mother," Kate interrupted with terse politeness. "I couldn't just grab the child and carry him off. That would be a crime."

"I'll tell you what is criminal, Katherine Blake—"

"Please don't," Kate broke in.

Irene took a sharp breath. "What's happened to you?" she demanded. "You're different."

"I'm older and wiser," Kate replied with a sigh.

"When are you joining your father in Washington?" Her mother pressed on.

"I'm not. He disinherited me, remember?"

"The senator didn't mean a thing by that, and you know it."

"He could have fooled me," Kate said.

"You're deliberately being difficult!"

Kate bit her lower lip. "I don't mean to be, Mother."

She let out her breath in a rush. "Maybe we should talk later. We don't seem to be getting anywhere."

"All right," Irene agreed stiffly, "but I wish you were the kind of daughter we could depend on."

And I wish you were the kind of mother I could call "Mom," Kate thought. *I wish I could cry on your shoulder and tell you how much I'm hurting right now.* "Goodbye, Mother," she said.

The following Monday morning Kate returned to college. Although she had a degree, she wanted to teach in elementary school, and that required a few credits she didn't have.

Soon, her life became a lonely round of going to class, studying, sleeping and eating. When she was at home, she invariably wore her bathrobe.

"You know," her friend Maddie Phillips remarked one night as she sat filing her nails and watching Kate watch a rerun, "you're going to seed. Look at you— you've got all the personality of a doorstop."

Kate gave the glamorous redhead a look meant to be quelling. "Gee, thanks, Maddie. I admire you, too."

Maddie shook her nail file at Kate. She owned a small travel agency and lived one floor down in a two-bedroom with a terrace. *"And,"* she rushed on, as though her friend hadn't spoken, "you're getting fat in the bargain."

Kate picked up the remote control for the TV set and pushed the volume button until Maddie's voice was drowned out completely. Never one to be ignored, Maddie scrambled out of her chair and plopped down beside Kate on the couch. She wrenched the control from her hands and turned off the TV.

"The trouble with you, Kate Blake, is that you're in denial."

Kate glared at her. "You've been reading too much pop psychology," she said. "I'm not denying anything."

"Oh, no? I'll bet you've put on ten pounds in the past month—true?"

Kate sighed. "True," she admitted.

"And you're not sleeping very well, either," Maddie went on.

There were shadows under Kate's eyes, and she knew it. "Can't deny that," she said.

Impulsively, for Maddie was nothing if not impulsive, she took Kate's hand in hers. "What happened down there in Australia?" she asked. "It's time you told somebody."

Kate felt tears pressing behind her eyes. She'd been back for six weeks, and there hadn't been a word from Sean—not a letter or a telephone call. Apparently he still believed Kate had planned to kidnap his son.

"I fell in love," she said, and then the whole story spilled out of her. She told Maddie everything, except for the intimate details.

"That's so romantic," Maddie murmured when the tale ended.

"Romantic? I love that man and he hates me, Maddie. What's romantic about that?"

Maddie ignored the question. "You've got to go back there. Or contact him."

Kate folded her arms. "Not on your life," she said stubbornly. "Sean's the one who's in the wrong, not me."

"Hell of a comfort that will be when the baby comes," Maddie said shrewdly.

Kate's gaze shot to her friend's face. She hadn't consciously considered the possibility that she might be pregnant, but now she was forced to. And she knew all the signs were there; she'd just been ignoring them.

Maddie folded her arms and nodded sagely. "Denial," she said.

"Oh, God," Kate replied, and she began to cry.

Maddie slipped an arm around Kate's shoulders. "Sean has a right to know," she said softly.

Kate shook her head. If Sean knew about the baby, there would be all sorts of problems. Hadn't he said he wouldn't have his children living on separate continents? No, it was better if he never learned he'd fathered another child.

"You're not being fair," Maddie insisted.

"Was it fair of Sean to accuse me of trying to steal his son?" Kate paused to sniffle. "He claimed to love me, Maddie, and yet he wouldn't even let me explain."

"There must have been a reason."

Kate sighed, remembering the kidnapping attempt against Gil, the one Sean had blamed on the senator. She had to admit, to herself at least, that he had more cause to worry than the average parent. "Maybe," she said grudgingly.

Maddie gathered up her purse and handed the TV control back to Kate. "Here. Watch reruns till your eyes cross," she told her friend. "See if I care."

Kate looked up at Maddie. "You do care," she said. "Thank you for that."

Maddie smiled sadly, touched Kate's shoulder, then left. Kate switched off the TV, crawled into bed and cried.

The next morning, a Saturday, her father returned from Washington and summoned her to his study in the fancy house on the hill. Because she had no classes that day, Kate put on her roomiest pair of jeans and a loose T-shirt and drove up there.

Her mother met her at the front door, elbowing aside a uniformed maid to do so. "Look at you," she said, running her eyes over Kate with an expression of horror. "You're a wreck!"

"You don't know the half of it, Mother," Kate replied, stepping past Irene to enter the house. "What does Daddy want?"

Irene made a face as she closed the door. "You needn't sound so cynical, Katherine. Your father is merely trying to bridge the gap between you, and it's more of an effort than *you've* made, I dare say."

Kate followed her mother down the hallway and into the familiar study.

"I want you to go back to Australia and fetch my grandson," the senator said, the moment he and his daughter were alone in that room full of books and expensive leather furniture.

Kate bit her lower lip, then answered, "I can't do that."

"Nonsense," John Blake retorted. "You simply pick the boy up when his father's not home, then the two of you get on a plane and come home."

Kate groped for a chair and fell into it. She felt dizzy and just a bit sick to her stomach. "You're serious, aren't you?" she whispered, her eyes round.

"Of course I'm serious," the senator replied.

"Why do you want Gil so badly?"

"He's my flesh and blood, that's why. He's all I have left of my firstborn child."

Kate closed her eyes for a moment. The room seemed

to be spinning around her. "It's really true," she marveled. "You *were* behind the kidnapping attempt."

"Harris forced me into that by denying me my grandchild..." the senator began.

Kate held up one hand in a plea for silence and eased herself out of her chair. "Please," she whispered. "I don't want to hear any more."

"Katherine!"

Kate stumbled out of the room, closed the door and leaned against it, as though to hold back something ugly.

After leaving her parents' house, she drove straight to the cemetery where Abby was buried, parked her car and made her way awkwardly over the slippery green grass to the family plot.

Abby's headstone was a giant angel, with a trumpet pressed to its lips. *Fitting,* Kate thought, kneeling nearby. "I thought you were so wonderful," she said sadly. "Know what, Abby? It hurts to find out you were only human."

A light breeze blew through the sunny graveyard, ruffling Kate's hair. She ran her hand gently over the place where her only sister lay. "I'm going to have Sean's baby," she went on. "I don't expect you or anyone else in the family to understand, but I had to tell someone."

Kate paused, looking up at the blue, blue sky with its lacy white clouds. "I'll never understand why you didn't want Sean, Abby. He's so wonderful—"

It seemed that Abby challenged her then, although Kate knew the exchange was happening only inside her own head. *If he's so wonderful, why did you leave him?*

Kate bit down on her lower lip, her eyes on the

ground. "I know now that I shouldn't have," she answered softly. "It was all a misunderstanding—we could have talked it out."

Give it up. You're Daddy's little girl and you always were. You wouldn't have been happy anywhere but right here in Seattle.

"That's not true," Kate argued. "I was happy in Australia. Happier than I've ever been."

Then go back. You have my blessing.

Kate shook her head. "I haven't the courage," she said.

Why not?

"I've been so wrong about everybody in my life—you, Brad, Daddy. The one time when I was right, I didn't stay and fight—I ran away like a coward. I'm afraid of doing that again."

After a long time, she rose, touched the face of the trumpeting angel and whispered, "Goodbye, Abby."

Sean nodded and left the cockpit. The passengers were still trailing out, and he had to struggle to keep himself from hurrying them along.

At last he was able to escape. His suitcase in one hand, Sean strode along the walkway and left the terminal. It was a chilly September day—down under it would be spring. Here it was the fall of the year, and the leaves were beginning to turn.

Sean shook his head. This part of the world was a strange place, whether the Yanks liked to admit it or not.

He got a cab right away, but he had to repeat the address twice before the driver understood. Sean grinned to himself. Everybody here had an accent—it was no wonder they didn't comprehend plain English.

* * *

Kate's glasses were riding on the tip of her nose as she read from her algebra textbook and got her prenatal vitamins down from the shelf at the same time. Without looking away from the book, she dumped a capsule onto the counter, lifted it to her mouth and swallowed it. She nearly choked and was gulping down water when the doorbell rang.

Muttering, she meandered into the living room. It was probably the Henderson kids selling candy or calendars so some team they were on could buy new uniforms.

When she opened the door, however, Sean was standing there, looking like an ad for flight school in his spiffy blue uniform. He took off his hat in a shy gesture and said, "Hello, Kate."

Kate's throat constricted around the prenatal vitamin capsule. "Hello," she managed, taking off her glasses.

Sean grinned slightly, bringing on a poignant pain in the region of Kate's heart. "May I come in?"

She stepped back, her glasses in one hand and her algebra book in the other. "Sure," she said, long after the fact.

Sean set his hat on a table. He had a bag, too, and he put that on the floor at his feet. "I was wrong," he said, just like that.

Kate stared at him. Even if she could have spoken, she wouldn't have known what to say.

He looked at Kate for a moment with his heart in his eyes, and then he went to the windows and stood with his back to her, gazing out at the city. "I'm living in San Francisco now," he told her.

At last Kate found her voice. "You're still with Austra-Air?"

Without turning around, Sean nodded. "Yes. So Gil and I are giving the States a chance to win us over."

Kate's heart was beating faster than it had since she'd returned from Australia. "Take him to Disneyland," she suggested softly. "That'll cinch it for you."

Now Sean turned. "I'm sorry, Kate," he said, meeting her eyes. "I should have trusted you."

"You're right," Kate said. "You should have."

"Will you give me a second chance?"

Kate had prayed to hear those words, but she hadn't really expected an answer. For that reason, she hadn't rehearsed a reply, and she just stood there, stricken.

Sean came closer, laying his hands gently on her shoulders. "Kate?" His voice was low and hoarse. "I'm ready to make some compromises, to prove I love you enough to make this thing work."

Kate swallowed. "Like what?" she managed.

"Like living in San Francisco. Like letting you adopt Gil if you want."

Kate was so moved that her voice came out sounding strangled and squeaky. "You'd do that? You'd make him legally my child?"

Sean nodded. "I would," he affirmed.

Tears welled in Kate's eyes—happy tears. Her arms went automatically around his neck. "What's my part of this bargain?" she asked with a half smile.

He chuckled. "Ah, sheila, I'm glad you asked that," he answered, slipping his arms around her thickening waist. "Come closer and I'll show you."

"I want a proposal first," Kate protested primly.

Sean laughed. "All right, then," he agreed. "Will you

marry me, Kate Blake? Will you share my life and my bed? Will you be a mother to my son?"

"I will," Kate vowed, raising one hand to prove the oath.

That was when Sean kissed her. At first it was a gentle, tentative kiss, but then she felt his body harden into a familiar readiness. His tongue plundered the depths of her mouth, and Kate's knees turned to mashed potatoes.

When he lifted her into his arms without breaking the kiss, she didn't demur. She wanted whatever he had to give her.

"There is one little thing I should mention," she said breathlessly when they reached the bedroom and Sean was lifting her sweatshirt off over her head.

He bent and kissed the rounded tops of each of her breasts. "What?" he asked.

Kate drew in a sharp breath as he unfastened her bra and quickly tossed it aside. "You're probably going to be mad," she warned.

Sean lifted her, so that she was forced to wrap her legs around his waist. That put her breasts at mouth level, and he took immediate advantage of the situation. "I'll get over it fast," he assured her between suckles.

Kate was moaning. "Maybe I should—oh, God— wait."

Sean turned to her other breast. "Tell me," he said.

"I'm pregnant," Kate blurted out.

He eased her slowly, gently to the bed, bending over her. "Damnedest thing," he murmured, shaking his head. "I could have sworn you just said you were pregnant."

"I did, and I am. That is, *we* did and I am."

Sean laughed, and the tears glistening in his eyes

were a touching contrast. "My God, sheila—that's wonderful."

Kate drew him down toward her lips and her body. Both were his to claim. "I'm very glad you think so, Captain Harris," she said, and then she kissed him, unbuttoning his shirt at the same time.

The warm, hairy hardness of his chest felt good under her palms. She squirmed as he unfastened and unzipped her jeans.

"I thought you had changed," he remarked when the kiss had ended. His lips were against her bare belly then, and Kate was trembling in anticipation.

"Thanks a lot," she muttered.

He laughed again. "As soon as you've gotten over having this one," he said, moving lower. "We'll start another."

Kate was already writhing slightly, for he was very near his destination. She felt the downy curtain part and she moaned. After that, all her words were incoherent.

Once the first shattering pinnacle had been reached, Kate lay gasping on the bed, watching Sean as he removed the rest of his clothes. When he was naked, he stretched out over her on the bed.

"I thought I'd die for missing you," he said hoarsely, and his eyes glinted in the half-darkness of the bedroom.

Kate ran her hands along his magnificent back. She didn't speak, for her body told him everything.

With a groan, Sean entered her, murmuring words of love and need as he completed that first long, delicious stroke.

Kate welcomed him, thrusting her hips upward to draw him into her very depths.

"You'll make a madman of me yet," he moaned, withdrawing slowly and then gliding into her again.

Fire had been ignited inside Kate, and the flames were rising higher and higher. She whimpered as her temperature climbed, and hurled herself at Sean in a wanton search for what only he could give her.

"That's it," he whispered, tucking his hands under her bottom to urge her on. "That's it, Katie-did—I want everything."

She was soaring toward a molten sky, borne high on tongues of fire. "Sean—Sean—"

He buried his face in her neck even as he buried his manhood in her depths. His strokes were the fierce lunges of a conqueror, and Kate's surrender was complete.

With a cry of jubilation, she exploded like a nova, and Sean was only moments behind her.

When it was over, they lay still. For Kate, Sean's rapid heartbeat and ragged breathing were music. She'd thought she'd never hold him like this again, never feel the unique planes and hollows of his body fitted to hers.

"The least you can do," she said when she was capable, "is buy me dinner."

Sean gave her a playful swat. "Buy you dinner, is it? I ought to turn you over my knee for not telling me about the baby sooner."

"I've only known about it for a few weeks myself," Kate defended. "Shall we send out for Chinese or walk down to the corner for fish and chips?"

"I'm not walking anywhere," Sean said. He'd slid down to her breast and was rolling his tongue around her nipple. "Besides, chow mein isn't what I'm hungry for."

Kate shifted slightly to give him better access. "We deliver," she said.

Later, when the loving was over, she told him about her estrangement with her father and her decision to become an elementary school teacher.

Sean thought teaching was a grand idea, since Kate liked kids so much, but he surprised her where the rift with her father was concerned. He said she should try to make things right, or she might come to regret it someday.

Chapter 12

The senator stepped uneasily through the front door of the gracious home overlooking San Francisco Bay. He held his hat in one hand and clutched the front of his overcoat closed as though he expected someone to snatch it away. Beside him, Irene slipped out of her snow-dusted mink coat and gave Kate a cautious kiss on the cheek.

"You look wonderful, darling," she said.

"Are you my grandparents?" Gil asked forthrightly.

Irene was crying, and the senator looked at the little boy with a helpless expression Kate had never seen on his face before.

"Yes," Sean said quietly when no one spoke. "These are your grandparents." He stood behind Gil, one hand resting on the boy's shoulder.

The senator's weary blue eyes moved from Kate's face to Sean's. "I apologize for everything," he said.

Sean nodded without speaking, took Kate's hand and led her out of the room.

"I wish I didn't have to leave for Honolulu tonight," he said, drawing her as close as he could, given her bulging stomach.

She laughed and laid both her hands on his cheeks. "Oh, you poor man," she teased.

Sean's hand rested on the rounded sides of Kate's stomach. "You'll take very good care of my daughter, won't you?"

"The best," Kate assured him.

He kissed her, and Kate was sorry he was going away. If they'd been alone, she might have taken him by the hand and led him up the stairs to their spacious bedroom.

"Keep that up and I'll have my way with you right here, Captain Harris," she said in a conversely prim voice.

He laughed and squeezed her bottom. "I'm shocked, Mrs. Harris," he scolded. "What would the PTA think if they heard their vice president carrying on like this?"

Kate shrugged. "Kiss me again," she said.

Sean obliged graciously.

When he'd left for the airport, Kate went back to the living room. Her mother was sitting in a chair next to the fireplace, watching fondly as Gil and the senator plundered the brightly wrapped gifts under the Christmas tree.

"No fair shaking," Kate protested.

The old man and the boy looked at her with similar smiles.

"Can I give Grandpa his present now, Mom?" Gil asked.

"No," Kate answered, settling into her favorite chair and spreading the colorful afghan she was knitting over her knees. "Christmas is still three days away."

"Scrooge," complained the senator.

"Please?" Gil wheedled.

Kate caved in. After all, it was Christmas and she was no disciplinarian, anyway. "All right, but just one," she conceded.

"Our gifts are arriving later," the senator confided to his daughter as Gil ran up the stairs to fetch the special set of Australian stamps he'd set aside for his grandfather.

"By boxcar," confirmed Irene.

Kate chuckled and tended to her knitting.

The snow had stopped in the early morning, two days later, when Sean crawled into bed beside her and drew her into his arms.

"Hello, Mrs. Harris," he said, his lips moving against her temple.

"Exactly who are you?" Kate retorted, yawning. But she snuggled closer.

He placed a warm hand on her stomach. "Very funny," he said. "Did you lay down the law to the senator, by the way?"

"Uh-huh," Kate said. "He won't be bothering me about coming back to work for him after this. I told him that being vice president of the PTA at Gil's school is the closest I'm ever going to get to politics."

"How did he react?" Sean asked, stretching and making himself comfortable beside Kate.

She giggled at the picture that came to her mind. "He

blustered, but I wasn't intimidated. After all, he was wearing Gil's Mickey Mouse ears at the time."

Sean laughed and stretched again. "I'm going to sleep," he announced.

"No, you're not," Kate replied.

* * * * *

WHAT A
WESTMORELAND WANTS

Brenda Jackson

To my husband, the love of my life
and my best friend, Gerald Jackson, Sr.

To everyone who enjoys reading
about the Westmoreland family,
this one is for you!

Cherish her, and she will exalt you;
embrace her, and she will honor you.
—*Proverbs* 4:8

Prologue

Callum Austell sat in the chair with his legs stretched out in front of him as he stared at the man sitting behind the huge oak desk. He and Ramsey Westmoreland had become friends from the first, and now he had convinced Ramsey that he was the man who would give his sister Gemma the happiness she deserved.

But Callum knew there was one minor flaw in his plans. One that would come back to haunt him if Gemma Westmoreland ever discovered that the trip to Australia he would offer her would be orchestrated for the sole purpose of getting her off familiar turf so that she would finally come to realize just how much he cared for her.

"I hope you know what you're doing," Ramsey said, interrupting Callum's thoughts. "Gemma will give you hell when she finds out the truth."

"I'll tell her before then, but not before she falls in love with me," Callum replied.

Ramsey lifted a brow. "And if she doesn't?"

To any other woman Callum's intense pursuit might seem like a romantic move, but Ramsey was convinced his sister, who didn't have a romantic bone in her body, wouldn't see things that way.

Callum's expression was determined. "She will fall in love with me." And then the look in his eyes almost became one of desperation. "Damn, Ram, she has to. I knew the first moment I saw her that she was the one and only woman for me."

Ramsey took a deep breath. He wished he'd had the same thoughts the first time he set eyes on his wife, Chloe. Then he would not have encountered the problems he had. However, his first thoughts when he'd seen Chloe weren't the least bit honorable.

"You're my friend, Callum, but if you hurt my sister in any way, then you'll have one hell of an angry Westmoreland to deal with. Your intentions toward Gemma better be nothing but honorable."

Callum leaned forward in his chair. "I'm going to marry her."

"She has to agree to that first."

Callum stood. "She will. You just concentrate on becoming a father to the baby you and Chloe are expecting in a couple of months, and let me worry about Gemma."

Chapter 1

Gem, I am sorry and I hope you can forgive me
one day.

—Niecee

Gemma Westmoreland lifted a brow after reading the
note that appeared on her computer after she'd booted it
up. Immediately, two questions sailed through her mind.
Where was Niecee when she should have been at work
over an hour ago and what was Niecee apologizing for?

The hairs on the back of Gemma's neck began standing up and she didn't like the feeling. She had hired
Niecee Carter six months ago when Designs by Gem
began picking up business, thanks to the huge contract
she'd gotten with the city of Denver to redecorate several of its libraries. Then Gayla Mason had wanted her
mansion redone. And, last but not least, her sister-in-

law, Chloe, hired Gemma for a makeover of the Denver branch of her successful magazine, *Simply Irresistible.*

Gemma had been badly in need of help and Niecee had possessed more clerical skills than the other candidates she'd interviewed. She had given the woman the job without fully checking out her references—something her oldest brother, Ramsey, had warned her against doing. But she hadn't listened. She'd figured that she and the bubbly Niecee would gel well. They had, but now, as Gemma quickly logged into her bank account, she couldn't help wondering if perhaps she should have taken Ramsey's advice.

Gemma had been eleven when Ramsey and her cousin Dillon had taken over the responsibility of raising their thirteen siblings after both sets of parents had been killed in a plane crash. During that time Ramsey had been her rock, the brother who'd been her protector. And now, it seemed, the brother she should have listened to when he'd handed out advice on how to run her business.

She pulled in a sharp breath when she glanced at the balance in her checking account. It was down by $20,000. Nervously, she clicked on the transaction button and saw that a $20,000 check had cleared her bank—a check that she hadn't written. Now she knew what Niecee's apology was all about.

Gemma dropped her face in her hands and felt the need to weep. But she refused to go there. She had to come up with a plan to replace that money. She was expecting invoices to come rolling in any day now from the fabric shops, arts and craft stores and her light fixtures suppliers, just to name a few. Clearly, she wouldn't have enough funds to pay all her debts. She needed to replace those funds.

She stood and began pacing the floor as anger consumed her. How could Niecee have done this to her? If she needed the money, all she had to do was ask. Although Gemma might not have been able to part with that much from her personal account, she could have borrowed the money from one of her brothers or cousins.

Gemma pulled in a deep frustrated breath. She had to file a police report. Her friendship and loyalty to Niecee ended the minute her former worker had stolen from her. She should have suspected something. Niecee hadn't been her usual bubbly self the last few days. Gemma figured it had to do with her trifling live-in boyfriend who barely worked. Had he put Niecee up to this? It didn't matter because Niecee should know right from wrong, and embezzling from your employer was wrong.

Sitting back down at her desk, Gemma reached for the phone and then pulled her hand back. Dang! If she called Sheriff Bart Harper—who had gone to school with both Ramsey and Dillon—and filed a report, there was no doubt in her mind that both Ram and Dillon would hear about it. Those were the last two people she wanted in her business. Especially since they'd tried talking her out of opening her interior design shop in the first place.

For the past year, things had worked out fairly well with her being just a one-woman show with her sisters, Megan and Bailey, helping out if needed. She had even pulled in her brothers Zane and Derringer on occasion, when heavy lifting had been involved. But when the big jobs began coming in, she had advertised in the newspapers and online for an administrative assistant.

She stood and began pacing again. Bailey was still taking classes at the university and wouldn't have that much money readily available, and Megan had mentioned just the other week that she was saving for a much-needed vacation. Megan was contemplating visiting their cousin Delaney, who lived in the Middle East with her husband and two children, so there was no way she could hit her up for a loan.

Zane and Derringer were generous and because they were bachelors they might have that kind of ready dough. But they had recently pooled all their funds to buy into a horse-breeding and -training franchise, together with their cousin Jason. She couldn't look in their direction now, due to that business venture. And all her other siblings and cousins were either in school or into their own businesses and investments.

So where was she going to get $20,000?

Gemma stood staring at the phone for a moment before it hit her that the thing was ringing. She quickly picked it up, hoping it was Niecee letting her know she was returning the money to her or, better yet, that the whole thing was a joke.

"Hello?"

"Hello, Gemma, this is Callum."

She wondered why the man who managed Ramsey's sheep farm would be calling her. "Yes, Callum?"

"I was wondering if I could meet with you sometime today to discuss a business proposition."

She lifted a brow. "A business proposition?"

"Yes."

The first thought that crossed her mind was that engaging in a business meeting was the last thing she was in the mood for today. But then she quickly realized that she couldn't let what Niecee did keep her from handling things with her company. She still had a business to run.

"When would you like to meet, Callum?"

"How about today for lunch."

"Lunch?"

"Yes, at McKay's."

She wondered if he knew that McKay's was her favorite lunch spot. "Okay, that'll work. I'll see you there at noon," she said.

"Great. See you then."

Gemma held the phone in her hand, thinking how much she enjoyed listening to Callum's deep Australian accent. He always sounded so ultrasexy. But then he was definitely a sexy man. That was something she tried not to notice too much, mainly because he was a close friend of Ramsey's. Also, according to Jackie Barnes, a nurse who worked at the hospital with Megan and who'd had a bad case of the hots for Callum when he first arrived in Denver, Callum had a girl waiting for him back in Australia and it was a very serious relationship.

But what if he no longer had that girl waiting for him back in Australia? What if he was as available as he was hot? What if she could forget that he was her oldest brother's close friend? What if…

Dismissing all such thoughts with a wave of her hand, she sat back down at her computer to figure out a way to rob Peter to pay Paul.

Callum Austell leaned back in his chair as he glanced around the restaurant. The first time he'd eaten here had been with Ramsey when he first came to Denver. He liked it then and now this would be the place where he would put into motion a plan some would think was way past due being executed. He would have to admit they were probably right.

He wasn't sure exactly when he decided that Gemma Westmoreland was destined to be *his* woman. Probably the day he had helped Ramsey build that barn and Gemma had arrived from college right after graduation. The moment she got out of her car and raced over to her older brother's arms for a huge hug. Callum had felt like he'd gotten hit over the head with a two-by-four, not once but twice. And when Ramsey had introduced them and she'd turned that wondergirl smile on him, he hadn't been the same since. His father and his two older brothers had warned him that it would be that way when he found the woman destined to be his, but he hadn't believed them.

That had been almost three years ago and she'd been just twenty-two years old. So he'd waited patiently for her to get older and had watched over her from afar. And each passing day she'd staked a deeper claim to his heart. Knowing how protective Ramsey was of his siblings, especially his three sisters, Callum had finally gotten up the nerve to confront Ramsey and tell him how he felt about Gemma.

At first Ramsey hadn't liked the idea of his best friend lusting after one of his sisters. But then Callum had convinced Ramsey it was more than lust and that he knew in his heart that Gemma was "the one" for him.

For six months, Ramsey had lived with Callum's family back in Australia on the Austell sheep ranch to learn everything he could so he could start his own operations in Denver. He had hung around Callum's parents and brothers enough to know how dedicated the Austell men were once they fell in love.

His father had given up on falling in love and was on his way back to Australia from a business meeting in the United States to marry an Australian woman when he'd met Callum's mother. She was one of the flight attendants on the plane.

Somehow the already engaged Todd Austell had convinced the Detroit-born Le'Claire Richards that breaking off with his fiancée and marrying her instead was the right thing to do. Evidently it was. Thirty-seven years later the two were still married, remained very much in love and had three sons and a daughter to show for it. Callum was the youngest of the four and the only one who was still single.

His thoughts shifted back to Gemma. Ramsey claimed that of his three sisters, Gemma was the one with the fiery temper. The one a man would least be able to handle. He'd suggested that Callum pray long and hard about making the right decision.

In the end, Callum had convinced Ramsey that he had made the right decision and that a hard-to-handle woman with a fiery temper was the kind he liked. He was more than certain that Gemma was the woman for him.

Now he had to convince Gemma… He'd have to be stealthy about his pursuit. He knew Gemma had no intention of engaging in a serious relationship after she had witnessed how two of her brothers, and several of her womanizing cousins, had operated with women over the years, breaking hearts in their wake. According to

Ramsey, Gemma Westmoreland was determined never to let a man break her heart.

Callum straightened up in his seat when he saw Gemma enter the restaurant. Immediately, the same feeling suffused his heart that always settled there whenever he saw her. He loved the woman. He no longer tried to rationalize why. It really didn't matter at this point.

As she walked toward him, he stood. She was probably 5'8", but just the right height for his 6'3" frame. And he'd always thought she had a rather nice figure. Her dark brown, shoulder-length hair was pulled back in a ponytail. He thought she had dazzling tawny-brown eyes, which were almost covered by her bangs.

Callum had worked hard not to give his feelings away. Because he'd always been on his best behavior around her, he knew she didn't have a clue. It hadn't been easy keeping her in the dark. She saw him as nothing more than her brother's best friend from Australia. The Aussie who didn't have a lot to say and was basically a loner.

He studied her expression as she got closer. She seemed anxious, as if she had a lot on her mind.

"Callum," she said and smiled.

"Gemma. Thanks for agreeing to see me," he said as he took her oustretched hand.

"No problem," she said, sitting down once he released her hand. "You said something about meeting to discuss a business proposition."

"Yes, but first how about us grabbing something to eat. I'm starving."

"Sure."

As if on cue, a waitress strolled over with menus and placed glasses of water in front of them. "I hope this place is acceptable," Callum said, moments later after taking a sip of his water.

"Trust me, it is," Gemma said, smiling. "It's one of my favorites. The salads here are fabulous."

He chuckled. "Are they?"

"Yes."

"That might very well be, but I'm not a salad man. I prefer something a lot heavier. Like a steak and the French fries I hear this place is famous for."

"No wonder you and Ramsey get along. Now that he's married to Chloe, I'll bet he's in hog heaven with all those different meals she likes to prepare."

"I'm sure he is. It's hard to believe he's married," Callum said.

"Yes, four months tomorrow and I don't recall my brother ever being happier."

"And his men are happy, too, now that Nellie's been replaced as cook," he said. "She never could get her act together and it worked out well for everyone when she decided to move closer to her sister when her marriage fell apart."

Gemma nodded. "I hear the new cook is working out wonderfully, although most of the guys still prefer Chloe's cooking. But she is happy just being Ramsey's wife and a mother-in-waiting. She doesn't have long now and I'm excited about becoming an aunt. Are you an uncle yet?"

It was his turn to smile. "Yes. My two older brothers and one sister are married with a child each. I'm used to being around kids. And I also have a goddaughter, who will be celebrating her first birthday soon."

At that moment the waitress returned. Callum resented the interruption.

* * *

Gemma appreciated the interruption. Although she had been around Callum plenty of times, she'd never noticed just how powerfully built he was. Her brothers and male cousins were all big men, but Callum was so much more manly.

And she had to listen carefully to what he said and stop paying so much attention to how he said it. His thick Australian accent did things to her. It sent a warm, sensual caress across her skin every time he opened his mouth to speak. Then there were his looks, which made her understand perfectly why Jackie Barnes and quite a number of other women had gone bonkers over him. In addition to being tall, with a raw, masculine build, he had thick chestnut-brown hair that fell to his shoulders. Most days he wore it pulled back into a ponytail. He'd made today an exception and it cascaded around his shoulders.

Gemma had once overheard him mention to her sister Megan that his full lips and dark hair came from his African-American mother and his green eyes and his square jaw from his father. She'd also heard him say that his parents had met on an airplane. His mother had been a flight attendant on his father's flight from the United States back to Australia. He'd told Megan it had been love at first sight, which made her wonder if he believed in such nonsense. She knew there was no such thing.

"So what do you think of Dillon and Pamela's news?"

Callum's question cut into her thoughts and she glanced up to meet his green eyes. She swallowed. Was there a hint of blue in their depths? And then there was his dimpled smile that took her breath away.

"I think it's wonderful," she said, suddenly feeling the need to take a sip of cold water. "There haven't been babies in our family in a long time. With Chloe expecting and now Pamela, that's two babies to spoil and I can't wait."

"You like children?"

She chuckled. "Yes, unfortunately, I'm one of those people who take to the precious darlings a little too much. That's why my friends call on me more often than not to babysit for them."

"You could always marry and have your own."

She made a face. "Thanks, but no thanks. At least no time soon, if ever. I'm sure you've heard the family joke about me never wanting to get serious about a man. Well, it's not a joke—it's the truth."

"Because of what you witnessed with your brothers while growing up?"

So he *had* heard. Any one of her brothers could have mentioned it, especially because she denounced their behavior every chance she got. "I guess you can say I saw and heard too much. My brothers and cousins had a reputation for fast cars and fast women. They thought nothing about breaking hearts. Ramsey usually had a steady girl, but Zane and Derringer were two of the worst when it came to playing women. As far as I'm concerned, they still are." Unfortunately, she'd overheard one of Zane's phone calls that very morning when she had stopped by to borrow some milk.

"I can clearly recall the times when Megan and I, and sometimes even Bailey, who was still young enough to be playing with her dolls, would be the ones to get the phone calls from love-stricken girls in tears after being mercilessly dumped by one of my brothers or cousins."

And they were females determined to share their teary-eyed, heart-wrenching stories with anyone willing to listen. Megan and Bailey would get them off the phone really quickly, but Gemma had been the bleeding heart. She would ease into a chair and take the time to listen to their sob stories, absorbing every heartbreaking detail like a sponge. Even to the point at which she would end up crying a river of tears right along with them.

She'd decided by the time she had begun dating that no man alive would make her one of those weeping women. And then there was this inner fear she'd shared with no one, the fear of falling in love and having the person abandon her one day…the way she felt whenever she thought about her parents. She knew she had no logical reason for feeling abandoned by them because she was certain if they'd had a choice they would have survived that plane crash. But still, as illogical as it might be, the fear was there for her and it was real. She was convinced there was no man worth a single Gemma Westmoreland tear or her fears, and intended to make sure she never shed one by never giving her heart to anyone. She would be celebrating her twenty-fifth birthday in a few months and so far she'd managed to keep both her heart and her virginity intact.

"And because of that you don't ever plan to get seriously involved with a man?"

She drew in a deep breath. She and her sisters had had this conversation many times and she was wondering why she was sitting here having it with Callum now. Why was he interested? It dawned on her that he probably wasn't; he was just asking to fill the time. "As far as I'm concerned that's a good enough reason. Those girls were in love with my brothers and cousins and assumed they loved them back. Just look what that wrong assumption did to them."

Callum took a sip of his water, deciding not to respond by saying that as far as he was concerned her brothers' behavior was normal for most men, and in some cases women. Granted, he hadn't been around Zane and Derringer while they had been in their teens and could just imagine some of the things they had gotten in to. Now, as grown men, he knew they enjoyed women, but then most hot-blooded men did. And just because a man might be considered a "player" somewhat before finally settling down with one woman— the one he chose to spend the rest of his life with—that didn't necessarily mean he was a man who totally disrespected women. In fairness to Zane and Derringer, they treated women with respect.

He wondered what she would think if she knew how his behavior had been before he'd met her. He hadn't considered himself a womanizer, although he'd dated a slew of woman. He merely thought of himself as a man who enjoyed life and wanted to have a good time with the opposite sex while waiting for the girl destined to share his life to come along. Once she had, he'd had no trouble bringing his fun-loving, footloose and fancy-free bachelor lifestyle to an end. Eventually, the same thing would happen to her brothers and cousins.

No wonder her brothers thought she was a lost cause, but he refused to accept that. He was determined to show her how things could be if she were to fall in love with a man committed to making her happy.

In a way, he felt he knew Gemma. He believed that beneath her rough and tough "I'll never fall in love" exterior was the heart of a woman who not only loved children but loved life in general. He also believed that she was a passionate woman. And that she was unknowingly reserving that passion for the one man capable of tapping into it. The same man destined to spend the rest of his life with her. Him.

The waitress delivered their food, and they engaged in chitchat while they ate their meal.

After they had finished eating and the waitress removed their plates, Gemma leaned back in her chair and smiled at Callum. "Lunch was wonderful. Now, about that business proposition?"

He chuckled, reached over and picked up the folder he had placed on an empty chair. He handed it to her. "This is information on the home I purchased last year. I would love you to decorate it for me."

Callum saw how her eyes lit up. She loved her work and it showed in her face. She opened the folder and carefully studied every feature, every detail of the house. He knew exactly what he was doing. He was giving her 9,200 feet of house to do with as she pleased. It was an interior designer's dream.

She lifted her gaze with a look of awe on her face. "This place is beautiful. And it's huge. I didn't know you had purchased a house."

"Yes, but it's still empty and I want to turn it into a home. I like what you did with Ramsey's place and thought you would be the ideal person for the job. I'm aware that because of the size of the house it will take up a lot of your time. I'm willing to pay you well. As you can see I haven't picked out any furniture or anything. I wouldn't know where to begin."

Now that much was true, Callum thought. What he

didn't tell her was that other designers had volunteered to decorate his new house, but he had bought it with her in mind.

She glanced back down at the papers in front of her. "Umm, eight bedrooms, six bathrooms, a huge kitchen, living room, dining room, family room, theater, recreation room and sauna. That's quite a lot of space for a single man."

He laughed. "Yeah, but I don't plan on staying single forever."

Gemma nodded, thinking that evidently Callum had decided to settle down and send for that girl back home. She glanced down at the papers again. She would love taking on this project, and he was right in thinking it would take up a lot of her time. But then she definitely needed the money.

"So, what do you think, Gemma?"

She glanced back up at him and smiled. "I think you just hired yourself an interior designer."

The smile that touched his face sent a tingling sensation flowing through her stomach. "I can't wait to see it."

"No problem. When can you get away?"

She pulled out her cell phone to check her calendar and her schedule for this week. Once she saw the place and gave him an official estimate, she could ask for a deposit, which would make up some of what Niecee had taken from her. "What about tomorrow around one?"

"That might be a bit of a problem."

"Oh." She figured he would probably be tied up at Ram's ranch doing something at that time, so without looking up she advanced her calendar another day. "What about Wednesday around noon."

He chuckled. "Twelve noon on Monday would be the earliest availability for me."

She nodded when she saw that time was free for her, although she wished she could see it sooner. "Monday at noon will be fine."

"Great, I'll make the necessary flight arrangements."

She put her phone back into her purse and glanced over at him. "Excuse me?"

"I said that I will make the necessary flight arrangements if we want to see the house Monday at noon. That means we'll need to fly out no later than Thursday morning."

Gemma frowned. "Thursday morning? What are you talking about? Just where is this house located?"

Callum leaned back in his chair and gave her a one kilowatt smile. "Sydney, Australia."

Chapter 2

Gemma didn't have to look in the mirror to know there was a shocked look on her face. And her throat felt tight, as if sound would barely pass through it if she tried to speak. To prove the point, she tried to utter a word and couldn't. So she just sat there and stared across the table at Callum like he had lost his ever-loving mind.

"Now that that's all settled, let's order some dessert," Callum said, picking up the menu.

She reached out, touched his hand and shook her head. "What's the matter?" he asked. "You don't want dessert?"

She drew in a deep breath, made an attempt to speak once more and was glad when sound came out. But to be absolutely sure he understood, she held up her hands in the shape of a T. "Time out."

He lifted an eyebrow. "Time out?"

She nodded. "Yes, time out. You lost me between

the flight on Thursday and Sydney, Australia. Are you saying this house that you want me to decorate is in Sydney, Australia?"

"Of course. Where else would it be?"

She fought hard not to glare at him; after all, he was a potential client. "I thought possibly in the Denver area," she said in what she hoped was a neutral tone.

"Why would you think that?"

She couldn't hold back her glare any longer. "Well, you've been in this country for almost three years now."

"Yes, but I've never said or insinuated to anyone that I wouldn't return home. I was here helping Ramsey out and now that he has the hang of things, I'm no longer needed. Now I can get back home and—"

"Get married," Gemma supplied.

He chuckled. "As I said earlier, I don't plan on staying single forever."

"And when do you plan on marrying her?"

"Her who?"

Gemma wondered why some men suddenly went daft when their girlfriends were mentioned. "The woman waiting for you back in Australia."

"Umm, I didn't know there was such a creature."

Gemma stared at him in disbelief. "Are you saying you don't have a fiancée or a sweetheart back in Australia?"

He smiled. "That's exactly what I'm saying. Where did you hear something like that?"

Normally Gemma wouldn't divulge her sources, but typically, Jackie knew what she was talking about, and that wouldn't be anything the woman would have made up. "Jackie Barnes. And everyone figured she got the information from you."

Callum shook his head. "She didn't get that from me, but I have an idea where it came from. Your brother Zane. I complained about Jackie making a nuisance of herself and he figured the best way to get rid of a woman like Jackie was just to let her believe I was already taken."

"Oh." She could see Zane doing something like that. If for no other reason than to shift Jackie's interest from Callum to him. Her brother was a womanizer to the nth degree. And Derringer wasn't any better. It was a blessing that the twins, Adrian and Aidan, were away at college, where the only thing on their minds was making the grade. "I assume Zane's plan worked."

"It did."

"In that case you were lucky," Gemma decided to say. "Some women would not have cared that you were spoken for. They would have taken it as a challenge to swing your interest their way."

Callum couldn't help but think of just where his interest had been for the past three years and knew no one could have succeeded in doing that. The woman sitting across the table was the one he intended to marry.

"And you actually assumed I have someone of interest back home?"

She shrugged. "Hey, that's what we all heard and I had no reason to assume differently. As far as I knew, you weren't dating anyone and whenever we had events you always came alone."

And tried hanging around you every chance I got, he thought.

"You were almost as much of a loner as Ramsey," Gemma added. "If your goal was to keep the women away, then it evidently worked for you."

He took a sip of his drink, wondering if the reason she had yet to pick up on his interest in her was because she figured he was already taken.

"Callum, about this trip to Australia?"

He knew where she was about to take the discussion and was prepared with a spiel to reel her in. "What about it? If you're having second thoughts, I understand. No sweat. I've already contacted a backup in case you couldn't do it. Jeri Holliday at Jeri's Fashion Designs has indicated she would love the job and will have her bags packed for Australia before I can blink an eye."

Over my dead body, Gemma thought as she sat up straight in her chair. Jeri Holliday had been trying to steal clients from her for years.

"I think she liked the fact that I'm offering $50,000, and half of that up-front."

His words froze her thoughts. "Come again?"

He smiled. "I said, considering that I'm asking the decorator to give up at least six weeks, I'm offering $50,000, just as a starting price."

Gemma could only stare at him once again in disbelief. She leaned closer to the table and spoke in a hushed tone, as if anyone sitting in close range could overhear their top-secret conversation. "Are you saying that you're paying $25,000 on acceptance of the job and the other half on completion; and that $50,000 does not include any of the materials? That's just for labor?"

"Yes, that's what I'm saying."

Gemma began nibbling on her bottom lip. The $25,000 would definitely boost her bank account, replacing what Niecee had stolen. And then to think there would be another $25,000 waiting when she completed everything. However, as good as it sounded there were a few possible conflicts.

"What do you see as the time line for this project, Callum?" she decided to ask him.

He shrugged wide shoulders. "I'll tell you the same thing I told Jeri. I think it will take a month to six weeks to take down all the measurements and get things ordered. I'd also like that person there to coordinate the selection of all the furniture. However, there's no rush on that."

Gemma began nibbling on her lips again. "The reason I asked is because there are two babies who will be born within a few months of each other and I'd like to be here for both births. If I can't make it back at the time of delivery then at least within a few days."

"No problem. In fact, I'll spring for the flight."

Gemma couldn't help but wonder why he was being so generous and decided to ask him.

"I've always believed in being fair when it came to those who worked for me," he said.

"In any case, I'm going to need to return myself to help out because Ramsey will be busy with Chloe and the baby," he continued. "I don't want him to worry about the ranch during that time, so I've already promised him that I would return. And although Dillon probably won't need me to do anything, he and Pamela are like family and I want to be here for their baby's arrival, too."

Gemma felt relieved. But still—Australia? That was such a long way from home. And for a month, possibly six weeks. The only other time she'd been away from home for so long was when she left for college in Nebraska. Now she was considering trekking off to another country. Heck, it was another continent.

She was suddenly filled with an anticipation she'd never felt before. She'd never been a traveler, but if she took Callum's job offer, she would get to see a part of the world she'd only read about. That was exciting.

"So are you still interested or do you want me to go with Jeri Holliday?"

She didn't hesitate. "I don't have a problem traveling to Australia and will be ready to fly out on Thursday. I just need to get my business in order. I'll be gone for a while and I'll need to let my family know."

It then occurred to her that her family might not like the idea of her going so far away. Ramsey had a tendency to be overprotective. But he had his hands full with Chloe expecting their baby at the end of November. He would be too busy to try to micromanage her life…thank goodness.

"Terrific. I'll make flight arrangements and will let you know when I have everything in order."

"All right."

Callum lifted up his soda glass in a toast. "Here's to adventures awaiting you in the outback."

Gemma chuckled as she lifted her glass in a toast, as well. "Yes, here's to adventures in the outback."

A few hours later back at her house, despite her outer calm, Gemma was trying to keep things together on the inside while she explained everything to her sisters, Megan and Bailey, as they sat together at the kitchen table. Megan was the oldest at twenty-six and Bailey was twenty-two.

"And why didn't you file a police report? Twenty

thousand dollars isn't a little bit of money, Gem," an angry Megan wanted to know.

Gemma drew in a deep breath. "I'm working with the bank's security team in trying to recover the funds. The main reason I didn't get Sheriff Harper involved is because he's close friends with both Dillon and Ramsey. He'll probably get a report of the incident from the bank, eventually, but I think he'd be more inclined to keep his mouth shut about it. It would appear more of an official matter then."

"Oh."

From the look on her sisters' faces and their simultaneous responses, she knew they had forgotten that one important piece of information. There wasn't too much a Westmoreland did in these parts that Dillon and Ramsey didn't know about. Sheriff Harper, who had gone to high school with Dillon and Ramsey, made sure of that.

"And I didn't want to hear, 'I told you so' from those two. Neither of them wanted me to start my own business when I did. So there was no way I was going to tell them what Niecee had done. Hiring her was my mistake and I'll have to deal with it in my own way."

"But will you make sure she doesn't get away with her crime? I'd hate for her to steal from some other unsuspecting soul."

"Yes, I'm going to make sure she doesn't do this again. And to think that I trusted her," Gemma said with a nod.

"You're too trusting," Megan said. "I've always warned you about that."

And she had, Gemma thought. So had her older

brothers. "So what do you think about me going to Australia?" She needed to change the subject.

Megan smiled. "Personally, I think it's cool and wish I could go with you, but I'm saving my time off at the hospital for that trip to visit Delaney in Tehran."

"I think that's cool, as well," Bailey said. "I'm still reeling over the fact that there's no woman waiting for Callum back in Sydney. If that's true, then why isn't he dating? I don't ever recall him having a girlfriend while he's been here in the States. He's nothing like Zane and Derringer."

"And he's such a cutie-pie," Megan added.

Gemma couldn't help smiling as she recalled how sexy he looked sitting across from her at lunch. "He'd already mentioned the job to Jeri Holliday, but it was contingent on whether or not I would accept his offer."

"And I'm sure she was ready to grab it," Bailey said with a frown.

"Of course she was. I wish the two of you could see the size of his house. I can't believe he'd buy such a place as a single man. Now that I've made up my mind about going to Australia, I need to let Ramsey know."

Gemma inhaled sharply at the thought of doing that, but knew it needed to be done. However, under no circumstances did Ramsey need to know that Niecee had embezzled $20,000 from her. She would let the bank's security team handle things.

"You don't have any appointments or projects scheduled for the next six weeks?" Megan asked as they helped her pack.

"No. This job offer came at a good time. I had thought about taking a well-deserved vacation anyway, but now it's back to work for me. I'll take some time off during the holidays."

"If Callum bought a house in Australia, does that mean he's moving back home?"

Gemma glanced over at Bailey. That thought hadn't occurred to her. "I guess so."

"What a bummer. I've gotten used to seeing him," Bailey said with a pout. "I'd begun thinking of him as another big brother."

Gemma drew in a deep breath. For some reason she'd never thought of him as another big brother.

She'd never felt the need to become as friendly with him as Megan and Bailey had, but she never knew why she'd been standoffish with him. She'd only accepted that that was the way things were. Why now, all of a sudden, did the thought of him returning to Australia to live and her not seeing him ever again seem like such a big deal?

The very thought made her uneasy.

Chapter 3

"Are you okay, Gemma?"

Gemma turned her head to glance over at Callum. What had the pilot just said? They were now cruising at an altitude of 36,000 feet. Was Callum inquiring as to how she felt because she'd suddenly turned green?

Now was not the time to tell him that she had an aversion to flying. Although she'd flown before, that didn't mean she liked it. In fact, she didn't. She'd told herself while packing that she could handle the eighteen hours it would take to get to Australia. Now she was having some pretty serious doubts about that.

"Gemma?"

She drew in a deep breath. "Yes, I'm fine."

"You sure?"

No, she wasn't sure, but he would be the last person to know. "Yes."

She turned her head to look out the window and

wondered if asking for a window seat had been a wise choice. All she could see were clouds and Callum's reflection. He smelled good, and she couldn't help wondering what cologne he was wearing. And he looked good, too. He had arrived to pick her up wearing a pair of jeans, a blue chambray shirt and Western boots. She'd seen him in similar outfits plenty of times, but for some odd reason he seemed different to her today.

"The attendant is about to serve snacks. Are you hungry?"

She turned and met his eyes. They were a beautiful green and she could swear that a strange expression shone in their dark depths. "No, I ate a good breakfast this morning with Ramsey and Chloe."

He lifted a brow. "You got up at five this morning to do that?"

She smiled. "Yes. All I had to do was set the alarm. I figured if I got up early, then by the time this plane leveled off in the sky I would be ready to take a nap."

He chuckled. "Does flying bother you?"

"Let's just say it's not one of my favorite things to do," she answered. "There're other things I prefer doing more. Like getting a root canal or something else equally as enjoyable."

He threw his head back and laughed, and she liked the sound of it. She'd known him for almost three years and this was the first time she recalled hearing him laugh. He'd always seemed so serious, just like Ramsey. At least that was how Ramsey used to be. She would be one of the first to say that marriage had changed her brother for the better.

"And then," she added in a soft, thoughtful tone. "My parents were killed in a plane crash and I can't help but think of that whenever I'm in the air." She paused a moment. "There was a time after their deaths that I swore I'd never get on a plane," she said quietly.

Callum did something at that moment she hadn't expected. He reached out and took her hand in his. His was warm and large and completely covered hers. "How did you overcome that fear?"

She shifted her gaze away from their joined hands to his face and sighed deeply. "I refused to live my life in fear of the unknown. So one day I went to Ramsey and told him I was ready to take my first plane ride. He was working with Dillon at Blue Ridge Land Management at the time and made arrangements to take me on his next business trip. I was fourteen."

A bright smile touched her lips. "He signed me out of school for a few days and I flew with him to New Mexico. My first encounter with turbulence almost sent me through the roof. But he talked me through it. He even made me write an essay on my airplane experience."

The flight attendant came around serving drinks and snacks, but Gemma declined everything. Callum took a pack of peanuts and ordered a beer. Gemma had asked for a pillow earlier and adjusted it against her neck as she reclined comfortably in her seat. She had to admit that the first-class seats on this international flight were spacious. And Callum had booked a double-seat row for just the two of them.

Gemma noticed that the attendant had given Callum one or two smiles more than was necessary. The attendant's obvious interest in her passenger made Gemma think of something. "Is it true that your parents met on a flight to Australia?"

He inclined his head to look at her. "Yes, that's true.

Dad was actually engaged to someone else at the time and was returning home to Australia to help plan his wedding."

"And he fell for someone else when he was already engaged?"

Callum heard the shock in her voice. Considering what she thought about men deliberately breaking women's hearts, he decided to explain. "From what I was told, he had asked this woman to marry him and it was to be a marriage of convenience."

She lifted a brow. "A marriage of convenience for whom?"

"The both of them. She wanted a rich husband and he wanted a wife to start a family. They saw it as the perfect union."

Gemma nodded. "So love had nothing to do with it?"

"No. He didn't think such a thing could exist for him until he saw my mother. He was hit between the eyes with a ton of bricks." Callum chuckled. "Those are his words, not mine."

"And what happened to the other woman? The one he'd been engaged to at the time?"

He could hear pity in her voice. "Not sure. But I know what didn't happen to her."

Gemma lifted a curious brow. "What?"

A smile touched his lips. "She didn't get the wedding she planned."

"And you find that amusing?"

"Actually, yes, because it was discovered months later that she was pregnant with another man's child."

Gemma gasped sharply and leaned her head closer to Callum's. "Are you serious?"

"Very much so."

"The same thing almost happened to Ramsey, but Danielle stopped the wedding," Gemma said.

"So I heard."

"And I liked her."

"I heard that, too. I understand that your entire family did. But then that goes to show."

She looked over at him. "What?"

"Men aren't the only ones who can be heartbreakers."

Surprise swept across her face at his remark. Gemma leaned back against her seat and released her breath in a slow sigh. "I never said they were."

"You didn't?" he asked smiling.

"No, of course not."

Callum decided not to argue with her about it. Instead, he just smiled. "It's time for that nap. You're beginning to sound a bit grouchy."

To Callum's surprise, she took one, which gave him the opportunity to watch her while she slept. As he gazed at her, he experienced the same intense desire that he'd always felt whenever he was close to her. At the moment, he was close, but not close enough. He couldn't help but study her features and thought her moments of peaceful bliss had transformed her already beautiful face into one that was even more striking.

He would be the first to admit that she no longer looked like the young girl he'd seen that first day. In three years, her features had changed from that of a girl to a woman and it all started with the shape of her mouth, which was nothing short of sensuous. How could lips be that full and inviting, he wondered, as his gaze moved from one corner of her mouth to the other.

Callum's gaze drifted upward from her mouth to her

closed eyes and the long lashes covering them. His gaze then moved to her cheekbones and he was tempted to take the back of his hand and caress them, or better yet, trace their beautiful curves with the tip of his tongue, branding her as his. And she *was* his, whether she knew it or not, whether she accepted it or not. She belonged to him.

He then noticed how even her breathing was, and how every breath drew his attention to the swell of her breasts that were alluringly hidden inside a light blue blouse. He'd always found her sexy, too sexy, and it had been hard not to want her, so he hadn't even bothered fighting the temptation. He had lusted after her from afar, which was something he couldn't help, since he hadn't touched another woman in almost three years. Once her place in his life had become crystal clear, his body had gone into a disciplined mode, knowing she would be the one and only woman he would make love to for the rest of his life. Now, the thought of that made his body go hard. He breathed in her scent, he closed the book he had been reading and adjusted his pillow. He closed his eyes and allowed his fantasies of her to do what they always did, take over his mind and do in his dreams what he couldn't yet do in reality.

Gemma slowly opened her eyes at the same moment she shifted in her seat. She glanced over at Callum and saw that he had fallen asleep. His head was tilted close to hers.

She would have to admit that at first his close proximity had bothered her because she assumed they would have to make a lot of unnecessary conversation during the flight. She wasn't very good at small talk or flirting. She'd dated before, but rarely, because most men had a tendency to bore her. She'd discovered that most liked talking about themselves, tooting their own horn and figured they were God's gift to women.

She pushed all thoughts of other men aside and decided to concentrate on this one. He was sitting so close that she could inhale his masculine scent. She had enough brothers and male cousins to know that just as no two women carried the same scent, the same held true for men. Each person's fragrance was unique and the one floating through her nostrils now was making funny feelings flutter around in her stomach.

Gemma found it odd that nothing like this had ever happened to her before, but then she couldn't recall Callum ever being this close to her. Usually they were surrounded by other family members. Granted, they weren't exactly alone now, but, still, there was a sense of intimacy with him sitting beside her. She could just make out the soft sounds of his even breathing.

She had been ready to go when he had arrived at her place. When she opened the door and he had walked in, her breath had gotten caught in her throat. She'd seen him in jeans more times than not, but there was something about the pair he was wearing now that had caused her to do a double take. When he'd leaned down to pick up her luggage, his masculine thighs flexed beneath starched denim. Then there were those muscled arms beneath the Western shirt. Her gaze had lingered longer than it should have on his body. She had followed him out the door while getting an eyeful of his make-you-want-to-drool tush.

She studied him now, fascinated by just what a good-looking man he was and how he'd managed to keep women at bay for so long. A part of her knew it hadn't just been the story Zane had fabricated about a woman waiting for him back in Australia. That tale might have kept some women like Jackie away, but it would not have done anything to hold back the bolder ones. It was primarily the way he'd carried himself. Just like Ramsey. In his pre-Chloe days, most women would have thought twice before approaching her brother. He radiated that kind of "I'm not in the mood" aura whenever it suited him.

But for some reason, she'd never considered Callum as unapproachable as Ramsey. Whenever they had exchanged words, he'd been friendly enough with her. A part of her was curious about why if he wasn't already taken; he'd held himself back from engaging in a serious relationship with a woman. Perhaps he wanted a wife who was from his homeland. That wouldn't be surprising, although it was ironic that his mother was American.

"Oh." The word slipped through her lips in a frantic tone when the plane shook from the force of strong turbulence. She quickly caught her breath.

"You okay?"

She glanced over at Callum. He was awake. "Yes. I hadn't expected that just then. Sorry if I woke you up."

"No problem," he said, straightening up in his seat. "We've been in the air about four hours now, so we were bound to hit an air pocket sooner or later."

She swallowed when the airplane hit a smaller, less forceful pocket of turbulence. "And they don't bother you?"

"Not as much as they used to. When I was younger, my siblings and I would fly with Mom back to the States to visit our grandparents. I used to consider turbulence as exciting as a roller-coaster ride. I thought it was fun."

Gemma rolled her eyes. "There's nothing fun about the feel of an airplane shaking all over the place like it's about to come apart."

He released a soft chuckle. "You're safe, but let me check your seat belt to be sure."

Before she could pull in her next breath, he reached out to her waist and touched her seat belt. She felt his fingers brush against her stomach in the process. At that precise moment, sensations rushed all through her belly and right up her arms.

She glanced over at Callum and found her gaze ensnared by the deep green of his eyes and those sensations intensified. She knew at that moment that something was happening between them, and whatever it was, she wasn't quite prepared for it.

She'd heard about sexual awareness, but why would it affect her now, and why with someone who was almost a total stranger to her? It wasn't as if this was the first time she and Callum had been around each other. But then…as she'd acknowledged to herself earlier, this was the first time they had been alone to this degree. She wondered if her new feelings were one-sided, or if he'd felt it, as well.

"You're belted tight," he said, and to her his voice seemed a bit huskier…or perhaps she was just imagining things.

"Thanks for checking."

"No problem."

Since they were both wide awake now, Gemma decided it was probably a good idea to engage in conversation. That would be safer than just sitting here and letting all kinds of crazy thoughts race through her mind, like what would happen if she were to check on his seat belt as he'd checked on hers. She felt heat infuse her face and her heart rate suddenly shot up.

Then her anxiety level moved up a notch when she thought his gaze lingered on her lips a little longer than necessary. Had that really been the case? "Tell me about Australia," she said quickly.

Evidently talking about his homeland was something he enjoyed doing if the smile tilting his lips was anything to go by. And they were a gorgeous pair. She'd noticed them before, but this was the first time she'd given those lips more than a passing thought.

Why all of a sudden was there something so compelling about Callum? Why did the thought of his lips, eyes and other facial features, as well as his hands and fingers, suddenly make her feel hot?

"You're going to love Australia," he said, speaking in that deep accent she loved hearing. "Especially Sydney. There's no place in the world quite like it."

She lifted a brow and folded her arms across her chest. She didn't want to get into a debate, but she thought Denver was rather nice, as well. "Nicer than Denver?"

He chuckled, as understanding lit his eyes. "Yes. Denver has its strong points—don't get me wrong—but there's something about Sydney that's unique. I'm not saying that just because it's where I was born."

"So what's so nice about it?"

He smiled again and, as if on cue, those sensations in her stomach fluttered and spread through her entire midsection.

"I hate to sound like a travel ad, but Australia is a cosmopolitan place drenched in history and surrounded by some of the most beautiful beaches imaginable. Close your eyes for a moment and envision this, Gemma."

She closed her eyes and he began talking in a soft tone, describing the beaches in detail. From his description, she could all but feel a spray of ocean water on her lips, a cool breeze caressing her skin.

"There're Kingscliff Beach, Byron Bay, Newcastle and Lord Howe, just to name a few. Each of them is an aquatic paradise, containing the purest blue-green waters your eyes can behold."

"Like the color of your eyes?" Her eyes were still closed.

She heard his soft chuckle. "Yes, somewhat. And speaking of eyes, you can open yours now."

She slowly lifted her lids to find his eyes right there. He had inched his head closer to hers and not only were his eyes right there, so were his lips. The thoughts that suddenly went racing through her mind were crazy, but all she would have to do was to stick out her tongue to taste his lips. That was a temptation she was having a hard time fighting.

Her breathing increased and she could tell by the rise and fall of his masculine chest, that so had his. Was there something significantly dangerous about flying this high in the sky that altered your senses? Zapped them real good and sent them reeling off course? Filled your mind with thoughts you wouldn't normally entertain?

If the answer to all those questions was a resounding yes, then that explained why her mind was suddenly filled with the thought of engaging in a romantic liaison with the man who was not only her client, but also her oldest brother's best friend.

"Gemma…" It seemed he had inched his mouth a little closer; so close she could feel his moist breath on her lips as he said her name in that deep Australian accent of his.

Instead of responding, she inched her mouth closer, too, as desire, the intensity of which she'd never felt before, made her entire body shiver with a need she didn't know she was capable of having. The green eyes locked on hers were successfully quashing any thoughts of pulling her mouth back before it was too late.

"Would either of you like some more snacks?"

Callum jumped and then quickly turned his face away from Gemma to glance up at the smiling flight attendant. He drew in a deep breath before responding. "No, thanks. I don't want anything."

He knew that was a lie the moment he'd said it. He *did* want something, but what he wanted only the woman sitting beside him could give.

The flight attendant then glanced over at Gemma and she responded in a shaky voice. "No, I'm fine."

It was only after the attendant had moved on that Callum glanced at Gemma. Her back was to him while she looked out the window. He suspected that she was going to pretend nothing had happened between them a few moments ago. There was no doubt in his mind that they would have kissed if the flight attendant hadn't interrupted them.

"Gemma?"

It took her longer than he felt was necessary to turn around and when she did, she immediately began talking about something that he couldn't have cared less about. "I was able to pack my color samples, Callum, so that you'll get an idea of what will best suit your home. I'll give you my suggestions, but of course the final decision will be yours. How do you like earth-tone colors? I'm thinking they will work best."

He fought the urge to say that what would work best would be to pick up where they'd left off, but instead he nodded and decided to follow her lead for now. In a way he felt good knowing that at least something had been accomplished today. She had finally become aware of him as a man. And he was giving her time to deal with that. He wouldn't push her, nor would he rush things for now. He would let nature take its course and with the degree of passion they exhibited a short while ago, he had no reason to think that it wouldn't.

"I happen to like earth-tone colors, so they will probably work for me," he said, although he truly didn't give a royal damn. The bottom line was whatever she liked would work for him because he had every intention of her sharing that house with him.

"That's good, but I intend to provide you with a selection of vibrant colors, as well. Reds, greens, yellows and blues are the fashionable hues now. And we can always mix them up to create several bold splashes. Many people are doing that now."

She continued talking, and he would nod on occasion to pretend he was listening. If she needed to feel she was back in control of things, then so be it. He relaxed in his seat, tilted his head and watched ardently as her mouth moved while thinking what he would love doing to that mouth if given the chance. He decided to think positive and concentrated on what he would do with that mouth *when* he got the chance.

A few moments after Callum closed his eyes, Gemma stopped talking, satisfied that she had talked him to sleep. She had discussed some of everything with him regarding the decorating of his home to make sure they stayed on topic. The last thing she wanted was for him to bring up what almost happened between them. Just the thought of how close they'd come to sharing a kiss, right here on this airplane, had her pulse racing something awful.

She had never behaved inappropriately with a client before and wasn't sure exactly what had brought it on today. She would chalk it up as a weak moment when she'd almost yielded to temptation. When she had noticed just how close their mouths were, it had seemed a perfectly natural thing to want to taste his lips. Evidently, he'd felt the same way about hers, because his mouth had been inching toward hers with as much enthusiasm as hers had moved toward his. She was grateful for the flight attendant's timely interruption.

Had the woman suspected what they had been about to do? The thought had made Gemma's head heat up with embarrassment. Her heart was racing and the palms of her hands felt damp just thinking about it. She readjusted the pillow behind her head, knowing she would have to regain control of senses jolted by too much turbulence. Callum was just a man. He was a client. A friend of her family. He was not someone she should start thinking about in a sexual way.

She had gone twenty-four years without giving any man a second thought and going another twenty-four the same way suited her just fine.

Chapter 4

Gemma glanced around the spacious hotel where she and Callum would be staying for the night—in separate rooms, of course. Once their plane had landed, she had given herself a mental shake to make sure all her senses were back under control. Fortunately, the rest of the flight had been uneventful. Callum had kept his lips to himself and she had kept hers where they belonged. After a while, she had begun feeling comfortable around him again.

They'd taken a taxi from the airport. Callum had informed her that a private car service would arrive the next morning to take them to his parents' home. Gemma assumed they would be staying with his parents for the duration of the trip.

She thought this hotel was beautiful and would rival any of the major chains back home. The suite was spacious with floor-to-ceiling windows that looked out onto Sydney, which at this hour was dotted with bright lights.

Because she had slept a lot on the plane, she wasn't sleepy now. In fact, she was wide awake, although the clock on the nightstand by the bed indicated that it was after midnight. It was hard to believe that on the other side of the world in Denver they were trailing a day behind and it was eight in the morning.

She strolled to the window and looked out. She missed Denver already, but she couldn't help being fascinated by all the things she'd already seen. Although their plane had landed during the night hours, the taxi had taken them through many beautiful sections of the city that were lit up, and showed just how truthful Callum had been when he'd said that there was no place in the world quite like Sydney.

Gemma drew in a deep breath and tried to ignore a vague feeling of disappointment. Even though she was glad Callum hadn't mentioned their interrupted kiss, she hadn't expected him to completely ignore her. Although they'd shared conversation since, most of it had been with him providing details about Sydney and with her going over information about the decorating of his home. The thought that he could control his emotions around her so easily meant that, although he had been drawn to her for that one quick instant, he didn't think she was worth pursuing. If those were his thoughts, she should be grateful, instead of feeling teed off. Her disappointment and irritation just didn't make any sense.

She left the window and crossed the hotel room to the decorative mirror on the wall to study her features. Okay, so she hadn't looked her best after the eighteen-hour plane flight, but she had taken a shower and had freshened up since then. Too bad he couldn't see her now. But overall, she hadn't looked awful.

Gemma couldn't help wondering what kind of woman would interest Callum. She was totally clueless. She'd never seen him with a woman before. She knew the types Zane and Derringer preferred dating—women who were all legs, beautiful, sophisticated, shallow, but easy to get into bed. For some reason she couldn't see Callum attracted to that type of woman.

There were times she wished she had a lot of experience with men and was not still a twenty-four-year-old virgin. There had been a number of times during her college days when guys had tried, although unsuccessfully, to get her into bed. When they had failed, they'd dubbed her "Ice Princess Gemma." That title hadn't bothered her in the least. She'd rather be known as an ice princess than an easy lay. She smiled, thinking that more than one frustrated stud had given up on seducing her. Giving up on her because she refused to put out was one thing, but ignoring her altogether was another.

A part of her knew the best thing to do was to relegate such thoughts to the back of her mind. It was better that he hadn't followed up on what had almost happened between them. But another part of her—the one that was a woman with as much vanity as any other female—hadn't liked it one bit and couldn't let it go.

A smile swept across her lips. Callum had suggested that they meet in the morning for breakfast before the car arrived to take them to his parents' home. That was fine with her, because she would be meeting his parents and she wanted to look her best. The last thing she wanted was for them to think he'd hired someone who didn't know how to dress professionally. So tomorrow she would get rid of her usual attire of jeans and a casual top and wear something a little more becoming.

She would see just how much Callum could ignore her then.

Callum got up the next morning feeling as tired as he'd been when he went to bed past midnight. He had tossed and turned most of the night, frustrated that he hadn't taken the opportunity to taste Gemma's lips when the chance to do so had been presented to him.

Every part of his body hardened with the memory of a pair of luscious lips that had been barely a breath away from his. And when she had tilted her head even more to him, placing her lips within a tongue reach, he had felt the lower part of his body throb.

The desire that had flowed between them had been anything but one-sided. Charged sensations as strong as any electrical current had surged through both their bodies and he had fought back the urge to unsnap her seat belt and pull her into his lap while lapping her mouth with everything he had.

He remembered the conversations they'd shared and how she'd tried staying on course by being the consummate professional. While she'd been talking, his gaze had been fixated on her mouth. He couldn't recall a woman who could look both sexy and sweet at the same time, as well as hot and cool when the mood suited her. He loved all the different facets of Gemma, and he planned on being a vital part of each one of them. How could any man not want to?

Minutes later, after taking a shower and getting dressed, he left his hotel room to walk a few doors down to where Gemma had spent the night. Just the thought that she had been sleeping so close had done something to him. He wondered if she had gotten a good night's sleep. Or had she tossed and turned most of the night, as he had? Probably not. He figured she had no idea what sexual frustration was all about. And if she did, he didn't want to know about it, especially if some other man ruled her thoughts.

The possibility of that didn't sit well with him, since he couldn't handle the thought of Gemma with any other man but him. He pulled in a deep breath before lifting his hand to knock on her door.

"Who is it?"

"Callum."

"Just a moment."

While waiting, he turned to study the design of the wallpaper that covered the expanse of the wall that led to the elevator. It was a busy design, but he had to admit that it matched the carpet perfectly, pulling in colors he would not have normally paid attention to.

He shook his head, remembering that Gemma had gone on and on about different colors and how her job would be to coordinate them to play off each other. He was surprised that he could recall any of her words when the only thoughts going through his mind had been what he'd like doing to her physically.

"Come on in, Callum. I just need to grab a jacket," she said upon opening the door.

He turned around and immediately sucked in a deep breath. He had to lean against the doorframe to keep from falling. *His* Gemma wasn't wearing jeans and a top today. Instead, she was dressed in a tan-colored skirt that flowed to her ankles, a pair of chocolate-suede, medium-heeled shoes and a printed blouse. Seeing her did something to every muscle, every cell and every pore of his body. And his gut twisted in a knot. She looked absolutely stunning. Even her hair was different. Rather than wearing it in a ponytail she had styled it to hang down to her shoulders.

He'd only seen her a few other times dressed like this, and that had been when they'd run into each other at church. He entered the room and closed the door behind him, feeling a gigantic tug in his chest as he watched her move around the room. He became enmeshed in her movements and how graceful and fluid they were.

"Did you get a good night's sleep, Callum?"

He blinked when he noticed that she stood staring at him, smiling. Was he imagining things or did he see amusement curving her lips? "I'm sorry, what did you ask?"

"I wanted to know if you got a good night's sleep. I'm sure it felt good being back home."

He thought about what she said and although he could agree that it was good being back home, it felt even better having her here with him. He'd thought about this a number of times, dreamed that he would share his homeland with her. He had six weeks and he intended to make every second, minute and hour count.

Apparently, she was waiting for his response. "Sleep didn't come easy. I guess I'm suffering from jet lag. And, yes, I'm glad to be home," he said, checking his watch. "Ready to go down for breakfast?"

"Yes, I'm starving."

"I can imagine. You didn't eat a whole lot on the plane."

She chuckled. "Only because I wasn't sure I could keep it down. There was a lot of turbulence."

And he'd known how much that bothered her. He was glad when she'd finally been able to sleep through it. He had watched her most of the time while she'd done so.

"I'm ready now, Callum."

He was tempted to reach out and take her hand in his, but he knew that doing such a thing would not be a smart move right now. He needed her to get to know him, not as her brother's best friend, but as the man who would always be a part of her life.

"Hey, don't look at my plate like that. I told you I was hungry," Gemma said, laughing. Her stack of pancakes was just as high as Callum's. He had told her this particular hotel, located in downtown Sydney, was known to serve the best pancakes. They not only served the residents of the hotel but locals who dropped in on their way to work. From where Gemma sat, she could see the Sydney Harbour Bridge in the distance. It was a beautiful sight.

"Trust me, I understand. I remember my mom bringing me here as a kid when I did something good in school," he said while pouring syrup onto his pancakes.

"Wow, you mean this hotel is *that* old?" Her eyes twinkled with mischief.

He glanced over at her as amusement flickered in his gaze. "Old? Just what are you trying to say, Gemma?"

"Umm, nothing. Sorry. I have to remember that you're my client and I have to watch what I say. The last thing I want to do is offend you."

"And be careful that you don't," he warned, chuckling. "Or all that information you provided yesterday on colors and designs would have been for naught. How you can keep that stuff straight in your head is beyond me."

He paused a moment. "And I talked to Ramsey last night. Everything is fine back in Denver and I assured him all was well here."

Gemma smiled as she took a sip of her coffee. "Did you tell him we were on the flight from hell getting here?"

"Not quite in those words, but I think he got the idea. He asked me if you fainted when the plane hit the first pocket of turbulence."

She made a face. "Funny. Did he mention how Chloe is doing?"

"Yes, she's fine, just can't wait for November to roll around." He smiled. "She has two more months to go."

"I started to call them last night when we got in, but after I took a shower and went to bed that did it for me. I hadn't thought I'd be able to sleep so soundly, but I did."

During the rest of their meal, Gemma explained to him how they managed to pull off a surprise baby shower for Chloe last month right under her sister-in-law's nose, and how, although Ramsey and Chloe didn't want to know the sex of the baby before it was born, Megan, Bailey and she were hoping for a girl, while Zane, Derringer and the twins were anticipating a boy.

Sipping coffee and sharing breakfast with Callum seemed so natural. She hadn't ever shared breakfast with him before…at least not when it had been just the two of them. Occasionally, they would arrive at Ramsey's place for breakfast at about the same time, but there had always been other family members around. She found him fun to talk to and felt good knowing he had noticed her outfit and even complimented her on how she looked. She had caught him staring at her a few times, which meant he couldn't ignore her so easily after all.

They had finished breakfast and were heading back toward the elevators when suddenly someone called out.

"Callum, it's you! I can't believe you're home!"

Both Callum and Gemma glanced around at the same time a woman threw herself at him and proceeded to wrap her arms around his waist while placing a generous smack on his lips.

"Meredith! It's good to see you," Callum said, trying to pry himself from the woman's grip. Once that was accomplished, he smiled pleasantly at the dark-haired female who was smiling up at him like an adoring fan. "What are you doing in town so early?"

The woman laughed. "I'm meeting some friends for breakfast." It was then that she turned and regarded Gemma. "Oh, hello."

The first thought that came into Gemma's mind was that the woman was simply beautiful. The second was that if it was the woman's intent to pretend she was just noticing Gemma's presence, then she had failed miserably, since there was no way she could have missed her, when she'd nearly knocked her down getting to Callum.

"Meredith, I'd love you to meet a good friend of mine," he said, reaching out, catching Gemma's hand and pulling her closer to his side. "Gemma Westmoreland. Gemma, this is Meredith Kenton. Meredith's father and mine are old school chums."

Gemma presented her hand to the woman when it became obvious the woman was not going to extend hers. "Meredith."

Meredith hesitated a second before taking it. "So, you're from the States, Gemma?"

"Yes."

"Oh."

She then turned adoring eyes on Callum again, and Gemma didn't miss the way the woman's gaze lit up when Callum smiled at her. "Now that you're back home, Callum, what about us doing dinner at the Oasis, going sailing and having a picnic on the beach."

For crying out loud. Will you let the man at least catch his breath, Gemma wanted to scream, refusing to consider that she was feeling a bit jealous. *And besides, for all you know, I might be his woman and if I were I wouldn't let him do any of those things with you. Talk about blatant disrespect.*

"I'm going to be tied up this visit," Callum said, easing Gemma closer to his side. Gemma figured he was trying to paint a picture for Meredith that really wasn't true—that they were a twosome. Any other time she might have had a problem with a man insinuating such a thing, but in this case she didn't mind. In fact, she welcomed the opportunity to pull the rug right out from under Miss Disrespect. Meredith was obviously one of those "pushy" women.

"And I'm only back home for a short while," he added.

"Please don't tell me you're going back over there."

"Yes, I am."

"When are you coming home for good?" Meredith pouted, her thin lips exuding disappointment.

Gemma looked up at Callum, a questioning look in her eyes. Was this the woman waiting for him that he told her didn't exist? He met her gaze and as if he read the question lingering there, he pulled her even closer to his side. "I'm not sure. I kind of like it over there.

As you know, Mom is an American, so I'm fortunate to have family on both continents."

"Yes, but your home is here."

He smiled as he glanced down at Gemma. He then looked back at Meredith. "Home is where the heart is."

The woman then turned a cold, frosty gaze on Gemma. "And he brought you back with him."

Before Gemma could respond, Callum spoke up. "Yes, I brought her back with me to meet my parents."

Gemma knew the significance of that statement, even if it was a lie. To say he had brought her home to meet his parents meant there was a special relationship between them. In truth, that wasn't the case but for some reason he didn't want Meredith to know that, and in a way she didn't want Meredith to know it, either.

"Well, I see my friends have arrived now," she said in a cutting tone. "Gemma, I hope you enjoy your time here in Sydney and, Callum, I'll talk to you later." The woman then beat a hasty retreat.

With his hand on her arm, Callum steered Gemma toward the elevator. Once they were alone inside the elevator, Gemma spoke. "Why did you want Meredith to assume we were an item?"

He smiled down at her. "Do you have a problem with that?"

Gemma shook her head. "No, but why?"

He stared at her for a few moments, opened his mouth to say something, then closed it. He seemed to think for a minute. "Just because."

She lifted a brow. "Just because?"

"Yes, just because."

She frowned up at him. "I'd like more of a reason

than that, Callum. Is Meredith one of your former girl-friends?"

"Not officially. And before you assume the worst about me, I never gave her a reason to think anything between us was official or otherwise. I never led her on. She knew where she stood with me and I with her."

So it was one of those kinds of relationships, Gemma mused. The kind her brothers were notorious for. The kind that left the woman broken down and broken-hearted.

"And before you start feeling all indignant on Mer-edith's behalf, don't waste your time. Her first choice of the Austells was my brother Colin. They dated for a few years and one day he walked in and found her in bed with another man."

"Oh." Gemma hadn't liked the woman from the first, and now she liked her even less.

The elevator stopped. They stepped off and Callum turned to her and placed his hand on her arm so she wouldn't go any farther. She hadn't expected the move and sensations escalated up her rib cage from his touch.

"I want to leave you with something to think about, Gemma," he said in that voice she loved hearing.

"What?"

"I know that watching your brothers and cousins operate with girls has colored your opinion of men in general. I think it's sad that their exploits have left a negative impression on you and I regret that. I won't speak for your brothers, because they can do that for themselves, but I can speak for myself. I'd never inten-tionally hurt any woman. It's my belief that I have a soul mate out there somewhere."

She lifted a brow. "A soul mate?"

"Yes."

Gemma couldn't help but wonder if such a thing really existed. She would be the first to admit that her cousin Dillon's first wife hadn't blended in well with the family, nor had she been willing to make any sacrifices for the man she loved. With his current wife, Pam, it was a different story. From the moment the family had met Pam, they'd known she was a godsend. The same thing held true for Chloe. Gemma, Megan and Bailey had bonded with their sister-in-law immediately, even before she and Ramsey had married. And just to see the two couples together, you would know they were meant for each other and loved each other deeply.

So Gemma knew true love worked for some people, but she wasn't willing to suffer any heartbreak while on a quest to find Mr. Right or her soul mate. But as far as Callum was concerned, she was curious about one thing. "And you really believe you have a soul mate?"

"Yes."

She noted that he hadn't hesitated in answering. "How will you know when you meet her?"

"I'll know."

He sounded pretty confident about that, she thought. She shrugged. "Well, good luck in finding her," she said as they exited the building and headed toward the parking garage.

She noted that Callum appeared to have considered her comment, and then he tilted his head and smiled at her. "Thanks. I appreciate that."

Chapter 5

"Wow, this car is gorgeous, but I thought a private car was coming for us."

Callum looked over at Gemma and smiled as they walked toward the car parked in the hotel's parking garage. "I decided to have my car brought to me instead."

"This is your car?" Gemma studied the beautiful, shiny black two-seater sports car.

He chuckled as he opened the door for her. "Yes, this baby is mine." *And so are you,* he wanted to say as he watched her slide her legs into the car, getting a glimpse of her beautiful calves and ankles. "I've had it now for a few years."

She glanced up at him. "Weren't you ever tempted to ship it to Denver?"

"No," he said with a smile. "Can you imagine me driving something like this around Ramsey's sheep farm?"

"No, I can't," she said, grinning when he got in on the other side and snapped his seat belt into place. "Is it fast?"

"Oh, yes. And you'll see that it has a smooth ride."

Callum knew she was sold on the car's performance moments later when they hit the open highway and she settled back in her seat. He used to imagine things being just like this, with him driving this car around town with the woman he loved sitting in the passenger seat beside him.

He glanced over at her for a second and saw how closely she was paying attention to everything they passed, as if she didn't want to miss anything. He drew in a deep breath, inhaling her scent right along with it, and felt desire settle into his bones. Nothing new there; he'd wanted Gemma since the first time he'd seen her and knew she would be his.

"This place is simply beautiful, Callum."

He smiled, pleased that she thought so. "More so than Denver?"

She threw her head back and laughed. "Hey, there's no place like home. I love Denver."

"I know." Just as he knew it would be hard getting her to leave Denver to move to Sydney with him. He would have returned home long ago, but he'd been determined not to until he had her with him.

"We're on our way to your parents' home?" she asked, interrupting his thoughts.

"Yes. They're looking forward to meeting you."

Surprise swept across her face. "Really? Why?"

He wished he could tell her the truth, but decided to say something else equally true. "You're Ramsey's sister. Your brother made an impression on them during the six months he lived here. They consider him like another son."

"He adores them, as well. Your family is all he used to write us about while he was here. I was away at college and his letters used to be so full of adventure. I knew then that he'd made the right decision to turn over the running of the family's real-estate firm to Dillon and pursue his dream of becoming a sheep rancher. Just as my father always wanted to do."

He heard the touch of pain in her voice and sensed that mentioning her father had brought back painful memories. "You were close to him, weren't you?"

When they came to a snag in traffic, he watched her moisten her lips before replying to his question. "Yes. I was definitely a daddy's girl, but then so were Megan and Bailey. He was super. I can still recall that day Dillon and Ramsey showed up to break the news to us. They had been away at college, and when I saw them come in together I knew something was wrong. But I never imagined the news they were there to deliver."

She paused a moment. "The pain wouldn't have been so great had we not lost our parents and Uncle Adam and Aunt Clarisse at the same time. I'll never forget how alone I felt, and how Dillon and Ramsey promised that, no matter what, they would keep us together. And they did. Because Dillon was the oldest, he became the head of the family and Ramsey, only seven months younger, became second in charge. Together they pulled off what some thought would be impossible."

Callum recalled hearing the story a number of times from Ramsey. He had hesitated about going to Australia because he hadn't wanted to leave everything on Dillon's shoulders, so he'd waited until Bailey had finished high school and started college before taking off for Australia.

"I'm sure your parents would be proud of all of you," he said.

She smiled. "Yes, I'm sure they would be, as well. Dillon and Ramsey did an awesome job and I know for sure we were a handful at times, some of us more than others."

He knew she was thinking about her cousin Bane and all the trouble he used to get into. Now Brisbane Westmoreland was in the Navy with dreams of becoming a SEAL.

Callum checked his watch. "We won't be long now. Knowing Mom, she'll have a feast for lunch."

A smile touched Gemma's lips. "I'm looking forward to meeting your parents, especially your mother, the woman who captured your father's heart."

He returned her smile, while thinking that his mother was looking forward to meeting her—the woman who'd captured his.

Surprise swept across Gemma's face when Callum brought his car to the marker denoting the entrance to his family's ranch. She leaned forward in her seat to glance around through the car's windows. She was spellbound, definitely at a loss for words. The ranch, the property it sat on and the land surrounding it were breathtaking.

The first thing she noticed was that this ranch was a larger version of her brother's, but the layout was identical. "I gather that Ramsey's design of the Shady Tree Ranch was based on this one," she said.

Callum nodded. "Yes, he fell in love with this place

and when he went back home he designed his ranch as a smaller replica of this one, down to every single detail, even to the placement of where the barns, shearing plants and lambing stations are located."

"No wonder you weren't in a hurry to return back here. Being at the Shady Tree Ranch was almost home away from home for you. There were so many things to remind you of this place. But then, on the other hand, if it had been me, seeing a smaller replica of my home would have made me homesick."

He keyed in the code that would open the electronic gate while thinking that the reason he had remained in Denver after helping Ramsey set up his ranch, and the reason he'd never gotten homesick, were basically the same. Gemma. He hadn't wanted to leave her behind and return to Australia, and he hadn't, except for the occasional holiday visit. And he truly hadn't missed home because, as he'd told Meredith, home is where the heart is and his heart had always been with Gemma, whether she knew it or not.

He put the car in gear and drove down the path leading to his parents' ranch house. The same place where he'd lived all his life before moving into his own place at twenty-three, right out of college. But it hadn't been unusual to sleep over while working the ranch with his father and brothers. He had many childhood memories of walks along this same path, then bicycle rides, motorcycle rides and finally rides behind the wheel of a car. It felt good to be home—even better that he hadn't come alone.

He fully expected not only his parents to be waiting inside the huge ranch house, but his brothers and their wives, and his sister and brother-in-law as well.

Everyone was eager to meet the woman whose pull had kept him working in North America as Ramsey's ranch manager for three years. And everyone was sworn to secrecy, since they knew how important it was for him to win Gemma's heart on his turf.

She was about to start getting to know the real Callum Austell. The man she truly belonged to.

When Callum brought the car to a stop in front of the sprawling home, the front door opened and a smiling older couple walked out. Gemma knew immediately that they were his parents. They were a beautiful couple. A perfect couple. Soul mates. Another thing she noted was that Callum had the older man's height and green eyes and had the woman's full lips, high cheekbones and dimpled smile.

And then, to Gemma's surprise, following on the older couple's heels were three men and three women. It was easy to see who in the group were Callum's brothers and his sister. It was uncanny just how much they favored their parents.

"Seems like you're going to get to meet everyone today, whether you're ready to do so or not," Callum said.

Gemma released a chuckle. "Hey, I have a big family, too. I remember how it was when I used to come home after being away at college. Everyone is glad to see you come home. Besides, you're your parents' baby."

He threw his head back and laughed. "Baby? At thirty-four, I don't think so."

"I do. Once a baby always a baby. Just ask Bailey."

Just a look into his green eyes let her know he still

wasn't buying it. He smiled as he opened the door to get out and said, "Just get ready for the Austells."

By the time Callum had rounded the car to open the door for her to get out, his parents, siblings and in-laws were there and she could tell that everyone was glad to see him. Moments later she stood, leaning against the side of his car, and watched all the bear hugs he was receiving, thinking there was nothing quite like returning home to a family who loved you.

"Mom, Dad, everyone, I would like you to meet Gemma Westmoreland." He reached out his hand to her and she glanced over at him a second before moving away from the car to join him where he stood with his family.

"So you're Gemma," Le'Claire Austell said, smiling after giving Gemma a hug. "I've heard quite a lot about you."

Surprise lit up Gemma's features. "You have?"

The woman smiled brightly. "Of course I have. Ramsey adores his siblings and would share tales with us about you, Megan, Bailey and your brothers, as well as all the other Westmorelands all the time. I think talking about all of you made missing you while he was here a little easier."

Gemma nodded and then she was pulled into Callum's dad's arms for a hug and was introduced to everyone present. There was Callum's oldest brother, Morris, and his wife, Annette, and his brother, Colin, and his wife, Mira. His only sister, Le'Shaunda, whom everyone called Shaun, and her husband, Donnell.

"You'll get to meet our three grands at dinner," Callum's mom was saying.

"I'm looking forward to it," Gemma replied warmly.

While everyone began heading inside the house, Callum touched Gemma's arm to hold her back. "Is something wrong?" He looked at her with concern in his green eyes. "I saw the way you looked at me when I called you over to meet everyone."

Gemma quickly looked ahead at his family, who were disappearing into the house and then back at Callum. "You didn't tell your family why I'm here."

"I didn't have to. They know why you're here." He studied her features for a moment. "What's going on in that head of yours, Gemma Westmoreland? What's bothering you?"

She shrugged, suddenly feeling silly for even bringing it up. "Nothing. I just remember what you insinuated with Meredith and hoped you weren't going to give your family the same impression."

"That you and I have something going on?"

"Yes."

He watched her for a moment and then touched her arm gently. "Hey, relax. My family knows the real deal between us, trust me. I thought you understood why I pulled that stunt with Meredith."

"I do. Look, let's forget I brought it up. It's just that your family is so nice."

He chuckled and pulled her to him. "We're Aussies, eight originals and one convert. We can't help but be nice."

She tossed him a grin before easing away. "So you say." She then looked over at the car as she headed up the steps to the house. "Do you need help getting our luggage?"

"No. We aren't staying here."

She turned around so quickly she missed her step

and he caught her before she tumbled. "Be careful, Gemma."

She shook her head, trying to ignore how close they were standing and why she suddenly felt all kinds of sensations flooding her insides. "I'm okay. But why did you say we're not staying here?"

"Because we're not."

She went completely still. "But—but you said we were staying at your home."

He caught her chin in his fingers and met her gaze. "We are. This is not my home. This is my parents' home."

She swallowed, confused. "I thought your home is what I'm decorating. Isn't it empty?"

"*That* house is, but I also own a condo on the beach. That's where we're staying while we're here. Do you have a problem with that, Gemma?"

Gemma forced herself to breathe when it became clear that she and Callum would be sharing living space while she was here. Why did the thought of that bother her?

She had to admit for the first time she was noticing things about him she'd never noticed before. And she was experiencing things around him that she hadn't experienced before. Like the way she was swept up in heated desire and the sensuous tickling in the pit of her stomach whenever he was within a few feet of her, like now...

"Gemma?"

She swallowed again as she met his gaze and the green eyes were holding hers with an intensity that she wasn't used to. She gave her head a mental shake. His family had to be wondering why they were still outside. She had to get real. She was here to do a job and she would do it without having these crazy thoughts that Callum was after her body, just because she'd begun having crazy fantasies about him.

"No, I don't have a problem with that." She pulled away from him and smiled. "Come on, your parents are probably wondering why we're still out here," she said, moving ahead and making an attempt to walk up the steps again.

She succeeded and kept walking toward the door, fully aware that he was watching every step she took.

Callum glanced around his parents' kitchen and drew in a deep breath. So far, things were going just as he'd hoped. From the masked smiles and nods he'd gotten from his family, he knew they agreed with his assessment of Gemma—that she was a precious gem. Even his three nephews, ages six, eight and ten, who were usually shy with strangers, had warmed up to her.

He knew that, for a brief moment, she had been confused as to why his family had taken so readily to her. What he'd told her hadn't been a lie. They knew the reason she was here and decorating that house he had built was only part of it. In fact, a minor part.

"When are you getting a haircut?"

Callum turned and smiled at his father. "I could ask you the same thing." Todd Austell's hair was just as long as his son's and Callum couldn't remember him ever getting his hair cut. In fact, it appeared longer now than the last time he'd seen it.

"Don't hold your breath for that to happen," his father said with joking amusement in his green gaze. "I love my golden locks. The only thing I love more is your mother."

Callum leaned against the kitchen counter. His mother, sister and sisters-in-law had Gemma in a corner and from their expressions he knew they were making *his woman* feel right at home. His brother and brothers-in-law were outside manning the grills, and his nephews were somewhere playing ball. His parents had decided to have a family cookout to welcome him and Gemma home.

"Gemma is a nice girl, Callum. Le'Claire and Shaun like her."

He could tell. He glanced up at his father. "And you?"

A smile crossed Todd Austell's lips. "I like her."

As if she felt Callum's gaze, she glanced over in his direction and smiled. His muscles tightened in desire for her.

"Dad?"

"Yes?"

"After you met Mom and knew she was the woman for you, how long did it take you to convince her of it?"

"Too long."

Callum chuckled. "How long was too long?"

"A few months. Remember, I had an engagement to break off and then your mother assumed that flying was her life. I had to convince her that she was sorely mistaken about that, and that I was her life."

Callum shook his head. His father was something else. Callum's was one of the wealthiest families in Sydney; the Austells had made their millions not only in sheep farming but also in the hotel industry. The hotel where he and Gemma had stayed last night was part of just one of several hotel chains that Colin was in charge of. Morris was vice president of the sheep-farm operation.

When Callum was home, he worked wherever he was needed, but he enjoyed sheep farming more. In fact, he was CEO of his own ranching firm, which operated several sheep ranches in Australia. Each was run by an efficient staff. He also owned a vast amount of land in Australia. He'd never been one to flaunt his wealth, although in his younger days he'd been well aware money was what had driven a lot of women to him. He had frustrated a number of them by being an elusive catch.

He glanced again at the group of women together and then at his father. "I guess it worked."

The older man lifted a brow. "What worked?"

"You were able to convince Mom that you were her life."

A deep smile touched his father's lips. "Four kids and three grandsons later, what can I say?"

A smile just as deep touched Callum's lips. "You can say that in the end Mom became your life as well. Because I think it's obvious that she has."

Chapter 6

The moment Gemma snapped her seat belt in place, a bright smile curved her lips. "Your family is simply wonderful, Callum, and I especially like your mom. She's super."

"Yes, she is," Callum agreed as he started the car's engine to leave his parents' home.

"And your dad adores her."

Callum chuckled. "You can tell?"

"How could I not? I think it's wonderful."

She was quiet for a moment. "I recall my parents being that way, having a close relationship and all. As I got older, although I missed them both, I couldn't imagine one living without the other, so I figured that if they had to die, I was glad they at least went together," she said.

Gemma forced back the sadness that wanted to cloud

what had been a great day. She glanced over at Callum. "And I love your parents' home. It's beautiful. Your mother mentioned that she did all the decorating."

"She did."

"Then why didn't you get her to decorate yours?"

"Mine?"

"Yes, the one you've hired me to do. I'm grateful that you thought of me, mind you, but your mother could have done it."

"Yes, she could have, but she doesn't have the time. Taking care of my dad is a full-time job. She spoils him rotten."

Gemma laughed. "Appears he likes spoiling her as well."

She had enjoyed watching the older couple displaying such a warm, loving attitude toward each other. It was obvious that their children were used to seeing them that way. Gemma also thought Callum's three nephews were little cuties.

"Is it far to the condo where you live?" she asked him, settling back against the car seat. When they walked out of Callum's parents' house, she noted that the evening temperature had dropped and it was cool. It reminded her of Denver just weeks before the first snowfall in late September. She then remembered that Australia's seasons were opposite the ones in North America.

"No, we'll be there in around twenty minutes. Are you tired?"

"Umm. Jet lag I think."

"Probably is. Go ahead and rest your eyes for a while."

Gemma took him up on his offer and closed her eyes for a moment. Callum was right, the reason she wanted to rest had to do with jet lag. She would probably feel this way until she adjusted to the change in time zone.

She tried to clear her mind of any thoughts, but found it impossible to do when she was drawn back to the time she had spent at Callum's parents' home. What she'd told him was true. She had enjoyed herself and thought his family was wonderful. They reminded her of her siblings.

She was close to her siblings and cousins, and they teased each other a lot. She'd picked up on the love between Callum and his siblings. He was the youngest and it was obvious that they cared deeply about him and were protective of him.

More than once, while talking to Callum's mom, she had felt his eyes on her and had glanced across the room to have her gaze snagged by his. Had she imagined it or had she seen male interest lurking in their green depths?

There had been times when the perfection of Callum's features had nearly stopped her in her tracks and she found herself at several standstills today. Both of his brothers were handsome, but in her book, Callum was gorgeous, and was even more so for some reason today. She could understand the likes of Meredith trying to come on to him. Back in Denver on the ranch, he exuded the air of a hardworking roughneck, but here in Sydney, dressed in a pair of slacks and a dress shirt and driving a sports car, he passed the test as the hot, sexy and sophisticated man that he was. If only all those women back in Denver could see him now.

She slowly opened her eyes and studied his profile over semi-lowered lashes as he drove the car. Sitting in a perfect posture, he radiated the kind of a strength most men couldn't fabricate, even on their best days.

His hair appeared chestnut in color in the evening light and hung around his shoulders in fluid waves.

There was something about him that infused a degree of warmth all through her. Why hadn't she felt it before? Maybe she had, but had forced herself to ignore it. And then there was the difference in their ages. He was ten years her senior. The thought of dating a man in close proximity to her age was bad enough; to consider one older, she'd thought, would be asking for trouble, definitely way out of her league.

Her gaze moved to his hands. She recalled on more than one occasion seeing those hands that were now gripping the steering wheel handle the sheep on her brother's ranch. There was an innate strength about them that extended all the way to his clean and short fingernails.

According to Megan, you could tell a lot about a man by his hands. That might be true, but Gemma didn't have a clue what she should be looking for. It was at times like this that her innocence bothered her. For once—maybe twice—she wouldn't mind knowing how it felt to get lost in the depth of a male's embrace, kissed by him in a way that could curl her toes and shoot sparks of pleasure all threw her. She wanted to be made love to by a man who knew what he was doing. A man who would make her first time special, something she would remember for the rest of her life and not forget when the encounter was over.

She closed her eyes again and remembered that moment on the plane when Callum had awakened and found her there, close to his face and staring at him. She remembered how he had stared back, how she had actually felt a degree of lust she hadn't thought she could feel and a swell of desire that had nearly shaken her to the core. She had felt mesmerized by his gaze, had felt frozen in a trance, and the only thing that would break it would be a kiss. And they had come seconds, inches from sharing one.

She knew it would have to be one of those kisses she'd always dreamed of sharing with a man. The kind that for some reason she believed only Callum Austell could deliver. Yes, the mind-blowing, toe-curling kind. A ripple of excitement sent shivers up her spine at the thought of being swept up in Callum's embrace, kissed by him, made love to by him.

She sucked in a quick breath, wondering what was making her think such things. What was causing her to have such lurid thoughts? And then she knew. She was attracted to her brother's best friend in the worst possible way. And as the sound of the car's powerful engine continued to roar under Callum's skillful maneuvering on the roadway, she felt herself fall deeper and deeper into a deep sleep with thoughts of Callum Austell getting embedded thoroughly into her mind.

Callum settled comfortably in the driver's seat as he drove the road with the power and ease he had missed over the years. Three in fact. Although he had returned home on occasion and had taken the car on the road for good measure whenever he did, there was something different about it this time. Because he had his future wife sitting beside him.

He smiled when he quickly glanced at her before returning his gaze to the road. She was *sleeping* beside him. He couldn't wait for the time when she would be sleeping with him. The thought of having her in his arms, making love to every inch of her body, filled him with a desire he didn't know it was possible to feel. But then Gemma had always done that to him, even when she hadn't known she was doing it.

Over the years he'd schooled himself well, and very few knew how he felt. Ramsey and Dillon knew, of course, and he figured Zane and Derringer suspected something as well. What had probably given Callum away was his penchant for watching Gemma the way a fox watched the henhouse, with his eye on one unsuspecting hen. It wasn't surprising that Gemma was totally clueless.

So far things were going as planned, although there had been a few close calls with his family when he thought one of them would slip and give something away. He wanted Gemma to feel comfortable around him and his family, and the last thing he wanted was for her to feel as if she'd deliberately been set up in any way. He wanted her to feel a sense of freedom here that he believed she wouldn't feel back in Denver.

For her to want to try new and different things, to embrace herself as a woman, topped his list. And for the first time, he would encourage her to indulge all her desires with a man. But not just any man. With him. He wanted her to see that not all men had only one thing in mind when it came to a woman, and for two people to desire each other wasn't a bad thing.

He wanted her to understand and accept that no matter what happened between them, it would be okay because nothing they shared would be for the short term. He intended to make this forever.

Callum pulled into the gated condo community and drove directly to his home, which sat on a secluded stretch of beach, prized for the privacy he preferred. He planned to keep this place even after their home was fully decorated and ready to move in. But first he had to convince Gemma that he was worth it for her to leave the country where she'd been born, the country in which her family resided, and move here with him, to his side of the world.

He brought his car to a stop and killed the ignition. It was then that he turned toward her, keeping one hand on the steering wheel and draping the other across the back of the passenger seat. She looked beautiful, sleeping as if she didn't have a care in the world—and in a way she didn't. He would shoulder whatever problems she had from here on out.

With an analytical eye he studied her features. She was smiling while she slept and he wondered why. What pleasing thoughts were going through her mind? It had gotten dark, and the lights from the fixtures in front of his home cast a glow on her face at an angle that made it look even more beautiful. He could imagine having a little girl with her mouth and cheekbones, or a son with her ears and jaw. He thought she had cute ears.

With a tentative hand he reached out and brushed his fingers gently across her cheeks. She shifted and began mumbling something. He leaned closer to catch what she was saying and his gut tightened in a ball of ravenous desire when she murmured in her sleep, "Kiss me, Callum."

Gemma felt herself drowning in a sea of desire she'd never felt before. She and Callum were not on the ranch in Denver, but were back on the plane. This time the entire plane was empty. They were the only two people onboard.

He had adjusted their seats to pull her into his arms, but instead of kissing her he was torturing her mouth inside, nibbling from corner to corner, then taking his tongue and licking around the lines of her lips.

She moaned deep in her throat. She was ready for him to take her mouth and stop toying with it. She needed to feel his tongue sucking on hers, tasting it instead of teasing it, and then she wanted their tongues to tangle in a delirious and sensual duel.

She began mumbling words, telling him to stop toying with her and asking that he finish what he'd started. She wanted the kiss she'd almost gotten before—a kiss to lose herself in sensual pleasure. Close to her ear she heard a masculine growl, sensed the passion of a man wanting to mate and breathed in the scent of a hot male.

Then suddenly she felt herself being gently shaken. "Gemma. Wake up, Gemma."

She lifted drowsy lids only to find Callum's face right there in front of hers. Just as it had been on the plane. Just as it had been moments earlier in her dream. "Callum?"

"Yes," he replied in a warm voice that sent delicious shivers up her spine. His mouth was so close she could taste his breath on her lips. "Do you really want me to kiss you, Gemma? You are one Westmoreland that I'll give whatever you want."

Chapter 7

Gemma forced the realization into her mind that she wasn't dreaming. This was the real deal. She was awake in Callum's car and he was leaning over her with his face close to hers and there wasn't a flight attendant to interrupt them if he decided to inch his mouth even closer. Would he?

That brought her back to his question. Did she want him to kiss her? Evidently, she had moaned out the request in her sleep and he'd heard it. From the look in the depth of his green eyes, he was ready to act on it. Is that what she wanted? He did say he would give her whatever she wanted.

More than anything, she wanted to be kissed by him. Although it wouldn't be her first kiss, she believed it would be the first one she received with a semblance of passion and desire on both sides. Before guys had wanted to kiss her, but she hadn't really cared if she kissed them or not.

This time she would act first and worry about the consequences of her actions later.

Holding his gaze, she whispered against his lips, "Yes, I want you to kiss me." She saw him smiling and giving a small nod of satisfaction before he leaned in closer. Before she could catch her next breath, he seized her mouth with his.

The first thing he did was seek out her tongue and the moment he captured it in his, she was a goner. He started off slow, plying her with a deep, thorough kiss as if he wanted to get acquainted with the taste and texture of her mouth, flicking the tip of his tongue all over the place, touching places she hadn't known a tongue could reach, while stirring up even more passion buried deep within her bones.

For a timeless moment, heat flooded her body in a way it had never done before, triggering her breasts to suddenly feel tender and the area between her thighs to throb. How could one man's kiss deliver so much pleasure? Elicit things from her she never knew existed?

Before she could dwell on any answers to her questions, he deepened the kiss and began mating with her mouth with an intensity and hunger that made her stomach muscles quiver. It was a move she felt all the way to her toes. She felt herself becoming feverish, hot and needy. When it came to a man, she'd never been needy.

He slanted his head, taking the kiss deeper still, while tangling with her tongue in a way she had dreamed about only moments earlier. But now she was getting the real thing and not mere snippets of a fantasy. He wasn't holding back on anything and his tongue was playing havoc with her senses in the process. It was a work of art, a sensuous skill. The way he'd managed to wrap his tongue around hers, only letting it go when it pleased him and capturing it again when he was ready to dispense even more pleasurable torture.

She had asked for this kiss and wasn't disappointed. Far from it. He was taking her over the edge in a way that would keep her falling with pleasure. His mouth seemed to fit hers perfectly, no matter what angle he took. And the more it plowed her mouth hungrily, the more every part of her body came alive in a way she wasn't used to.

She moaned deep in her throat when she felt the warmth of his fingers on her bare thigh and wondered when had he slid his hand under her skirt. When those fingers began inching toward her center, instinctively she shifted her body closer to his. The move immediately parted her thighs.

As if his fingers were fully aware of the impact they were having on her, they moved to stake a claim on her most intimate part. As his fingers slid beneath the waistband of her panties, she released another moan when his hand came into contact with her womanly folds. They were moist and she could feel the way his fingertips were spreading her juices all over it before he dipped a finger inside her.

The moment he touched her there, she pulled her mouth away from his to throw back her head in one deep moan. But he didn't let her mouth stay free for long. He recaptured it as his fingers caressed her insides in a way that almost made her weep, while his mouth continued to ply her with hungry kisses.

Suddenly she felt a sensation that started at her midsection and then spread throughout her body like tentacles of fire, building tension and strains of sensuous pressure in its wake. Her body instinctively pushed against his hand just as something within her snapped and then exploded, sending emotions, awareness and all kinds of feeling shooting all through her, flooding her with ecstasy.

Although this was the first time she'd ever experienced anything like it, she knew what it was. Callum had brought her to her first earthshaking and shattering climax. She'd heard about them and read about them, but had never experienced one before. Now she understood what it felt like to respond without limitations to a man.

When the feelings intensified, she pulled her mouth from his, closed her eyes and let out a deep piercing scream, unable to hold it back.

"That's it. Come for me, baby," he slurred thickly against her mouth before taking it again with a deep erotic thrust of his tongue.

And he kept kissing her in this devouring way of his until she felt deliciously sated and her body ceased its trembling. He finally released her mouth, but not before his tongue gave her lips a few parting licks. It was then that she opened her eyes, feeling completely drained but totally satisfied.

He held her gaze and she wondered what he was thinking. Had their business relationship been compromised? After all, he was her client and she had never been involved with a client before. And whether she'd planned it or not, they were involved. Just knowing there were more kisses where that one came from sent shivers of pleasure down her spine.

Better yet, if he could deliver this kind of pleasure to her mouth, she could just imagine what else he could do to other parts of her body, like her breasts, stomach, the area between her legs. The man possessed one hell of a dynamic tongue and he certainly knew how to use it.

Heat filled her face from those thoughts and she wondered if he saw it. At least he had no idea what she was thinking. Or did he? He hadn't said anything yet. He was just staring at her and licking his lips. She felt she should say something, but at the moment she was speechless. She'd just had her very first orgasm and she still had her clothes on. Amazing.

Callum's nostrils flared from the scent of a woman who'd been pleasured in the most primitive way. He would love to strip her naked and taste the dewy essence of her. Brand his tongue with her intimate juices, lap her up the way he'd dreamed of doing more times than he could count.

She was staring at him as if she was still trying to figure out why and how this thing had happened. He would allow her time to do that, but what he wouldn't tolerate was her thinking that what they'd shared was wrong, because it wasn't. He would not accept any regrets.

The one thing he'd taken note of with his fingers was that she was extremely tight. With most men that would send up a red flag, but not him because her sexual experience, or lack thereof, didn't matter. However, if she hadn't been made love to before, he wanted to know it.

He opened his mouth to ask her, but she spoke before he could do so. "We should not have done that, Callum."

She could say that? While his hand was still inside

of her? Maybe she had forgotten where his fingers were because they weren't moving. He flexed them, and when she immediately sucked in a deep breath as her gaze darkened with desire, he knew he'd succeeded in reminding her.

And while she watched, he slid his hand from inside of her and moments later he brought it to his lips and licked every finger that had been inside her. He then raked one finger across her lips before leaning down and tracing with his tongue where his finger had touched her mouth before saying, "With that I have to disagree." He spoke in a voice so throaty he barely recognized it as his own.

Her taste sent even more desire shooting through him. "Why do you feel that way, Gemma?"

He saw her throat move when she swallowed with her eyes still latched on his. "You're my client."

"Yes. And I just kissed you. One has nothing to do with the other. I hired you because I know you will do a good job. I just kissed you because—"

"I asked you to?"

He shook his head. "No, because I wanted to and because you wanted me to do it, too."

She nodded. "Yes," she said softly. "I wanted you to."

"Then there's no place for regrets and our attraction to each other has nothing to do with your decorating my home, so you can kill that idea here and now."

She didn't say anything for a moment and then she asked, "What about me being Ramsey's sister? Does that mean anything to you?"

A smile skidded across his lips. "I consider myself one of Ramsey's closest friends. Does that mean anything to you?"

She nervously nibbled on her bottom lip. "Yes. He will probably have a fit if he ever finds out we're attracted to each other."

"You think so?"

"Yes," she said promptly, without thinking much about his question. "Don't you?"

"No. Your brother is a fair man who recognizes you as the adult you are."

She rolled her eyes. "Are we talking about the same Ramsey Westmoreland?"

He couldn't help but grin. "Yes, we're talking about the same Ramsey Westmoreland. My best friend and your brother. You will always be one of his younger sisters, especially since he had a hand in raising you. Ramsey will always feel that he has a vested interest in your happiness and will always play the role of your protector, and understandably so. However, that doesn't mean he doesn't recognize that you're old enough to make your own decisions about your life."

She didn't say anything and he knew she was thinking hard about what he'd said. To reinforce the meaning of his words, he added. "Besides, Ramsey knows I would never take advantage of you, Gemma. I am not that kind of guy. I ask before I take. But remember, you always have the right to say no." A part of him hoped she would never say no to any direction their attraction might lead.

"I need to think about this some more, Callum."

He smiled. "Okay. That's fine. Now it's time for us to go inside."

He moved to open the door and she reached out and touched his hand. "And you won't try kissing me again?"

He reached out and pushed a strand of hair away from her face. "No, not unless you ask me to or give me an indication that's what you want me to do. But be forewarned, Gemma. If you ask, then I will deliver because I intend to be the man who will give you everything you want."

He then got out of the car and strolled to the other side to open the door for her.

He intended to be the man who gave her everything she wanted? A puzzled Gemma walked beside Callum toward his front door. When had he decided that? Before the kiss, during the kiss or after the kiss?

She shook her head. It definitely hadn't been before. Granted, they'd come close to kissing on the plane, but that had been the heat of the moment, due to an attraction that had begun sizzling below the surface. But that attraction didn't start until… When?

She pulled in a deep breath, really not certain. She'd always noticed him as a man from afar, but only in a complimentary way, since she'd assumed that he was taken. But she would be the first to admit that once he'd told her he wasn't, she'd begun seeing him in a whole different light. But she'd been realistic enough to know that, given the ten-year difference in their ages and the fact he was Ramsey's best friend, chances were that even if she was interested in him there was no way he would reciprocate that interest.

Or had it been during the kiss, when he had shown her just what a real kiss was like? Had he detected that this was her first real kiss? She'd tried following his lead, but when that lead began taking her so many different places and had made her feel a multitude of emotions and sensations she hadn't been used to, she just gave up following and let him take complete control. She had not been disappointed.

Her first orgasm had left every cell in her body feeling strung from one end to the other. She wondered just how many women could be kissed into an orgasm? She wondered how it would be if she and Callum actually made love. The pleasure just might kill her.

But then, he might have decided that he was the man to give her whatever she wanted after the kiss, when she was trying to regain control of her senses. Did he see her as a novelty? Did he want to rid her of her naïveté about certain things that happen between a man and a woman?

Evidently, he thought differently about how her oldest brother saw things. Well, she wasn't as certain as he was about Ramsey's reaction. She was well aware that she was an adult, old enough to call the shots about her own life. But with all the trouble the twins, Bane and Bailey had given everyone while growing up, she had promised herself never to cause Ramsey any unnecessary grief.

Although she would be the first to admit that she had a tendency to speak her mind whenever it suited her and she could be stubborn to a fault at times, she basically didn't cross people unless they crossed her. Those who'd known her great-grandmother—the first Gemma Westmoreland—who'd been married to Raphel, said she had inherited that attitude from her namesake. That's probably why so many family members believed there was more to the story about her great-grandfather Raphel and his bigamist ways that was yet to be uncovered. She wasn't as anxious about uncovering the truth as Dillon had been, but she knew Megan and some of her cousins were.

She stopped walking once they reached the door and Callum pulled a key from his pocket. She glanced around and saw that this particular building was set apart from the others on a secluded cul-de-sac. And it was also on a lot larger than the others, although, to her way of thinking, all of them appeared massive. "Why is your condo sitting on a street all by itself?" she asked.

"I wanted it that way for privacy."

"And they obliged you?"

He smiled. "Yes, since I bought all the other lots on this side of the complex as buffers. I didn't want to feel crowded. I'm used to a lot of space, but I liked the area because the beach is practically in my backyard."

She couldn't wait to see that, since Denver didn't have beaches. There was the Rocky Mountain Beach that included a stretch of sand but wasn't connected to an ocean like a real beach.

"Welcome to my home, Gemma."

He stood back and she stepped over the threshold at the same exact moment that he flicked a switch and the lights came on. She glanced around in awe. The interior of his home was simply beautiful and unless he had hidden decorating skills she wasn't aware of, she had to assume that he'd retained the services of a professional designer for this place, too. His colors, masculine in nature, were well-coordinated and blended together perfectly.

She moved farther into the room, taking note of everything—from the Persian rugs on the beautifully polished walnut floors, to the decorative throw pillows on the sofa, to the style of curtains and blinds that covered the massive windows. The light colors of the window treatments made each room appear larger in dimension and the banister of the spiral staircase that led to another floor gave the condo a sophisticated air.

When Callum crossed the room and lifted the blinds, she caught her breath. He hadn't lied when he'd said the beach was practically in his backyard. Even at night, thanks to the full moon overhead, she could see the beautiful waters of the Pacific Ocean.

Living away from home while attending college had taken care of any wanderlust she might have had at one time. Seeing the world had never topped her list. She was more than satisfied with the one hundred acres she had acquired on her twenty-first birthday—an inheritance for each of the Westmorelands. The section of Denver most folks considered as Westmoreland Country was all the home she'd ever known and had ever wanted. But she would have to admit that all she'd seen of Sydney so far was making it a close second.

Callum turned back to her. "So what do you think?"

Gemma smiled. "I think I'm going to love it here."

Chapter 8

The next morning, after taking his shower, Callum dressed as he gazed out his bedroom window at the beautiful waters of the ocean. For some reason he believed it was going to be a wonderful day. He was back home and the woman he intended to share his life with was sleeping under his roof.

As he stepped into his shoes, he had to admit that he missed being back in Denver, working the ranch and spending time with the men he'd come to know over the past three years. During that time Ramsey had needed his help and they'd formed a close bond. Now Ramsey's life had moved in another direction. Ramsey was truly happy. He had a wife and a baby on the way and Callum was happy for his friend.

And more than anything he intended to find some of that same happiness for himself.

As he buttoned up his shirt, he couldn't help but

think about the kiss he and Gemma had shared last night. The taste of her was still on his tongue. He'd told her that he wouldn't kiss her again until she gave the word, and he intended to do everything within his power to make sure she gave it—and soon.

The one thing he knew about Gemma was that she was stubborn. If you wanted to introduce an idea to her, you had to make her think that it had been *her* idea. Otherwise, she would balk at any suggestion you made. He had no problems doing that. When he put his seduction plan into motion, he would do it in such a way that she would think she was seducing him.

The thought of such a thing—her seducing him— had his manhood flexing. Although his feelings for Gemma were more than sexual, he couldn't help those nightly dreams that had plagued him since first meeting her. He'd seen her stripped bare—in his dreams. He'd tasted every inch of her body—in his dreams. And in his dreams he'd constantly asked what she wanted. What she needed from him to prove that she was his woman in every way.

Last night after he'd shown her the guestroom she would be using and had brought in their luggage, she had told him she was still suffering from jet lag and planned to retire early. She had quickly moved into her bedroom and had been sequestered there ever since. That was fine. In time she would find out that, when it came to him, she could run but she most certainly couldn't hide.

He would let her try to deny this thing that was developing between them, but she would discover soon enough that he was her man.

But what he wanted and needed right now was another kiss. He smiled, thinking his job was to make sure she felt that she needed another kiss as well. And as he walked out of his bedroom he placed getting another kiss at the top of his agenda.

Gemma stood in her bare feet in front of the window in Callum's kitchen as she gazed out at the beach. The view was simply amazing. She'd never seen anything like it.

One year while in college, during spring break weekend, she and a few friends had driven from Nebraska to Florida to spend the weekend on the beach in Pensacola. There she had seen a real beach with miles and miles of the purest blue-green waters. She was convinced that the Pacific Ocean was even more breathtaking and she'd come miles and miles away from home to see it.

Home.

Although she did miss home, she considered being in Australia an adventure as well as a job. Because of the difference in time zones, when she'd retired last night, she hadn't made any calls, but she intended to try to do so today. Megan was keeping tabs on the bank situation involving Niecee. With the money Callum had advanced her, her bank account was in pretty good shape, with more than enough funds to cover her debts. But she had no intention of letting Niecee get away with what she'd done. She had yet to tell anyone else in the family, other than Megan and Bailey, about the incident and planned on keeping things that way until the funds had been recovered and were back in her bank account.

She took another sip of her coffee, thinking about the kiss she and Callum had shared last night. Okay, she would admit it had been more than off the chain and the climax was simply shocking. Just the thought gave her sensuous shivers and was making her body tingle all over. What Callum had done with his tongue in her mouth and his fingers between her legs made her blush.

It had been hard getting to sleep. More than once she had dreamed of his tongue seeking hers and now that she was fully aware of what he could do with that tongue and those fingers, she wanted more.

She drew in a deep breath, thinking there was no way she would ask for a repeat performance. She could now stake a claim to knowing firsthand what an orgasm was about with her virginity still intact. Imagine that.

She couldn't imagine it when part of her dream last night dwelled on Callum making love to her and taking away her innocence, something she'd never thought of sharing with another man. The thought of being twenty-four and a virgin had never bothered her. What bothered her was knowing that there was a lot more pleasure out there that she was missing out on. Pleasure she was more than certain Callum could deliver, with or without a silver platter.

All she had to do was tell him what she wanted.

"Good morning, Gemma."

She turned around quickly, surprised that she had managed to keep from spilling her coffee. She hadn't heard Callum come down the stairs. In fact, she hadn't heard him moving around upstairs. And now he stood in the middle of his kitchen, dressed in a way she'd never seen before.

He was wearing an expensive-looking gray suit. Somehow he had gone from being a sheep-ranch manager to a well-groomed, sophisticated and suave businessman. But then the chestnut-brown hair flowing around his shoulders gave him a sort of rakish look.

She wasn't sure what to make of the change and just which Callum Austell she most preferred.

"Good morning, Callum," she heard herself say, trying not to get lost in the depths of his green eyes. "You're already dressed and I'm not." She glanced down at herself. In addition to not wearing shoes, she had slipped into one of those cutesy sundresses Bailey had given as a gift for her birthday.

"No problem. The house isn't going anywhere. It will be there when you're ready to see it. I thought I'd go into the office today and let everyone know that I'm back for a while."

She lifted a brow. "The office?"

"Yes, Le'Claire Developers. It's a land development company similar to Blue Ridge Land Management. But also under the umbrella of Le'Claire are several smaller sheep ranches on the same scale as Ramsey's."

"And you are…"

"The CEO of Le'Claire," he said.

"You named it after your mother?"

He chuckled. "No, my father named it after my mother. When we all turned twenty-one, according to the terms of a trust my great-grandfather established, all four of us were set up in our own businesses. Morris, being the firstborn, will inherit the sheep farms that have been in the Austell family for generations as well as stock in all the businesses his siblings control. Colin is CEO of the chain of hotels my family owns. The one we stayed in the other night is one of them. Le'Shaunda received a slew of supermarket chains, and I was given a land development company and several small sheep ranches. Although I'm CEO, I have a staff capable of running things in my absence."

Gemma nodded, taking all this in. Bailey had tried telling her and Megan that she'd heard that Callum was loaded in his own right, but she really hadn't believed her. Why would a man as wealthy as Bailey claimed Callum was settle for being the manager of someone else's sheep ranch? Granted, he and Ramsey were close, but she couldn't see them being *so* close that Callum would give up a life of wealth and luxury for three years to live in a small cabin on her brother's property.

"Why did you do it?" she heard herself asking.

"Why did I do what?"

"It's obvious that you have money, so why would you give all this up for three years and work as the manager of my brother's sheep ranch?"

This, Callum thought, would be the perfect time to sit Gemma down and explain things to her, letting her know the reason he'd hung around Denver for three years. But he had a feeling just like when his father had tried explaining to his mother about her being his soul mate and it hadn't gone over well, it wouldn't go over well with Gemma, either.

According to Todd Austell, trying to convince Le'Claire Richards it had been love at first sight was the hardest thing he ever had to do. In fact, she figured he wanted to marry her to rebel against his parents trying to pick out a wife for him and not because he was truly in love with her.

Callum was sure that over the years his mother had pretty much kissed that notion goodbye, because there wasn't a single day that passed when his father didn't show his mother how much he loved her. Maybe that's why it came so easily to Callum to admit that he loved a woman. His father was a great role model.

But still, when it came to an Austell falling in love, Callum had a feeling that Gemma would be just as skeptical as his mother had been. So there was no way he could tell her the full truth of why he had spent three years practically right in her backyard.

"I needed to get away from my family for a while," he heard himself saying, which really wasn't a lie. He had been wild and reckless in his younger years, and returning home from college hadn't made things any better. The death of his grandfather had.

He had loved the old man dearly and he would have to say that his grandfather had spoiled him rotten. With the old man gone, there was no one to make excuses for him, no one to get him out of the scrapes he got into and no one who would listen to whatever tale he decided to fabricate. His father had decided that the only way to make him stand on his own was to make him work for it. So he had.

He had worked on his parents' ranch for a full year, right alongside the other ranch hands, to prove his worth. It had only been after he'd succeeded in doing that that his father had given him Le'Claire to run. But by then Callum had decided he much preferred a ranch-hand bunk to a glamorous thirty-floor high rise overlooking the harbor. So he had hired the best management team money could buy to run his corporation while he returned to work on his parents' ranch. That's when he'd met Ramsey and the two had quickly become fast friends.

"I understand," said Gemma, cutting into his thoughts.

He lifted a brow. He had expected her to question him further. "You do?"

"Yes. That's why Bane left home to join the Navy.

He needed his space from us for a while. He needed to find himself."

Brisbane was her cousin Dillon's baby brother. From what Callum had heard, Bane had been only eight when his parents had been killed. He had grieved for them in a different way than the others, by fighting to get the attention he craved. When he'd graduated from high school, he had refused to go to college. After numerous brushes with the law and butting heads with the parents of a young lady who didn't want him to be a part of their daughter's life, Dillon had convinced Bane to get his life together. Everyone was hoping the military would eventually make a man of him.

Callum decided that he didn't want to dig himself in any deeper than he'd be able to pull himself out of when he finally admitted the truth to Gemma. "Would you like to go into the office with me for a while today? Who knows? You might be able to offer me a few decorating suggestions for there as well."

Her face lit up and he thought at that moment, she could decorate every single thing he owned if it would get him that smile.

"You'd give me that opportunity?"

He held back from saying, *I'll give you every single thing you want, Gemma Westmoreland.* "Yes, but only if it's within my budget," he said instead.

She threw her head back and laughed, and the hair that went flying around her shoulders made his body hard. "We'll see if we can work something out," she said, moving toward the stairs. "It won't take long for me to dress. I promise."

"Take your time," he said to her fleeting back. He peeped around the corner and caught a glimpse of long, shapely legs when she lifted the hem of her outfit to rush up the stairs. His body suddenly got harder with a raw, primitive need.

He went over to the counter to pour a cup of the coffee she'd prepared, thinking he hadn't gotten that kiss yet, but he was determined to charm it out of her at some point today.

"Welcome back, Mr. Austell."

"Thanks, Lorna. Is everyone here?" Callum asked the older woman sitting behind the huge desk.

"Yes, sir. They are here and ready for today's meeting."

"Good. I'd like you to meet Gemma Westmoreland, one of my business associates. Gemma, this is Lorna Guyton."

The woman switched her smile over to Gemma, who was standing by Callum's side. "Nice meeting you, Ms. Westmoreland," the woman said, offering Gemma her hand.

"Same here, Ms. Guyton." Gemma couldn't help but be pleased with the way Callum had introduced her. Saying she was a business associate sounded a lot better than saying she was merely the woman decorating one of his homes.

She glanced around, taking mental note of the layout of this particular floor of the Le'Claire Building. When they had pulled into the parking garage, she had definitely been impressed with the thirty-floor skyscraper. So far, the only thing she thought she would change with respect to the interior design, if given the chance, was the selection of paintings on the various walls.

"You can announce us to the team, Lorna," Callum

said, and placing his hand on Gemma's arm, he led her toward the huge conference room.

Gemma had caught the word *us* the moment Callum touched her arm and wasn't sure which had her head suddenly spinning more—him including her in his business meeting or the way her body reacted to his touch.

She had assumed that since he would be talking business he would want her to wait in the reception area near Lorna's desk. But the fact that he had included her sent a degree of pleasure up her spine and filled her with an unreasonable degree of importance.

Now if she could just stop the flutters from going off in her stomach with the feel of his hand on her arm. But then she'd been getting all kinds of sensations—more so than ever—since they had kissed. When he'd walked into the kitchen this morning looking like he should be on the cover of *GQ* magazine, a rush of blood had shot to her head and it was probably still there. She'd had to sit beside him in the car and draw in his scent with every breath she took. And it had been hard sitting in that seat knowing what had happened last night while she'd been sitting there. On the drive over, her body had gone through some sort of battle, as if it was craving again what it once had.

"Good morning, everyone."

Gemma's thoughts were interrupted when Callum swept her into the large conference room where several people sat waiting expectantly. The men stood and the women smiled and gave her curious glances.

Callum greeted everyone by name and introduced Gemma the same way he had in speaking to Lorna. When he moved toward the chair at the head of the table, she stepped aside to take a chair in the back of the room. However, he gently tightened his grip on her arm and kept her moving toward the front with him.

He then pulled out the empty chair next to his for her to sit in. Once she had taken her seat, he took his and smiled over at her before calling the meeting to order in a deep, authoritative voice.

She couldn't help but admire how efficient he was and had to remind herself several times during the course of the business meeting that this was the same Callum who'd managed her brother's sheep farm. The same Callum who would turn feminine heads around town when he wore tight-fitting jeans over taut hips and an ultrafine tush, and sported a Western shirt over broad shoulders.

And this was the same Callum who had made her scream with pleasure last night…in his car of all places. She glanced over at his hand, the same one whose fingers were now holding an ink pen, and remembered just where that hand had been last night and what he'd been doing with those fingers.

Suddenly, she felt very hot and figured that as long as she kept looking at his hands she would get even hotter. Over the course of the hour-long meeting, she tried to focus her attention on other things in the room like the paintings on the wall, the style of window treatments and carpeting. Given the chance, she would spruce things up in here. Unlike the other part of the office, for some reason this particular room seemed a little drab. In addition to the boring pictures hanging on the walls, the carpeting lacked any depth. She wondered what that was all about. Evidently, no one told the prior interior designer that the coloring of carpet in a business often set the mood of the employees.

"I see everyone continues to do a fantastic job for me in my absence and I appreciate that. This meeting is now adjourned," Callum said.

Gemma glanced up to see everyone getting out of their seats, filing out of the room and closing the door behind them. She turned to find Callum staring at her. "What's wrong? You seemed bored," he said.

She wondered how he'd picked up on it when his full attention should have been on the meeting he was conducting. But since he had noticed…

"Yes, but I couldn't help it. This room will bore you to tears and I have a bucket full of them." She glanced around the room. "Make that *two* buckets."

Callum threw his head back and laughed. "Do you always say whatever suits you?"

"Hey, you did ask. And yes, I usually say whatever suits me. Didn't Ramsey warn you that I have no problem giving my opinion about anything?"

"Yes, he did warn me."

She gave him a sweet smile. "Yet you hired me anyway, so, unfortunately, you're stuck with me."

Callum wanted nothing more than to lean over and plant a kiss firmly on Gemma's luscious lips and say that being stuck with her was something he looked forward to. Instead, he checked his watch. "Do you want to grab lunch before we head over to the house you'll be decorating? Then while we eat you can tell me why you have so many buckets of tears from this room."

She chuckled as she stood up. "Gladly, Mr. Austell."

Chapter 9

"Well, here we are and I want you to tell me just what you can do with this place."

Gemma heard Callum's words, but her gaze was on the interior of a monstrosity of a house. She was totally in awe. There weren't too many homes that could render her speechless, but this mansion had before she'd stepped over the threshold. The moment he'd pulled into the driveway, she'd been overwhelmed by the architecture of it. She'd known when she'd originally seen the design of the home on paper that it was a beauty, but actually seeing it in all its grandiose splendor was truly a breathtaking moment.

"Give me the history of this house," she said, glancing around at the elegant staircase, high sculptured ceilings, exquisite crown molding and gorgeous wood floors. And for some reason she believed Callum knew

it. Just from her observation of him during that morning's meeting, she'd determined that he was an astute
businessman, sharp as a tack, although he preferred
sporting jeans and messing with sheep to wearing a
business suit and tweaking mission statements.

Over lunch she'd asked how he'd managed to keep
up with his business affairs with Le'Claire while working for Ramsey. He'd explained that he had made trips
back home several times when his presence had been
needed on important matters. In addition, the cottage
he occupied in Denver had a high-speed Internet connection, a fax machine and whatever else was needed
to keep in touch with his team in Australia. And due to
the difference in time zones, six in the evening in Denver was ten in the morning the next day in Sydney. He'd
been able to call it a day with Ramsey around five, go
home and shower and be included in a number of critical
business meetings by way of conference call by seven.

"This area is historic Bellevue Hills and this house
was once owned by one of the richest men in Australia.
Shaun told me about it, thought I should take a look at
it and make the seller an offer. I did."

"Just like that?" she asked, snapping her fingers for
effect.

He met her gaze. "Just like that," he said, snapping his.

She couldn't help but laugh. "I like the way you
think, Callum, because, as I said, this place is a beauty."

He shifted his gaze away from her to look back at
the house. "So, it's a place where you think the average
woman would want to live?"

She placed her hands on her hips. "Callum, the average woman would die to live in a place like this. This
is practically a mansion. It's fit for a queen. I know

because I consider myself the average woman and I would."

"You would?"

"Of course. Now, I'm dying to take a look around and make some decorating suggestions."

"As extensive as the ones you made at lunch regarding that conference room at Le'Claire?"

"Probably," she said with a smile. "But I won't know until I go through it and take measurements." She pulled her tape measure out of her purse.

"Let's go."

He touched her arm and the moment he did so, she felt that tingling sensation that always came over her when he touched her, but now the sensations were even stronger than before.

"You okay, Gemma? You're shivering."

She drew in a deep breath as they moved from the foyer toward the rest of the house. "Yes, I'm fine," she said, refusing to look at him. *If only he knew the truth about how she was feeling.*

Callum leaned against the kitchen counter and stared over at Gemma as she stood on a ladder taking measurements of a particular window. She had long ago shed her jacket and kicked off her shoes. He looked down at her feet and thought she had pretty toes.

They had been here a couple of hours already and there were still more measurements to take. He didn't mind if he could continue to keep her up there on a ladder. Once in a while, when she moved, he'd get a glimpse of her gorgeous legs and her luscious-looking thighs.

"You're quiet."

Her observation broke into his thoughts. "What I'm doing is watching you," he said. "Having fun?"

"The best kind there is. I love doing this and I'm going to love decorating this house for you." She paused a second. "Unfortunately, I have some bad news for you."

He lifted a brow. "What bad news?"

She smiled down at him. "What I want to do in here just might break you. And, it will take me longer than the six weeks planned."

He nodded. Of course, he couldn't tell her he was counting on that very thing. "I don't have a problem with that. How is your work schedule back in Denver? Will remaining here a little longer cause problems for you?"

"No. I finished all my open projects and was about to take a vacation before bidding on others, so that's fine with me if you think you can handle a houseguest for a little while longer."

"Absolutely."

She chuckled. "You might want to think about it before you give in too easily."

"No, you might want to think about it before you decide to stay."

She glanced down at him and went perfectly still and he knew at that moment she was aware of what he was thinking. Although they had enjoyed each other's company, they had practically walked on eggshells around each other all day. After lunch he'd taken her on a tour of downtown and showed her places like the Sydney Opera House, the Royal Botanic Gardens and St. Andrew's Cathedral. And they had fed seagulls in Hyde Park before coming here. Walking beside her seemed natural, and for a while they'd held hands. Each time he had touched her she had trembled.

Did she think he wasn't aware of what those shivers meant? Did she not know what being close to her was doing to him? Could she not see the male appreciation as well as the love shining in his eyes whenever he looked at her?

Breaking eye contact, he looked at his watch. "Do you plan to measure all the windows today?"

"No, I'd planned to make this my last one for now. You will bring me back tomorrow, though, right?"

"Just ask. Whatever you want, it's yours."

"In that case, I'd like to come back to finish up this part. Then we'll need to decide on what fabrics you want," she said, moving to step down from the ladder. "The earlier the better, especially if it's something I need to backorder."

He moved away from the counter to hold the ladder steady while she descended. "Thanks," she said, when her bare feet touched the floor. He was standing right there in front of her.

"Don't mention it," he said. "Ready to go?"

"Yes."

Instead of taking her hand, he walked beside her and said nothing. He felt her looking over at him, but he refused to return her gaze. He had promised that the next time they kissed she would ask for it, but she'd failed to do that, which meant that when they got back to his place he would turn up the heat.

"You all right, Callum?"

"Yes, I'm fine. Where would you like to eat? It's dinnertime."

"Doesn't matter. I'm up for anything."

He smiled when an idea popped into his head. "Then how about me preparing dinner tonight."

She lifted a brow. "Can you cook?"

"I think I might surprise you."

She chuckled. "In that case, surprise me."

Whatever you want, it's yours.

Gemma stepped out of the Jacuzzi to dry herself while thinking that Callum had been saying that a lot lately. She wondered what he would think of her if she were to tell him that what she wanted more than anything was another dose of the pleasure he'd introduced her to last night.

Being around him most of the day had put her nerves on edge. Every time he touched her or she caught him looking at her, she felt an overwhelming need to explore the intense attraction between them. His mouth and fingers had planted a need within her that was so profound, so incredibly physical, that certain parts of her body craved his touch.

She'd heard of people being physically attracted to each other to the point of lust consuming their mind and thoughts, but such a thing had never happened to her. Until now. And why was it happening at all? What was there about Callum—other than the obvious—that had her in such a tizzy? He made her want things she'd never had before. She was tempted to go further with him than she had with any other man.

In a way she had already done that last night. There was no other man on the face of this earth who could ever lay a claim to fingering her. But Callum had done that while kissing her senseless, stirring a degree of passion within her that even now made her heart beat faster just thinking about it.

She shook her head, and tried to get a grip but failed to do so. She couldn't let go of the memories of how her body erupted in one mind-shattering orgasm. Now she knew what full-blown pleasure was about. But she knew that she hadn't even reached the tip of the iceberg and her body was aching to get pushed over that turbulent edge. The thought that there was something even more powerful, more explosive to experience sent sensual shivers through her entire being.

There were a number of reasons why she should not be thinking of indulging in an affair with Callum. And yet, there were a number of reasons why she should. She was a twenty-four-year-old virgin. To give her virginity to Callum was a plus in her book, because, in addition to being attracted to him, he would know what he was doing. She'd heard horror stories about men who didn't.

And if they were to have an affair, who would know? He wasn't the type to kiss and tell. And he didn't seem bothered by the fact that his best friend was her brother. Besides, since he would be returning to Australia to live, she didn't have the worry about running into him on a constant basis, seeing him and being reminded of what they'd done.

So what was holding her back?

She knew the answer to that question. It was the same reason she was still a virgin. She was afraid the guy she would give her virginity to would also capture her heart. And the thought of any man having her heart was something she just couldn't abide. What if he were to hurt her, break her heart the way her brothers had done to all those girls?

She nibbled on her bottom lip as she slipped into her dress to join Callum for dinner. Somehow she would have to find a way to experience pleasure without the possibility of incurring heartache. She should be able to make love with a man without getting attached. Men did it all the time. She would enter into the affair with both eyes open and not expect any more than what she got. And when it was over, her heart would still be intact. She wouldn't set herself up like those other girls who'd fancied themselves in love with a Westmoreland, only to have their hearts broken.

It should be a piece of cake. After all, Callum had told her he was waiting to meet his soul mate. So there would be no misunderstanding on either of their parts. She wasn't in love with him and he wasn't in love with her. He would get what he wanted and she would be getting what she wanted.

More of last night.

A smile of anticipation touched her lips. She mustn't appear too eager and intended to play this out for all it was worth and see how long it would last. She was inexperienced when it came to seduction, but she was a quick study.

And Callum was about to discover just how eager she was to learn new things.

Callum heard Gemma moving around upstairs. He had encouraged her to relax and take a bubble bath in the huge Jacuzzi garden tub while he prepared dinner.

Since they'd eaten a large lunch at one of the restaurants downtown near the Sydney Harbour, he decided to keep dinner simple—a salad and an Aussie meat pie.

He couldn't help but smile upon recalling her expression when she'd first seen his home, and her excitement about decorating it just the way she liked. He had gone along with every suggestion she made, and although she had teased him about the cost, he knew she was intentionally trying to keep prices low, even though he'd told her that doing so wasn't necessary.

His cell phone rang and he pulled it off his belt to answer it. "Hello."

"How are you doing, Callum?"

He smiled upon hearing his mother's voice. "I'm fine, Mom. What about you?"

"I'm wonderful. I hadn't talked to you since you were here yesterday with Gemma, and I just want you to know that I think she's a lovely girl."

"Thanks, Mom. I think so, too. I just can't wait for her to figure out she's my soul mate."

"Have patience, Callum."

He chuckled. "I'll try."

"I know Gemma is going to be tied up with decorating that house, but Shaun and I were wondering if she'll be free to do some shopping with us next Friday," his mother said. "Annette and Mira will be joining us as well."

The thought of Gemma being out of his sight for any period of time didn't sit well with him. He knew all about his mother, sister and sisters-in-law's shopping trips. They could be gone for hours. He felt like a possessive lover. A smile touched his lips. He wasn't Gemma's lover yet, but he intended to be while working diligently to become a permanent part of her life—namely, her husband.

"Callum?"

"Yes, Mom. I'm sure that's something Gemma will

enjoy. She's upstairs changing for dinner. I'll have her call you."

He conversed with his mother for a little while longer before ending the call. Pouring a glass of wine, he moved to the window that looked out over the Pacific. His decision to keep this place had been an easy one. He loved the view as well as the privacy.

The house Gemma was decorating was in the suburbs, sat on eight acres of land and would provide plenty of room for the large family he wanted them to have. He took a sip of wine while his mind imagined a pregnant Gemma, her tummy round with his child.

He drew in a deep breath, thinking that if anyone would have told him five years ago that he would be here in this place and in this frame of mind, he would have been flabbergasted. His mother suggested that he have patience. He'd shown just how much patience he had for the past three years. Now it was time to make his move.

"Callum?"

The sound of her voice made him turn around. He swallowed deeply, while struggling to stay where he was, not cross the room, pull her into his arms and give her the greeting that he preferred. As usual, she looked beautiful, but there was something different about her this evening. There was a serene glow to her face that hadn't been there before. Had just two days in Australia done that to her? Hell, he hoped so. More than anything, he wanted his native land to grow on her.

"You look nice, Gemma," he heard himself saying.

"Thanks. You look nice yourself."

He glanced down at himself. He had changed out of his suit, and was now wearing jeans and a pullover shirt. She was wearing an alluring little outfit—a skirt that fell a little past her knees, a matching top and a cute pair of sandals. He looked at her and immediately thought of one word. *Sexy.* Umm, make that two words. *Super sexy.* He knew of no other woman who wore her sexuality quite the way Gemma did.

His gaze roamed the full length of her in male appreciation, admiring the perfection of her legs, ankles and calves. He had to have patience, as his mother suggested and tamp down his rising desire. But all he had to do was breathe in, take a whiff of her scent and know that would not be an easy task.

"What are you drinking?"

Her words pulled his attention from her legs back to her face. "Excuse me? I missed that."

A smile curved her lips. "I asked what you're drinking."

He held up his glass and glanced at it. "Wine. Want some?"

"Sure."

"No problem. I'll pour you a glass," he said.

"No need," she said, walking slowly toward him. He felt his pulse rate increase and his breathing get erratic with every step she took.

"I'll just share yours," she said, coming to a stop in front of him. She reached out, slid the glass from his hand and took a sip. But not before taking the tip of her tongue and running it along the entire rim of the glass.

Callum sucked in a quick breath. Did she know how intimate that gesture was? He watched as she then took a sip. "Nice, Callum. Australia's finest, I assume."

He had to swallow before answering, trying to retain control of his senses. "Yes, a friend of my father owns a winery. There's plenty where that came from. Would you like some more?"

Her smile widened. "No, thank you. But there is something that I do want," she said, taking a step closer to him.

"Is there?" he said, forcing the words out of a tight throat. "You tell me what you want and, as I said yesterday and again today, whatever you want I will deliver."

She leaned in closer and whispered, "I'm holding you to your word, Callum Austell, because I've decided that I want you."

Chapter 10

Gemma half expected Callum to yank her down and take her right there on the living room floor. After all, she'd just stated that she wanted him, and no one would have to read between the lines to figure out what that meant. Most men would immediately act on her request, not giving her the chance to change her mind.

Instead, Callum deliberately and slowly put his glass down. His gaze locked with hers and when his hands went to her waist he moved, bringing their bodies in close contact. "And what you want, Gemma, is just what you will get."

She saw intense heat in the depths of his eyes just seconds before he lowered his mouth to hers. The moment she felt his tongue invade her mouth, she knew he would be kissing her senseless.

He didn't disappoint her.

The last time they'd kissed, he had introduced her to a range of sensations that she'd never encountered before. Sensations that started at her toes and worked their way up to the top of her head. Sensations that had lingered in her lower half, causing the area between her legs to undergo all kinds of turbulent feelings and her heart all kinds of unfamiliar emotions.

This kiss was just as deadly, even more potent than the last, and her head began swimming in passion. She felt that drowning would soon follow. Blood was rushing, fast and furiously, through her veins with every stroke of his tongue. He was lapping her up in a way that had her entire body shuddering from the inside out.

Callum had encouraged her to ask for what she wanted and was delivering in full measure. He wasn't thinking about control of any kind and neither was she. He had addressed and put to rest the only two concerns she had—his relationship with her brother and her relationship with him as a client. Last night, he'd let her know that those two things had nothing to do with this—the attraction between them—and she was satisfied with that.

And now she was getting satisfied with this—his ability to deliver a kiss that was so passionate it was nearly engulfing her in flames. He was drinking her as if she were made of the finest wine, even finer than the one he'd just consumed.

She felt the arms around her waist tighten and when he shifted their positions she felt something else, the thick hardness behind the zipper of his jeans. When she moved her hip and felt his hard muscles aligned with her curves, the denim of his jeans rubbing against her bare legs, she moaned deep in her throat.

Callum released Gemma's mouth and drew in a deep breath and her scent. She smelled of the strawberry bubble bath she had used and whatever perfume she had dabbed on her body.

He brushed kisses across her forehead, eyebrows, cheeks and temples while giving her a chance to breathe. Her mouth was so soft and responsive, and it tasted so damn delicious. The more he deepened the kiss, the more responsive she became and the more accessible she made her mouth.

His hands eased from her waist to smooth across her back before cupping her backside. He could feel every inch of her soft curves beneath the material of her skirt and top, and instinctively, he pulled her closer to the fit of him.

"Do you want more?" he whispered against her lips, tasting the corners of her mouth while moaning deep in his throat from how good she tasted.

"Yes, I want more," she said in a purr that conveyed a little catch in her breathing.

"How much more?" He needed to know. Any type of rational thought and mind control was slipping away from him big time. It wouldn't take much to strip her naked right now.

He knew for a fact that she'd rarely dated during the time he'd been in Denver. And although he wasn't sure what she did while she was in college, he had a feeling his Gemma was still a virgin. The thought of that filled him with intense pride that she would give him the honor of being her first.

"I want all you can give me, Callum," she responded in a thick slur, but the words were clear to his ears.

He sucked a quick gulp of air into his lungs. He

wondered if she had any idea what she was asking for. What he could give was a whole hell of a lot. If he had his way, he would keep her on her back for days. Stay inside her until he'd gotten her pregnant more times than humanly possible.

The thought of his seed entering her womanly channel, made the head of his erection throb behind his zipper, begging for release, practically pleading for the chance to get inside her wet warmth.

"Are you on any type of birth control?" He knew that she was. He had overheard a conversation once that she'd had with Bailey and knew she'd been taking oral contraceptives to regulate her monthly cycle.

"Yes, I'm on the pill," she acknowledged. "But not because I sleep around or anything like that. In fact, I'm..."

She stopped talking in midsentence and was gazing up at him beneath her long lashes. Her eyes were wide, as if it just dawned on her what she was about to reveal. He had no intention of letting her stop talking now.

"You're what?"

He watched as she began nervously nibbling on her bottom lip and he almost groaned, tempted to replace her lip with his and do the nibbling for her.

He continued to brush kisses across her face, drinking in her taste. And when she didn't respond to his inquiry, he pulled back and looked at her. "You can tell me anything, Gemma. Anything at all."

"I don't know," she said in a somewhat shaky voice. "It might make you want to stop."

Not hardly, he thought, and knew he needed to convince her of that. "There's nothing you can tell me that's going to stop me from giving you what you want. Nothing," he said fervently.

She gazed up into his eyes and he knew she believed him. She held the intensity in his gaze when she leaned forward and whispered, "I'm still a virgin."

"Oh, Gemma," he said, filled with all the love any man could feel for a woman at that particular moment. He had suspected as much, but until she'd confessed the truth, he hadn't truly been certain. Now he was, and the thought that he would be the man who carried her over the threshold of womanhood gave him pause, had him searching for words to let her know just how he felt.

He hooked her chin with his fingers as he continued to hold her gaze. "You trust me enough with such a precious gift?"

"Yes," she said promptly without hesitation.

Filled with both extreme pleasure and profound pride, he bent his head and kissed her gently while sweeping her off her feet into his arms.

When Callum placed her on his bed and stepped back to stare at her, one look at his blatantly aroused features let Gemma know that he was going to give her just what she had asked for. Just what she wanted.

Propped up against his pillow, she drank him in from head to toe as he began removing his shoes. Something—she wasn't sure just what—made her bold enough to ask. "Will you strip for me?"

He lifted his head and looked over at her. If he was shocked by her request, he didn't show it. "Is that what you want?"

"Yes."

He smiled and nodded. "No problem."

Gemma shifted her body into a comfortable position as a smile suffused her face. "Be careful or I'll begin to think you're easy."

He shrugged broad shoulders as he began removing his shirt. "Then I guess I'll just have to prove you wrong."

She chuckled. "Oooh, I can't wait." She stared at his naked chest. He was definitely built, she thought.

He tossed his shirt aside and when his hand went to the zipper of his jeans, a heated sensation began traveling along Gemma's nerve endings. When he began lowering the zipper, she completely held her breath.

He slid the zipper halfway down and met her gaze. "Something I need to confess before I go any further."

Her breath felt choppy. "What?"

"I dreamed about you last night."

Gemma smiled, pleased with his confession. "I have a confession of my own." He lifted his brows. "I dreamed about you, too. But, then, I think it was to be expected after last night."

He went back to slowly easing his zipper down. "You could have come to my bedroom. I would not have minded."

"I wasn't ready."

He didn't move as he held her gaze. "And now?"

She grinned. "And now I'm a lady-in-waiting."

He threw his head back and laughed as he began sliding his pants down his legs. She scooted to the edge of the bed to watch, fascinated when he stood before her wearing a skimpy pair of black briefs. He had muscular thighs and a nice pair of hairy legs. The way the briefs fit his body had her shuddering when she should have been blushing.

All her senses suddenly felt hot-wired, her heart began thumping like crazy in her chest and a tingling sensation traveled up her nerve endings. She felt no shame in staring at him. The only thing she could think of at that moment was that *her* Aussie was incredibly sexy.

Her Aussie?

She couldn't believe her mind had conjured up such a thought. He wasn't hers and she wasn't his. At least not in *that* way. But tonight, she conceded, and whenever they made love, just for that moment, they would belong to each other in every way.

"Should I continue?"

She licked her lips in anticipation. "I might hurt you if you don't."

He chuckled as he slid his hands into the waistband of his briefs and slowly began easing them down his legs. "Oh my…" She could barely get the words past her throat.

Her breasts felt achy as she stared at that part of his anatomy, which seemed to get larger right before her eyes. She caught a lip between her teeth and tried not to clamp down too hard. But he had to be, without a doubt, in addition to being totally aroused and powerfully male, the most beautiful man she'd ever seen. And he stood there, with his legs braced apart, his hands on his hips and with a mass of hair flowing around his face, fully exposed to her. This was a man who could make women drool. A man who would get a second look whenever he entered a room, no matter what he was wearing. A man whose voice alone could make woman want to forget about being a good girl and just enjoy being bad.

She continued to stare, unable to do anything else, as

he approached the bed. She moved into a sitting position to avoid being at eye level with his erection.

Gemma couldn't help wondering what his next move would be. Did he expect her to return the favor and strip for him? When he reached the edge of the bed, she tilted her head back and met his gaze. "My turn?"

He smiled. "Yes, but I want to do things differently."

She lifted a confused brow. "Differently?"

"Yes, instead of you stripping yourself, I want to do it."

She swallowed, not sure she understood. "You want to take my clothes off?"

He shook his head as a sexy smile touched his lips. "No, I want to strip your clothes off you."

And then he reached out and ripped off her blouse.

The surprised look on her face was priceless. Callum tossed her torn blouse across the room. And now his gaze was fixed on her chest and her blue satin push-up bra. Fascinated, he thought she looked sexy as hell.

"You owe me for that," she said when she found her voice.

"And I'll pay up," he responded as he leaned forward to release the front clasp and then eased the straps down her shoulders, freeing what he thought were perfect twin mounds with mouth-watering dark nipples.

His hand trembled when he touched them, fondled them between his eager fingers, while watching her watch him, and seeing how her eyes darkened, and how her breath came out in a husky moan.

"Hold those naughty thoughts, Gemma," he whispered when he released her and reached down to remove her sandals, rubbing his hands over her calves and ankles, while thinking her skin felt warm, almost feverish.

"Why do women torture their feet with these things?" His voice was deep and husky. He dropped the shoes by the bed.

"Because we know men like you enjoy seeing us in them."

He continued to rub her feet when he smiled. "I like seeing *you* in them. But then I like seeing you out of them, too."

His hand left her feet and began inching up her leg, past her knee to her thigh. But just for a second. His hand left her thigh and shifted over to the buttons on her skirt and with one tug sent them flying. She lifted her hips when he began pulling the skirt from her body and when she lay before him wearing nothing but a pair of skimpy blue panties, he felt blood rush straight to his heads. Both of them.

But it was the one that decided at that moment to almost double in size that commanded his attention. Without saying a word, he slowly began easing her panties down her thighs and her luscious scent began playing havoc with his nostrils as he did so.

He tossed her panties aside and his hands eased back between her legs, seeing what he'd touched last night and watching once again as her pupils began dilating with pleasure.

And to make sure she got the full Callum Austell effect, he bent his head toward her chest, captured a nipple in his mouth and began sucking on it.

"Callum!"

"Umm?" He released that nipple only to move to the other one, licking the dark area before easing the tip between his lips and sucking on it as he'd done to the other one. He liked her taste and definitely liked the sounds she was making.

Moments later he began inching lower down her body and when his mouth came to her stomach, he traced a wet path all over it.

"Callum."

"I'm right here. You still sure you want me?" His fingers softly flicked across her womanly folds while he continued to lick her stomach.

"Oh, yes."

"Are there any limitations?" he asked.

"No."

"Sure?"

"Positive."

He took her at her word and moved his mouth lower. Her eyes began closing when he lifted her hips and wrapped her legs around his neck, lowered his head and pressed his open mouth to her feminine core.

Pleasure crashed over Gemma and she bit down to keep from screaming. Callum's tongue inside her was driving her crazy, and pushing her over the edge in a way she'd never been pushed before. Her body seemed to fragment into several pieces and each of those sections was being tortured by a warm, wet and aggressive tongue that was stroking her into a stupor.

Her hands grabbed tight to the bedspread as her legs were nudged further apart when his mouth burrowed further between her thighs and his tongue seem to delve inside her deeper.

She continued to groan in pleasure, not sure she would be able to stop moaning even when he ceased doing this to her. She released a deep moan when the pressure of his mouth on her was too much, and the erotic waves she was drowning in gave her little hope for a rescue.

And then, just like the night before, she felt her body jackknife into an orgasm that had her screaming. She was grateful for the privacy afforded by the seclusion of Callum's condo.

"Gemma."

Callum's deep Australian voice flowed through her mind as her body shuddered nearly uncontrollably. It had taken her twenty-four years to share this kind of intimacy with a man and it was well worth the wait.

"Open your eyes. I want you to be looking at me the moment I make you mine."

She lifted what seemed like heavy lids and saw that he was over her, his body positioned between her legs, and her hips were cupped in the palms of his hands. She pushed the thought out of her mind that she would never truly be his, and what he'd said was just a figure of speech, words just for the moment, and she understood because at this moment she wanted to be his.

As she gazed up into his eyes, something stirred deep in her chest around her heart and she forced the feeling back, refusing to allow it to gain purchase there, rebuffing the very notion and repudiating the very idea. This was about lust, not love. He knew it and she knew it as well. There was nothing surprising about the way her body was responding to him; the way he seemed to be able to strum her senses the same way a musician strummed his guitar.

And then she felt him, felt the way his engorged erection was pressed against her femininity and she kept her gaze locked with his when she felt him make an attempt to slide into her. It wasn't easy. He was trying to stretch her and it didn't seem to be working. Sweat popped on his brow and she reached up and wiped his forehead with the back of her hand.

He saw her flinch in pain and he went still. "Do you want me to stop?"

She shook her head from side to side. "No. I want you to make it happen, and you said you'll give me what I want."

"Brat," he said. When she chuckled, he thrust forward. When she cried out he leaned in and captured her lips.

You truly belong to me now and I love you, Callum wanted to say, but knew that he couldn't. Instead, after her body had adjusted to his, he began moving. Every stroke into her body was a sign of his love whether she knew it or not. One day when she could accept it, she would know and he would gladly tell her everything.

He needed to kiss her, join his mouth to hers the same way their bodies were joined. So he leaned close and captured her mouth, kissing her thoroughly and hungrily, and with a passion he felt through every cell in his body. When she instinctively began milking his erection, he deepened the kiss.

And when he felt her body explode, which triggered his to do likewise, he pulled his mouth from hers to throw his head back to scream her name. *Her name.* No other woman's name but hers, while he continued to thrust in and out of her.

His body had ached for this for so long, his body had ached for her. And as a climax continued to rip through them, he knew that, no matter what, Gemma Westmoreland was what he needed in his life and there was no way he would ever give her up.

Chapter 11

Sunlight flitting across her face made Gemma open her eyes and she immediately felt the hard muscular body sleeping beside her. Callum's leg was thrown over hers and his arms were wrapped around her middle. They were both naked—that was a given—and the even sound of his breathing meant he was still asleep.

The man was amazing. He had made love to her in a way that made her first time with a man so very special. He'd also fed her last night the tasty meal he'd prepared, surprising her and proving that he was just as hot in the kitchen as he was in the bedroom.

She drew in a deep breath, wondering which part of her was sorer, the area between her legs or her breasts. Callum had given special attention to both areas through most of the night. But with a tenderness that touched her deeply, he had paused to prepare a warm, soothing soak for her in his huge bathtub. He hadn't made love to her since then. They'd eaten a late dinner, and returning to bed, he had cuddled her in his arms, close to his warm, masculine body. His hands had caressed her all over, gently stroking her to sleep.

And now she was awake and very much aware of everything they'd done the night before. Everything she'd asked him for, he had delivered. Even when he had wanted to stop because last night was her first time, she had wanted to experience more pleasure and he had ended up making it happen, giving her what she wanted. And although her body felt sore and battered today, a part of her felt that last night had truly been worth it.

Deciding to get a little more sleep, she closed her eyes and immediately saw visions of them together. But it wasn't a recent image. She looked older and so did he and there were kids around. Whose kids were they? Certainly not theirs. Otherwise that would mean…

Her eyes sprang open, refusing to let such an apparition enter her mind. She would be the first to admit that what they'd shared last night had overwhelmed her, and for a moment she'd come close to challenging everything she believed about relationships between men and women. But the last thing she needed to do was get off-track. Last night was what it was—no more, no less. It was about a curious, inexperienced woman and a horny, experienced man. And both had gotten satisfied to the nth degree. They had both gotten what they wanted.

"You're awake?"

Callum's voice sent sensations running across her skin. "Who wants to know?"

"The man who made love to you last night."

She shifted her body, turned to face him and immediately wished she hadn't. Fully awake he was sexy as sin. A half asleep Callum, with a stubble chin, drowsy eyes and long eyelashes, could make you come just looking at him.

"You're the one who did that to me last night, aren't you?"

A smile curved his lips. "I'm the one who plans to do that to you every night."

She chuckled, knowing he only meant every night she remained in Australia. She was certain he knew that when they returned to Denver things would be different. Although she had her own little place, he would not be making late-night booty calls on her Westmoreland property.

"You think you have the stamina to do it every night?"

"Don't you?"

She had to admit that the man's staying power was truly phenomenal. But she figured, in time, when she got the hang of it, she would be able to handle him. "Yes, I do."

She then reached out and rubbed a hand across his chin. "You need a shave."

He chuckled. "Do I?"

"Yes." Then she grabbed a lock of his hair. "And…"

"Don't go there. I get my hair trimmed, never cut."

She smiled. "That must be an Austell thing, since I see your father and brothers evidently feel the same way. Don't be surprised if I start calling you Samson."

"And I'll start calling you Delilah, the temptress."

She couldn't help but laugh. "I wouldn't know how to tempt a man."

"But you know how to tempt me."

"Do I?"

"Yes, but don't get any ideas," he said. "Last night you made me promise to get you to your new office by ten o'clock."

Yes, she had made him promise that. He'd told her she could set up shop in the study of the house. He would have a phone installed as well as a fax machine and a computer with a high-speed Internet connection. The sooner she could get the materials she needed ordered, the quicker she could return to Denver. For some reason, the thought of returning home tugged at her heart. This was her third day here and she already loved this place.

"You do want to be on the job by ten, right?"

A smile touched her lips. "Yes, I do. Have you decided when and if you're returning to Denver?" She just had to know.

"Yes, I plan to return with you and will probably stay until after Ramsey and Chloe's baby is born to help out on the ranch. When things get pretty much back to normal for Ramsey, then I'll leave Denver for good and return here."

She began nibbling on her bottom lip. This was September, and Chloe was due to deliver in November, which meant Callum would be leaving Denver a few months after that. Chances were there would be no Callum Austell in Denver come spring.

"Umm, let me do that."

She lifted her gaze to his eyes when he interrupted her thoughts. "Let you do what?"

"This."

He leaned closer and began gently nibbling on her lips, then licking her mouth from corner to corner.

When her lips parted on a breathless sigh, he entered her mouth to taste her fully. The kiss grew deeper, hotter and moments later, when he pulled his mouth away, he placed his fingers to her lips to stop the request he knew she was about to make.

"Your body doesn't need me that way, Gemma. It needs an adjustment period," he whispered against her lips.

She nodded. "But later?"

His lips curved in a wicked smile. "Yes, later."

Callum was vaguely aware of the information the foreman of one of his sheep ranches was giving to him. The report was good, which he knew it would be. During the time he'd been in Denver, he'd pretty much kept up with things here as well as with Le'Claire. He'd learned early how to multitask.

And he smiled, thinking how well he'd multi-tasked last night. There hadn't been one single part of Gemma he hadn't wanted to devour—and all at the same time. He'd been greedy, and so had she. His woman had more passion in her body than she knew what to do with, and he was more than willing to school her in all the possibilities. But he also knew that he had to be careful. He didn't want her to start thinking that what was between them was more lust than love. His goal was to woo her every chance he got, which is why he'd hung up with the florist a few moments ago.

"So as you can see, Mr. Austell, everything is as it should be."

He smiled at the man who'd been talking for the past ten minutes, going over his sheep-herding records. "I figured they would be. I appreciate the job you and your men have done in my absence, Richard."

A huge grin covered the man's face. "We appreciate working for the Austells."

Richard Vinson and his family had worked on an Austell sheep ranch for generations. In fact, upon Callum's grandfather's death, Jack Austell had deeded over five hundred acres of land to the Vinson family in recognition of their loyalty, devotion and hard work.

A few minutes later, Callum was headed back to his car when his phone rang. A quick check showed it was a call from the States, namely Derringer Westmoreland. "Yes, Derringer?"

"Just calling to see if you've given any more thought to becoming a silent partner in our horse-breeding venture?"

Durango Westmoreland, part of those Atlanta Westmorelands, had teamed up with a childhood friend and cousin-in-law named McKinnon Quinn, and bought a very successful horse-breeding and -training operation in Montana. They had invited their cousins, Zane, Derringer and Jason, to become part of their outfit as Colorado partners. Callum, Ramsey and Dillon had expressed an interest in becoming silent partners. "Yes. I'm impressed with all I've heard about it, so count me in."

"Boy, you're easy," Derringer teased.

His words made Callum think about Gemma. She had said the same thing to him last night, but during the course of the night he'd shown her just how wrong she was. "Hey, what can I say? Are you behaving yourself?"

Derringer laughed. "Hey, now what can I say? And

speaking of behaving, how is that sister of mine? She hasn't driven you crazy yet?"

Callum smiled. Gemma had driven him crazy but in a way he'd rather not go into with her brother. "Gemma is doing a great job decorating my place."

"Well, watch your wallet. I heard her prices can sometimes get out of sight."

"Thanks for the warning."

He talked to Derringer a few moments longer before ending the call. After he married Gemma, Ramsey, Zane, Derringer, the twins, Megan and Bailey would become his in-laws, and those other Westmorelands, including Dillon, his cousins-in-law. Hell, he didn't want to think about all those other Westmorelands, the ones from Atlanta that Ramsey and his siblings and cousins were just beginning to get to know. It didn't take the Denver Westmorelands and the Atlanta Westmorelands long to begin meshing as if they'd had a close relationship all their lives.

Callum's father had been an only child and so had his father before him. Todd Austell probably would have been content having one child, but Le'Claire had had a say in that. His father had known that marrying the American beauty meant fathering at least three children. Callum chuckled, remembering that, according to his father, his birth had been a surprise. Todd had assumed his daddy days were over, but Le'Claire had had other ideas about that, and Todd had decided to give his wife whatever she wanted. Callum was using that same approach with Gemma. Whatever this particular Westmoreland wanted is what she would get.

After Callum snapped his seat belt in place, he checked his watch. It was a little past three and he would be picking Gemma up around five. He'd wanted to take her to lunch, but she'd declined, saying she had a lot of orders to place if he wanted the house fully decorated and ready for him to move in by November.

He really didn't care if he was in that house, still living in his condo on the beach or back in Denver. All that mattered to him was that Gemma was with him—wherever he was. And as he turned the ignition to his car, he knew that making that happen was still his top priority.

"Will there be anything else, Ms. Westmoreland?"

Gemma glanced up at the older woman Callum had introduced her to that morning, Kathleen Morgan. "No, Kathleen. That's it. Thanks for all you did today."

The woman waved off her words. "I didn't do anything but make a lot of phone calls to place those orders. I can just imagine how this place is going to look when you finish with it. I think Mr. Austell's decision to blend European and Western styles will be simply beautiful. One day this house will be a showplace for Mr. Austell and his future wife. Goodbye."

"Goodbye." Gemma tried letting the woman's words pass, but couldn't. The thought of Callum sharing this house with a woman—one he would be married to— bothered her.

She tossed her pencil on the desk and glanced over at the flowers that had been delivered not long after he'd dropped her off here. A dozen red roses. Why had he sent them? The card that accompanied them only had his signature. They were simply beautiful, and the fragrance suffused her office.

Her office.

And that was another mystery. She had assumed she

would have an empty room on the main floor of the house with a table and just the bare essentials to operate as a temporary place to order materials and supplies. But when she'd stepped through the door with Callum at her back, she had seen that the empty room had been transformed into a work place, equipped with everything imaginable, including a live administrative assistant.

She pushed her chair back and walked across the room to the vase of flowers she'd placed on a table in front of a window. That way she could pause while working to glance over at them and appreciate their beauty. Unfortunately, seeing them also made her think of the man who'd sent them.

She threw her head back in frustration. She had to stop thinking of Callum and start concentrating on the job he'd hired her to do. Not only had he hired her, he had brought her all the way from Denver to handle her business.

But still, today she'd found herself remembering last night and this morning. True to his word, he had not made love to her again, but he had held her, tasted her lips and given her pleasure another way. Namely with his mouth. He had soothed her body and brought it pleasure at the same time. Amazing.

She turned when her cell phone rang and quickly crossed the room to pick it up. It was her sister Megan. "Megan, how are you doing?" She missed her sisters.

"I'm fine. I have Bailey here with me and she says hello. We miss you."

"And I miss you both, too," she said honestly. "What time is it there?" She placed her cell phone on speaker to put away the files spread all over her desk.

"Close to ten on Monday night. It's Tuesday there already, right?"

"Yes, Tuesday afternoon around four. Today was my first day on the job. Callum set a room up at the house for me to use as an office. I even have an administrative assistant. And speaking of administrative assistants, has the bank's security team contacted you about Niecee?"

"Yes, in fact I got a call yesterday. It seems she deposited the check in an account in Florida. They are working with that bank to stop payment. What's in your favor is that you acted right away. Most businesses that are the victims of embezzlement don't find out about the thefts until months later, and then it's too late to recover the funds. Niecee gave herself away when she left that note apologizing the next day. Had she been bright she would have called in sick a few days, waited for the check to clear and then confessed her sins. Now it looks like she'll be getting arrested."

Gemma let out a deep sigh. A part of her felt bad, but then what Niecee had done was wrong. The woman probably figured that because Gemma was a Westmoreland she had the money to spare. Well, she was wrong. Dillon and Ramsey had pretty much drilled into each of them to make their own way. Yes, they'd each been given one hundred acres and a nice trust fund when they'd turned twenty-one, but making sure they used that money responsibly was up to them. So far all of them had. Luckily, Bane had turned his affairs over to Dillon to handle. Otherwise, he would probably be penniless by now.

"Well, I regret that, but I can't get over what she did. Twenty thousand dollars is not small change."

A sound made Gemma turn around and she drew

in a deep breath when she saw Callum standing there, leaning in the doorway. And from the expression on his face, she knew he'd been listening to her and Megan's conversation. How dare he! She wondered if he would mention it to Ramsey.

"Megan, I'll call you back later," she said, placing her phone off speaker. "Tell everyone I said hello and give them my love."

She ended the call and placed the phone back on her desk. "You're early."

"Yes, you might say that," he said, crossing his arms across his chest. "What's this about your administrative assistant embezzling money from you?"

Gemma threw her head back, sending hair flying over her shoulders. "You were deliberately eavesdropping on my conversation."

"You placed the call on speaker and I just happened to arrive while the conversation was going on."

"Well, you could have let me know you were here."

"Yes, I could have. Now answer the question about Niecee."

"No. It's none of your business," she snapped.

He strolled into the room toward her. "That's where you're wrong. It *is* my business, on both a business and a personal level."

A frown deepened her brow. "And how do you figure that?"

He came to a stop in front of her. "First of all, on a business level, before I do business with anyone I expect the company to be financially sound. In other words, Gemma, I figured that you had enough funds in your bank account to cover the initial outlay for this decorating job."

She placed her hands on her hips. "I didn't have to worry about that since you gave me such a huge advance."

"And what if I hadn't done that? Would you have been able to take the job here?"

Gemma didn't have to think about the answer to that. "No, but—"

"No buts, Gemma." He didn't say anything for a minute and it seemed as if he was struggling not to smile. That only fueled her anger. What did he find so amusing?

Before she could ask, he spoke. "And it's personal, Gemma, because it's you. I don't like the idea of anyone taking advantage of you. Does Ramsey know?"

Boy, that did it! "I own Designs by Gems—not Ramsey. It's my business and whatever problems crop up are *my* problems. I know I made a mistake in hiring Niecee. I see that now and I should have listened to Ramsey and Dillon and done a background check on her, as they suggested. I didn't and I regret it. But at least I'm—"

"Handling your business." He glanced at his watch. "Ready to go?" he asked, walking away and heading for the door, turning off the light switch in the process. "There's a nice restaurant not far from here that I think you'll like."

Gemma spun around to face him. "I'm not going anywhere with you. I'm mad."

Callum flashed her a smile. "Then get over it."

Gemma was too undone…and totally confused. "I won't be getting over it."

He nodded. "Okay, let's talk about it then."

She crossed her arms over her chest. "I don't want to talk about it, because it's none of your business."

Callum threw his head back and laughed. "We're back to that again?"

Gemma glared at him. "We need to get a few things straight, Callum."

He nodded. "Yes, we do." He walked back over to her. "I've already told you why it's my business and from a business perspective you see that I'm right, don't you?"

It took her a full minute, but she finally said, "Yes, all right. I see that. I'll admit that you are right from a business perspective. That's not the way I usually operate but…"

"You were robbing Peter to pay Paul, I know. However, I don't like being Peter or Paul. Now, as far as it being personal, *you* were right."

She lifted a brow. "I was?"

"Yes. It was your business and not Ramsey's concern. I admitted it and told you that you handled it. That was the end of it," he said.

She gave herself a mental shake, trying to keep up with him. He had scolded her on one hand, but complimented her way of handling things on the other. "So you won't mention it to Ramsey?"

"No. It's not my place to do that…unless your life is in danger or something equally as dire, and it's not." He looked down at her and smiled. "As I said, from the sound of the conversation you just had with Megan, you handled this matter in an expeditious manner. By all accounts, you will be getting your money back. Kudos for you."

A smile crossed Gemma's lips. She was proud of

herself. "Yes, kudos for me." Her eyes narrowed. "And just what did you find amusing earlier?"

"How quickly you can get angry just for the sake of doing so. I'd heard about your unique temperament but never experienced it before."

"Did it bother you?"

"No."

Gemma frowned, not sure how she felt about that. In a way she liked that Callum didn't run for cover when her temper exploded, as it did at times. Zane, Derringer and the twins were known to have had a plate aimed at their heads once or twice, and knew to be ready to duck if they gave her sufficient cause.

"However, I would like you to make me a promise," he said, breaking into her thoughts.

She lifted a curious brow. "What?"

"Promise that if you ever find yourself in a bind again, financial or otherwise, you'll let me know."

She rolled her eyes. "I don't need another older brother, Callum."

He smiled and his teeth flashed a bright white against his brown skin. "There's no way you can think we have anything close to a brother-sister relationship after last night. But just in case you need a little reminder..."

He pulled her into his arms, lowered his head and captured her mouth with his.

Chapter 12

Gemma's face blushed with anticipation as she walked into Callum's condo. Dinner was fantastic, but she liked being back here alone with him.

"Are you tired, Gemma?"

He had to be kidding. She glanced over her shoulder and gave him a wry look. He was closing the door and locking it. "What makes you think that?"

"You were kind of quiet at dinner."

She chuckled. "Not hardly. I nearly talked your ears off."

"And I nearly talked yours off, too."

She shook her head. "No, you didn't. You were sharing how your day went, and basically, I was doing the same." *While sitting there nearly drooling over you from across the table.* Now that they were alone, she wondered if she would have to tell him what she wanted or if he already had a clue.

"So Kathleen worked out well for you?"

"Yes," she said, easing out of her shoes. "She's a sweetheart and so efficient. She was able to find all the fabric I need and the cost of shipping won't be bad. I really hadn't expected you to set up the office like that. Thanks again for the roses. They were beautiful."

"You thanked me already for the flowers, and I'm glad you liked them. I plan to take you to the movies this weekend, but how would you like to watch a DVD now?"

She studied his features as he walked into the living room. Was that what he really wanted to do? "A movie on DVD sounds fine."

"You got a favorite?"

She chuckled as she dropped down on the sofa. "And if I do, should I just assume you have it here?"

He sat in the wingback chair across from her. "No, but I'm sure it can be ordered through my cable company. As I said, whatever you want, I will make it happen."

In that case. She stood from the sofa and in bare feet she slowly crossed the room and came to a stop between his opened legs. "Make love to me, Callum."

Callum didn't hesitate to pull Gemma down into his lap. He had been thinking about making love to her all day. That kiss in her office had whetted his appetite and now he was about to be appeased. But first he had to tell her something before he forgot.

"Mom called. She's invited you to have lunch and go shopping with her, my sister and my sisters-in-law next Friday."

Surprise shone on Gemma's face. She twisted around in his arms to look up at him. "She did?"

"Yes."

"But why? I'm here to decorate your house. Why would they want to spend time with me?"

Callum chuckled. "Why wouldn't they? You've never been to Australia and I gather from the conversations the other day they figured you like to shop like most other women."

"The same way men like watching sports. I understand that sports are just as popular here in this country as in the States."

"Yes, I played Australian rules football a lot growing up. Not sure how my body would handle it now, though," he said, adjusting her in his lap to place the top of his chin on the crown of her head. "I also like playing cricket. One day I'm going to teach you how to play."

"Well, you must have plans to do that during the time I'm here, because once I return home it's back to tennis for me."

Callum knew Gemma played tennis and that she was good at it. But what stuck out more than anything was her mentioning returning home. He didn't intend for that to happen, at least not on a permanent basis. "How can you think of returning to Denver when you still have so much to do here?"

She smiled. "Hey, give me a break. Today was my first full day on the job. Besides, you hired Kathleen for me. She placed all the orders and I even hired the company to come in and hang the drapes and pictures. Everything is moving smoothly. Piece of cake. I'll have that place decorated and be out of here in no time."

He didn't say anything for a moment, thinking he definitely didn't like the sound of that. Then he turned her in his arms. "I think we got sidetracked."

She looked up at him. "Did we?"

"Yes. You wanted to make love."

She tilted her head. "Umm, did I?"

"Yes."

She shook her head, trying to hide a grin, which he saw anyway. "Sorry, your time is up."

He stood with her in his arms. "I don't think so."

Callum carried her over to the sofa and sat down with her in his arms. "We have more room here," he said, adjusting her body in his lap to face him. "Now tell me what you want again."

"I don't remember," she said, amusement shining in her gaze.

"Sounds like you need another reminder," he said, standing.

She wrapped her arms around his neck. "Now where are you taking me?"

"To the kitchen. I think I'd like you for dessert."

"What! You're kidding, aren't you?"

"No. Watch me."

And she did. Gemma sat on the kitchen counter, where he placed her, while he rummaged through his refrigerator looking for God knows what. But she didn't mind, since she was getting a real nice view of his backside.

"Don't go anywhere. I'll have everything I need in a sec," he called out, still bent over, scouring his fridge.

"Oh, don't worry, I'm not going anywhere. I'm enjoying the view," she said, smiling, her gaze still glued to his taut tush.

"The view is nice this time of night, isn't it?" he asked over his shoulder.

She grinned as she studied how the denim of his

jeans stretched over his butt. He thought she was talking about the view of the ocean outside the window. "I
think this particular view is nice anytime. Day or night."

"You're probably right."

"I know I am," Gemma said, fighting to keep the
smile out of her voice.

Moments later Callum turned away from the refrigerator and closed the door with his hands full of items.
He glanced over at Gemma. She was smiling. He arched
a brow. "What's so funny?"

"Nothing. What you got there?"

"See for yourself," he said, placing all the items on
the counter next to her.

She picked up a jar. "Cherries?"

A slow smile touched his lips at the same time she
saw a hint of heat fill his green eyes. "My favorite fruit."

"Yeah, I'll bet."

She picked up another item. "Whipped cream?"

"For the topping."

She shook her head as she placed the whipped cream
back on the counter and selected another item. "Nuts?"

"They go well with cherries," he said, laughing.

"You're awful."

"No, I'm not.

She picked up the final item. "Chocolate syrup?"

"That's a must," he said, rolling up his sleeve.

Gemma watched as he began taking the tops off all
the containers. "So what are you going to do with all
that stuff?"

He smiled. "You'll see. I told you that you're going
to be my dessert."

She blinked when she read his thoughts. He was
serious.

"Now for my fantasy," he said, turning to her and placing his hands on her knees as he stepped between them, widening her legs as he did so. He began unbuttoning her shirt and when he took it off her shoulders he neatly placed it on the back of the kitchen chair.

He reached out to unsnap the front of her bra, lifting a brow at its peach color. He'd watched her put it on this morning and when he asked her about it, she told him she liked matching undies.

"Nice color."

"Glad you like it."

Gemma couldn't believe it a short while later when she was sitting on Callum's kitchen counter in nothing but her panties. He then slid her into his arms. "Where are we going now?"

"Out on the patio."

"More room?"

"Yes, more room, and the temperature tonight is unusually warm."

He carried her through the French doors to place her on the chaise longue. "I'll be back."

"Okay." Anticipation was flowing through her veins and she could feel her heart thudding in her chest. She'd never considered herself a sexual being, but Callum was proving just how passionate she could be. At least with him. She had a pretty good idea just what he planned to do and the thought was inciting every cell in her body to simmer with desire. The thought that couples did stuff like this behind closed doors, actually had fun being together, being adventurous while making love, had her wondering what she'd been missing all these years.

But she knew she hadn't been missing anything because the men she'd dated in the past hadn't been

Callum. Besides being drop-dead gorgeous, the man certainly had a way with women. At least he had a way with her. He had made her first time memorable; not only in giving her pleasure but in the way he had taken care of her afterwards.

And then there were the flowers he'd sent today. And then at dinner, she had enjoyed their conversation where not only had he shared how his day had gone, but had given her a lot of interesting information about his homeland. This weekend he had offered to take her sailing on his father's yacht. She was looking forward to that.

While sitting across from him during dinner, every little thing had boosted up her desire for him. She couldn't wait to return here to be alone with him. It could be the way he would smile at her over the rim of his wineglass, or the way he would reach across the table and touch her hand on occasion for no reason at all. They had ordered different entrées and he had hand-fed her some of his when she was curious as to how his meal tasted.

Callum returned and she watched as he placed all the items on the small table beside her. The patio was dark, except for the light coming in from the kitchen and the moonlight overhead. They had eaten breakfast on the patio this morning and she knew there wasn't a single building on either side of them, just the ocean.

He pulled a small stool over to where she lay on her back, staring up at him. "When will you be my dessert?" she tried asking in a calm voice, but found that to be difficult when she felt her stomach churning.

"Whenever you want. Just ask. I'll give you whatever you want."

He'd been telling her that so much that she was beginning to believe it. "The ocean sounds so peaceful and relaxing. You'd better hope I don't fall asleep," she warned.

"If you do, I'll wake you."

She looked up at him, met his gaze and felt his heat. She'd told him last night there were no limitations. There still weren't. It had taken her twenty-four years to get to this point and she intended to enjoy it for all it was worth. Callum was making this a wonderful experience for her and she appreciated him for being fascinating as well as creative.

He moved off the stool just long enough to lean over her to remove her panties. "Nice pair," he said, while easing the silky material down her thighs and legs.

"Glad you like them."

"I like them off you even better," he said, balling them up and standing to put them into the back pocket of his jeans. "Now for my dessert."

"Enjoy yourself."

"I will, sweetheart."

It seemed that her entire body responded to his use of that endearment. He meant nothing by it—she was certain of it. But still, she couldn't help how rapidly her heart was beating from hearing it and how her stomach was fluttering in response to it.

While she lay there, she watched as Callum removed his shirt and tossed it aside before returning to his stool. He leaned close and she was tempted to reach out and run her fingertips across his naked chest, but then decided she wouldn't do that. This was his fantasy. He'd fulfilled hers last night.

"Now for something sweet, like you," he said, and

she nearly jumped when she felt a warm, thick substance being smeared over her chest with his fingers and hands in a sensual and erotic pattern. When he moved to her stomach the muscles tightened as he continued rubbing the substance all over her belly, as if he was painting a design on her.

"What is it?"

"My name."

His voice was husky and in the moonlight she saw his tense features, the darkness of the eyes staring back at her, the sexy line of his mouth. All she could do was lie there and stare up at him speechlessly, trying to make sense of what he said. He was placing his name on her stomach as if he was branding her as his. She forced the thought from her mind, knowing he didn't mean anything by it.

"How does it feel?" he asked as his hand continued spreading chocolate syrup all over her.

"The chocolate feels sticky, but your hands feel good," she said honestly. He had moved his hands down past her stomach to her thighs.

He didn't say anything for a long moment, just continued to do what he was doing.

"And this is your fantasy?" she asked.

His lips curved into a slow smile that seemed to heat his gaze even more. "Yes. You'll see why in a moment."

When Callum was satisfied that he had smeared enough chocolate syrup over Gemma's body, he grabbed the can of whipped cream and squirted some around her nipples, outlined her belly button, completely covered her feminine mound, and made squiggly lines on her thighs and legs.

"Now for the cherries and nuts," he said, still holding her gaze.

He then proceeded to sprinkle her with nuts and place cherries on top of the whipped cream on her breasts, navel and womanly mound. In fact, he placed several on the latter.

"You look beautiful," he said, taking a step back and looking down at her to see just what he'd done.

"I'll take your word for it," she said, feeling like a huge ice-cream sundae. "I just hope there isn't a colony of ants around."

He laughed. "There isn't. Now to get it off you."

She knew just how he intended to do that, but nothing prepared her for the feel of his tongue when he began slowly licking her all over. Every so often he would lean up and kiss her, giving her a taste of the concoction that was smeared all around his mouth, mingling his tongue with hers. At one point he carried a cherry with his teeth, placed it in her mouth and together they shared the taste.

"Callum…"

Callum loved the sound of his name on her lips and as he lowered his mouth back down to her chest, he could feel the softness of her breasts beneath his mouth. And each nipple tasted like a delicious pebble wrapped around his tongue. Every time he took one into his mouth she shivered, and he savored the sensation of sucking on them.

He kissed his way down her stomach and when he came to the area between her legs, he looked up at her, met her gaze and whispered, "Now I will devour you."

"Oh, Callum."

He dropped to his knees in front of her and homed in

to taste her intimately. She cried out his name the moment his tongue touched her and she grabbed hold of his hair to hold his mouth hostage. There was no need, since he didn't plan to go anyplace until he'd licked his fill. Every time his tongue stroked her clitoris, her body would tremble beneath his mouth.

She began mumbling words he was certain had no meaning, but hearing her speak incoherently told him her state of mind. It was tortured, like his. She was the only woman he desired. The only woman he loved.

Moments later when she bucked beneath his mouth when her body was ripped by a massive sensual explosion, he kept his tongue planted deep inside her, determined to give her all the pleasure she deserved. All the pleasure she wanted.

When the aftershocks of her orgasm had passed, he pulled away and began removing his jeans. And then he moved his body in position over hers, sliding between her open legs and entering her in one smooth thrust.

He was home. And he began moving, stroking parts of her insides that his tongue hadn't been able to reach, but his manhood could. And this way he could connect with all of her now. This way. Mating with her while breathing in her delicious scent, as the taste of her was still embedded in his mouth.

The magnitude of what they were sharing sent him reeling over the top, and he felt his own body beginning to explode. He felt his release shoot straight into her the moment he called out her name.

Instinctively, her body began milking him again, pulling everything out of him, making him moan in pleasure. And he knew this was just a part of what he felt for her. And it wasn't lust. It was everything love was based on—the physical and the emotional. And he hoped she would see it. Every day she was here he would show her both sides of love. He would share his body with her. He would share his soul. And he would continue to make her his.

He was tempted to tell her right then and there how he felt, let her know she was his soul mate, but he knew he couldn't. Not yet. She had to realize for herself that there was more between them than this. She had to realize and believe that she was the only woman for him.

He believed that would happen and, thankfully, he had a little time on his side to break down her defenses, to get her to see that all men weren't alike, and that he was the man destined to love her forever.

"So what do you think of this one, Gemma?" Mira Austell asked, showing Gemma the diamond earrings dangling from her ears.

"They're beautiful," Gemma said, and truly meant it.

The Austell ladies had picked her up around ten and it was almost four in the afternoon and they were still at it. Gemma didn't want to think about all the stores they had patronized or how many bags they had between the five of them.

Gemma had seen this gorgeous pair of sandals she just had to buy and also a party dress, since Callum had offered to take her to a club on the beach when she mentioned that she enjoyed dancing.

This particular place—an upscale jewelry store— was their last stop before calling it a day. Le'Claire suggested they stop here, since she wanted a new pair of pearl earrings.

"Gemma, Mira, come look at all these gorgeous

rings," Le'Shaunda was saying, and within seconds they were all crowded around the glass case.

"I really like that one," Annette said, picking out a solitaire with a large stone.

"Umm, and I like that one," Le'Claire said, smiling. "I have a birthday coming up soon, so it's time to start dropping hints."

Gemma thought Callum's mother was beautiful and could understand how his father had fallen in love so fast. And no wonder Todd gave her anything she wanted. But then Callum gave her anything she wanted as well. Like father, like son. Todd had trained his offspring well. Last weekend Callum had treated her to a picnic on the beach, and another one was planned for this weekend as well. She had enjoyed her time with him and couldn't help but appreciate the time and attention he gave to her when he really didn't have to do so.

"Gemma, which of these do you like the best?" Le'Claire asked.

Gemma pressed her nose to the glass case as she peered inside. All the rings were beautiful and no doubt expensive. But if she had to choose…

"That one," she said, pointing to a gorgeous four-carat, white-gold, emerald-cut ring. "I think that's simply beautiful."

The other ladies agreed, and each picked out their favorites. The store clerk even let everyone try them on to see how each ring looked on their hands. Gemma was amused by how the others said they would remind their husbands about those favorites when it got close to their birthdays.

"It's almost dinnertime, so we might as well go

somewhere to get something to eat," Le'Shaunda said. "I know a wonderful restaurant nearby."

Le'Claire beamed. "That's a wonderful idea."

Gemma thought it was a wonderful idea as well, although she missed seeing Callum. He had begun joining her for lunch every day at her office, always bringing good sandwiches for her to eat and wine to drink. They usually went out to a restaurant in town for dinner. Tonight they planned to watch a movie and make love. Or they would make love and then watch a movie. She liked the latter better, since they could make love again after the movie.

"Did Callum mention anything to you about a hunting trip in a couple of weeks?" Annette asked.

Gemma smiled over at her. "Yes, he did. I understand all the men are leaving for a six-day trip."

"Yes," Mira said as if she was eager for Colin to be gone. The other woman glanced over at Gemma and explained. "Of course I'm going to miss my husband, but that's when we ladies get to do another shopping trip."

Everyone laughed and Gemma couldn't keep from laughing right along with them.

Chapter 13

"Hello," Gemma mumbled into the telephone receiver.

"Wake up, sleepy."

A smile touched Gemma's lips as she slowly forced her eyes fully open. "Callum," she whispered.

"Who else?"

She smiled sleepily. He had left two days ago on a hunting trip with his father and brothers and would be gone for another four days. "I've been thinking about you."

"I've been thinking about you, too, sweetheart. I miss you already," he said.

"And I miss you, too," she said, realizing at that moment just how much. He had taken her to a party at his friend's home last weekend and she had felt special walking in with him. And he'd never left her side. It was nice meeting some of the guys he'd gone to college with.

And the night before leaving to go hunting he'd taken her to the movies again. He filled a lot of her time when she wasn't working, so yes, she did miss him already.

"That's good to hear. You had a busy day yesterday, right?"

She pulled herself up in bed. "Yes, but Kathleen and I were able to make sure everything would be delivered as planned."

"Don't forget, you promised to take a break and let me fly you to India when I get back."

"Yes, and I'm looking forward to it, although I hope there isn't a lot of turbulence on that flight."

"You never know, but you'll be with me and I'll take care of you."

Her smile widened. "You always do."

A few moments later they ended the call, and she fluffed her pillow and stretched out in the bed. It was hard to believe that she had been in Australia four weeks already. Four glorious weeks. She missed her family and friends back home, but Callum and his family were wonderful and treated her like she was one of them.

She planned to go shopping with his mother, sister and sisters-in-law again tomorrow, and then there would be a sleepover at Le'Claire's home. She genuinely liked the Austell women and had had some rather amusing moments when they'd shared just how they handled their men. It had been hilarious when Le'Claire even gave pointers to Le'Shaunda, who claimed her husband could be stubborn at times.

But nothing, Gemma thought, could top all the times she'd spent with Callum. They could discuss anything. When she'd received the call that Niecee had been arrested, she had let him handle it so that her emotions wouldn't stop her from making sure the woman was punished for what she had done. And then there were the flowers he continued to send her every week, and the "I'm thinking of you" notes that he would leave around the house for her to find. She stared up at the ceiling, thinking that Callum was definitely not like other men. The woman he married would be very lucky.

At that moment a sharp pain settled around her heart at the thought of any other woman with Callum, sharing anything close to what they had shared this past month. To know that another woman, his soul mate, would be living with him in the house she was decorating almost made her ill.

She eased to the edge of the bed, knowing why she felt that way. She had fallen in love with him. "Oh, no!"

She dropped back on the bed and covered her face with her hands. How did she let that happen? Although Callum wouldn't intentionally break her heart, he would break it just the same. How could she have fallen in love with him? She knew the answer without much thought. Callum was an easy man to love. But it wasn't meant for her to be the one to love him. He had told her about his soul mate.

She got out of bed and headed for the bathroom, knowing what she had to do. There was no way she would not finish the job she came here to do, but she needed to return home for at least a week or two to get her head screwed back on straight. Kathleen could handle things until she returned. And when she got back, she'd be capable of handling a relationship with Callum the way it should be handled. She would still love him, but at least she would have thought things through and come to the realization she couldn't ever be the number one woman in his life. She'd have to be satisfied with that.

A few hours later she had showered, dressed and packed a few of her things. She had called Kathleen and given her instructions as to what needed to be done in her absence, and assured the older woman that she would be back in a week or so.

Gemma decided not to call Callum to tell him she was leaving. He would wonder why she was taking off all of a sudden. She would think of an excuse to give him when she got home to Denver. She wiped the tears from her eyes. She had let the one thing happen to her that she'd always sworn would never happen.

She had fallen in love with a man who didn't love her.

Callum stood on the porch of the cabin and glanced all around. Nothing, he thought, was more beautiful than the Australian outback. He could recall the first time he'd come to this cabin as a child with his brothers, father and grandfather.

His thoughts drifted to Gemma. He knew for certain that she was his soul mate. The last month had been idyllic. Waking up with her in his arms every morning, making love with her each night, was as perfect as perfect could get. And he was waiting patiently for her to realize that she loved him, too.

It would be then that they would talk about it and he would tell her that he loved her as well, that he'd known for a while that she was the one, but had wanted her to come to that realization on her own.

Callum took a sip of his coffee. He had a feeling she was beginning to realize it. More than once over the past week he'd caught her staring at him with an odd look on her face, as if she was trying to figure out something. And at night when she gave herself to him, it was as if he would forever be the only man in her life. Just as, when he made love to her, he wanted her to believe that she would forever be the only woman in his.

"Callum. You got a call. It's Mom."

Morris's voice intruded on his thoughts and he reentered the cabin and picked up the phone. "Yes, Mom?"

"Callum, it's Gemma."

His heart nearly stopped beating. He knew the ladies had a shopping trip planned for tomorrow. "What's wrong with Gemma? What happened?"

"I'm not sure. She called and asked me to take her to the airport."

"Airport?"

"Yes. She said she had to return home for a while, and I could tell she'd been crying."

He rubbed his forehead. That didn't make any sense. He'd just spoken to her that morning and she was fine. She had two pregnant sisters-in-law and he hoped nothing had happened. "Did she say why she was leaving, Mom? Did she mention anything about a family crisis?"

"No, in fact I asked and she said it had nothing to do with her family."

Callum pulled in a deep breath, not understanding any of this.

"Have you told her yet that you're in love with her, Callum?"

"No. I didn't want to rush her and was giving us time to develop a relationship before doing that. I wanted her to see from my actions that I loved her and get her to admit to herself that she loved me, too."

"Now I understand completely," Le'Claire said softly.

"You do?"

"Yes."

"Then how about explaining things to me because I'm confused."

He heard his mother's soft chuckle. "You're a man, so you would be. I think the reason Gemma left is because she realizes that she loves you. She's running away."

Callum was even more confused. "Why would she do something like that?"

"Because if she loves you and you don't love her back then—"

"But I do love her back."

"But she doesn't know that. And if you explained about waiting for a soul mate the way you explained it to me, she's probably thinking it's not her."

The moment his mother's words hit home, Callum threw his head back in frustration and groaned. "I think you're right, Mom."

"I think I'm right, too. So what are you going to do?"

A smile cascaded across Callum's lips. "I'm going after my woman."

Chapter 14

Ramsey Westmoreland had been in the south pasture most of the day, but when he got home he'd heard from Chloe that Gemma was back. She'd called for Megan to pick her up at the airport. And according to what Megan had shared with Chloe, Gemma looked like she'd cried during the entire eighteen-hour flight.

He was about to place a call to Callum to find out what the hell had happened when he received a call from Colin saying Callum was on his way to Denver. The last thing Ramsey needed in his life was drama. He'd had more than enough during his affair with Chloe.

But here he was getting out of his truck to go knock on the door to make sure Gemma was all right. Callum was on his way and Ramsey would leave it to his best friend to handle Gemma from here on out because his sister could definitely be Miss Drama Queen. And seeing that she was here at Callum's cabin and not at her own place spoke volumes, whether she knew it or not. However, for now he would play the dumb-ass, just to satisfy his curiosity. And Chloe's.

He knocked on the door and it was yanked open. For a moment he was taken aback. Gemma looked like a mess, but he had enough sense not to tell her that. Instead, he took off his hat, passed by her and said in a calm tone. "Back from Australia early, aren't you?"

"Just here for a week or two. I'm going back," she said in a strained voice, which he pretended not to hear.

"Where's Callum? I'm surprised he let you come by yourself, knowing how afraid you are of flying. Was there a lot of turbulence?"

"I didn't notice."

Probably because you were too busy crying your eyes out. He hadn't seen her look like this since their parents' funeral. Ramsey leaned against a table in the living room and glanced around. He then looked back at her. "Any reason you're here and not at your own place, Gemma?"

He knew it was the wrong question to ask when suddenly her mouth quivered and she started to sob. "I love him, but he doesn't love me. I'm not his soul mate. But that's okay. I can deal with it. I just didn't want to ever cry over a man the way those girls used to do when Zane and Derringer broke up with them. I swore that would *never* happen to me. I swore I would never be one of them and fall for a guy who didn't love me back."

Ramsey could only stare at her. She actually thought Callum didn't love her? He opened his mouth to tell her just how wrong she was, then suddenly closed it. It was not his place to tell her anything. He would gladly let Callum deal with this.

"Sorry, Ram, but I need to be alone for a minute." He then watched as she quickly walked into the bedroom and closed the door behind her.

Moments later Ramsey was outside, about to open the door to his truck to leave when a vehicle pulled up. He sighed in relief when he saw Callum quickly getting out of the car.

"Ramsey, I went to Gemma's place straight from the airport and she wasn't there. Where the hell is she?"

Ramsey leaned against his truck. Callum looked like he hadn't slept for a while. "She's inside and I'm out of here. I'll let you deal with it."

Callum paused before entering his cabin. Ramsey had jumped into his truck and left in a hurry. Had Gemma trashed his place or something? Drawing in a deep breath, he removed his hat before slowly opening the door.

He strolled into the living room and glanced around. Everything was in order, but Gemma was nowhere in sight. Then he heard a sound coming from the bedroom. He perked up his ears. It was Gemma and she was crying. The sound tore at his heart.

Placing his hat on the rack, he quickly crossed the room and opened his bedroom door. And there she was, lying in his bed with her head buried in his pillows.

He quietly closed the door behind him and leaned against it. Although he loved her and she loved him, he was still responsible for breaking her heart. But, if nothing else, he'd learned over the past four weeks that the only way to handle Gemma was to let her think she was in control, even when she really wasn't. And even if you had to piss her off a little in the process.

"Gemma?"

She jerked up so fast he thought she was going to tumble out of the bed. "Callum! What are you doing here?" She stood quickly, but not before giving one last swipe to her eyes.

"I could ask you the same thing, since this is my place," he said, crossing his arms over his chest.

She threw her hair over her shoulder. "I knew you weren't here," she said as if that explained everything. It didn't.

"So you took off from Australia, left a job unfinished, got on a plane although you hate flying to come here. For what reason, Gemma?"

She lifted her chin and glared at him. "I don't have to answer that, since it's none of your business."

Callum couldn't help but smile at that. He moved away from the door to stand in front of her. "Wrong. It is my business. Both business and personal. It's business because I hired you to do a job and you're not there doing it. And it's personal because it's you and anything involving you is personal to me."

She lifted her chin a little higher. "I don't know why."

"Well, then, Gemma Westmoreland, let me explain it to you," he said, leaning in close to her face. "It's personal because you mean everything to me."

"I can't and I don't," she snapped. "Go tell that to the woman you're going to marry. The woman who is your soul mate."

"I am telling that to her. You are her."

She narrowed her eyes. "No, I'm not."

"Yes, you are. Why do you think I hung around

here for three years working my tail off? Not because I needed the job, but because the woman I love, the woman who's had my heart since the first day I saw her, was here. The woman I knew the moment I saw her that she was destined to be mine. Do you know how many nights I went to this bed thinking of you, dreaming of you, patiently waiting for the day when I could make you belong to me in every possible way?"

He didn't give her a chance to answer him. Figured she probably couldn't anyway with the shocked look on her face, so he continued. "I took you to Australia for two reasons. First, I knew you could do the job, and secondly, I wanted you on my turf so I could court you properly. I wanted to show you that I was a guy worth your love and trust. I wanted you to believe in me, believe that I would never break your heart because, no matter what you thought, I was always going to be there for you. To give you every single thing you wanted. I love you."

There, he had his say and he knew it was time to brace himself when she had hers. She shook her head as if to mentally clear her mind and then she glanced back up at him. And glared.

"Are you saying that I'm the reason you hung around here and worked for Ramsey and that you took me to Australia to decorate your house and to win me over?"

She had explained it differently, but it all came down to the same thing. "Yes, that about sums it all up, but don't forget the part about loving you."

She threw her hands up in the air and then began angrily pacing the room while saying, "You put me through all this for nothing! You had me thinking I was decorating that house for another woman. You had me thinking that we were just having an affair that would lead nowhere."

She stopped pacing and her frown deepened. "Why didn't you tell me the truth?"

He crossed the room to stand in front of her. "Had I told you the truth, sweetheart, you would not have been ready to hear it, nor would you have believed it. You would have given me more grief than either of us needed," he said softly.

A smile then crossed his lips. "I had threatened to kidnap you, but Ramsey thought that was going a little too far."

Her eyes widened. "Ramsey knew?"

"Of course. Your brother is a smart man. There's no way I could have hung around here for three years sniffing around his sister and he not know about it."

"Sniffing around me? I want you to know that I—"

He thought she'd talked enough and decided to shut her up by pulling her into his arms and taking her mouth. The moment his tongue slid between her lips he figured she would either bite it or accept it. She accepted it and it began tangling with hers.

Callum deepened the kiss and tightened his hold on Gemma and she responded by wrapping her arms around his neck, standing on tiptoes and participating in their kiss the way he'd shown her how to do. He knew they still had a lot to talk about, and he would have to go over it again to satisfy her, but he didn't care. He would always give her what she wanted.

Callum forced his mouth from hers, but not before taking a quick lick around her lips. He then rested his forehead against hers and pulled in a deep breath. "I love you, Gemma," he whispered against her temple.

"I loved you from the moment I first saw you. I knew you were the one, my true soul mate."

Gemma dropped her head to Callum's chest and wrapped her arms around his waist, breathing in his scent and glowing in his love. She was still reeling from his profession of love for her. Her heart was bursting with happiness.

"Gemma, will you marry me?"

She snatched her head up to look into his eyes. And there she saw in their green depths what she hadn't seen before. Now she did.

"Yes, I'll marry you, but..."

Callum chuckled. "There's a but?"

"Yes. I want to be told every day that you love me."

He rolled his eyes. "You've hung around my mom, sister and sisters-in-law too much."

"Whatever."

"I don't have a problem doing that. No problem at all." He sat down on the bed and pulled her down into his lap. "You never answered my question. What are you doing here and not at your place?"

She lowered her head, began toying with the buttons on his shirt and then glanced up and met his gaze. "I know it sounds crazy, but I came home to get over you, but once I got here I had to come here to feel close to you. I was going to sleep in this bed tonight because I knew this is where you slept."

Callum tightened his arms around her. "I got news for you, Gemma. You're *still* sleeping in this bed tonight. With me."

He eased back on the bed and took her with him, covering her mouth with his, kissing her in a way that let her know how much love he had for her. He adjusted their bodies so he could remove every stitch of her clothing and then proceeded to undress himself.

He returned to the bed and pulled her into his arms, but not before taking a small box from the pocket of his jacket. He placed his knee on the bed and pulled her into his arms to slide a ring on her finger. "For the woman who took my breath away the moment I saw her. To the woman I love."

Tears clouded Gemma's eyes when she gazed down at the beautiful ring Callum had placed on her finger. Her breath nearly stopped. She remembered the ring. She had seen it that day when she'd gone shopping with the Austell women and they had stopped by that jewelry store. Gemma had mentioned to Le'Claire how much she'd liked this particular one.

"Oh, Callum. Even your mom knows?" She had to fight back tears as she continued to admire her ring.

"Sweetheart, everybody knows," he said, grinning. "I had sworn them to secrecy. It was important for me to court you the way you deserved. You hadn't dated a whole lot, and I wanted to show you that not all guys were heartbreakers."

She wrapped her arms around his neck. "And you did court me. I just didn't know that's what you were doing. I just figured you were being nice, sending me those flowers, taking me to the movies and those picnic lunches on the beach. I just thought you were showing me how much you appreciated me..."

"In bed?"

"Yes."

"And that's what I was afraid of," he said, pulling her closer to him. "I didn't want you to think it was all about sex, because it wasn't. When I told you I would give you anything and everything you wanted, Gemma, I meant it. All you had to do was ask for it, even my love, which is something you already had."

She rested her head on his bare chest for a moment and then she lifted her head to look back at him. "Do you think you wasted three years living here, Callum?"

He shook his head. "No. Being here gave me a chance to love you from afar while watching you grow and mature into the beautiful woman you are today. I saw you gain your independence and then wear it like a brand of accomplishment in everything you did. I was so proud of you when you landed that big contract with the city, because I knew exactly what you could do. That gave me the idea to buy that house for you to decorate. That will be our home and the condo will become our private retreat when we want to spend time at the beach."

He paused a moment. "I know you'll miss your family and all, and—"

Gemma reached up and placed a finger to his lips. "Yes, I will miss my family, but my home will be with you. We will come back and visit and that will be good enough for me. I want to be in Sydney with you."

Callum didn't say anything for a moment and then asked. "What about your business here?"

Gemma smiled. "I'm closing it. I've already opened another shop in Sydney, thanks to you. Same name but different location."

Her smile widened. "I love you, Callum. I want to be your wife and have your babies and I promise to always make you happy."

"Oh, Gemma." He reached out and cupped her face with both hands, lightly brushing his lips against hers before taking it in a hard kiss, swallowing her breath in the process.

He shifted to lie down on the bed and took her with him, placing her body on top of his while he continued to kiss her with a need that made every part of his body feel sensitive.

He tore his mouth away from hers to pull in a much-needed breath, but she fisted her hands in his hair to bring his face closer, before nibbling on his lips and licking around the corners of his mouth. And when he released a deep moan, she slid her tongue into his mouth and begin kissing him the way she'd gotten used to him kissing her.

Callum felt his control slipping and knew this kiss would be imprinted on his brain forever. He deepened the kiss, felt his engorged sex press against the apex of her thighs, knowing just what it wanted. Just what it needed.

Just what it was going to get.

He pulled his mouth away long enough to adjust her body over his. While staring into her eyes, he pushed upward and thrust into her, immediately feeling her heat as he buried himself deep in her warmth. He pulled out and thrust in again while the hard nipples of her breasts grazed his chest.

And then she began riding him, moving her body on top of his in a way that had him catching his breath after every stroke. Together, they rode, they gave and took, mated in a way that touched everything inside of him; had him chanting her name over and over.

Then everything seemed to explode and he felt her body when it detonated. He soon followed, but continued hammering home, getting all he could and making her come again.

"Callum!"

"That's it, my love, feel the pleasure. Feel our love."

And then he leaned up and kissed her, took her mouth with a hunger that should already have been appeased. But he knew he would always want this. He would always want her, and he intended to never let her regret the day she'd given him her heart.

Totally sated, Gemma slowly opened her eyes and, like so many other times over the past weeks, Callum was in bed with her, and she was wrapped in his embrace. She snuggled closer and turned in his arms to find him watching her with satisfied passion in the depth of his green eyes.

She smiled at him. "I think we broke the bed."

He returned her smile and tightened his arms around her. "Probably did. But it can be fixed."

"If not, we can stay at my place," she offered.

"That will work."

At that moment the phone rang and he shifted their bodies to reach and pick it up. "That's probably Mom, calling to make sure things between us are all right."

He picked up the phone. "Hello."

He nodded a few times. "Okay, we're on our way."

He glanced over at Gemma and smiled. "That was Dillon. Chloe's water broke and Ramsey rushed her to the hospital. Looks like there's going to be a new Westmoreland born tonight."

It didn't take long for Callum and Gemma to get to the hospital, and already it was crowded with Westmorelands. It was almost 3:00 a.m. If anyone was curious as to why they were all together at that time of the morning, no one mentioned it.

"The baby is already here," Bailey said, excited. "We have a girl, just like we wanted."

Callum couldn't help throwing his head back and laughing. Good old Ram had a daughter.

"How's Chloe?" Gemma asked.

"Ramsey came out a few moments ago and said she's fine," Megan said. "The baby is a surprise."

"Yes, we didn't expect her for another week," Dillon said, grinning. He glanced over at his pregnant wife, Pam, and smiled as he pulled her closer to him. "That makes me nervous."

"Has anyone called and told Chloe's father?"

"Yes," Chloe's best friend, Lucia, said, smiling. "He's a happy grandpa and he'll be here sometime tomorrow."

"What's the baby's name?" Callum asked.

It was Derringer who spoke up. "They are naming her Susan after Mom. And they're using Chloe's mom's name as her middle name."

Gemma smiled. She knew Chloe had lost her mother at an early age, too. "Oh, that's nice. Our parents' first grand. They would be proud."

"They *are* proud," Dillon said, playfully tapping her nose.

"Hey, is this an engagement ring?" Bailey asked loudly, grabbing Gemma's hand.

Gemma glanced up at Callum and smiled lovingly. "Yes, we're getting married."

Cheers went up in the hospital waiting room. The Westmorelands had a lot to celebrate.

Zane glanced over at Dillon and Pam. "I guess now

we're depending on you two to keep us male Westmorelands in the majority."

"Yeah," Derringer agreed.

"You know the two of you could find ladies to marry and start making your own babies," Megan said sweetly to her brothers. Her suggestion did exactly what she'd expected it to do—zip their lips.

Callum pulled Gemma closer into his arms. They shared a look. They didn't care if they had boys or girls—they just wanted babies. There were not going to be any hassles getting a big family out of them.

"Happy?" Callum asked.

"Extremely," she whispered.

Callum looked forward to when they would be alone again and he bent and told her just what he intended to do when they got back to the cabin.

Gemma blushed. Megan shot her sister a look. "You okay, Gem?"

Gemma smiled, glanced up at Callum and then back at her sister. "Yes, I couldn't be better."

Epilogue

There is nothing like a Westmoreland wedding, and this one was extra special because guests came from as far away as Australia and the Middle East. Gemma glanced out at the single ladies, waiting to catch her bouquet. She turned her back to the crowd, closed her eyes and threw it high over her head.

When she heard all the cheering, she turned around and smiled. It had been caught by Lucia Conyers, Chloe's best friend. She glanced across the room and looked at the two new babies. As if Susan's birth had started a trend, Dillon and Pam's son, Denver, came early, too.

"When can we sneak away?"

"You've waited three years. Another three hours won't kill you," she jokingly replied to her husband of two hours.

"Don't be so sure about that," was his quick response.

Their bags were packed and he was going to take her to India, as they'd planned before. Then they would visit Korea and Japan. She wanted to get decorating ideas with a few Asian pieces.

Callum took his wife's hand in his as they moved around the ballroom. He had been introduced to all the Atlanta Westmorelands before when he was invited to the Westmoreland family reunion as a guest. Now he would attend the next one as a bona fide member of the Westmoreland clan.

"How soon do you want to start making a baby?"

Gemma almost choked on her punch. He gave her a few pats on the back and grinned. "Didn't mean for you to gag."

"Can we at least wait until we're alone?"

"To talk about it or to get things started?"

Gemma chuckled as she shook her head. "Why do I get the feeling there will never be a dull moment with you?"

He pulled her closer to him. "Because there won't be. Remember I'm the one who knows what a Westmoreland wants. At least I know what my Westmoreland wants."

Gemma wrapped her arms around his neck. "I'm an Austell now," she said proudly.

"Oh, yes, I know. And trust me—I will never let you forget it."

Callum then pulled her into his arms and in front of all their wedding guests, he kissed her with all the love flowing in his heart. He had in his arms everything he'd ever wanted.

* * * * *

We hope you enjoyed reading
Just Kate
by *New York Times* bestselling author
LINDA LAEL MILLER
and
What a Westmoreland Wants
by *New York Times* bestselling author
BRENDA JACKSON

Originally MIRA Books and
Harlequin® Desire stories!

From passionate, suspenseful and dramatic
love stories to inspirational or historical,
Harlequin offers different lines to
satisfy every romance reader.

New books in each line
are available every month.

BAC2HALO0119

They'd never talked about how they were always overlapping each other with dating other people.

It was an odd thing to notice.

Why had Sabrina noticed?

Sabrina Douglas was his best girl friend. Girl, space, friend. But Flynn felt a definite stir in his gut.

For the first time in his life, sex wasn't off the table for him and Sabrina.

Which meant he needed his head examined.

After the tasting, Sabrina chattered about her favorite cheeses and how she couldn't believe they didn't serve wine at the tour.

"What kind of establishment doesn't offer you wine with cheese?" she exclaimed as they strolled down the boardwalk. Which gave him a great view of her ass—another part of her he'd noticed before, but not like he was noticing now.

Not helping matters was the fact that he didn't have to wonder what kind of underwear she wore beneath that tight denim. He knew.

They'd been friends and comfortable around each other for long enough that no amount of trying to forget would erase the image of her wearing a black thong that perfectly split those cheeks into two biteable orbs.

"What do you think?" She spun and faced him, the wind kicking her hair forward, a few strands sticking to her lip gloss. He reached her in two steps. Before he thought it through, he swept those strands away, ran his fingers down her cheek and tipped her chin, his head a riot of bad ideas.

With a deep swallow, he called up ironclad Parker willpower and stopped touching his best friend. "I think you're right."

His voice was as rough as gravel.

"You're distracted. Are you thinking about work?"

"Yes," he lied through his teeth.

"You're going to have to let it go at some point. Give in to the urge." She drew out the word *urge*, perfectly pursing her lips and leaning forward with a playful twinkle in her eyes that would tempt any mortal man to sin.

And since Flynn was nothing less than mortal, he palmed the back of her head and pressed his mouth to hers.

Don't miss what happens next!
Best Friends, Secret Lovers *by Jessica Lemmon,*
part of her Bachelor Pact series!

Available February 2019 wherever
Harlequin® Desire books and ebooks are sold.

www.Harlequin.com

HARLEQUIN® *Desire*

Family sagas...scandalous secrets...burning desires.

Save **$1.00**

on the purchase of ANY

Harlequin® Desire book.

Available wherever books are sold, including most bookstores, supermarkets, drugstores and discount stores.

Save **$1.00**

on the purchase of any Harlequin® Desire book.

Coupon valid until March 1, 2019.
Redeemable at participating outlets in the U.S. and Canada only.
Not redeemable at Barnes & Noble stores. Limit one coupon per customer.

52616222

5 65373 00076 2 (8100)0 12408

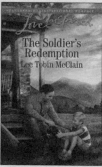

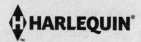